Book Description:

THUG PASSION - THUG LOVE, is the story of Timmy, a somewhat sexually confused and very curious young man, who by chance meet three good friends on a hot summer's day. That meeting would result in a considerable change in his life forever.

One of those friends, Tyree, the most dynamic of the trio, falls head over heels in love with him; this leads to eventual sexual advances which at first were spurned by Timmy, but later reciprocated.

Timmy later found himself battling those deep lustful thoughts, which plagued his mind for years, about his real true feelings for Tyree.

Timmy, had to admit to himself, but couldn't fully explain why things were the way they were; but finally came to grips with the realization of his relationship with Tyree, and spent years living a secret life of love and passion, with him; even though he had a beautiful wife and several lovely children.

1

I0571225

He prodded and quickly shifted his position, evading my hand as I try to grab his balls "

Timmy: " motha fucka! ..... mm-mm-mmmphf .... Oh Fuck! - AAIGHT! .... aiight .... mmmph, mmph, I surrender "

Tyree: "see...I tole you" He gloated and dug into my sides once more.

Timmy: "fuck you Tyree...cccctt, ooh, ... SHIT"

Tyree: " you can't be surrenderin' 'n cussin' like dat in front o' grown folk, you surrender or what? "

Timmy: " yes, yes,...yes, I surrender .... lemmi go"

Tyree: " you sure? "

Timmy: "yes, you, tha boss, you tha master, jus move yo' hand, please"

Tyree: "well you best behave yo'self now" Without warning, he straddled me; kneeling on the sofa and pinning me between the back of the seat and his stomach.

Tyree: "I want you boi...."

Timmy: "you got me"

Tyree: "I ain't talkin' like dat .... am talkin' 'bout some o' dat"

Timmy: "some o' what .... I ain't GOTS nothin' to give you"

Tyree: "am serious, 'specially from I seen how you tore dat nigga Marlon up, .movin' dat booty like dat" Pretending to be uninterested in his quest, I suddenly changed the subject, asking as I toyed with his belly button;

Timmy: "Tyree, you say you love me...why?"
Tyree: "dang son, you gon ask dat now!"
Timmy: "tell me...a need to hear" He hastily got off me, tilted my chin up, knelt before me and looked deep in my eyes before he bowed his head, shook it slowly from side to side, sighed heavily then looked back at me.

Tyree: "Timmy, I ain't got no more words to explain it to you, I ain't got no more ways I, I, don't know what to tell you except that I love you, am torn apart e'rry day jus thinkin' 'bout you...datz what I do all day every day -jus think about you".ain't nothin' mo' dat I know dat I could say, you jus gotta let time prove me right or wrong...but I do love you...more than you eva know"

Timmy: "what is it about me dat you love?"

Tyree: "dang son, datz 'errythang...shiit; from yo' temper, how yo' chest move up 'n down when you mad, da way you walk, them very hairy, slightly bow legs, yo tight little muscular butt, all dat pretty black hair on yo' butt, stomach, yo' pubes, under yo' arms, them hairy ballz, dat nice l'il 'stache, thick eyebrows 'n

3

lips, yo' bright dark brown eyes, rich coco 'n cream complexion, da way you talk. dang son, Ioknow. jus da way you squeeze me back when I hold you. I know son, e'rrythang.jus e'rrythang, fo' real - I jus saw you 'n wuz like wow! .this kid is bangin'.'n on top o' dat you fresh - 'n intelligent too...its too good. Son you what I been lookin' fo' all this time"

"Thug Passion – Thug Love"
(Volume 1)
By D.Lowe

Edited by – Mr. M.G.

visit:
www.ThugPassion.us
and
www.ThugLove.us

Acknowledgements:

"This Book is Dedicated to My Beauitful DL Brothers."
- OneLove ...

Published by
DNA eBooks Publishing Company
P.O. BOX 314
New York, NY 10037

www.DNAeBooks.com

Publisher@DNAeBooks.com

ISBN: 978-0-9832476-0-9

DNA eBooks Publishing Company

DNA eBooks Publishing Group

*Thank You Very Much for
Purchasing My eBook and
Thank You So Much for Supporting
all Our Authors and Writers.*

*Feel Free to Contact and Email Me:
DLowe@DNAeBooks.com*

visit – DNAeBooks.com

**MEET OUR WRITERS and AUTHORS,
WATCH VIDEOS and MUCH MORE:**
Special Offers, Exclusive Content and More

**Our Website is the Place to HangOut
for all Reading Groups,
and for all of Us who Enjoy Reading.**

**The DNA eBooks Publishing Group
Can Bring Authors / Writers to Your Events.
email us: Events@DNAeBooks.com**

**Sign Up and be on Our VIP Email List
email us: VIPList@DNAeBooks.com**

http://www.dnaebooks.com/short-form/

**For information:
The DNA eBooks Publishing Group
P.O. BOX 314
New York City, NY 10037**

"Thug Passion – Thug Love"
(Volume 1)
By D.Lowe

(Chapter 1)

I was born and raised on Harlem's East side, New York City of a Dominican mother and an African American father. We are a large closely knit family consisting of seven children of which I am the sixth. I have four brothers and two sisters in the order of :- A boy, a girl, a girl, a boy, then three boys. That would be: - Ramon, Marla, Elise, Antonio { Ant }, Thomas { Tommy - my twin brother }, myself Timothy {Timmy} and my little brother Peter being the baby of the family. Our childhood was a most happy period as many summers, during breaks from school, mom and dad would send us to the Dominican Republic or Washington D.C. to visit our grandparents and other relatives. There were other happy family moments like a day at the beach, Coney Island, once a month Saturday Matinees [where just us kids would go and raise hell as a seven crew gang - nothing really detrimental to anyone mind you, just kid pranks] and so on, but nothing could take the place of those long trips we had out of state or abroad.

It was great fun to be traveling back and forth like that and we would spend two or three weeks, then fly back to New York City to spend the rest of the summer before finally preparing for the new school year in September. We were not rich, but mom, who is the Chief Administrator at a major hospital, and dad, who is a motorman plying the New Haven rail lines, would work so hard, most times they did not even see each other as husbands and wives should. All this, just to make sure that we did not lack anything that was necessary. Of course, we never had all the things that we wanted but we did in fact have all the things that we needed. They were a couple who raised us to understand that hard work has its great reward and that we should always work hard to attain our goals. Dad would always drill in us the idea of "an honest days work for an honest days pay" ; that we must always respect our women and be the fathers that we should be to our kids. I can distinctly remember that, and, especially Tommy and I, would always snicker when he said that part about our kids .... it did seem to us to be the funniest thing - our having kids. However, they were hardworking parents who had struggled, skimped and saved enough to have bought a brownstone, which is where we are living.

As the years went by, my two sisters and eldest brothers had married and moved out leaving just Pete, Tommy and I. When Tommy and I did so very well in school, mom and dad decided to gear us for a higher level of education, like they'd done with my sister Marla. College was set on the agenda and when Tommy and I succeeded at College Level Education Program, the family was enthusiastic; we'd be going to college. Of the offers, we accepted a college in California where we'd be close to Marla, who was an Anesthesiologist at a hospital in Los Angeles.

However, when the time finally came, I realized I didn't want to go, and I didn't even know why. That decision caused so much discord - mom and dad viewed it as more than rebellion and I thought surely they were going to disown me. On a daily basis, I had to suffer the indignity of how much of a bum I'd turn out to be. I was chastised much to my shame and embarrassment but still, I did not want to go. Tommy was at a complete loss and in the months leading up to leaving, would quiz me daily, wanting to know if I'd changed my mind and why I'd made such a decision.

His desire to go was just as strong as when we first decided we'd attend the same college. He was very disappointed and didn't want to go alone but for some reason, I just could not see it in myself to go. Those were tense and tedious months and when the day finally came, although I'd refused to go, mom and dad bought two tickets. I was convinced within myself that they'd bought the second ticket in the hope that when they sent me to accompany Tommy and I saw what there was to offer, I'd change my mind. Even with that amount of hope and prodding, I still didn't go. I stayed for the first two weeks Tommy was in college before returning home.

From then on, my life would change considerably. I wasn't working, I had many idle days and eventually worked here and there for a few months at a time, much to the disgust of my parents. Dad took it the hardest and I think that was one of the reasons why in these, his later years, he worked so much overtime. He couldn't bear to see me so often and in those long winter months, I stayed home a lot. Whenever he was home I'd avoid him as much as I could but there were times when I couldn't. Like the times he'd come home from work tired, and when he walked into the house and saw me, he'd put on the most horrid, extremely disagreeable face. He wouldn't speak to me much, if any at all. That made for a much longer, colder and unpleasant winter. I didn't have many friends; I am a sociable person, but for the most part it was always just me, Tommy and Pete [except for acquaintances that I had encountered during my school years, and to a lesser extent, after I'd finished school]. It was, therefore, only natural that after he left for college, Pete and I would get considerably closer.

Pete, though two years my junior, being only sixteen going on seventeen, had formed such a very close bond, he was kind of like Tommy to me - so much so, he would come talk to me about anything, confiding in me, seeking my brotherly and friendly advice before even confronting our parents with any problems he might have. He was more into his schoolwork than girls though and had never told me of having any girlfriend. I, on the other hand, was enjoying my teenage years. I had the girls I wanted, and never had a problem getting them; I don't think I would be conceited in saying that I am a handsome young man who has always been able to get the girls of my choice - even some that were already taken. That had never been, nor is it now my " modus operandi " but there were times during my school years that I've done it. While it might be argued that women are the ones that find themselves being admired and pursued by men, I have to differ and say I've been ogled, seduced and told that I was alluring many times - and by older women too. Not-with-standing, I was never ready to settle down and thus was still, as they say, "sowing my wild oats."

Not seeking new friends, I would occupy my

time between jobs by playing video games with Pete, soccer (wherever there was a game), but most of all - lots of basketball in the park.

Basketball was my preferred game and I had excelled at both in high school, but have an affinity for basketball in particular, to the extent I was promoted from junior to varsity at school. This was the game that would always draw me to the park as there was almost always at least a pick up game to get into. Every week I was sure to be there on Mondays and Wednesdays and a few times I would go late on a Saturday and or Sunday.

It was one of those days - a steamy summer Saturday afternoon when I first met my friends Tyree, Ardee and Aji. It was so muggy that Saturday that when I got to the park there was hardly anyone on the basketball courts. It was, after all, 104 degrees that day so I guess most of the ballers stayed away in exchange for some cool air conditioned place like the movies or just stayed home; but it was a beautiful day, a nice day to be out. The guys there weren't playing nor did it appear they wanted to. They just sat around on the benches chatting so I went onto one of the courts away from them and the shade of the trees and practiced my shots.

Thirty minutes had gone by without any competition and I was soaking wet so I took my jersey off and sat on my ball in the most shaded corner of the court for a few minutes until my thirst demanded a quencher. I got up taking my ball with me and went across the street and down the block to get a bottle of water. On my return, there were these three guys on the court taking turns just dribbling their ball. I sat on my ball again and squirted some water on my head and let it run all the way down my chest and back down into my shorts, took a sip and decided to just watch them. They were all older than me. I was only eighteen at the time but I thought there couldn't be any harm in trying to see if these guys would let me play with them.

Finally, I stood up after about fifteen minutes and I could feel my boxers and shorts uncomfortably clinging to my sweaty wet body. That was when I recognized that those are the guys who play regularly in here, they were some of the players from one of the teams that play the "Business Matches" on some weekends - they were good.

As I got up and walked toward them to ask if I could play, the tallest of them [Guy #1] who was now swiftly headed in my direction, looked at me kind of strange as he walked past me on his way to the other end of the court where their bags were. He took three bottles of water out and headed back to join the other two. Seeing that, I went over and asked if I could join in. They pretty much ignored me, except for the tallest, who was now holding the ball; he was a few feet away with his back to me, he turned and faced me, looked at me rather cockily...scanning me curiously up and down...then suddenly chucked the ball with both hands at me.

Instinctively, I caught and shoot; his eyes followed the ball as it left my fingers and........ "ssswoosh" - all net. After I made the basket, he turned to look back at me, exposed a wry grin....then told his two friends to pass the ball back to him. He made a bounce pass very wide to my left, I chased and caught it before it went out of bounds, spun to my right, then let it go just a few feet outside the arc and..... - basket - [again]. He raised his eyebrows and looked at the other fellows as I, displaying my own bit of cockiness, watching with my hands akimbo as if to say..." yeah, that's me - I can do that ". He never figured I could make that shot under such conditions but I know this court and can almost see the basket with my eyes closed. After all, this was what I did every time I went there, so I had no doubt about taking the shot or any fear that it might not go in.

I stood proudly, still waiting for an answer but rather than address me, he cocked his head to one side and eyed me like a lizard, then ordered his friends saying,..... " Yo let this l'il nigga play.....I know his l'il azz think he got game but, he gon be took to school today " .

As he continued to eye me with a boastful insidious grin, I held his gaze. I had seen them play a few times and I knew they were very good but I wasn't scared, I knew I could play with them and I wanted to. Eventually, he said " yo, come play then " ...... as though it was beneath their dignity to have someone such as myself play with them. Anyway, that was how I became a member of the "A Team", as they are known. As I picked the ball up, I thought " L'il nigga! ". Who does he think he is, he was talking like I was some little kid. I could see he was tall and very muscular - and - yes, they're all tall and muscular - and I was a bit shorter and a little smaller but..."Little ". Anyway, I wanted to play with them so I disregarded all that and stood a little distance away from them. He walked slowly over to me and spoke in a low raspy voice.

Guy #1:   " whatz yo' name shorty? "

A frown creased my brow and I tilted my head

slightly upward and gave him a cockeyed look.
Who was he calling " Shorty " .....it infuriated
me somewhat, he realized this and grinned
wryly then rephrased the statement;

Guy #1:   " ma bad...aiight, whatz
yo' name? "

thats better, I thought and replied;

Timmy: " whatz yo' name? "

Guy #1:   " where yo' twin at?...you
always together "

he asked quickly, discarding my question but at
the same time I was curious that he was asking
about Tommy.

Timmy: " you know Tommy? "

Guy #1:   " naaw,....not really -
but, y'all be together alla time "

Timmy: " he live in LA, he go to
school there "

Guy #1:   " oh! ...... so what, you
ready to do this? "

Timmy: " no doubt "

He introduced himself as Tyree, his friends as Ardee and Aji then told them I was going to play with them; I could see they were taken aback by his demand and they asked in unison.

Ardee & Aji: " WHO! ...... the kid? "

Tyree: " YEAAH ...... y'all got a problem wit it? "

They didn't respond, just shrugged their shoulders, looked at each other and turned away.

And so we played.   I'm sure they were impressed with my skills because when the game was over, Tyree threw his arms around my shoulders as we walked out of the park and would stroke my head from time to time like I was some little kid. I didn't like anyone stroking my head so when he tried to do that again I shifted my head to the side. Realizing that, he looked down at me and as our gaze met he smiled and stroked my head again.

And so it began. We would meet almost every Saturday and sometimes on Sundays too, and when it was over, we would hang around eating ice cream - or something like that - for a while before I'd call it a day and go home.

There was this particular Sunday though, after the game, when I walked with them to get slurpees. As we left the store and continued ambling down the sidewalk in the summer heat with Ardee and Aji yapping and enjoying their slurpees, Tyree fell silent for a moment. Then suddenly, he stopped, I hesitated; Ardee and Aji paused and turned around looking at us. Standing alongside him, I then looked up at him, wondering what was wrong and before I could ask, he offered;

Tyree: " me 'n the fellas gon kick it at ma crib fo' a while, ... wanna come chill wit us? "

Timmy: " mmmm - yeah! "

Ardee and Aji looked at him like he had lost his mind or something, they seemed shocked or troubled at the idea of him inviting me. He was cool though so I really had no misgivings about going .... the other fellas are good funny company too, but for whatever reason, I liked him best - in spite of the cockiness about his game.

Tyree: " aiight, come on then "

And so we continued on.

When we got to his apartment, I was surprised at the large collection of books he had on a shelf in the living room. At a quick glance, I noticed the topics were well varied, consisting of: Foreign Languages, World Travel, History and Cultures, Business Management, Human Anatomy, Health and Fitness - to name a few. He was a reader, it seemed, and as an avid reader myself, I had to comment.......

Timmy: " Whoaa, you got madd books son "

.......as I continued to scan the shelves quickly.

Tyree: " I try to catch up on stuff, ... "

He replied modestly, and added;

Tyree: " you like readin'? "

Timmy: " every chance I get "

Now Ardee spoke for the first time in a long while.

Ardee: " yeah, but don't get fired on yo' first job like him "

Timmy: " you lost yo' job 'cause

you wuz readin'? "

Then, with a chuckle, Ardee opined;

Ardee: " ..... hell yeah, they
wuzn't payin' him fo' no shit like dat, he
                    s'posed to sort tha damn
mail 'n deliver them to who ever "

Timmy: " Daamn! "

Tyree: " man, Ioknow how I
even ...... I jus got caught up in the damned
                         paper "

We all had a good laugh at his expense.

The apartment was clean and neatly kept,
except for the jumbled pile of paperwork at his
computer desk. We spent the next couple hours
just relaxing and talking until I decided to
leave. From that weekend on, I would chill out
at his crib with them until I was ready to go
home.   As time went by, Ardee and Aji seemed
to be more comfortable with me around at the
crib, so all was good.

Tyree: Twenty one years old: Six feet,
one inch tall. Smooth, dark chocolate
complexion, corn rows, well groomed beard

21

and sideburns [that make him appear older than he really is]. He even had pearly white teeth and a beguiling smile that raised the left side and lowered the right side corner of his lips; dark brown eyes, moustache and pierced ears with a small tattoo on his well formed left breast bearing a heart and the name " Tyrone " - I wondered who that was. He's a definite charmer; works out religiously five days a week....... the owner of an envious six pack and a sturdy upright and military-like gait.   A most handsome and classy dresser; fastidious, patient, kind, thoughtful, loves kids, loves to read, has a very keen sense of humor, as well as a deep interest in cultures, languages and history; very perceptive, unassuming manners [except for his basketball prowess] - not to be pushed.

Then there is:-

Ardee: Twenty three years old: Five feet, eleven inches, mocha complexion, braided hair, two tattoos, pierced ears, works out with Tyree five days a week. Ruggedly handsome; strong and tough type; appears hostile but is really approachable once you get to know him; always helpful. Swaggering gait; he is very hardworking and can be diabolically cruel when upset,.... and although seeming otherwise, he will, on rare occasions, display witticism and an intellectual capacity not thought to be in his arsenal; also has a softer side which he hardly ever shows ..... but jovial most of the time. and finally:-

Aji: Twenty years old: A straightforward individual; five feet, nine inches [as myself]. Hazel eyes, very creamy chocolate complexion, pierced ears [like myself], one tattoo. Dressy but not flamboyant and an avid shopper who always has the latest in fashion; will talk your ears off once he gets to know you,....and poke fun at you, if he likes you. Otherwise, always unheard but is always the one to pull a prank and is a very sly instigator. Kind, caring and thoughtful, loves children. By no means a sap, but not as aggressive as the others and is the most likely of the trio to display frivolousness. Somewhat self-centered and tends to be cocky sometimes.

We would always team up with whomever we could find at the courts in the park for a quick pick up game but whenever we had any serious games, this guy Garnet [but everybody calls him "Chawklit"] would always be the sixth man on our team. He is Tyree's long time friend; its just that he never seemed to hang with us most of the time, or for too long. He's the eldest of the lot of us, being twenty four, a recently married, City Transit worker and lives with his wife and young daughter in the Bronx.

So, there you have it, " my bball boyz "; and we would always be chilling together smoking [although I'm not that much a smoker] and without a doubt, playing basketball and just regular hanging out till whenever.

(Chapter 2)

It was an early August Saturday afternoon, when me and Pete were home watching the history channel; the phone rang and he picked it up;

Pete: " hello,......yeah, what up?.... where you at? .... oh, we chillin' "

I broke into his conversation inquiring who it was, he answered;

Pete: " Tyree"

but kinda sarcastically, stretching the "e" in his name while rolling his eyes.

Pete: " why he always be callin you?"

Timmy: " negro,......gimmi tha phone, whatchu mean - datz ma boi "

Pete: " whuteva "

He retorted under his breath, but I paid him no mind.

Tyree: " whaddup ma dude......whatchu doin? "

I responded cheerfully, glad to get his call. Pete was watching me carefully, a streak of apparent discontent in his demeanor; I continued to ignore him and proceeded with the conversation, enjoying my friend.

Timmy: " nothin'...jus chillin' wit Pete watchin some TV "

I replied, looking at Pete and trying to bring him back into my good graces. Tyree exclaimed:

Tyree: " yo, its Saturday son, what! - you ain't hittin' the courts, tha fellaz is ready "

Timmy: " whenever y'all ready dawg "

I responded cheerfully;

Tyree: " son,.....we been ready......we been ova here waitin' on yo' azz "

Timmy: " aiight, aiight.... don't hit the panic button "

he then lied boastfully trying to assure me ....

Tyree: " ain't nobody
panikin'.....but you need to get yo' narrow azz
ova
                    here now "

Timmy: " yea, yea, ... not
anything special, ama be there "

I grabbed my shorts and sneakers, jumped into
them in a flash and threw a white wifebeater
over one shoulder. Pete had stepped out of the
room and was now just walking back in sipping
from a bottle of water. He inquired if I was
going out and where; I told him I was heading
to the basketball court over at the park to play
with the fellas; he looked disappointed. Most
times he would choose to come with me to the
game but, today he seem somewhat
preoccupied and wanted to hang around me all
day. Still, I invited him but he declined with a
sad face, even so, I told him I had to go.

Pete: " why you gotta go
today....you ain't gotta go "

Timmy: " man....you know we
play just about every Saturday....
                    ....I juss forgot 'cause we
wuz here watchin' TV "

Pete: " can't you miss one

Saturday? "

Timmy: " Noo! ...... c'mon, get
ready "

Pete: " I don't feel like goin'
nowhere today "

Why is it that I think he was acting strange?.....
was something wrong?..... anyway, my mind
was now awash with heroic moments of past
games, highlighted by the sometimes dramatic
game winning baskets I'd made; I had to leave.

Timmy: " you used to come
watch us sometimes, 'n you see we have madd
                          fun playin'..... why you
stop coming anyway? "

His reply was only his unusual forelorn look.
Still bent on going, I urged....

Timmy: " them fellas is waitin'
and we runnin' late..... lets go "

Pete: " I ain't goin'..... "

Timmy: " stop playin' "

I demanded.

Pete: " I got madd homework
and research..... "

I knew he was lying, so I prompted him more.

Timmy: " stop bitchin' and come
on or ama leave without you "
Pete: " fo'get you then "

he responded angrily and turned away as I
walked toward the door. Something seemed
out of place; he was awfully quiet most of the
time today and while I would have loved to
continue to spend some more time with him, I
had to go take care of this game first. I realized
that something was bothering him..... but he'll
tell me about it when he's ready, I'll just
wait...although I wondered what it could be.
Never-the-less, I stopped, gave him a hug as I
went toward the door, he just stood with his
arms by his sides, I let go, tried to search his
face but he merely looked away - I hurried off
to the park.

We made up two teams with some of the
regular guys that we usually play with in the
park; one team wearing shirts, the other -
shirtless. I said I'd join the shirtless team
because Tyree and them fellas was on the other.
Tyree was making some fuss about my not

29

joining his team. I was only trying to mess with his head anyway; besides, everybody was crying broke so we'd only be playing for fun. I thought to myself, well, since Tyree seemed so pissed about my saying I wanted to play on the other team, I was really going to do it and have a good laugh on him when it was all over.

Now, I gotta tell you: When we're playing serious games, we play for six packs, each team would bring a duffle bag, back-packs or some other bag large enough to carry the beers that would be the prize and set it at the score-keeper's feet until after the game. We played hard. I especially, played Tyree very hard and caused him to miss quite a few of his shots. We had a very good game and my team won by eight points. All-in-all we had fun, as usual, and then hung around talking after the game.

Finally as it was getting near 7:00 p.m., Ardee figured we should all go chill over at Tyree's and everyone agreed. As we ambled along the sidewalk, Tyree asked Ardee if he had money to get him a bottle of water, saying he was very thirsty. Normally he would ask me but he had not spoken a word to me directly since the game.....I'm cracking up inside because I know that he mad that I caused his team to lose the game - he hates to lose.

Ardee: " nigga, you know I don't
start back working for another good two
                    to three weeks ..... I ain't
got shit "

Aji: " ask yo' boi Timmy, dat
mofucka always got that paper ....
                    ....I swear dat nigga be
runnin' number or some shit "

Tyree: " who.....wit his broke
azz! "

He hissed between his teeth and gave a snide
laugh. Now I was in stitches; knowing that I
had money, had played against them, made
them lose and now he was thirsty and without
money. He glared at me, stopped bouncing
the ball off the sidewalk pavement and in one
swift stroke, using both hands, he tossed the
ball towards me bouncing it off my chest. Now
that was uncalled for. I didn't think the loss was
that much of an issue for him to do that and
stared at him in amazement for a moment then
looked him dead in the eye and replied.

Timmy: " man, fuck you ..... ain't
nobody mo' broke than yo' azz ....
                    ....yo' baby momma gets all
yo' mothafuckin' money 'n then some;
                    'n e'rrybody know you

whipped too .... "

I jeered, as I jumped and danced at my own comeback and taunted in a sing-song.

Timmy: " .... slave to the mighty pussy .... Liana, Wonder Woman with tha
                      Wunda Puss-say "

Making a wry grin, he replied softly.

Tyree: " Oh! - a nigga got jokes,....a nigga havin' fun "

Timmy: " man you a sore loser - 'tain't like we wuz playin' fo' money -
                      damn! "

Tyree: " I see a certain negro is against me but datz cool,....at least I know
                      who ma frienz is from today "

I turned my head, looking at Ardee and Aji in amazement at that statement but they.....strangely, cast their gaze across the street.

Timmy: " now, now, see .... a nigga feelins' hurt .... they start shit n' then
                      can't take some heat "

Tyree: " its aaight tho'.... I know how to stand on ma own - I ain't got no brother, no sister "

Tyree mused, nodding his head; I charged;

Timmy: " who talkin' 'bout you? "

Tyree: " one thing I ain't - 'n datz dumb; ama get you mothafucka, ama getchu - ama get you "

Timmy: " bitch you ain't gettin' nobody "

Ardee: " oh shit, see.... they at it again Aji.... "

now all of a sudden these two were my companions again.

Ardee: " .... these niggaz gonna throw down one a these days "

Timmy: " y'all trippin'.......he ain't gon do shit to nobody "

We continued like that for a few minutes before Aji, appearing fed up with it, quickly interjected;

Aji: " damn, y'all need to
shut the fuck up; am hungry like a
                    mothafucka,.....am
thinkin' 'bout somethin' to eat "

as a matter of fact, we were all supposed to be
hungry, I know I was, so Aji was making sense
this time.

Tyree: " chicken restaurant right
there at the end of the block "

Timmy: " I know ama get me
some - wit some fries too "

Ardee: " dat place gon be
crowded like a mo'fucka .... but get me and Aji
                    some too dawg "

Timmy: " AIIGHT! "

I hollered back as I'd started to race ahead of
them down the block when Tyree roared

Tyree: " WHAT!.....YOU
AIN'T GETTIN ME SOME TOO SON? "

I made a quick " U " turn, sprinted back up to
them and with arms widespread, I leaned my
head to one side, looked Tyree in the eye and

jokingly asked.

Timmy: " THA FUCK!......what,
is you ma bitch now......am fuckin' you
                              now? "

Tyree: " Oh, it gon be like dat
now dawg? .... "

He posed with a strange grin.

Timmy: " like what? "

Tyree: " you tryin' to jump
down a nigga throat "

Timmy: " yeah! its like dat ....
you gon do somethin' 'bout it? "

Tyree: " yo, B .... why you gon
be like dat - I thought we wuz boyz "

Timmy: " negro, I don't even
know yo' azz .... "

Ardee: " oh we know dat "

Aji: " about time tho'.... you
know datz his bitch right "

Timmy: " why you...... "

Becoming more disgusted with the frequency of these kinds of diatribes, I looked at both of them and shook my head saying.

Timmy: " ......yo, why y'all always gotta be on dat fucked up shit like dat!
                    - enough wit dat shit awready - aiight. How would you like if
                    a nigga wuz to come atchu like dat.....c'mon now "

I protested in disgust; those two were always insinuating something nasty had happened or was happening between Tyree and me.

Ardee: " I don't give a fuck ....
although, ... can't no nigga steps to me like
                    dat 'cause I'd be da first to
fuck him in his azz 'n send him runnin'
                    like a l'il biatch "

Aji: " knowamsayin' "

Timmy: " wha kinda shit is dat! "

What kind of response was that from them, I thought; he probably was trying to say "he'd be the first to fuck him up". I immediately tried to put it out of my mind and turned my attention back to Tyree.

Timmy: " jus be chill son I
gotchu .... you know I gotchu my nigga,
                    don't pay them durtyazz
mo'fuckaz no mind "

Tyree: " I know dawg, ... they a
bunch o' ill-bred mo'fuckaz anyways,
                    you know they ain't been brought
up no better "

Ardee: " see, ... can't nobody
say nothin' 'bout this boi 'n he dont insult 'n
                    degrade a nigga entire
family tree "

Aji: " ain't dat funny
Ardee...considerin' he ain't got no class his'self"
Tyree: " y'all need to get off ma
dick .... ma dude, go get dat chicken
                    'cause these starvin'
mo'fucka can't do withoutchu "

Timmy: " knowamsayin' .... jus
don't let them drag you down in they shit
                    son.... "

I trumped and stepped off adding.....

Timmy: " ....wit dat fucked up
talk - "

......in a barely audible tone, then finished by proudly announcing,

Timmy: " ..... 'cause me 'n you know it ain't even like dat "

Tyree: " I feel you dawg "

I said trying to allay any possible fears that he himself may have been harboring because of those unkind statements the two were always making.

They were all my good friends, and I really liked them a lot but just couldn't stand that pair always making those kinds of snide references. Trying to erase the memory of those remarks, I raced back down the road ahead of them to go place my order, hoping there wasn't a long line in there this evening although that is usually the case.

To my surprise, it wasn't overcrowded as it usually is at this hour but there were lots of customers. As luck would have it, Elise, whom I used to mess with long ago, was now working there and although I'd broken up with her, she's still been giving me the eye. Quite unbeknownst to the other customers, she sped up my order of chicken and fries and I was able pay my bill in no time and hurry out to find the boys waiting outside on the sidewalk for me.

Ardee: " nigga you back awready? "

Timmy: " Elise hooked me up yo "

Ardee: " you must still be fuckin' dat long haired bitch "

Timmy: " naaw, we ain't did shit in a minit - she still want this tho' "

Tyree: " so you gon hit it again? "

Timmy: " am thinkin' I might take one more last stab at it "

Ardee: " yo,....the chick fine as hell - can get any dick she want,...what make you think you can jus jump in 'n out o' dat pussy like dat? "

Timmy: " 'cause I got it like dat dawg...I know I got it like dat "

I boasted, staring him in the face.

Ardee: " am jus sayin'...... "

Timmy: " 'n am sayin' you ain't
sayin' nothin'.....I knows my game son "

He shrugged,
Ardee: " if you say so dawg "

Tyree: " awright; enough wit
the pussy talk, we ain't tryin'a eat no pussy,
                    we dealin' wit food "

Timmy: " right "

I concurred, pleased at Tryee's interjection.
Suddenly he asked;

Tyree: " so where the drinks at?
"

Timmy: " at yo' house! "

Tyree: " at ma house!.... what
ma house got to do..... "

Ardee: "c'mon dawg, you know
you shoulda bought somethin' to
                    drink...what !...you tryin' to
choke a brotha "

Timmy: " I don't believe this shit
...y'all talkin' 'bout drink like am s'posed
                    to buy e'rrything; what
'bout y'all? "

Ardee: " " y'all ! "....we ain't got
no mo'fuckin' money - you the buyer "

Timmy: " well am sorry but the
money was just enough to get this
                    shit...besides, this negro
s'posed to have shit at his crib to
                    drink.......sssshit "

Tyree: " yeah, I got drink fo' ya
- right here "

He grinned, grabbing his dick as he made three
rapid forward thrust of his pelvis [Michael
Jackson style] and roared loudly. Ardee and
Aji was cracking up; I didn't find it at all funny
and shot back my opinion.

Timmy: " man, datz some fucked
up homo/faggot shit right there..... fuck
                    all y'all "

He then smiled roguishly, pointing at me,

Tyree: " yeaah,.... ama getchu"

Sometimes I wondered why I bothered with their company but it seemed beyond me to stay away. At this point we were at Tyree's building and about to enter the elevator. Suddenly, as Aji moved to step into the elevator, Tyree stretched his hand forward, denying both him and Ardee access and playfully demanded;

Tyree: " stand back varlet,....
nobody enter this elevator be'fo' ma dawg.... "
Aji: " tha Fuu!...... "

Tyree: " after you your Majesty
"

He offered with a wave of that same right hand.

Ardee: " whateva, jus so long as you hold onto dat chicken good "

I could only grin as I stepped forward, I thought that was funny. We were all in, I hit the #12 button and we were on our way up to Tyree's crib. During the ride, he just kept looking at me and nodding his head while smiling. I swear, sometimes this dude can be as mischievous as Aji.

As soon as we got in the apartment and I bent over to put the food on the coffee table Tyree grabbed me from behind by my waist in a vice-like grip and started to hump and grind on my butt.

Tyree: " see, you bendin' ova already....ama give you " homo'faggot " shit "

Timmy: " DA FUCK!....what is wrong witchu nigga....yo, yo....I ain't.... "

Quickly pulling away and turning to Ardee with a knitted brow....

Timmy: " .... yo....y'all need to stop dat shit - you cause this shit "

Swallowing hard on a mouthful of chicken he'd taken from the bucket, Aji interrupted in the sleaziest of statements and in a manner suggesting boredom.....

Aji: " you ever notice how dese two niggaz be always bitchin 'N
                    carryin' on? "

..... which I found to be very irksome; and to top it off, Ardee was equally as disdainful as he replied in like fashion,

Ardee: " Uh uh... I see it dawg...like a real nigga 'n his bitch,...back and

forth, back and
forth...fo' sho' "

Timmy: " nigga fuck you! "

I exclaimed in vehement protest; and he added
further insult to the injury;

Ardee: " you know what they
say "

he offered haughtily, turning to Aji; and they
both smiled while looking each other in the
eyes.....then replied loudly in unison.

Ardee & Aji: " Tha Truth Hurts! "

They snickered, continuing to look into each
others eyes,...... then gave each other a pair of
high fives. That irritated me to the point I
wanted to step to them both and pop them in
their fucking grills; instead, I just gave them a
very dirty look and angrily blurted out....

Timmy: " why y'all mofuckaz
always gotta be ridin' my azz on some
                         faggot shit...y'all must be
some homos or shit... Bitchazz
                         mothafuckaz ..... y'all
can kiss my black azz "

..... and took a seat. The second that sentence left my lips I regretted saying it, just for the fact that I knew one of them was going to take up the part I said about "riding my ass" and sure enough, Aji, with his head bowed and eyes cast downwards calmly offered.

Aji: " Yo I aint da one tryin' to ride yo azz...you need to see yo boi
                    'bout that...he da one wuz grindin' on yo a... "

Ardee immediately flashed him a stone cold killer look and he instantly balked, like a deer caught in the headlights. Quickly changing the subject he softly asked Tyree who throughout that exchange had never said a word, nothing, not one thing in defense.

Aji: " where da drinks at? "

Tyree: " where da fuck you think it at!....in tha
                    fridge.....dumbazzmo'fucka "

Aji: " go get it then "

Tyree: " you go get that shit yo'self - pussyazz nigga "

Was he now treating Aji in this manner because

of the way they'd treated me?....I kinda think so.
Aji: " if I didn't know Ma
Gladys I'da tole you somethin' 'bout yo'
                        mamma "

Tyree: " bwoi, suck ma dick "

Tyree replied, stepping off to go do the usual,
the after the game routine of rolling two blunts;
a regular one for himself and a baby blunt for
me.

As he sat there calmly and quietly rolling the
blunts I pondered the fact that he never had my
back like I thought he would during all those
nasty comments Ardee and Aji made...and he
knew it wasn't even like that; somehow, I just
could not get over it. I was so pissed, I just sat
there looking at Tyree and never even touched
the chicken. When he finally lifted his eyes and
looked at me, it was a real long sympathetic yet
somewhat questioning stare,.... and he said;

Tyree: " dawg, you ain't gonna
eat yo' chicken "

Timmy: " nigga,......FUCK YOU
TOO! "

Tyree: " aaaww c'mon dawg,
you know them boyz always be fuckin'

witchu...they don't mean nothin' by dat shit....knowimsayin' "

He came over and sat next to me, playfully but firmly putting me in a headlock.

I was still kinda mad and was trying to shove him off when Ardee tactfully suggested I eat my chicken before I smoke that blunt. They all knew I'm not a big smoker or drinker so you could say that in spite of all that earlier rigmarole, they still had my best interest at heart. They continued to eat,... and I now began to eat; we all ate and drank, talked sports, Basketball of course, and smoked blunts. When I got done with my blunt, I was floating high above the clouds; I heard a chuckle and opened my eyes,

Tyree: " ma dawg lit da fuck up "

he said with a tender smile. I got to my feet......and straight up; I was feeling good, so good I put the CD player on and started to play some music. After a while Tyree got up, went into the kitchen and returned with a bottle of Hennesy and three glasses. Ardee looked up and saw it; he immediately threw out a playful accusation.

Ardee: " Oh!...so you been hidin'
shit from me son "

Tyree: " negro, I ain't been
hidin' nothin', Liana gave me that as a present
                        last Fathers' Day
and it been juss sittin' there "

Ardee: " last Fathers' Day!...... "

Ardee exclaimed sarcastically;

Ardee: " ..... you sure she didn't
leave dat here last night or somethin' "

I thought that was funny and had to put my
little bit in.

Timmy: " yea - 'n maybe she
left her panties here too "

Ardee: " ooh! so they still
fuckin' then; dawg, I thought you said it wuzn't
                        gon work "

Suddenly Aji sat up in his seat, alert like a
canine sensing something, and asked softly;

Aji: " Hello! ...... ain'tchu
lissenin' ma boi done seen her panties "

Aji chortled and before I could reply, Tyree nailed him.

Tyree: " any panties he seen up in here wuz yo's - you mean you ain't
                                missed it yet "

Quickly turning his head to the side and raising one leg as he put a fist up to his lips and made a face, indicating he felt the blow, Ardee choked on his first sip;

Ardee: " O-ooh ..... daamn, dat wuz wikkid ..... I see blood oozin' "

and Tyree concluded with a broad grin as Aji strangely remained silent. Then suddenly changing his demeanor, becoming quite stern, he offered;

Tyree: " on some real shit tho - it ain't even like dat son.....although e'rry
                                time she come thru' to pick up Yani she be tryin' to get some....I
                                ain't wit dat no mo'...I can't handle no mo of her drama - 'n I
know it got a lot to do wit her parents. I know we... "

Aji: " y'all know dis negro lyin' - right! "

49

Aji quipped with a sly grin ..... looking at Ardee
...

Aji: " datz da only pussy he
be gettin' "

Tyree: " you know I get any
pussy I want, even yo' sista "

Aji: " bruh - I ain't got no
sister - remember "

he quickly fired back;

Tyree: " well, I ain't gon say
nothin' 'bout yo' momma.... but you da
                          virgin-azz mo'fucka who
ain't neva had none since the first day
                          you saw a sunrise -
you neva even seen what one look like .....
                          wit all them bitches dat
be trippin' ova yo' azz "

Aji gave him a smirk.

Timmy: " Oooohu!.....dat hurts "

I roared, raising both knees and holding my
stomach as I rocked back and forth in my seat.
Everything had been extra funny these last

couple minutes since I finished my blunt and I knew I was probably louder than usual but I didn't care. Still tickled by Tyree's retort, Ardee put his head between his knees and snickered, then I laughed so hard I thought I was going to vomit.

Aji: " think y'all funny, dontchu...well y'all can suck ma nine inch dick   'cause you bitches ain't got a clue...c'mon,...who first? "

Tyree: " ooou, somebody gettin' nasty. Still, I can hook you up   tho'...whatchu want, one o' ma fitty cent or fi dolla ho's? "

Aji smirked and then snorted....

Aji: " FUN-NAY, very funny "

......and that ended the banter.

We spent hours there just hanging out, talking about every and any funny thing when Tyree hit the subject of Marie the new Pharmacist working at the pharmacy not tco far from my house. They were all talking about how fine looking she was and then Aji blurted out that he had seen me and her on several occasions...at the bus stop and once in Starbucks holding hands. I did tell Tyree about her but didn't want to say anything to Ardee and Aji yet because I didn't know just how far it was going to go. I had no idea he'd seen us, he'd never approached us. I really liked her but I didn't want to be so quick as to say we were a couple or anything. Tyree smiled wryly at Aji's comment, shook his head and to my defence jumped in.

Tyree: " don't hardly no shit gets by you...do it! "

Aji just sat there looking smug without saying a word. Ardee was quick to enquire;

Ardee: " fo' real son....you hittin' dat, datz yo' peeps?....how come you ain't
                    tole us nothin' dawg?"

Tyree: " hell yeah he hittin' it....ain'tchu dawg....I know ma dawg be hittin'
                    that "

Tyree offered, before he gave me a very tight hug from behind then changed it to another playful headlock and began poking his finger in my ribs; that started a little tussle which he tried to turn into another of his regular full scale Saturday rough and tumbles with me. He knew very well I'm ticklish and he'd always do this kind of clowning around when we were here with the other fellas on Saturdays or Sundays. I tried to get serious but he kept on and I.....

Timmy: " Yo, stop!.....stop playin'.... stop B! ...stop or ama hurt - Yo!... what tha-fuck "

....I managed between giggles,

Tyree: " you gon do what? "

Timmy: " aaaarrrghhh...da fuck, yo, yo...Tyree, aha-a-ha haaw.... y'all tell him tc stop "

Ardee: " we ain't gettin' involved in y'allz shit, we got better sense than dat "

Timmy: " oh-ma-gaawd!......yo, B...c'mon...aak, aha haa ahh...c'mon dawg lemmi go...ple...Da fuck, Tyreee Aaaghhh "

Tyree: " Yeah....see, I gotchu...mmph, what....whatchu gonna do now? "

Timmy: " aah ha,...I ain't...o-oh oww...I ain't comin' back ova here "

Aji: " give him a break son,
see you makin' the man begin to drool all
                          ova his self "

Ardee: " yeah, bwoi in
stitches...I think he might pass out "

With that, he reluctantly released me saying,

Tyree: " you damned lucky they
begged fo' you or I wuz gon tickle tha
                  shit outta you "

Timmy: " I swear,......one o' these
days ama fuck you up "

Aji: " you ain't gon do
shit...you jus frontin' "

Ardee: " right...nigga love dat
shit....rubbin' all up against you "

Timmy: " See!........there you go
wit dat shit again, y'all...... "

Ardee: " we see you love
wigglin' yo' l'il azz up against the brotha "

Timmy: " Nigga-fuck-
you......y'allz two a buncha mo'fuckin' faggots "

Tyree: " yo, y'all need to leave ma dawg tha fuck alone "

Ardee: " pshaw...you know he love dat shit too "

Timmy: " see whatchu cause!.....you always be doin' this shit - I tole you   to stop "

Aji: " don't get mad dawg, you know we jus fuckin' witchu "

Aji responded with a sincere look saying how much I should know that they have nothing but love for me. I couldn't help but smile,..... and shook my head; they were always funny, jovial,.......although nasty and sarcastic at times; but they were very good friends.

Tyree went back to the kitchen and returned in a couple of minutes with a Margarita he had made just for me - looking very official in a margarita glass.

We'd been hanging out for a couple hours and I was " lit ", ... we were all " lit " but me even moreso; what with that blunt and two margaritas, I was feeling good - maybe too good. So there I was,.... just sitting there.... and

Tyree went over to the CD Player and put in a CD he said he burned the day before. As the audio came on, he was playing " Shawty is a ten " .... I did like that joint. He walked over and stood directly in front of me looking down at me, his crotch in my face and a very devilish expression on his.

Timmy: " What! "

I quizzed, looking up at him through my half closed eyes, he said nothing. I then got up and safely made my way to the bathroom without stumbling,.... I really had to take a leak. I took care of business, came back out and as I was going by Tyree, he suddenly grabbed me by the waist from behind, all pasted to my butt; I didn't much like how he did that but said nothing, he enquired,

Tyree: " you ok ma dawg? "

I was ok,

Timmy: " am aiight "

and said so; but he still held onto me like that and asked again;

Tyree: " you sure you good? "

only this time, he was doing so breathing in my ear.

Timmy: " yea-am-aiight -
LEMMI GO NIGGA! "

I answered and twisted my body pulling away from his grip and throwing myself back down on chair.

Tyree: " daayum.....why you trippin' like dat dawg "

Timmy: " well get off me bro -
what the fuck is wrong witchu! "

Tyree: " awright!-awright! "

He offered quickly and apologetically, although wearing a smile to couple with the mischievous gleam in his eyes. There was silence, an uneasy one but I just returned to my seat. The silence lasted several minutes and I was half here and half there with thoughts of all kinds of funny things, even from long past, coming back to mind. When I took a conscious look at my surroundings several minutes later, everyone was sitting, just sprawled out....Aji, his head leaning completely on Ardee's left shoulder, the bottle of Hennesy two thirds empty. The two had either been dozing off or they were knocked out. Tyree came over, sat on my lap and I immediately looked over at Ardee and Aji on the sofa, shoving him off and wondered if they had seen that kind of intimate thing he just did.

Timmy: " you drunk dawg? "

I asked.

Tyree: " naw dawg...but you is tho'...ha ha haa "

He got back up and pulled me off the chair but my legs were somewhat wobbly. I wasn't ready to stand so he caught me, hugging me around the waist. We were so close, like too close, it felt strange. He brought his face closer to mine and seemed to be strangely searching into my eyes; I didn't want to look back into his but there was something in his gaze that made me wanna look back and.....when I did, I instantly tried to break away from his crushing yet gentle grip but could not.

Timmy: " c'mon dawg, let me down .... lemmi go-o "

I protested softly but he roughly spun me around, his body smothering me and his his pubic area - again - pasted to my butt. I could feel his manhood - hard and demanding against my rear, I knew it for sure because it generated such heat. I think I might have been in a panic mode as I kept trying to get him off me but in the tussle I tripped on the edge of the area rug and was falling to the floor, but he still didn't let go of me. Those little thuds and the tussle aroused Ardee and Aji who, when I looked up from the floor, were looking at us. A pair of devious grins greeted this nervous and strangely terrified teenager.

Timmy: " get off me nigga...get offa me...get da fuck off me ..... yo!, I
                    swear .... "

Oh, those two were very alert now.....and grinning from ear to ear. I think my feeling at that point was embarrassment mingled with fear but Tyree would not get off my back and no matter how hard I tried, I could neither toss him or turn myself face-up. By now the fellas were laughing real hard and that was making me quite irate; plus, Tyree was now trying to pull my wife beater over my head to muffle my verbal protests. He finally succeeded but I never-the-less continued to fight back as hard as I could while still hollering for him to get off me - but now he had me in a body scissors too. I couldn't get away. He rasped in my ear;

Tyree: " see how you wuz
trippin'.....I got yur azz now tho'......whatchu
                    gon do - huh! "

Timmy: "
Ummph!,...get...offa...MMPHF....yo, yo,....what
da fuck "

Tyree: " whatchu gon do -
huh! "

Timmy: " Black....mmph, I
swear....get....offa....MMPHF.... yo, yo....what
                    da fuck.... I ain't
playin' - STOP! "

Tyree: " why - whatchu gon
do! "

he boasted; I roared as hard and as loud as I
could....

Timmy: " MMRRRMPHF...GET
- UGH...GET OFF MA.....DA FUCK -
                    YO!........GET OFFA
MA AZZ NIGGA "

..... albeit muffled, and I felt quite undignified.
His whole demeanor suddenly changed, no
more smile, no more mischievous look. Of all
things, he looked like he was hurt, he asked;

Tyree: " why you gotta be so serious...am jus playin' witchu "

Timmy: " yo,..... two people play - I wuzn't playin' - aiight! "

Tyree: " dang son,....you ma boi,.... I wuz jus havin' some fun witchu "

Timmy: " c'mon B.... you see I wuzn't playin'.... "

                          then he seemed to regain his composure.

Tyree: " you so scared o' yo' l'il butt...what you scared ama stick you?

"He chortled and grabbed me again.

Timmy: " nigga, am tellin' you - get off me 'n stop wit dat shit "

Next thing I knew, he was trying to pull the back of my shorts down and quickly succeeded in doing so. He wrestled me to the floor and got back on top of me with my shorts almost halfway down my thighs;

Timmy: " Whatchu doin'! - get offa me! "

He was oblivious to all my warnings and demands; he now had me in a " Full Nelson " ; I tried to wiggle out of it but with absolutely no success. Holding me with his left hand, he then used his right hand to smack my bare butt timely and hard - but not hurtful. I agreed he was playing around but......my butt!....my bare butt! - and on top of that, the fellas were right there, gawking and snickering.

Timmy: " Tyree...son, stop, this ain't no joke...da fuck yo "

Tyree: " what y'all think, should I tap his l'il azz? "

He asked in a grating panting voice; Ardee was the first to respond;
Ardee: " hell yeah... fresh fish...give him dat jailhouse/prison shit "

Aji gave a strange and sickingly satisfied smile ..... and bit his lower lip before puckering, licking them and then went on to seal his blunt, slowly moistening it in his mouth. I couldn't tell if his move was one of taunting or nonchalance. He then made a loud cackle, his shoulders jerking as he did and,.... in rather matter-of-fact fashion, softly provoked,

Aji: " inmate, this yo' first

night ..... whatz yo' numba - you know
                        who bitch you is now? "

Now I was in full panic mode. They all seemed
quite serious and in complete unison with this
travesty Tyree was inflicting on me and I feared
something dreadful was about to happen to me.
Would Tyree really rape me as they were
indicating?...somehow I just couldn't see him
doing that to me - and though this was no
prison, I was held prisoner.... and I was really
scared. I couldn't escape his grip either, no
matter how hard I'd tried,..... and I thought: If
this thing was really going to happen to me, it
would be three against one and although I
wasn't a punk, it definitely would be no contest.
Ardee had eagerly gotten out of his seat and
was now standing over us; now I was more
scared than irate. I began to tell myself that this
was just a terrible nightmare I was having but
then Ardee hissed between clenched teeth,.....

Ardee: " get dat son,... then call
the whole block "

Now I was sure I was dreaming. I could hear
myself pleading......

Timmy: " Tyree,...whatchu doin'
bro, this shit ain't right "

...... but he discarded my pleas with common indifference. Rather, he seemed frenzied and cruel.....even sounded like it.

Tyree: " you beggin' convict?... oh, you want me to spare you fo' anotha   night? "

Still scared out of my wits, I swallowed hard......

Timmy: " yes,...mmph yes, don't do nothin' to me "

.....I begged - but to no avail. I felt groping hands clawing at my bare butt; all my embarrassment had long morphed into morbid fear as clammy hands tried to separate my butt cheeks. As I fought against the intrusion and locked my cheeks tightly, fingers were pressed so hard against my flesh, pulling against the hairs on my butt, that it began to sting. I was getting nowhere in this fight but I couldn't give up like this and tried to summon up my last ounce of courage - but there was no escape. My physical objection a failure, I had to try something else. Trying to sound even tougher and more menacing, I hollered;

Timmy: " Shit ain't funny Black...it ain't fuckin' funny - aiight,......you can   stop now "

But they were deaf to my protests. Instead, I
only received a snarling, merciless, sickening
rant from Tyree.

Tyree: " what, you mean you
don't want me to... "

Timmy: " Yo!...da fuck....STOP
- AIIGHT! "

Tyree: " all dat noise ain't gon
stop me boi, ama take dat l'il booty...hand
                    me some grease y'all "

Aji sat silently but was totally enjoying my
humiliation. I fixed pleading eyes on him and
he fully understood but just laughed out loud
and tapped both feet on the floor as though in
excitement and continued his snicker. I had no
recourse, it was now up to me to appeal to
Tyree's sanity;

Timmy: " Tyree...whatchu doin'
son - don't ... "

Tyree: " sshhh, don't cry... ama
be gentle witchu.... "

That didn't deter him any and he continued as

Ardee sicced him on.

Ardee: " oooh, Pretty Thug gon
get his booty tapped "

Tyree: " am goin' up in it right
now, watch "

Of all the good things I thought of this trio, was
this what they were really willing to do to me?
My butt exposed and his hands roaming all over
me, I began to feel pity for myself and tears
welled up in my eyes. I'd come to the
conclusion that there was no escape and told
myself that I would have to face this calamity
but I knew I was going to deal with them if they
didn't kill me first. However, seeing all my
toughness didn't avail anything, I began to
plead in earnest again, hoping to appeal to that
man deep inside Tyree that I knew had great
love and respect for me in the past.

Timmy: " how you gon do
somethin' like this to me bro...you ma boi "

Tyree: " datz why ama tap this
l'il booty; then ama send you home cryin'
                              to yo' mama "

My hopes were completely dashed when I
heard that.

Timmy: " pleeze son, don't
do.......Aj, you mean you ain't even got ma back
                    bro? "

I pleaded verbally, but it was Tyree who
answered with a snorting, sickening sound,

Tyree: " uh-uh-uh, ha-ha....I got
yo' back,....he-he-he....right here, phat
                    back too "

followed by Ardee with a chorus of snickers.
Aji - he merely pulled hard on his blunt then
exhaled, clouding his face in thick swirls of
smoke that slowly danced a spiral up over his
head. When he finally responded, he simply
offered;

Aji: " 'tain't nothin' 'bout no
backin' up...you gon jus have to give it up
                    son "

I couldn't believe it; but I did hear it. With that,
I was sure my fate was sealed. I knew it surely
would be the end of me because Tyree suddenly
seemed to be a totally different person and was
completely indifferent to anything I'd said or
done to prevent this....

(Chapter 3)

Ardee had become more excited and began to make embarrassing comments.

Ardee: " ooh shit! lookit all dat hair on this nigga'z azz, ...oh-ma-gaaa,
                   .... DAMN! "

He exclaimed, much to my utter disgust. I was in no way ashamed of my body but to have two men........

Aji: " oh, you just had to see some shit like dat, didn'tchu ... you need
                   to sit yo' azz down 'n leave ma boi alone "

Aji seethed with calm disdain. Ardee paid no attention to Aji and quickly got up, bent over me and was pulling my butt cheeks open despite my efforts to muscle up and lock them tight. Tyree seemed all the more spurred on and was even more aggressive as he tried to fix himself in a position to look between my butt cheeks too. But I was wiggling way too fiercely for him to get in that position; wiggling to get free and pull my shorts back up. Then Ardee started to make some disparaging comments;

Ardee: " see how he be grindin'
under you dawg, he want you to take dat
                    azz ..... "

That was a lie, I was doing no such thing and
his comments infuriated me.

Timmy: " get ... offa ... me nigg,
I swear ... yo Black "

Aji: " y'all need to stop dat
shit; don't you see it ain't a joke no more? "

Well it never was, at least not to me; but fingers
were still intrusive,

Tyree: " stop squirmin' ... you
ain't goin' nowhere - you sexy l'il thang "

Timmy: " Tyree, let me up ...
Tyree ... Tyree, yo I ain't playin' "

Hell-bent on having his way, Tyree started
gyrating on my bare butt with his breathing
heavy and irregular in my right ear. I quickly
turned away from Ardee's and Aji's gaze,
putting my face toward the other side of the
room and heard Ardee goading Tyree on ....
sending him into a higher state of paroxysm.

Ardee: " Yeaah ..... get dat azz

son .... tear it ..... oh shit - yea, stab it like
                                dat "

Eventually turning my face back the other way,
I saw Ardee wasn't laughing anymore, his face
was intense with ardor, egging Tyree on. It was
so shameful; why was Tyree doing this to me,
why? ... I couldn't imagine. To make matters
worse, not even Aji would really say or do
anything forceful in my defense.

Ardee: " tap dat virgin azz son? "

Tyree: " fresh fish - hellyea, he
gon get it "

Ardee: " ooow, I know datz gon
be tight "

Tyree: " he fightin' like a big
catch son..... fix ma dick right at dat hole &
                            lemmi force this dick up in
him "

Bending over us, Ardee took a quick step
closer.

From where I finally summoned the strength I
cannot say; I was so embarrassed and irate that
my nose was flaring and my eyes were

beginning to well up with tears again. I could feel blood rushing .... I knew I was about to murder these negroes [somehow]. I knew Tyree sensed it all and suddenly got off me...... he tried to help pull my shorts back up but I violently slapped his hands away. I sat there on the floor for a moment.

Aji: " y'all still think dat shit wuz so funny - don'tchu "

Neither of them said anything. I sat there fuming, I couldn't look any of them in the eye but I saw Ardee dash off to the bathroom. Everyone was silent and after a minute or so, I got up and stomped my way to the bathroom completely and without care barrelling into Ardee, who just so happened to be coming out, sending him off balance and tumbling to the floor; I then violently slammed the door shut behind me.

My chest was heaving like mad and I was shaking all over. I sat on the toilet cupping my face in my palms with both elbows on my thighs trying to figure out why my best friend would embarrass me like that - and in the presence of Ardee and Aji. I mean, us four were close as anything; we'd been hanging out for quite a while now and although I am the youngest they never made me feel unwelcomed or unwanted in any way .... matter of fact, I'd been seeing them for a few years playing ball and been kinda hanging around with the crowd of other fellas in their presence, especially since Tommy went off to college. How could he, why would he .... pull my clothes down, exposing me and have Ardee groping and poking his fingers between my bare butt cheeks, looking up my butt like that. I couldn't make any sense of it and neither could I think straight, especially since I was smoking and drinking. I could recall him doing lots of crazy things, especially when we hung out at his crib smoking and drinking, but this was beyond anything rational.

I had no idea how long I'd been sitting on that toilet, or even overhearing the buzz of seemingly heated conversation out in the living room, but I was brought back to my immediate surroundings with a knock on the bathroom door. It was Tyree inquiring softly.

Tyree: " yo, you aiight ma dawg? "

I wouldn't even speak to that piece of dirt....

Tyree: " ...... yo Timmy, Timmy! "

......still, I made no response. He then slowly opened the door, came up to me and gently placed a hand on my shoulder

Timmy: " get yo' hands offa me!
"

I demanded as I shrugged, displacing his hand from my shoulder then finally looked him in the eye.

Tyree: " you mad at me dawg? "

What the hell does he think?.

Timmy: " move! ..... get outta ma way "

Tyree: " Timmy - dawg ..... am so sorry.....am sorry "

I could see there was self reproach but I was beyond irate,

Timmy: " oh you sorry awright - a sorry motha fucka "

Tyree: " you got a right to be mad at me dawg but I didn't mean ..... "

Timmy: " yo, this yo' house but
am tellin' you ... move tha fuck outta ma
                         way or ama do somethin'
to you "

I was deeply hurt. He hesitated, gloom
overwhelming his entire face.

Timmy: " you a fucked up nigga,
you know dat ..... yeah, you a fucked up
                         nigga 'n I ain't got nothin'
to do witchu no mo' "

Devastation overcame him, he tried to speak
but his lip twiched and quivered; this normally
oratory man couldn't seem to find a word,.....
any words,.....and dropped his gaze to the floor
and bowed his head in apparent shame before
he eventually managed an utterance.

Tyree: " Timmy ...... dawg .... I,
I neva .... "

Timmy: " yeaah .... see how
dat shit feel "

I rebuked, as I purposely bumped into him on
my way out then plopped myself back down on
my chair in the living room. When I looked
across the room at Ardee and Aji, neither of
them would meet my gaze. The atmosphere

was different in the place from then on; you could hear a pin drop ..... the stench of mendacity was intense as Ardee and Aji attested they didn't think I was or would be upset over " that little prank " they'd pulled on me.

Timmy: " oh, y'all think am stupid; ya'll mothafuckaz is grimy. Dat wuz   some fucked up shit 'n y'all wuz laughin' but datz cool tho' ...   y'all gon see ... "

Petrified with horror and astonishment that I'd become so boisterous, Ardee got up and was slowly walking over to me when I raised my fists and stopped him in his tracks; he knew better than to want to spar with me; if he grabbed me, now that was a different thing.

Timmy: " yea, come near me mother fucka, come closer so I can murder   yo' azz "

Raising both hands up against his chest, open palms towards me in appeasement and backing away, he pleaded;

Ardee: " calm down dawg, ... don't make the neighbours hear us; they   gon complain "

He had some nerve, trying to tell me what to do ... trying to calm me down after all he'd done. I held my stance, still waiting, daring him to approach me - I shouted,

Timmy: " Fuck them, ... 'n fuck you too .... fuck all o' y'all - I ain't got
                                nothin' to hide "

Aji: " ma dude, please ..... I know you mad but, don't make the
                                neighbours have nothin'
over us "

Timmy: " I ain't no us,...they ain't got shit ova me! "

Aji: " aiight, aiight - I know but they still gon look atchu as bad as
                                they look at us "

Probably my first rational thought in the last several minutes; I paused and thought for a moment. I really didn't want to create a scandal and plopped myself back down in my chair still fuming.

A few minutes went by; Ardee pretended to have dozed off and only Aji was left to glance at me now from time to time, with the abject

look of woefulness. Good. I thought to myself
... serves them right; but I was still deeply
upset with that ... that Tyree, and wondered
why I didn't break my chair over his head when
he wasn't looking and run to his kitchen for a
steak knife. I knew I really couldn't get him
any other way. He was looking so
uncomfortable sitting over there at his computer
desk pretending to straighten up a mass of
paper he had cluttering it; as he sensed me
looking at him, he swirled his chair around and
made a nervous grin.

Tyree: " sup ma dawg ..... you
want another Margarita - or some more
                              chicken? "

He enquired pensively.

Timmy: " NIGGA!.... "

Tyree: " sssssssh! dawg pl..... "

He begged, raising both hands to chest level,
his clammy palms looking at me. I tried to
compose myself,

Timmy: " Yo, I ain't said I
wanted shit from you...did I?...... I don't need
                              nothin' from you ....
know what, let me get da fuck up outta

77

this bitch "

I snarled as I got up and stomped my way toward the door.

Tyree: " don't leave ma daw......I gotta talk to you B......lemmi talk......yo,   I wuz jus playin' "

Timmy: " ma-an -FUCK YOU! "

I retorted and stormed by him flinging the door wide open on my way out. He'd followed behind me trying to catch the door but was late - it closed with a very loud bang behind me. He continued out into the hallway and down to the elevator pleading with me quietly not to go, trying to hold onto my wrist, but the look I gave him made him quickly withdraw his hand. Still, he kept telling me to come back so we could sit down and talk this over "rationally" but, I flatly told him no and not to even try to touch me.

Tyree: " Ti-Timmy, wait......wait!, waa-it "

He whispered, his voice trailing off as he scurried alongside me on my way to the

elevator but I continued to ignore his pleas.
Even so, he continued to beg like a dog,
looking over his shoulders every now and then
to see if anyone had come out of their
apartment into the hallway.

Tyree: " please, don't go ma
dawg.......gimmi a chance to talk to you...... "

Timmy: " what! so you can
embarrass me some mo' bro? "

Tyree: " Noo, no.......to
apologize, I........ "

Wouldn't this be just what you'd expect, the
elevator was stopping on almost every floor on
its way up.

Timmy: " Ooh.....this fuckin'
elevator - c'mon bitch "

I seethed, senselessly banging on the door.
Looking over his shoulder again then finally
turning around to face me, he gently stroked my
arm.

Timmy: " you best stay away
from me nigga - I warned you "

I seethed,

Tyree: " please Timmy, we can talk 'bout this like grown men "

What was he implying, that I was acting immaturely; I clenched my fists in rage and gritted my teeth. Where is this damned elevator.

Timmy: " am warnin' you nigga, back up offa me...... "

Realizing my anger, he stepped back;

Tyree: " awright, awright "

I'd reduced his booming baritone voice to mere whimpers and whispers now.

Timmy: " ......'n stay tha fuck back "

Suddenly the elevator bell rang, it had reached our floor. He clammed up and I remained aloof; it was empty and there was nobody getting off on this floor. As the door opened I quickly and gladly slid right in, he followed hot on my heels and I was about to bolt back out but he barred the door and was about to hold me when, I think, he remembered the camera installed. Instead, he continued to plead with me to come back upstairs.

Tyree: " Timmy, don't do this
ma dawg "

Timmy: " ohma gawd - nigga
why is you followin' me, way you follow
                         me out here "

Tyree: " dawg, if you'da jus let
us talk, I know we can settle this "
Timmy: " it settled awready, I
know what to do - ama stay tha fuck away
                         from yo' azz "

His face twisted with torment,

Tyree: " ooh, ... don't do dat
dawg, I ..... mmphf "

he said, stopping short of saying something that
was probably too painful to utter or something
he thought might infuriate me even more.
Instead, he chose to get closer to me, up in my
face ... whispering;

Tyree: " please Timmy, please,
if you'd jus gimmi a chan.... "

At that moment the elevator reached the lobby
and I stepped toward its opening door but he

put his hand out and blocked my way again. I flashed him a fierce look, then backed off and looked him up and down. He relented and stepped back, humiliated; he was expecting me to say something more but I got off leaving him with mouth agape and a troubled look on his face. I stood waiting to see if he would follow me from here on, if he did I was prepared to start a fight. He held his ground, and with a puzzled and troubled look, started to scratch his beard..... the elevator door began to close and I looked away; seconds later I looked up to see the indicator lights showing that it was ascending. That scratching of his beard I've come to know by now means: " What the hell am I to do now " but that wasn't my problem, I knew what I had to do. I continued out to the front of the building and turned onto the sidewalk only to sense a little later someone coming up close behind me. It was Tyree, he'd changed his mind about going back up to his apartment and was now following me again. When he caught up to me, he tried to appear normal as we passed people going up and down the walkway; I said nothing but he was persistent;

Tyree: " talk to me dawg, its jus the two of us now we can ..... "

without looking at him, I warned.

Timmy: " there ain't no " we " to
do or say nothin' ..... you did what you
                          wanted 'n now ama do
what I want "

Tyree: " can't we jus sit out here
'n talk fo' a minit son ..... I really ..... "

Stopping now to look him in the eye,

Timmy: " nigga, I know you a
smart boi - I know you get it - I don't
                          wanna talk to you "

Tyree: " Timmy, I know what I
did wuz wrong but, you ma boi 'n .... "

Timmy: " Yo!....... you need to
leave me tha fuck alone befo' I do somethin'
                          out here to tarnish yo' precious
image "

Whether it was fear or awe, he stopped dead in
his tracks - speechless, for the first time since
he caught up to me,.......and I left him standing
there ..... fazed, forlorn and by himself. I
continued along the side walk and down the
block without looking back, vowing never to
see or speak to any of them again.

(Chapter 4)

A week went by and I never made a single attempt to call any of the fellas. When Tyree called on that Saturday, quite likely for me to come over for the basketball game, I didn't feel like talking to him and turned the phone over to voicemail.

Two more weeks went by with the fellas calling me almost on a daily basis but I just couldn't bring myself to speak to any of them. I just hung out with Pete during the day and visited some girl at night.

Two more weeks went by and the following Sunday Pete and I went shopping to get him a pair of sneakers. Pete was eager and ahead of me as we were about to enter the third store. Suddenly he bumped into someone,... it was Aji who was bearing two shopping bags in one hand and a cigarette and lighter in the other. Apparently happy to see me, he dropped his bags at his feet and excitedly fell upon me, greeting me with a crushing hug; I didn't hug him back .... it was an awkward feeling. When he did let go, he was beaming from ear to ear;
Aji: " whatzup ma dude? "
he said in an almost whisper. I wanted no part of him and could feel contempt swelling within

me. I was in that apartment again, surrounded by mocking faces, lurid minds, and sweaty indiscriminate hands with intrusively probing fingers. I was trying hard to repel them from my mind; I didn't want to stay too bitter, it would only serve to eat at me. I tried forgiveness but I couldn't evoke it - and tried to be civil but could only manage a half smile and a curt response:

Timmy: " chillin' "

and remained stoic. There was now an uneasiness about him and his eyes slowly and guiltily left mine and he turned to Pete, greeted him warmly with a "whatzup" and promptly turned back around proceed to hug me again - a hug like a long lost brother and, as a matter of fact, this time quite as though nothing had ever happened; he asked.

Aji: " damn, whatzup witchu dawg ...e'rrybody be askin' fo you ... 'boutchu "

I said nothing; he continued,

Aji: " daamn dawg I miss you - we miss you .... Tyree here, Ardee too, he tryin' on some sneakers "

Timmy: " oh word! ..... aiight "

I replied, not knowing what else to say. Before I could move, he firmly grabbed my arm and turned around, eagerly pulling me deeper into the store while Pete gave me one of his puzzled looks. What the hell, I thought, as I let myself be pulled along with Pete in tow. Upon seeing me, Tyree shot to his feet and came right over to us with that trademark pearly-white lopsided guilty smile. I sensed he was about to give me a hug but thought otherwise; he resorted instead to a firm yet gentle hand shake that lingered a bit too long; so much so, that I slowly but gently eased my hand out of his before he ever so quietly but sheepishly said in soft raspy voice.

Tyree: " can I holla atchu fo' a quick minit dawg? "

Damn, he looked pitiful. I'd never ever seen him look like that ..... never at any time. I really didn't want to talk to him; not right here, not right now but I didn't know if he would make a scene if I said "no"; I thought of Pete in our midst and..... I just said yes. He quickly stepped aside to a corner and I followed; as I turned around I noticed that Pete wasn't looking at sneakers but just watching us. I felt kinda nervous and somewhat irritated, although I wasn't sure why. I only knew that I wanted him to say what he had to say .... and quickly. As he brightened up the little corner with another big smile and opened his mouth to speak, I noticed that Pete had now turned back around and was giving his attention to the sneakers on the shelf.

Tyree: " yo ma dawg, Ioknow how to say it.... I ... I know you think the worst of me now and I can't blame you but,.... I need to talk to you dawg...... to seriously letchu know dat am sorry - to apologize ..... "

I cut him off right there now that I'd gathered what he wanted to talk to me about, but I wasn't comfortable standing in the store with him right now and quickly blurted;

Timmy: " apology accepted "

and stepped away but he held my arm.

Timmy: " whatchu doin'? "

I exclaimed, looking at him with raised brows.

Tyree: " am sorry "

He said, letting go of my arm.

Tyree: " I appreciate dat you accept my apology but I'd really like for you to gimmi a chance can I talk to you ... mano-a-mano ... one on one, to try to explain - make it up to you.... "

Make it up to me,.....I pierced his gaze with raised eyebrows.... a deflated look shrouded his face,.....he offered softly,

Tyree: " ......possibly!...... "

I couldn't find the words to say what I really wanted and I'd begun to feel more awkward than anything.

Timmy: " Ioknow bruh "

Tyree: " if I could only do this one thing - this one thing to not have me etched in yo' mind as...... "

Although he kept his voice low, he was getting really sentimental and I certainly didn't want anyone to just walk by and see and hear how soft and sentimental he was at that moment - talking to another man; I suddenly realized it. Even so, I found myself retaliating with bitter sarcasm, posing.....

Timmy: " as what!.....as being foul, untrustworthy, indifferent to -   fucked up! You unworthy of any real true friendship. I wuz beginin' to look atchu and

                              regard you as ma friend...... "

Tyree   " I know dawg, I know - but I am yo' friend dawg..... "

Timmy: " Ha! "

..... and had to stop as I found my temper flaring.

Tyree: " Timmy, if you only knew how much you a friend to me you wouldn't......let me at least have a chance to explain ma'self 'n..... "

The man looked like he wanted to cry;

Timmy: " I, ... yo ... "

Tyree: " don't be mad at me no mo' dawg, ... please, at least gimmi a chance to talk to you "

the whole thing was getting too awkward, I told him;

Timmy: " yo, lets talk about it later "

Tyree: " later when? - today? "

his face brightened at the sound of hope, the look of distraught melting a bit and that got me flustered.

Timmy: " IOKNOW NIGGA! "
I snapped, not really sure who or what I was
mad at.....

Tyree: " ss-ss-sssh!   "
.....but the sight and thought of him telling me
to be quiet made me realize I was mad at
everyone, him most all.

Tyree: " Dang dawg .... why
you gotta be mad at me again fo' .... whadid I
do now "
He asked, sounding like a kid just caught in
mischief. I then caught myself trying to still the
rage inside me.....

Timmy: " aiight, aiight "
.....then just ignored him and walked away. I
joined Pete and hastened him to choose his
sneakers. I did this especially to hurry him out
of that store as fast as I could ... before the
fellas were done and ready to leave. As we
were about to leave, Pete declared he had to go
say goodbye to Tyree first, ... I reluctantly let
him, hoping not to let on that the real fuss was
between me and the fellas. As I stood by the
door on the outside waiting, I watched as Pete
gave him a hug then walked off looking back
over his shoulder at him several times. Tyree
just stood there looking quite sad and forsaken
- and I thought, " good ".... as Pete and I
headed off down the street; were I alone, I'd
have just hopped in the first and nearest cab and

disappeared out of their sight.

As we strode along the sidewalk, Pete enquired anxiously of me as to all that back and forth in the store. I quickly dispelled any further curiosity by explaining that Tyree merely wanted to talk to me about something he said was serious and important. I wasn't quite sure that he believed it but he was wise enough to let it go at that and we continued on, doing more shopping down the block. When we were done, we stopped for a bite at a fast food restaurant before going home.

Every now and then my mind would wander back to Tyree and for some strange reason, I came to realize for the first time that I really wasn't mad at him at all. I'd viewed him as my friend,.... and still did. I was deeply upset by what he'd done but somehow I was still regarding him as my friend. I'd told him I accepted his apology but the question I had to ask myself was: Did I really forgive him? It didn't take me long to conclude that I did but then, that begged another question: Why? This latter question I wrestled with all day and could not come up with an answer.

Later that night, I had trouble sleeping, images

of that mauling moment still running through my head. I finally opened my eyes, it was 1:42 a.m. - that hour and still I couldn't fall asleep! I figured ..... what the hell ... I'll go see what Tyree has to say as well as make him know exactly how I feel and what I thought about what he'd done to me.

A sudden leap to my feet and I found myself hastily putting my sneakers on; I tossed one of my basketball jerseys over my shoulder and grabbed a bottle of water out of the fridge as I snuck out, carefully and as silently as I could, pulling the front door shut. I continued down the sidewalk deep in thought until I was halfway down the fourth block before I realized that I'd left my wallet in my pants pocket. Now I could not get on the bus but instead of turning back, I elected to keep on walking. I wish I'd remembered it though because it was still only 2:00 a.m., and if stopped by the cops I wouldn't even have any kind of identification.... not to mention, I didn't have my phone...I'd left that to charge. I continued slowly on, acutely aware of my night surroundings and its activities.

I was near Tyree's building now and found my heart racing unusually. The lobby was well lit and bare except for two tenants.

After riding the elevator up to Tyree's apartment, I stood there a couple seconds and wondered if I should really ring his bell at this hour. I figured since I'd come this far already, why not? So I did......four quick but distinct rings. I waited and no one answered; I rang again once and moments later I could see that someone was looking through the peep hole. The locks turned, the door quickly swung open and Tyree was standing there in his boxers, groggy eyed with an enormous, well pitched tent which he made no attempt to conceal.

Tyree: " whatup dawg! ..... "

He asked, his voice gruffy, a faint smile creasing his lips.

Timmy: " I know its late bruh but I ...... "

I started to apologize;

Tyree: " .... whatchu - come in, come in .... lock the door "

but he brushed it aside. I continued.

Timmy: " .....you said you wanted to talk to me so .... "

Tyree: " yo dawg, Iemmi take a quick piss, ...I gotta go "

He begged as he hurried off to the bathroom reminding me,

Tyree: " lock tha door behind you "

I locked the door and followed him into the

living room where I could hear him emptying his bladder like water running off a broken storm drain on a roof. I sat there on the sofa with my shoulders down and my arms hanging between and squeezed by my thighs. I looked around at that very spot,... the spot of the greatest embarrassment of my life and all I could feel for myself was a tinge of self-pity. I dwelt on the sad recollection of the moment and was almost completely transported when I heard,

Tyree: " so whatz up dawg,...I know you still mad at me but am glad you came "

Suddenly the words came tumbling out of my mouth....

Timmy: " yo, Ioknow why you did... "

Tyree: " I CAN'T HEAR WHATCHU SAYIN' DAWG "

..... he thundered from the bathroom as I tried to speak louder.

Timmy: " am sayin' I know its late,...maybe I should come back another...... "

Tyree: " come talk dawg, what...you scared of?.... "

The bathroom door was still open, I got up and inched a little closer and hesitating halfway, trying to explain to him that it wasn't really my intended plan to come over at this hour.

Tyree: " come ova here dawg, I

still ain't hearin' nothin' you sayin' "
He encouraged again. I gingerly inched my
way over to the bathroom door not wanting to
get too close but he invited;
Tyree: " come in,....you can
come in "
again, I inched closer,.....and I peeked in, he
was standing over the toilet still urinating, his
boxers a pool of shimmering red sateen
surrounding his ankles. I hesitated as he turned
slightly to his left and looked over his left
shoulder...
Tyree: " come in dawg .... "
he offered yet again, sounding almost annoyed
at my delay. Turning around to face me fully
with a grin;
Tyree: " what! - you scared? "
he asked, in a playful tone this time.
Timmy: " hell no! "
I bravely replied,.... lying but, still only made a
half a step more forward. I wasn't very scared,
if at all, ... I think I was just overcome with
some sort of anticipation. He smiled again,
then turned his head around as he jiggled his
dick. He lingered for a moment then suddenly
turned around to face me; I turned my gaze
away. Brushing against me as if he was going
to go by, he said;
Tyree: " .... you ain't gotta be
scared son .... you ma dawg, I ain't gon do
nothin' to you "

trying to assure me. In retrospect, I guess he was being kind phrasing it like that, considering I'd come visiting alone at that hour of the night after what he'd done to me. It was only now that he bent down and started to pull his boxers up,.....and I saw his dick...huge and rigid. I mean, I've seen all of the fellas at one time or another and they've seen me so it was nothing strange. There had been instances where we've ended up in Men's Rooms on several occasions, the movies, the park restroom and so on but I've never seen it hard, and out, before - and this, for whatever reason, felt strange.

Why was I thinking about his dick, I thought - then tried to brush the image aside. I stood there as he washed his hands, and then when he tried to get by me on his way out, instead of stepping back out the door or moving to the side so he could pass, I inadvertently moved in the same direction he did and we bumped into each other in the narrow confines of the bathroom. His naked stomach brushed against me. I quickly stepped backwards and almost fell into the bathtub but he caught me by the elbow and yanked me toward him with such power, our bodies bumped again and I felt his dick rub against me just below my navel. It was another very awkward moment and I pulled away from his grip and backed away until I was just outside the bathroom door.

As he went by he calmly said;

Tyree: " come, ... siddown dawg "

I followed and we sat in the living room next to each other for a minute before I realized that he'd been drinking, I could smell liquor on his breath. I asked him,

Timmy: " is you drunk? "

he made a frown and looked at me in disbelief.

Tyree: " drunk! "

Timmy: " I, ... amean if you wuz drinkin' "

Tyree: " yeah, what? "

Timmy: " nothin' .... am jus askin' "

I answered, trying to be casual but now aware that the question was probably silly, unwarranted or both. I began to nibble on my thumbnail and looked away up to the ceiling and across the room.

Tyree: " you aiight dawg? "

Timmy: " uh huh "

Tyree: " you behavin' odd "

I didn't know what he was implying but the question got under my skin. I was about to try and hide it by asking what he wanted to talk about but he asked again,

Tyree: " you aiight? "

Timmy: " yes! "

I replied irritated. He eyed me questioningly

with a frown and asked again.

Tyree: " you sure you aiight son...amean.... "

That did it, I lost my cool - and wasn't sure I knew why.

Timmy: " yo!....whats yo' pro'lem.....whatchu stressin' me fo'? "

Tyree: " dang son, I ain't tryin' to stress you ... why you sayin' dat? "

Timmy: " yo, whatchu wanna talk to me 'bout? "

He shuffled and fixed himself sideways in the seat in order to face me.

Tyree: " Timmy, I know I done somethin' dat I had no business doin' but you ain't gotta .... "

Timmy: " look, you tole me you wanna say somethin' .... whats up? "

Tyree: " yeah, yeah but chill out ... what, you didn't get dat pussy or somethin' "

He teased with a grin. I had to smile, I was snapping at him for no apparent reason and he was trying to lighten the atmosphere.

Tyree: " you want me make you a drink? ... a margarita? "

Timmy: " yea "

I replied sharply.

Tyree: " aiight, jus relax right there - ama fix you one "

As he got to his feet, he looked down at me again and said,

Tyree: " I know somethin' ain't right ... you sure you good? "

Timmy: " uh huh...yea, am good "

I replied rather nonchalantly;

Tyree: " naaw, somethin' you ain't tellin' me.... "

he pressed, gnawing at his inner lower lip. I said nothing and he continued to stand there towering over me. Finally he spoke again,

Tyree: " so what is it? "

Timmy: " you gon make dat drink or what! "

I demanded authoritatively.

Tyree: " ok, ok, ... gimmi "

He conceded and turned about.

As he walked to the kitchen to make the drink, I found myself smiling, bemused at my attitude. Why was I so edgy?. Leaning back in the chair with my hands behind my head, I chuckled at the thought of having seen him naked in the bathroom earlier and just now watching as he walked to the kitchen with his boxers wedged between his butt cheeks. He must have sensed that I was looking, as he began to spread one leg kinda wide as he went, tugging at his boxers and pulling it out. I felt exceptionally comfortable and even more at ease than ever before as I sat there. The now somewhat darkened room, the steady ticking of the clock on the wall, the hum of the air conditioning unit in the window and the constant drip from the faucet were at a steady rhythm; only my strangely racing heartbeat pounding in my ears was out of sync, disturbing the orchestra of other sounds.

Tyree: " almost done now "
He chimed from the kitchen, breaking the otherwise stillness.
Timmy: " what? "
I asked, as I if didn't hear - and I didn't know why.
Tyree: " I'm almost done "
I didn't answer, but found myself smiling as I eased my sneakers off with my feet and settled back more comfortably in my soft seat.

As I continued to wait while he made my drink, I pulled my feet up onto the sofa and snuggled up in the fetal position with my head on the cushion against the arm-rest. As he was approaching, I sat up and watched him return with a margarita in one hand and a mug in the other, his seemingly semi hard dick rolling from side to side in his boxers, creating a shimmering effect as he moved under the light in the foyer and entered the living room.

He handed me the margarita and sat at his computer desk across the room from me sipping his mug, I presumed tea, with his back to me. Suddenly, he swung around in the swivel chair and faced me, looking me in the eye - a very sorrowful look, his dark eyes pleading, and before he even apologized again, I knew he was sincere.

Tyree: " yo, ma dawg, I know what i done made you hurt....'n datz the last thing I'd ever want.....I shouldn'ta done it - Ioknow what came over me; all I know is when I seen yo' face afterwards............mmphf....... "
He paused, sighed heavily and bowed his head; then continued again.

Tyree: " ....'n then you lock yo'self in the bathroom........wouldn't even talk to me....brush my hand away when I touched you - and you just stomped yo' way out.........slammin' the door like dat. I wuz like - DAMN!, homey ain't gon even wanna see me again......but when you said what you said 'n left me standin' out there in front o' the building - then never returned none o' ma calls or even answer when I call - I wuz like, ... he don't wanna see me no mo' - don't wanna talk to me "
Good, I thought; he did feel what I wanted him to feel: embarrassed, rejected and dismayed.

Timmy: " ma-aan, whatchu did somethin' like dat fo'. You seen what Ardee did tho' .... he wuz grabbin' on ma butt, forcin' his finger up in ......dat wuz some fucked up shit son .... fo' real .... I wasn't feelin' dat shit ....

100

knowamsayin'; I wuz gonna do somethin' to
him B... you know dat, right? .... I wuz....datz
wuz tha most fucked up.... "
I lamented as tears almost welled up in my eyes
[when I get mad I can feel the blood rush to my
nose, my hands begin to shake and my eyes
well up with tears]. He realized I was having
difficulty just talking about it and tried to
comfort me.
Tyree: " I think I know how you
feel son 'n am truly sorry - I am "
Timmy: " dat shit hurt .... he neva
had to do no shit like dat "
Tyree: " its my fault, I take all
blame fo' dat.....truly dawg, am so sorry I hurt
you...from the bottom of my heart, I mean it...
just tell me
                          what I need to do to
make it up to you... "
Timmy: " make up? what can
you do to undo dat? "
Tyree: " Ioknow, but if it mean
anything - Ardee tole me he real sorry .... "
Timmy: " he got good reason to
... motha fucka. How you think he woulda felt
if I'da done dat to him "
Tyree: " I know .... but am
willin' to do anything to make you feel better ...
I mean it. Tell me whatchu want me to do, jus
tell me "
He implored as he got down on one knee in

front of me and sandwiched one of my hand between his palms.

Timmy: " man you be doin' some real crazy shit sometimes; still, we boyz ... knowamsayin' so I ain't neva really tripped or nothin'

not, not .... even like dat night .... Independence Day, ... when you wuz standin' between me and Aji with yo' arm 'round my shoulder...you....you wuz....I ain't even talkin' 'bout dat tho'....dat wasn't nothin'.....but DAT shit in the living room with them fellaz right there 'n shit ...you shouldn'ta ... yo...... "

Tyree: " I see you hurt dawg, 'n I know you pissed 'cause I see you wipin' yo' eyes - I know tears wellin' up; I know datz happenin' 'cause you mad 'n I know how you be when you mad... but I'm beggin' you, ...dawg, don't botha sayin' nothin' to Ardee..... its ma fault, I 'cause you that pain - I hope you gon forgive me 'cause .. I neva meant wuz to hurtchu - I swear "

He got up, turned the reading lamp in the corner on, then sat back down, real close to me, kinda sideways again. I had to turn my head to the side to look in his eyes but then I just looked away again. He got up again, this time squatting in front of me and took both my hands in his two; I looked up and gazed into a pair of pitiful puppy dog eyes.

Tyree: " I missed you ma dawg

....you ma boi and I love you, you know dat?.....right! just tell me you forgive me, tell me dawg so I can know "

He pleaded again with those puppy dog eyes. I missed him too but I was way too mad to be anywhere near any of them at the time because my temper would not allow me not to do something violent, something that I now think I'd really have regretted. I didn't respond to anything Tyree said but as I looked down at the floor I could see the head of his dick hanging out the leg of his boxers; I started to laugh. He looked at me real puzzled asking,

Tyree: " what? "
Timmy: " nothin' "

I lied successfully.

Tyree: " whatz so funny? "
Timmy: " nothin'.....nothin' "

I did it again,........but I couldn't stop laughing; to the point where I swallowed a sip of margarita and it went down the wrong way. It caused me to start coughing incessantly. I guess I must have given the whole thing away by probably glancing downward again because this time he saw and looked down too - his big ol' dick hanging out one leg of his boxers.

Tyree: " shiiit..that ain't nothin'
B.... "

He said shamelessly, both verbally and in his demeanor. I laughed all the more, but he merely shrugged his shoulders nonchalantly and replied,

Tyree: " 'tain't like I got somthin' you ain't got ...... besides, you ma dawg, 'tain't nothin' to me fo' you to see me like this ... I walks

        'round ma crib half nekid alla time anyways .... dat don't upset you, do it? "

Timmy: " Ioknow "

I answered, shrugging off the question.

Tyree: " if it bother you I can go put somethin' mo' on "

Timmy: " naw .... not really ... amean ... amsayin'... if datz how you do "

Tyree: " you sure? "

Timmy: " dang son, I ain't tryin' to tell you how to be .... you in yo' house "

Tyree: " datz ... datz, jus me son .... I, am jus .... "

Timmy: " jus nasty, datz what you is "

I rebuked in jest and took another sip, careful not to choke this time. He grinned;

Tyree: " no, amean ... if it make you feel uncomfort ... "

Tyree: " do you son, I ain't trippin'; its yo' tripe, if you wanna let it hang out "

I replied,........ laughing again. He started laughing too, then plopped himself down next to me and gave me such a tight hug, he'd pulled our cheeks together. We were like that for a couple of seconds and out of nowhere, he brought his face around and kissed me on my lips - not long, just a little bit lingering. The whole thing felt indescribably and incredibly strange and I felt something unusual surge through me - strongly. I was completely astonished.

Timmy: " what da!... "

Tyree: " am sorry, am sorry .... I shouldn'ta done dat but I couldn't help it - am sorry "

He begged, and quickly got up.

Timmy: " whatchu do dat fo'? "

I found myself asking him, not knowing what else to say or do.

Tyree: " sorry dawg ... it jus came ova me ... am sorry ..... you mad? "

Timmy: " not really mad like dat but amsayin' ... amean, Ioknow ... whatchu askin' me dat for? "

Tyree: " now ... you gon get mad 'n leave again - right? "

Timmy: " no "

I answered softly, shifting my head down.....and not knowing how to look up at him again, ...look him in the eye.

I didn't even know I'd answered him until I heard myself. I felt oddly excited and aroused, and knew I wasn't even mad ... why wasn't I mad after what he'd just done? He'd kissed me on my lips and that was not normal - it just wasn't, not for me, at any rate. I was supposed to be mad but I wasn't; nor was I distressed. On the contrary, I was excited, extremely excited. I tried to calm myself with the thought that it was just an over-zealous, spontaneous act on his part simply because I said I wasn't mad; an overly friendly gesture that he'd made with no ulterior motive. I was also glad that things were now back to normal but offended - no.

As I cast my eyes toward him with my head still down, I noticed that his dick was hard again...rock hard - and strangely, for the first time, found that mine was rock hard as well [and it had been like that for quite a while now]. I was all aflutter.....nervous with excited anticipation. In anticipation of what? I quietly questioned myself before he interrupted my swirling thoughts.

Tyree: " we still boyz then dawg ... you still ma dawg? .... or is you really still mad at me? "

Timmy: " negro, we ALWAYS been boyz ... 'tain't been nothin' else "
I replied, feeling suddenly relieved and elated yet trying to conceal my exuberance by not looking him in the eye. He grabbed me in a crushing hug;

Tyree: " datz ma dawg yo "

he trumpeted ecstatically. He pulled me up off
the sofa and hugged me again, very close this
time; and I wondered if he'd felt my hard dick
against him. I was doing everything to hide it,
and I eased my lower half off him when he tried
to get closer. I quickly finished the remainder
of my drink and asked him to make me another.
When he did and brought it to me, I asked;
Timmy: " yo, Tyree.... ama sleep
ova here tonight .... if datz cool witchu .... all
you gotta do is jus gimmi some extra sheets 'n
am

                              good ... ama jus open
this day bed up "
Tyree: " hellyeah son.....any time
you want son "
I said that lying through my teeth. He replied
jubilantly, his eyes lighting up as he gave a big
smile.
Tyree: " ama hook you up "
Deep down I suddenly realized that I really
wouldn't mind laying down on his bed. Still, I
asked,
Timmy: " aiight, where the sheets
at? "
and he sat next to me again;
Tyree: " son, you ain't really
gotta sleep out here "
Timmy: " naw, naw....I ain't
tryin'a put you outta yo' bed "
Tyree: " is you fo' real son I

107

got a *real* nice, big comfortable bed, wit the very/best quality mattress in there, covered over wit six

hundred thread count sateen - 'n you think ama have you sleep out here? ...naaw ..... hell-no, we ain't havin' dat ... you ain't gon sleep out here on dat dawg .... c'mon now "

The strangest things were happening inside me. I was giddy with excitement; his response sent those warm waves of delight through me. He got to his feet and pulled me up by my hands but I didn't want to stand because my brick hard dick had lost none of its power and was still trying to fight its way out of my shorts. I was abashed; even so, I stood. And in another moment of closeness, he caressed my left cheek and kissed me, this time taking my entire lower lip into his mouth. My body shuddered with excitement but I pulled away, exclaiming softly ......

Timmy: " whatchu doin' this for? "

......because for some reason I couldn't let on that I had the desire for him doing such a thing to me.

Tyree: " you didn't like dat? "

Timmy: " Ioknow "

There I was, lying yet again. After all that was exposed between us, I still couldn't find it within me to be candid.

Tyree: ' you wanna do it again?
"

I avoided the question by asking again;

Timmy: " whatchu did dat fo'
tho'? "

He gave no answer. Hoping I'd hear an answer
that would give credence to my innermost
thoughts, that I did like this feeling yet knowing
full well, and deep within, the vexing it would
cause my soul later; I languished in silence. I
was without a sane thought, dizzy with delight
and wanting the moment to go on without end.

Breaking my thoughts, he quickly pulled me
close up against his groin where I could feel his
huge warm pulsating dick between us; he gave
me a long lingering tongue kiss. I didn't pull
away this time; I readily succumbed to his
overpowering but passionate aggression and
found myself moaning softly in rapturous
delight.

When he pulled away, I searched his face and
eyes long and hard while my heart thundered in
my chest. What was this I thought ..... where
would it take me? I'd never been kissed by a
man before....... to be honest, I'd never even
thought about something like that.

Another kiss erased all sanity from my being

and I just reveled in the splendor of it, knowing quite well that even in this, my most strangest of moments of sexual intimacy...[well, it was sexual, although we only kissed], I could not honestly say I felt sickened by it, that it didn't feel good, and I mean......real good too.   I didn't know just what to expect from us being together like this. Mind you I wasn't naive to two men being together like this, but I didn't know how far this was going. At any rate, I just knew I was not afraid to be with him even after what had just happened those several weeks earlier.

He led me by the hand to the bathroom and I followed willingly. He turned the shower on and began to peel my shorts off. I was trembling and my dick was still hard; the trembling I could hide but my dick served as open evidence that I was enjoying every minute of what he was doing.

Maybe I should just let go - not try to hide anything ... just let him, but something in me would still fight.   He kissed me again,.....urgently; hugged me tightly and kissed my neck. He traced his lips along my neck and ear then back to my lips; he came back again, this time the tip of his hot tongue, wetting as it went along my cheek and up to my ear,......
when I felt his hot breath in my ear, his hard

dick, his body against me ... my hand left my side and cradled the back of his head begging him to devour my neck. He was demanding, I was submissive...... I succumbed. I was helpless in the arms of another MAN.

He whispered in my ear.
Tyree: " you scared ..... you afraid? "
I could only muster a whimper;
Tyree: " don't be scared, I ain't gon hurtchu "
Timmy: " aiight "
I managed to mutter breathlessly.
Tyree: " don't be scared "
I was on weary and uncontrollably wobbly knees and couldn't fall;
Timmy: " oooh, mmmph "
he was making mince-meat of my insides, churning my brain, making puree, stirring it into submissive liquid nothingness.
Tyree: " son, oh Timmy .... if you only knew how long I been wantin' to jus hold you like this .... I love you Timmy .... you hear me what am
                    sayin' to you dawg? "
I could only mutter a weak but delighted,
Timmy: " uh huh "
Tyree: " eh? "
I suspect he couldn't hear me on account of the shower;

111

Timmy: "Ye-es"
I said over the tepid streams of water beating
against the tub, enveloped tightly in his arms
and clouded in mind and shrouded in the misty
steam filling the bathroom.

I completely submitted myself to his bidding as
he directed me under the water stream and
began gently washing my body. My du-rag and
head were soaking wet and I could taste my
salty perspiration mingled with the water as it at
first slowly trickled down my face then in great
profusion, wetting my lips with the blandness
of plain water. I put my head directly under the
stream to completely wash away the saltiness
then opened my eyes to look at him. His face, a
picture of gentle, thoughtful agreeableness and
pleasant inquisitive serenity as he studied my
body with each stroke of his lathered hand. His
lips were slightly agape, head slightly bowed
and droplets of water trickled from the canyons
of cornrows to his forehead and down the side
of his nose. He lathered my body ever so
gently, massaging my pecs and slowly moving
down to my midsection. He made a soapy swirl
around my hairy belly button, seeming to
deliberately delay his hand movement before
going further southward to comb my pubic
hairs with his fingers.

My body tensed in hunger and anticipation of a

more intimate touch - and when he finally touched my hard dick, the heavy weight of my heart was lifted. Using two fingers, he gently and slowly peeled the foreskin back revealing the crimson head beneath; he then made a fist with my dick in his palm and pulled forward, folding foreskin back over then with a tight hold, peeled it back over the head of my dick. He did it again, gently, teasingly,.... pulling it back and forth a few more times.

Timmy: " cccccccctt a-ummmm "
Tyree: " you like dat? "
Timmy: " uh-uh "

He lathered the head lovingly for what seemed like several minutes and my arms found his shoulders and my palms the back of his neck. My head was heavy, I couldn't stay up, and my forehead found a resting place against his.

I thought his intent was to bring me to an eruptive climax but he suddenly stopped. I opened my eyes and gazed down between us at the biggest dick I'd ever seen, pointing at me threateningly; he was as huge as he was long, ten inches at least!

As I continued to secretly marvel at his manhood, he slowly turned me around and began to lather my back starting at the shoulders. It had been an almost silent operation since we entered the bathroom but now as he was lathering my lower back, going down to my butt cheeks - I kinda froze, a natural reaction I guess, and clenched them. A sudden movement from his left hand peeling over my dick again seemed to soothe me and I relaxed as he used a forefinger to stroke underneath my dick's head.

A few seconds of toying with my dick like that and he again suddenly abandoned it to palm a butt cheek with his soapy right hand. I was much calmer now and didn't flinch; then his hand strayed from soaping my already soapy cheeks to slipping deep between them in a fluid motion; involuntarily I tensed..... his hand paused;
Tyree: " I know you scared dawg ..... but don't be, I love you, I do ... I wouldn't do nothin' to hurtchu - you know dat, don'tchu? "
he offered reassuringly..... and I uttered a somewhat scared and feeble but slightly high-pitched....
Timmy: " uhhuh "
...... and tried to relax. Continuing to reassure, he went back to lathering my lower back,.....then sneakily edged his way back down to my butt. I let him and he slipped all four fingers between them, moving it up and down,.....ever so slowly bringing the lead forefinger closer to my hole.....

Timmy: " M-mm-mmmm "

.......and I found myself stiffening a bit.

Tyree: " let me wash you dawg, don't be scared "

Timmy: " mm-m uh-huh "

I uttered, a quaking falsetto mingled with fear and want. He shuffled closer behind me, causing me to lose my balance and catch myself against the tiled wall. His body that close to me, I could feel his hard dick against my thigh and his urgent yet not so intruding, this time, finger rubbing back and forth against my butt hole. Suddenly, a pained yet delighted sound escaped his lips....

Tyree: " Mmmh! "

..... and I felt him caress my shoulder with his cheek. As he gently stroked, I could feel his hot breath before he put an arm around my waist and pulled me off the wall and brought my back up against his hardness. I inhaled deeply and tilted my head backwards as he kept up the one-fingered butt hole lathering. His soapy fingers continued to massage my butt hole, and when he pressed hard against it, I began to swoon as I entered a state of uncontrollable emotion.....a state I'd never before experienced and as much as I tried, I couldn't suppress a loud, delirious yet curious moan.

Timmy: " O-ooohmmph! "

Tyree: " Oooh ye-ees! "

My knees offered me little support,
Tyree: " you gon be awright
dawg,....you gon be aiight "
.....and Tyree quickly rinsed me off and dried
my head with my du-rag still on. He used his
hands to remove most of the water from my
body and indicated I should step out of the tub;
I did,......and just stood there while he turned
the water off, then held me by my shoulders
from behind....
Tyree: " you cool my dawg?.....
"
Timmy: " uh-huh "
.....He kissed my neck, placed his hands on my
hips and gently urged me out of the bathroom,
following me to the bedroom with his two
hands never leaving my hips.   As I stood, he
began to massage from my damp chest to my
feet with a little baby oil before he said for me
to lay on the bed.....When I did, he turned me
over on my stomach, then stood over me.
Tyree: " Daayum dawg, ...you
is gorgeous, - beautiful - DAMN!, YOU IS
ONE HAIRY MO'FUCKA TOO,...... I could
eat you up "
He whispered in amazement and delight as he
slowly began to move his strong expert hands
over my body, caressing and teasing every
muscle, soothing me to the point I could almost
fall off to sleep, for he had completed his task
of bathing my body and mind.

His hands now began roaming my body
differently - up and down, up and down.....
investigating every pore it seemed; then he
finally stopped at my butt, holding and
squeezing each cheek, all his fingers between
them except for his thumb ....

Tyree: " you aiight my dawg?"

Timmy: " uh uh "

....was all I could manage, my throat had gone
completely dry.

Tyree: " you know what ama do
now? "

...... he asked raspily;

Timmy: " Idunno "

Tyree: " ama give you somethin'
you never had before "

Timmy: " I don't care.... you can
do whatever you want"

I had no idea exactly what that was but so far
everything had only given me a sexual
awakening I'd never had before and I was
content to undergo this ecstatic experiment. To
my delight, he wasted no time, and although I
didn't know exactly how far this was going, the
anticipation of him doing some other new thing
to me tonight had my poor little heart just about
ready to bust out of my chest and my aching
dick competing for relief. He passionately
kissed my butt cheeks over and over before
spreading them wide open and burying his face,

tongue first, right on my butt hole. My body
shuddered violently;

Tyree: " daang,....you aiight
son? "

Timmy: " yeaah "

Tyree: " boi, ... you is covered
in goose pimples "

Timmy: " its yo' fault "

I replied lazily. He continued briefly but gently
and stopped abruptly .... I thought I was going
to fall out of my skin as my body twisted in
every which way while I swear my toes curled
and locked in that position...then he started
again, this time ravenously and noisily.

Timmy: " ccccctt....oh shit - do it
dawg, do it.......oooh.....shit....don't stop, don't
stop - Oh! ccccctt N-Ngh!, damn son, oh, oh,
o-ooh ma-gaaw - don't stop! "

Tyree: " you like dat shit "

He quizzed, his voice muffled, his face still
buried between the crack of my butt.

Timmy: " Yes, Yes, yes, ... oh
yes ..... Tyreeee ..... oh fuck yes, ... sshit,
mmm,, ngh, ghfn, ... ooh, oh shit .... whatchu
doin' to me son,

                            whatchu .... oh yea, you
got me, you got me dawg "

He finally stopped after several minutes. I was
breathless, my body was alive, being set afire
by the touch of his warm tongue. It ached for

him ......I ached for him, I craved this new feeling of his half naked body so intimately close against mine. Oh man, was this ever a weird feeling; I simply couldn't believe this was me - I was enjoying what he was doing to me and wanted more; talk about " whack."

As I lay there comfortably sprawled out on his bed I watched as he stepped out of his wet boxers and I again gazed in silent awe at the size of his dick ... big ol' thing with a large vein on the top of it running from his densely clustered black pubic hairs to just behind its large menacing mushroom head.

Standing right next to me at the side of the bed he held it, pointed it threateningly at me, squeezed and shook it, then swung his body from side to side causing a plopping sound. I felt something moist land on my right cheek. When I wiped my cheek it was slippery, then I looked and saw a long trail of precum leading from the head of his dick and collected into a glistening little ball two or so inches long from the tip of his dick. He looked down at it then eyed me provocatively;

Tyree: " see what you cause son .... you want it? "

Timmy: " yo, ... get away! "

he had that thing on his right forefinger holding it up over me.

Tyree: " wanna try it? "
He said grinning mischievously.
Timmy: " its yos' ..... you have it!"
Tyree: " pretty thug; scoot yo' sexyazz self ova "
He teased as he put one knee on the bed.
Timmy: " you got room "
Tyree: " move ova and let me lay down next to yo fineazz "

He purred tantalizingly and climbed on top of me as though there wasn't room for him to lay next to me - but I didn't mind one bit. He started to kiss my neck, my lips, my nose and eyes. He drew a sloppy wet tongue across an ear then came back and stuck it in. He gripped my shoulders from under my armpits and gyrated slowly at first, then started to thrust fast and ravenously. I hugged his neck, then cupped the back of his head.

From the back of his head, with one hand, I roamed his back, carefully caressing and searching every inch of it, mesmerized at the feeling of exploring another male's body that intimately and amazed at the enjoyment the newfound feeling gave. He was driving me out of my mind with a desire I'd never felt before .... and the only compelling thing I felt was to wrap my thigh around his waist and search for his mouth and stick my tongue in ... and I did. He began to gyrate and clung tightly onto me, breathing rapidly as his dick pulsated between us and..... as I gently kissed his neck, he expelled a deep, hungry moan.

This was a night like none other; a night I don't think I'll forget: I was kissed by a man and I kissed him back; I'd had a man grind up on top of me and of all the unthinkable, disgusting thoughts I'd held prior, I'd had a man play with my butt hole and even lick it.

Could I ever sleep again tonight?, I asked myself; that I doubted. We separated moments later and as I lay there in the fetal position, Tyree snuggled up behind me, nibbling at my neck and ear; thereafter we just lay motionless and wordless as time elapsed but I couldn't find sleep. Some more time went by and he whispered:

Tyree: " you asleep son? "
Timmy: " no, ... I can't fall asleep "

Tyree: " me neither ... 'n its yo' fault "
Timmy: " yeah!,......how you figure? "
Tyree: " I ain't gon try to explain it but I know its you "
Timmy: " you can't explain it but

you know its me ... dat don't even make no sense "

Tyree: " ok, dat wuz a lie ..... its 'cause I want you 'n can't have you "

Timmy: " but you got me now - I see this whatchu always wanted "

He said nothing, just sighed heavily.

Tyree: " I ain't talkin' like dat. Maan, ma shit gon hurt like a mothafucka tomorrow "

He added thoughtfully as we lay there butt naked, our legs intertwined; my thoughts going everywhere and couldn't come up with an answer to that comment.

Timmy: " how come? "

Tyree: " you don't wanna know "

Timmy: " whatchu mean, am serious ... how come? "

Exhaling deeply, he chuckled and looked at the clock on the night table;

Tyree: " dang, look at the time "

It was 4:42, exactly three hours since I last saw the time. I posed the question again.

Timmy: " how come - why? "

Again he chortled, and.....and this time replied;

Tyree: " Mr. Johnson storage tank full 'n overflowin' "

I sat up and looked across at him.

Timmy: " what! "

Tyree: " 'cause all dat nutt

backed up in there from way back "
Timmy: " oh!: " way back " ...
from like when? "
Tyree: " from December "
He said softly;
Timmy: " December! ...... datz
like almost a year "
Tyree: " c'mon now, it ain't no
year "
Timmy: " aiight, aiight, ... half a
year, nine months - whateva ... datz been
months "
Tyree: " I know "
Timmy: " 'n it make you hurt like
dat alla time? "
Tyree: " well, ... especially if I
get aroused 'n don't do nothin' ..... "
Now I felt really terrible. He went on to
explain.
Tyree: " .... then like tha next
day -   it start to hurt like a mo'fucka "
Timmy: " bro, you need some
serious lovin' ... you need help "
Tyree: " I need yo' help "
He whispered and snuggled up behind me.

I have no idea what time I eventually fell asleep
but it was broad daylight when I was awakened
by the warm caress of Tyree's gentle kiss on my
cheek. Feeling strangely buoyed, I gazed
through groggy eyes at his smiling face,......and

as the memory of last night came flooding back, I smiled back at him.

Timmy: " what time is it? "

Tyree: " slow down son, you got someplace you gotta go? "

Timmy: " naaw I don't think so "

Tyree: " well, lay yo' azz back down 'cause I made you some breakfast "

Timmy: " thanks but, what time is it ... move so I can see the clock "

Tyree: " its eleven 'o clock "

Timmy: " Ooh! "

Tyree: " well we did go to bed late "

He tried to force me to have breakfast in bed but I didn't want to. I told him I'd rather sit in the kitchen and have it with him .

Timmy: " Don't get me wrong, I appreciate it but I'd rather eat in the kitchen witchu ... maybe next time "

Tyree: " next time! "

I couldn't believe I said that; deep down was I hoping to do this again? I must be ... it just flowed from my mouth like that - it must have been a suppressed thought. Tyree's eyes sparkled; he grinned, bent over the bed and hugged me tightly.

Tyree: ' you da boss dawg ... N - E - thang you say....anything! "

He exclaimed joyfully with his arms spread wide. I just smiled and shook my head thinking how crazy he can be but to be completely honest, I was feeling happy too.

As soon as I got up to put my shorts back on, he grabbed me from behind. I'd turned my back to him, which was quite the normal thing a guy usually does in the presence of another male when he's naked. For me though, I usually face the crowd whenever I found myself in a situation like this. I'd do that because of the looks or laughs I would receive from the other guys seeing my hairy butt. I thought this situation to be rather peculiar at this point though, considering I wasn't really bothered because he'd more than seen my butt earlier; the dick was not a problem, I readily realized that ..... was I trying to show off my butt? It was too much psychoanalyzing and I just shook my head hoping I would physically remove it.

Not rapt in thought anymore, I became acutely aware of Tyree's eyes on me. I turned around to face him while pulling my shorts up and found he was smiling gratifyingly.
Tyree: " you is gorgeous, ... you know dat "
He beamed, coming up behind me to throw his arms around me, trapping mine at my sides; he snuggled his chin in my clavicle and humped my butt like mad while he groped my already hard dick.

Tyree: " dat wuz a compliment
.... won'tchu even acknowledge it? "
I said nothing, and just mused at his
ferociousness around my naked body.
Tyree: " boi,.... don'tchu hear
me talkin' to you? "
He said nibbling my ear, he was getting playful
again and I really think I loved it.
Timmy: " whatchu want me to
say ... I .... "
Tyree: " ok, ok dawg ... I see
you ain't there yet "
Timmy: " what! ... " there "
where? "
Tyree: " it don't matter now,
fo'get it "
Timmy: " you crazy "
Tyree: " I know dat too. You
ready to have some breakfast wit a crazy dude
then? "
Timmy: " you ain't jus crazy, ...
you silly too "
Tyree: " anything you say - my
sexy, hairy butt shawty "
Timmy: " oh my gaa .... negro
will you stop "
I muttered, gently shoving him out of the way
and quickly heading for the kitchen where I
took a seat at the table, pretending to be tired or
offended by hearing him say that about my
butt,.....but I did like the compliment. It was

the first time I'd ever had any man do that, and it was contrary to what I'd heard all those times I happened to be in the locker-room or at my school.

I started on the breakfast of eggs scrambled with ham, cheese, pepper and onions [his favourite, he said]. There was also orange juice and coffee. He'd placed the bread on the kitchen counter, he said, since he didn't know if I'd rather have it toasted or what.

Tyree: " so what will it be Your Highness ..... your wish is my command "

Timmy: " negro .... you is silly ... you know dat "

I laughed, then went back to having my breakfast only to notice a little later that he wasn't eating but just sitting there looking at me like I was doing something crazy ...

Timmy: " what! "

Tyree: " Dang son! .... you was hungry "

I just smiled and continued to eat but he just sat there watching me.

Timmy: " ain'tchu gon eat? "

I asked with a wide-eyed smirk.

Tyree: " uh! ..... uh-huh "

Timmy: " so whatchu lookin' at then - eat! "

Tyree: " ma bad, as your Highness wishes ..... but, shawty, you fine in every way, I jus couldn't help ..... "

Timmy: " you makin' me nervous
"

Tyree: " aiight, aiight, ... hand
me a slice o' dat toast "

He said grinning; then took a small bite;

Timmy: " datz better "

I encouraged as I took another morsel to my
mouth.

Tyree: " I love you Timmy "

He offered with a mouthful. Hearing this again,
I felt awkward and didn't quite know what to
say; but, I was revelling in the compliment.
Finally, I responded,

Timmy: " you make it sound so
serious "

Tyree: " but I am serious, I ain't
playin' ..... "

he replied gruffly, food still in his mouth.

Tyree: " if you gimmi the
chance ama prove it to you "

I didn't say anything ..... I didn't know what to
say and he surmised as much and dropped the
subject. We continued having our breakfast in
silence.

(Chapter 5)

I didn't visit Tyree's for the next couple of days but we called and talked to each other every day, sometimes even way into the night. He wanted to know why I had not come over since, was I disappointed, did I have second thoughts ... stuff like that, but I assured him that wasn't the case and that I just wanted to chill out for a minute and clear my head and think about the things that had happened, how I felt and how I was going to deal with it. He told me he wasn't rushing me, but that I shouldn't, in his words: " just don't stay away from me ". I reassured him that would not be the case.

Everything seemed to speed by so fast since August, especially since me and Tyree. It was already the last day of October and since the weather was still so strangely pleasant, the fellas had scheduled our final Big Game Day of this year for this Saturday. This would be our last meaningful game and I was feeling happy about everything: Things had been going real good with me and Marie since we started dating; I'd been going to school, training to be an X-ray Technician, specializing in Imaging Technologies [including CT and MRI]. Plus my nineteenth birthday was coming up on November 30. That made me reflect,

December 31 would be Tyree's, followed by
Pete's on the first of January.

Yes, I was happy indeed; the only thing in my
life that was giving me any feeling of
misgivings was this " THING " between Tyree
and me . I mean, I'd been intimate with only
women all my life, it's only natural ... and it's
been beautiful; I had pussy for the taking any
day of the week that I felt like it but this..... this
latest thing just kept resonating in my brain.
Other than that, I think I was a very happy man.

As time went by, I tried to keep as busy as I
could, spending a lot more time with Pete. We
went sightseeing and shopping with visiting
relatives, taking in a movie here and there -
just about anything to avoid thinking too much
about the things that weighed so heavily on my
mind. And before I knew it, it was Saturday: "
Big Game Day "; we would be playing for cash
- not beer.

These types of games are conducted like a
business in some respects. There is the
"Keeper" [the man who holds the beer, or cash,
in safekeeping]; he is paid three hundred
dollars or three six packs by the winning team.
The ref gets two hundred dollars or two six
packs - depending on what the prize is.
Contribution to the pool is:

In the case of a "Beer Match":.........every player from each team contributes three six packs.

In the case of a "Cash Match" :.........every player from each team contributes four hundred dollars.

These matches are played five times each year during the summer, three beer games and two cash. Cash Match to us is like the NBA playoffs and the " Keeper " and his back up man comes to the game strapped when it's a cash match.

The game was a rout for our team, 57 to their lowly 35. I made it rain threes that afternoon, eleven of thirteen; it's like everything I was putting up was falling, just net and the noisy crowd was loving every minute of it.

To the business end of it: We made absolutely sure there was no " Po po " [police] around, collected our money from " Keeper ", paid him and the Referee, then walked out of the park over to Malik's Suburban where we piled in so we could split the winnings in private. That was four thousand dollars [minus " Keeper's " and Ref's], so we had a sweet three thousand, five hundred dollars between us.

We then drove over to the Wholesale Liquor Store and the fellas bought a few cases of beer. Malik said he had other things he had to do, so he was only going to be able to drop us off at Tyree's and elected to wait outside in his ride. Tyree wouldn't spend too much because, as he secretly told me, he was cutting back on spending, hoping to buy a house and was just waiting on a response from some company or other about an investment he'd made. Anyway, I, of course, couldn't buy anything because I was under age. Never-the-less, to feel like a part of the whole thing, I insisted and threw in a couple of dollars, much to Tyree's chagrin.

As we exited the the vehicle I was surprised to see a grinning Laurie Mosely standing outside the Liquor Store. As always, he was very glad to see us, especially me. Although two years younger than me, of all the people I was acquainted with back in High School, he was the only one I could call a friend.

Like myself, his father was black but from the Dominican Republic; his mother, however, was from the Philippines. He was usually at every game we played, cheering and rooting for us. He was what some people might refer to as a "Blatino." He had a dark caramel complexion, a small but muscular body, and jet black hair. He had mainly inherited his father's physical appearance, a handsome black specimen with unusual, kinda slanted eyes. His hair though, was more of his mother's, black and curly but

coarse like his dad's and he kept his low cut at
all times.

Tyree: " whatchu doin' hangin'
out outside a Liquor Store? "
Laurie: " waitin' fo' Dominic, ...
he in the store gettin' somethin' .... where y'all
goin'? "
Neither of them replied to his question; instead,
Ardee joked;
Ardee: " whatchu think .....
'boutchu waitin' fo' Dominic ..... you oughta be
home wit yo' mamma "
and Tyree quickly added;
Tyree: " yea, how old is you
anyways? "
Laurie: " I ain't no l'il kid "
he frowned at Tyree, then looked at me for
confirmation....
Laurie: " I oknow wha you talkin'
'bout "
..... but not really wanting to say anything, I
merely chuckled. Tyree eyed him cockily and
retaliated.....
Tyree: " oh, you a grownazz
man now huh? .....all tough 'n shit "
.......as Laurie fidgeted with his hand under his
wifebeater seeming to dig at his belly button.
Laurie: " why y'all actin' like
y'all old folks ..... 'bout " oughta be home wit
yo' mamma ".... am grown "

He shot back, dropping his wifebeater back down over his naked lower belly and covering his bright red over-sized red shorts. Tyree scanned him from head to toe.....

Tyree: " dude, you ain't no grown - only thing grown 'boutchu is ..... "

......grinning strangely as he stroked his goatee. Tyree seemed willing to spend time talking to him but Malik cut the chat short by hollering at us from across the street to hurry; and as the pair of Ardee and Tyree gave each other a stealthy look then turned to head inside the store giving Laurie the " once over ", I could have sworn I heard Ardee mutter.....

Ardee: " the only thing grown 'bout dat l'il thugazz nigga is dat phat back on him "

.... to which Tyree replied,

Tyree: " you seen dat shit too - daamn! "

My mind was awash with what I thought I'd just heard but my old friend was there with me and I turned my attention to him. While they shopped inside, I waited outside and began to chat with Laurie, trying to catch up on what he'd been doing. (I'd heard he'd gotten a woman pregnant while still in school).

Timmy: " so whatz good son? "

Laurie: " jus chillin' .... whatz good witchu? .....damn a nigga can't even see you no mo'..... "

Timmy: " am .... "
Laurie: " whatz up wit dat, you
jus like yo' boyz - them niggaz jus be keepin'
to themself "
Timmy: " you know how I do "
I replied with a shrug.
Timmy: " so wuz all dat shit
'bout you gettin' somebody pregnant true? "
His smile bore guilt,
Laurie: " man,.....tha shit jus
happened "
and he immediately shifted the topic.
Timmy: " ..... so you hangin' out
wit Dominic, what y'all gon do? "
For a moment, he appeared a bit flustered by
the question before stammering;
Laurie: " I, ... er, we ..... you
mean right now? "
Timmy: " yea, what kinda
question dat? "
I've know Laurie since High School but there
was something odd about his behaviour right
now and I couldn't quite put my finger on it. I
decided to leave it alone but was wondering
what he wanted to do with himself when he
finished school, so I asked;
Timmy: " so whatchu gon do -
after school amean? "
his demeanor wasn't as marked as when I'd
asked the earlier question because he quickly
clarified that.

Laurie: " am, ... am tryin' to
have Dominic look out fo' me 'cause he already
got a high position in dat city job "
Timmy: " dat would be nice. If
you pass the test maybe he can "
Laurie: " he said he workin' up to
supervisor soon. As soon as I graduate ama put
in my application ..... dat way I can help out my
                     moms, my sister and
ma little brother - knowamsayin' "
Timmy: " yeaah, ... I hope
things work out fo' you bro "
Laurie: " real talk ..... if dat don't
work, am gon join the Navy "
Timmy: " whatchu wanna do
there? "
Laurie: " I dunno, ama have to
see whats open by the time am ready. Be nice
to get a job down there tho', they got good
benefits "
That reply didn't seem positive, I'd have
thought he would know exactly what he wanted
to do but - I wished him the best anyway.
Timmy: " dat would be cool .....
gotta make dat papa, ... earn yo' own money.
If its the Navy, you get a chance to see the
world 'n
                     you can learn some
kinda skill too "
Laurie: " knowamsayin' "
Usually a smiling, soft-spoken and reserved

guy, it was the first opportunity I had of talking to him one on one in a long time and except for my question about Dominic, he was really forthcoming. We kept up our conversation, with him telling me that he was in the Dominican Republic for Christmas but we didn't get any further with that subject as Laurie alerted me to the fellas who came walking out of the store with their purchase.

Laurie: " yo Timmy, yo boyz ready, see Big Dude lookin' ova here "
Timmy: " oh! ..... aiight ..... "
I said goodbye .....
Timmy: " yea, I see you "
giving each other a slap and a hug as Tyree eyed us. I then joined the fellas in the van and headed for Tyree's.

As soon as we got into the apartment, Tyree, who seemed happier than I can ever remember seeing him so far, put on the CD player and was again playing that remix of " Shorty is a Ten " ; he seemed to be stuck on that song for no sooner had it finished, he hit the replay button.

Ardee and Aji declared that they were hot and sticky and decided they were going to shower here. Ardee was the first to hit the shower so us three were all sitting on the living room floor, Aji yakking his head off until Ardee came out of the bathroom butt naked, drying his hair.

I was surprised to see Ardee do that considering I was present but he seemed quite unabashed. Just then Tyree, who had been sitting there digging at his sweaty crotch, got up and walked over to me; suddenly he wiped his funky-smelling fingers across my nose and mouth.

Ardee and Aji chuckled but Ardee was the one who seemed most amused by it. I just hoped Tyree wasn't about to start some more of that embarrassing mess in front of the fellas again. I swung at him......

Timmy: " Yo what tha fuck!....ama do somethin' to you. Stop playin' " ......and he adeptly dodged it, grinning as he skittered away toward the living room doorway; then Aji had the nerve to calmly tell me,
Aji: " it wuzn't all dat bad son "
I was mad as hell;
Timmy: " what the fuck you talkin' 'bout! - you wuzn't gon appreciate anybody doin' dat to you "
and about to curse both of them out when Ardee quickly interceded, asking Aji;
Ardee: " nigga, what you standin' 'round fo' ..... "
Aji: ' calm down son, keep yo' drawz on "

Tyree chortled at the pun.....and I think especially seeing that Ardee was naked. I gave him a dirty look as Ardee reminded,

Ardee: " ...otha people need to use the bathroom too - get yo' sweaty azz in there "

He continued to dry the rest of his body, putting much emphasis on his crotch, pubic area and butt when Tyree advised

Tyree: " y'all ain't gonna come up in here 'n use up a whole bunch of my towels, you best believe dat "

Timmy: " y'all got dat!.....'n I ain't gon be usin' dat one after you done scrubbed yo' durty azz wicdit "

Tyree was choking with laughter, and as Ardee tossed the towel towards my face Tyree caught it in mid-air and threw it back at him.

Ardee: " nigga what you know 'bout my azz ... my shit is clean, I just got outta the sho-wA ... it be yo' sweaty, hairy azz dat be dirty

                    right about now "

he boasted as he danced around naked, his dick moving sinuously. He had a big dick too, though not as big as Tyree's, and it had a very distinctive curve. I'd never seen him completely naked before, nor had I ever seen a dick with such an utter distinct bend. It was Tyree who broke my thoughts, putting up a defense on my behalf.......

Tyree: " Yo, ...mothafucka, you need to leave my dawg da fuck alone ...... aaight! "

Ardee: " negro ...... fuck-you-too "

he intoned and sauntered off to the bathroom, closing the door behind him as Tyree stood there, his hand again down the front of his shorts still digging himself.

As I got up off the floor, stretching and flexing my tired muscles, I smiled at the fact that he had my back. As I opened my eyes, I saw Tyree walking up to me; he pulled his hand from his crotch, wiped his fingers between my lips and kissed me. I swooned at his musky scent; his fingers were salty, sweaty.....and I found the scent delightfully overwhelming. Before I could succumb any further, I pulled away, remembering the two now in the bathroom.

He eyed me most provocatively, licking his lips, smiling playfully and feeling on his semi hard dick.

Timmy: " what is wrong witchu? ...... "

I exclaimed, scared, and making a nervous plea as I quickly stepped away from him, glancing back at the bathroom door, making my voice as audible as I could over the sound of water beating the bathtub floor, while yet backing away. I begged with arms raised up to my chest, palms turned outwards facing him and beseeched.

Timmy: " please, please, ... don't come no closer - No!, no ..... mmmph ..... ohmagawd; Tyree, stop - remember Aj 'n Ardee in the

                          bathroom ..... Tyree, don't do this, ... please ...... "

He paid no attention to my pleas; I continued to beg.

Timmy: " .... tha fuck, Tyree, ... what is wrong witchu .... yo, yo, yo! "

I was petrified but just as I was wondering what Ardee was doing in the bathroom so long, out he comes trying to hide his hard dick with both hands. Tyree held his stomach and roared with laughter as Ardee rummaged through his back-pack before finally coming up with a pair of clean shorts. He hurriedly got into them, turning his back to us and forcing his dick down toward his crotch before quickly taking a seat on the sofa. He looked at Tyree who went back to playing that song for the fifth time, then wryly declared.

Ardee: " ma dude, you gonna wear that song out. Seriously tho' you need to get dat nigga outta yo' bathroom befo' he finish dat

                          wata "

Tyree: " you wanna go first son
"

He advised, so I jumped up, just in time to see
Aji coming out draped in a towel. I wasted no
time getting under the water and got a good
cleansing. The water felt so refreshing I could
have stayed longer but Tyree needed to use it
too plus, he just might make one of his crazy
decisions - like joining me in the shower.
When I was done, I realized there was no towel
and that I'd also left my clean shorts out there in
my bag; so I called out to Tyree to get me a
fresh towel and bring my shorts too. He came
in with the shorts and a sky blue monogrammed
bath sheet bearing his initials " T. J. D." in a
darker shade of blue. He quickly closed the
door, then grabbed my butt and started to
fondle me all over. I begged him;
Timmy: " Tyree, pleeease, not
now - not now, oh ma Gaaa ..... Tyreee "
he eyed me up and down, smiled and puckered
his lips then exited the bathroom. That was a
relief. I hurriedly dried myself, put my shorts
on and stepped out - still drying my upper
body. Ardee looked up at me, his mouth agape
in shock.
Ardee: " tha fuck - Aj, you see
dat,......this nigga gave us some ol' rag to dry off
with...but fo' this l'il nigga right here, ... noo
....he
                    brung out da " Royal

142

Hilton " shit ..... monogrammed 'n all .... I bet
dat shit new too "
Rolling his eyes in mock dissatisfaction, he
mumbled,

Aji: " knowamsayin' "
Tyree: " so what if it's new? "
Ardee: " afta all these years ......
'n ma boi treatin' me like some durty ol' grease
rag "
Aji: " yeah, I see dawg, ...
we ain't nobody "

he continued to poke more indirect fun at me as
I listened in amusement, delighted at my newly
found status.

Ardee: " this mus be how them
women feel when they nigg.... "
Aji: " yep, used, misused and
abused "

Aji jumped in and finished his statement.
Tyree had not said a word all this time but,
now, quickly shot back;

Tyree: " used 'n abused! -
nigga, is I fuckin' any o' y'all? "
Aji: " oooh! ..... datz cold "
Ardee: " well, excuse-fuckin'-
me, "

then feigning a woman's sorrow and distress in
a like situation, Aji fell upon Ardee's shoulders
and sobbed;

Aji: " he treated us like some
discarded durty rag .... "

Ardee: " afta all tha good years
we done gave him "

Tyree: " sorryazz mo'fuckaz "
enthused by their melodrama and tickled almost
to tears, I chortled;

Timmy: " aah you done hurt they
feelins' "

Tyree: " feelins' .... they ain't
got no feelins', they inanimate earthen objects "

Aji: " who you callin'
objects? "
Aji asked, sitting up alertly.

Ardee: " we object to dat "

Tyree: " well, you the one
hollarin' ..... mus got somethin' to do with you "
Removing his head from Ardee's shoulder, Aji
turned his head toward us and cut eyes at Tyree
saying,

Aji: " next thang you know,
one of these days he gonna just spit in our
mothafuckin' faces "

Tyree: " yep ..... fo' fuckin' wit
ma dawg "
Tyree shot back triumphantly before turning his
gaze to me and adding;

Tyree: " they jus hatin' 'cause
you love me dawg "
Ardee and Aji shot to their feet, Ardee turning
an indifferent gaze at Aji,

Ardee: " what he bitchin' 'bout
now Aj? "

Aji: " lo-ve bro - but, as we
all know, ... he ain't gettin' none "
Ardee: " oh, datz why he so
ornery "
Ardee responded trying to sound sarcastic as
they sat down in unison. Aji drew closer to
him, they puckered their lips and gestured
kissing and I thought: There they go again with
that mock gay thing; it was insulting - and
Tyree would say nothing.
Timmy: " dat shit is nasty .....
y'all is da illest bunch of durtyazz mofuckaz -
but y'all know dat awready "
I retorted, as Tyree walked to the bathroom and
took what must have been the quickest shower
anyone had ever taken. He returned to the
living room where all the banter had now
ceased and we were quietly chatting about the
game and drinking beer. He proceed to hastily
put away a clutter of seemingly important
papers he'd mistakenly left laying on his desk
and joined us.

We hung out there, sprawled out on the floor
and furniture, still talking about the game.

It was now 12:11 a.m; we decided to call it a
night. As we collected our bags to leave, I was
the last heading toward the door and took a
quick look behind to see Tyree with a

bewildered and disappointed expression. He shrugged his shoulders questioningly and seemed even more dismayed when I turned back around and continued on out the door. As we walked down the hallway leading to the elevator, I looked back again to catch him gawking at me from his doorway until I stepped into the elevator car and disappeared out of his view.

When we finally got to the corner of the block where we would split up to take our separate route home, I gladly exchanged handshakes and hugs with Ardee and Aji;
Aji: " get home safe dawg "
Timmy: " yeah bro, as soon as I get in ama tear some food up, brush ma teeth 'n go press out dat mattress "
My lie made me feel guilty but what else could I do. Ardee teased......
Ardee: " don't press it too hard or you might leave somethin' on dat mattress dat nobody gon wanna sleep on "
...... that immediately shadowed my feeling of guilt and I shot back,
Timmy: " I ain't gotta do dat, I got somewhere warm to leave mine "
and not caring much for my boastful comment, Aji ribbed, throwing up his hands.........
Aji: " yea, yea,.....I know - whateva "

..........and we parted but as I knew they were far enough down the road, I quickly doubled back to Tyree's.

I'd only buzzed his apartment number for a few seconds when he buzzed me in. I was surprised at the quick response and figured he must have been in the kitchen. As I entered the Lobby, a lady got off the elevator and I hurried to grab it. On my way up, all I could think about was Tyree and the surprisingly exciting and arousing things that he'd done to me before, this amazing thing that occurred between us that had me thinking about it constantly ever since.

Glad to reach his floor, I bolted out of the elevator and hastened down the corridor toward his apartment, almost ringing his doorbell in my mind. I was only a few yards from his apartment when the door suddenly opened a crack and he stuck his head out.

Like a thief, I lengthened my strides and found myself going through the doorway before he'd even fully pulled his head back in. He was waiting for me...... and as soon as I stepped in, he quietly closed and locked the door behind me. He'd barely done so when he hugged me tightly from behind and kissed my neck before he turned me around and kissed my lips passionately..... I didn't resist.

Tyree: " I knew you wuz comin'
back dawg - I jus knew..... "
He muttered between kisses,......
Tyree: " mmmm-you-feel-good-
against-me "
.......and if I knew what to say, I didn't.
Tyree: " yes!...... my l'il
sexy...... "
He rasped softly and hungrily as he began to
undress me with fervor. I bravely slid my hand
inside the front of his boxers, searching for and
finding his dick. It got even harder as I eagerly
tried to pull it out of his boxers; my own dick
was already hard in hopeful anticipation of
more of the magic he had conjured on my naive
but receptive body and mind when I was last
here.

I needed to talk to him about what happened,
where we were going with this and so on, but
my passion would have none of it right now
and so I let him lead the way to do whatever he
wanted.
Tyree: " I want you Timmy .....
I want you in the worst way, you know dat? "
Timmy: " yea .... I know dat
now "
Tyree: " so, ... so, you ready to
lemmi get it now? "
Timmy: " yea.....I think so "
I replied kinda nervously.

148

Tyree: " don't say it like dat son, you gotta be sure.......tell me you sure "
He prompted,......and I tried to find the words to reply.
Timmy: " yeah, ... I ..... I want you to do it but am ..... "
The next moment his lips and tongue were obstacles in my mouth and we were shuffling along the floor, me going backwards as he bent over me, continuing to shower me with receptive kisses.

When I next realized my location, we were a tightly tangled pair in the bed kissing, hugging,......... ....and fondling each other. Like a rug, he laid me out on his bed and began to vacuum my entire body with his tongue; licking my arm pits, neck, ears, back, thighs, kissing my feet, even sucking my toes before working his way back up to my quivering butt hole. His hot tongue flickering in and out between my cheeks, I was almost disoriented as my fistful of his silky soft blue sheet began to come loose, pulling the pillows with it. I nearly screamed from the sheer delight but somehow managed a hiss and a moan that left my mouth agape in ecstatic awe.
Timmy: " ccccttt aaaahmmm - ooh! "
Tyree: " mm-mm, yeah son - love it "

Timmy: " sssssssh-it!..... son! "
Tyree: " mmph, yea
babyboi......lemmi wet dat, keep dat leg up there
"

My hole was a sloppy mess, I could feel the
oozing but it wouldn't be there for long as my
hungry dawg kept lapping it back up.
Tyree: " mmmm - damn-you-
taste-good-son "
He gurgled,
Timmy: " O-ooooowoou "
and I tried to imagine what else I could do to
spread my legs wider. A leg could go but so
far.....and mine was at its limit. I was now
hanging over the edge of one side of the bed
with my hands on the floor for support while he
was now on his stomach, moving me even more
with his tugboat of a tongue.

With the blood rushing to my head, I thought I
was about to pass out when he yanked me back
onto the bed and effortlessly flipped me over
onto my back. Wasting no time, he began
licking my balls. This had my already
contorting body in additional rapturous delight.

He even sucked my dick, peeling the foreskin
over in his mouth with each movement and
giving me a delight I'd never gotten when
having this done to me by a woman. I was so
beside myself with passion that at one point

only my shoulders and the soles of my feet were touching the bed and just when I thought I wouldn't be able to bear the intensity of it any more, he stopped, and having straddled me, he got on all fours and whispered erotically while gently kissing and nibbling my ear .....

Tyree: " I want you so bad dawg - from tha very first day I seen you ...... I wanted you; did you know dat too? "

Timmy: " Mmm-noo "

I managed,

Tyree: " well I do......I wantchu "

...... panting as he continued to devour my neck and ear, leaving my body limp with surrender. I felt so vulnerable,.....never had I felt this kind of helplessness before

Tyree: " so we gon do this? "

Timmy: " Ioknow, ... I .... "

I replied timidly, wanting more yet dreading what it would be.

Tyree: " ain't nobody gonna know dawg "

He assured but I don't think that's what I was concerned about. Nevertheless, I responded to his words of assurance.

Timmy: " you sure? "

Tyree: " course am sure, I ain't tellin' nobody ....datz why you scared? "

he muttered between kisses, nibbling and

licking my ears and neck.

Timmy: " I ain't scared "

I lied boldly but he somehow knew it and asked,

Tyree: " so why you keep bitin' yo' lips 'n rubbin' yo' arms? "

I was definitely unaware of that but I found that I was doing just that. I was so nervously helpless and felt so awkward but he soothingly stroked my cheek and gently showered me with endless little kisses on my lips before he comforted my fears;

Tyree: " you ain't gotta lie to me dawg, if you scared jus lemmi know .... 'tain't no thang - still scared? "

Timmy: " l'il bit "

Tyree: " still wanna try? "

Timmy: " uh huh ..... if you want "

Tyree: " hellyeah ..... but, what aboutchu? ..... you wanna let me try? "

Tyree: " I wantchu son but am willin' to wait till you ready - amean I wish you wuz ready now but .... "

Timmy: " Ioknow ...... if you wanna do it "

I replied almost frustrated. Here I was with him and feeling this strange way - not knowing if I could or how to make up my mind about it. My body ached and I just wanted to hug him tight, tongue kiss him and wrap my legs about his waist but still he sought my permission.

Tyree: "its up to you boo "

Timmy: " jus do it "

Tyree: " aiight, it gon hurt a l'il
bit at first "

He grinned and quickly got to his knees

Timmy: " li'l bit? "

I asked, considering the size of his dick;

Timmy: " don't do nothin' rough
"

I rasped and swallowed my saliva; I was dying
from the anticipation.

He pulled out the drawer of his night stand and
brought out a small bottle of lubricant, lubed
my butt hole and his big mushroom-like dick-
head, then ever-so-slowly slid his dick between
my butt cheeks and right up against my hole;
his dick felt very warm and rigid. He applied
pressure and told me to poke my butt up and try
to keep it there. The harder he forced himself
down, the more I had to poke my butt up but
after several painful attempts, he still was not
able to penetrate.

We took a fifteen minute rest, kissing and
cuddling before he decided to try again. He
told me to relax, take a deep breath, and just let
myself go.

Tyree: " you too tense; jus think
of somethin' nice ..... somethin' you like - a

nice place, somethin' like dat "

Timmy: " datz gon help? "

Tyree: " trust me, ... it will "

There were still more unsuccessful tries but l
was getting more and more relaxed; then, after
a couple more tries, and to my great surprise, he
suddenly busted through. The pain was so
intense, I shot up off the bed.

Tyree: " you aaight boo"

Timmy: " Ooowwwu .....oou, a-
wooo ..... ooh .... dat shit is too big yo .... it
hurted son "

I pleaded from my destination of flight on the
floor and reiterated.

Timmy: " Oooh ..... dat shit is too
big yo ..... it hurt "

Tyree: " but I wuz takin' it easy
"

Timmy: " dat shit hurted like a
bitch ...... damn! "

Tyree: " its gon be aiight "

Timmy: " aiight! .... " I
exclaimed, looking at him in shock. That thing
felt like he had just split me open in several
places.

Timmy: " ...... - dat hurt like a
mo'fucka "

Tyree: " its awright boo, c'mon,
...... get back in da bed dawg, don't be scared "

Easy for you to say. I thought. I'd never felt a
pain like that. It wasn't just my butt hole, it

shook my entire body and I still felt the impact of his penetration. I had to ask myself, why was I even thinking of getting back in the bed with him. I wasn't sure if I had the answer but I did as he coaxed, and he started kissing me again.

I returned his kiss for the first time, ravenously sucking on his tongue and lips while I caressed and squeezed his slippery dick. He moaned with pleasure and I gently rubbed his dick head; his eyes rolled back and he flung his legs and arms wide as he began to gyrate, grinding his hard dick in my fist. It was the oddest but coolest feeling, holding somebody else's, but even moreso, Tyree's.

It wasn't long before he asked .....
Tyree: " ready to try again? "
I was apprehensive; I was more than willing to lay next to him and cuddle and kiss, but that dick was fearsome.
Timmy: " I want to but it's burnin' .... I think you musta bust somethin' "
Tyree: " naaw "
he assured me, then said,
Tyree: " come lay down here and lemmi take a look at dat pretty booty hole "
I willingly and unashamedly spread my legs wide, allowing him to inspect my hole.
Tyree: " naaaw .... ain't nothin'

bust dawg, you prolly bruised a l'il bit but datz all "

Timmy: " you sure? "

Tyree: " I wouldn't lie 'bout dat son .... it's aiight "

Timmy: " damn son, ... feel like you tore ma shit, it burnin' like a mo'fucka "

Tyree: " aiight ma dawg, come lie down, I wanna feel you next to me - nice 'n warm "

As I got back into bed and he tried again several times, he was still unable to penetrate me so he lubed my butt with a lot of that gooey stuff and said he was just gonna hump me instead.

He was on my back, covering me like a stallion. He poked and gyrated, moving his dick back and forth, up and down the crack of my butt cheeks and, at times, against my hole - while gripping my shoulders (having snaked his arms below my arm pits). It felt good having his dick there rubbing against my butt hole like that but I was scared of another penetration so I suggested we just cuddle and kiss. He agreed and said we should just do as I suggested and try another time whenever I felt in the mood.

I could see how much he wanted it, how frustrated he was at not being able to get in, but he was thoughtful and patient; he didn't try to force me any more and he just decided to wait.

As he lay on his back with his hands behind his head, I lay on my stomach between his open legs and began to gently play with his dick. He was enjoying it so much that he began gyrating and moaning as I continued giving him what pleasure I could but my hand was getting very tired; he realized this, and started to fuck my fist.

About three or four minutes later, he lubed up his dick with my hand still on it and continued to grind it .... grind it .... and grind it .... and was now frantically out of control.

Tyree: " damn dawg, ... you got da sweetest, softest hands ..... ooh yeah son, right there ..... jus like dat, yea ..... yeaah ..... yea ccccttt

Timmy: " you like dat? "

Tyree: " oh yeaah ..... don't stop, keep playin' wit dat shit "

Timmy: " this mo'fucka is big "

Making no comment, he continued gyrating. Even when it slipped from my hand for a moment, he was involuntarily grinding and muttering in delight.

Tyree: " fuck! ..... damn yo, ccctt.... fuck, cccctt .....o-ooohh yeaaa, oooh, yeah, hold it tighter .... cccctt.....oh fuck, yea

son, ye-eaaaah ......
                          mmphf, cccct, awh,
nghf ..... "
I was more than pleased with the job I was
performing.
Tyree: " ..... oh fuck, ... aaaw
fuck, watch it son, watch it .... ama .... ssshhit,
oh shit, damn dawg ..... oh damn - Timmy,
Timmy - son "
Timmy: " what! "
I asked boastfully, knowing that I'd reduced
him to a state of moaning, groaning, and
begging.
Tyree: " Timmy ..... yo, shawty
..... oh daamn, Timmy ....A-A-Aaaaaarrghhh,
aaah Ngh "
He groaned as the first burst of cum erupted,
landing on my forehead and oozing down my
face. I wasn't disgusted by it; as a matter of
fact, I was pleased with my handy [pun
intended] work.

He continued to pump and grind in a frenzy,
raising his head to look; the spasms caused his
head to move like a bobble head doll and as his
eyes rolled back, he let his head slump back
onto the pillow, delirious with joy and, no
doubt, much satisfaction as he continued to
mutter and mumble uncontrollably.
Tyree: " ..... fuck! .... here it
comes son, here it comes; you gon make it

skeet ..... ooh ssshhiit boo .... NGHF, mmmphf, ooh, ooh, ooooohh

.... Daaamn ......
PHWEEEW, ... maan! "
I watched through one eye, being blinded by the previous salvo, as he continued to release salvo after salvo over his head and onto the pillow, the sheets, and his chest as he gripped the sides of the mattress and kept grinding his dick into my fist.... the last volley of cum had jettisoned up to his shoulder while the rest just kept oozing out above my fist that was still gripping his dick.

Timmy: " Daayum ..... you wuz loaded son "
I muttered in amazement at the amount he'd let off.

I gently squeezed the head and rubbed it a little and his body went into a spasm. He grabbed my hand to stop me, and when I did, he just lay there pleasantly spent with his eyes closed, wearing a smile of contentment, his head lapsed to one side.

I found that experience so very exciting, I just laid there watching him and looking at all that cum. I had never seen anybody come before, but the amount that he let off, I was almost sure it had to be some kind of record. And to know that I had subdued him like that - this big strong muscular man - gave me a feeling of accomplishment and satisfaction.

I went to the bathroom and cleaned myself off with a washcloth and warm water, then went back to the bedroom and began to clean Tyree off - still mesmerised by his nude body and huge, yet semi-hard dick. As soon as I was finished cleaning him off, he opened his eyes and pulled me on top of him and sucked and stretched my lower lip, tangling his tongue with mine, then looking up at me...

Tyree: " son, dat was da best hand job I eva had in my whole life; I don't like jerking off, quit doin' it years ago but .... "

Timmy: " you really liked it? "

Tyree: " I love how you do it, yo' hands nice n' soft ...... you made it feel like the real shit "

Timmy: " am glad you liked it 'cause ..... "

Tyree: " son "

he said, taking my hand and pulling me to him. Looking deep in my eyes, sincerity all over his face, he continued;

Tyree: " ......I ain't had no pussy or azz in like eight months B..... yo, dat shit was da bomb. Tha only thing dat coulda been better,

                    wuzs dat tight l'il hairy booty you won't let me get up in "

160

he grinned. That comment made me feel somewhat disappointed. I knew then that I didn't completely please him as he wanted nor even like I'd hoped to. Knowing he had tried to penetrate me several times, I guessed the fault was mine ..... it just didn't work .... it was way harder than I thought it would be - and I wanted to let him know that;

Timmy: " I .... I tried ... I was trying .... I wanted it to work too .... but dat shit is big yo, ... it hurted like a mo'fucka "

He didn't say a word, he just laid there;

Timmy: " so you gon be mad at me now because ..... "

Tyree: " hell no dawg, ... don't even trip, I ain't mad atchu "

Timmy: " oh, 'cause I wuz wonderin' if you gon cause somethin' like dat .... "

now he suddenly sat up, looked at me puzzled and demanded;

Tyree: " whatchu mean: ' like dat ' ..... 'n I ain't tryin' to stress you or nothin'..... but, don't make it look trivial, datz a very important part of a relationship "

....and then he ended up talking about a relationship.

Timmy: " 'relationship? ' ..... you tryin' to say we gon be in a relationship? "

Tyree: " aiight, aiight dawg, ma bad ..... we can take this slow. I wanted it, I

still do .... I ain't gonna lie, but we can go slow.
Ama
                                    wait till wheneva you
is ready boo. Dat ok witchu? "
Timmy: " ama think 'bout it "

As we lay there I tried hard to think about the
relationship part of the argument but couldn't
come to any decision. However, I noticed that
his dick never went completely soft, and as we
lay there cuddling and kissing, he always
sought to poke his finger up my butt hole. But
each time he tried I got so tense, he resorted to
just rubbing his fingers against it. That felt so
very good, I wanted to feel his finger in me and
eventually began to poke my butt up to meet it
so that I could be penetrated. I think he
realized this and soon after, asked me if I would
try again to have him penetrate me with his
dick; I told him yes.

He applied more lubrication to my butt and
tried for several minutes but, again, it didn't
work.

Frustrated beyond endurance, he decided that
he should just try humping me again and I
agreed. I gladly rolled over on my stomach and
let him hump away. As he worked his dick
between the crack of my butt cheeks, and
sometimes between my thighs,

I'd put my hand under my stomach to fondle my own dick. Each time he would move his dick from between my thighs to between my butt cheeks, I'd come to the verge of ejaculation but then he would, quite unwittingly, shift it again to my thighs. It had gotten to the point where I was actually visualizing that the dick was really in my butt and therefore starting to gyrate and poke it up, coordinating with his movements. He was enjoying this as much as I was, I think, and for quite a long time, kept working his dick between my butt cheeks and not going back to my thighs.

As we continued, he was becoming more and more frenzied, his movements more agitated and impassioned with desire. He gripped my shoulders even harder as he moaned, grunted, and sucked my earlobe, panting like a horse. I was beyond excitement and continued to ride with him the wave he'd started. I was poking it up, pretending he was inside me and grinding in sync with him when, quite unexpectedly, his dick busted right through me; I screamed and involuntarily tightened up, but I couldn't get away.

Timmy: " Ooow, Tyreee! "
Tyree: " Ooh yeaaaah bwoi...ccctt, mmmph "

I pleaded, but having the head of his dick

163

fastened securely inside me transformed him into wild delirium. I had to scratch and claw and was just barely able to get him out of me just as he was about to erupt; his whole body shuddered and he roared like a lion;

Tyree: "
Aaaarrrrrhhh.....shiiit...mmmph, rrrrraah - ma boo "

and quickly got up, shooting copious amounts of hot sperm on my shoulder and butt, the last of which came oozing down between my butt cheeks and onto my hole before he lay his limp exhausted body on top of me - motionless. Yes, there I was with my hand under my dick, and... full of my own cum.

After a few minutes, he exhaled deeply and enquired.

Tyree: " damn!...you aiight son? "

Timmy: " you bust me open son .... I felt dat shit ..... ohmagaawd, ... Damn! "

Tyree: " com'here .... you aiight ma dawg? "

He asked tenderly, rolling me over on my side to face him. He looked at me lovingly, and I looked at him with amazement at his aggressive pursuit and the wild excitement I'd felt for the short time his dick was inside me.

Timmy: " nigga, yo' dick is big

.... ohmagawd,.... ma azz is tore up "
Tyree: " it wuz jus tha head dat
got in; you sorry we did this....is you mad at
me? "
Timmy: " noo,....I ain't mad
atchu...its jus dat...I, I neva thought it woulda
hurt so much "
Tyree: " am sorry you had to
feel pain; did you like it tho'...amean...you'd do
it again? "
Timmy: " it felt good, I ain't gon
lie...amean da first part...but when you popped
me wit dat shit....yo!..... dat shit is big son,...yo'
dick is

                            way too big "
Tyree: " don't think 'bout it no
mo'........ "
I was pained but happy he had at least made
one penetration.
Tyree: " .... I love how you wuz
doin' tho' .... you wuz throwin' it back "
That made me feel a bit embarrassed - me
throwing my butt back at him. I knew I was
doing it but hearing him say it made me kinda
bashful. I put on a brave face and tried to erase
the feeling.
Timmy: " damn B...dat shit wuz
crazy...omagawd "
Tyree: " you sweet,...you know
dat boi?...I wish I coulda tear this outta tha
frame! "

Timmy: " another time we can do
it,...jus so long as don't nobody know "
Tyree: " stop trippin', how
anybody gon know...I ain't tellin' nobody, you
gon tell somebody? "
Timmy: " is you crazy! "
Tyree: " well, there you go...you
ain't tellin' 'n I ain't tellin' so you ain't got
nothin' to worry 'bout "
Timmy: " I hope so 'cause I don't
want nobody lookin' at me like am some kinda
faggot or somethin' "
Tyree: " don't think 'bout it no
mo'...aiight dawg. I don't think I can but, lets
try 'n see if we can get some sleep - its late "
Timmy: " yeah, aiight "
As he snuggled up close behind me, pasting his
groin against my naked butt, he threw an arm
across my chest and whispered,
Tyree: " dawg you wakin' up
every - amean every - thing inside me "
his breath hot on the back of my neck,
Tyree: " ma sexyazz shawty "
I smiled and shuffled back even closer against
him and held onto the hand across my chest. I
felt so good, even moreso when he slipped his
warm leg between mine.

(Chapter 6)

FEAR OF FEARS

I was awakened by the phone on the night-stand
and realized that Tyree was not in bed. There
was the aroma of bacon cooking and Tyree
hollered from the kitchen for me to answer the
phone....

Timmy: " hello "

Aji: " hello, Tyree .... who
this ...Timmy? ...nigga, it's six o' clock in tha
mornin', whatchu doin' over there...you slept
over there -

                don't lie to me "

I panicked, and without replying to Aji's
question, hurried to Tyree in the kitchen to
hand him the phone. When he took the phone I
could still hear Aji yakking away like an
excited parrot. Tyree spoke calmly,

Tyree: " 'sup Aj....what!. negro,
why is you questionin' me.......you a lawyer or
somethin'...... mind yo' own damned bi'nizz; yo,
son I'm busy right now. Man, even if it's so, dat
ain't got nothin' to do witchu.... well, you da
one sayin' it, I ain't tole you nothin' like dat.
Furthermore, y'all sleep ova here, wouldn't be
nothin' if he did wanna sleep ova here too....so
anyway....whatchu want.....wha!..... yo azz is
too nosy....yo, am busy .... holla atchu lata "

I left the kitchen and went back to the bedroom, fretting that Aji might catch on to what happened last night .... and hoped Tyree wouldn't be pressured into telling him anything.....naaw, I thought, he wouldn't do that.

Eventually, he brought the phone back to the bedroom and told me that Aji was coming over. Suddenly my appetite for breakfast was gone. I didn't want to see Aji - not right now, not today, and I began to argue with Tyree as to why he even invited him over at this particular time. He tried to assure me that he didn't but he knew Aji was coming over anyway. I was petrified, and Tyree tried to calm me down.

Timmy: " what da fuck you gettin' me into B...why you had to go tell him our bi'nizz for...now he gon tell Ardee too 'n then he comin' ova here...FUCK! "

Tyree grabbed both of my hands and tried to look me in the eyes but I turned away; how could he betray something so secret between us. He pulled me close to his stomach and hugged me...
Tyree: " chill out dawg, chill out.....calm down, calm down 'n lissen "

After a few minutes, I somehow composed myself and as Tyree squatted in front of me sitting on the bed with my face in my hands, he said he had something to tell me, something equally secret and important..

Tyree: " Timmy I'd neva do nothin' to hurt you, I couldn't see you hurt; aiight, lissen...lissen up dawg .....it don't matter if he come ova...it don't even matter if he tell Ardee..... it don't matter; just calm down dawg, please, calm down 'cause I need to tell you somethin'...oh, son!.... Timmy .....mmph......see....you see Aji, datz Ardee's shawty...they peeps....so don't even.... "
Timmy: " whatchu say? "
I looked at him in total amazement;
Timmy: " since when....you mean they be like..... fuckin' 'n shit "
Tyree: " Uh, huh...yup, yup...they peeps "
Timmy: " ooh shit "
Tyree: " so you gon eat this breakfast now ... or what dawg? "
Timmy: " aiight .... but I need to shower first ....oh shiit, me head is really spinnin' now "
He chuckled in amusement at my shock from finding out this secret I'd been so close to and didn't even know it. I walked off to the bathroom; maybe I could wash my confusion

away.

After my shower, I sat at the kitchen table with Tyree, still stunned by the news. I was eating but couldn't tell if I was dead or alive. All this time I'd been around these fellas and didn't know this? I searched the meandering paths of my mind; surely I must have seen some little thing that would offer a clue....was I so completely naive?

My cell phone rang, interrupting my thoughts. It was Pete.
Pete: " where you at,....you neva came home last night...I was waitin' all night fo' you, I gotta tell you somethin' "
Timmy: " I'm at Tyree's....what you gotta tell me....what's up! ..... come ova here?....."
I looked across the table at Tyree, chin propped up by his hands with elbows on the table, studying my face....he nodded his approval;
Timmy: " yo Pete, come 'bout noon,....aiight "
I said, looking at Tyree again for another okay and he nodded again, noon was fine with him too.

Just as I was putting the phone away, Tyree spoke; it sounded dreamy as though his words were coming from a far away place. I turned around to see him, elbows still on the table, his chin cupped in the palm of his hands and a distant look in his eyes; it was evident his mind was far away.

Tyree: " I love you son,....you know dat, right? .... "

Timmy: " you crazy "

Tyree: " will you stop sayin' dat "

He quickly replied, a hint of annoyance in his tone. I really didn't know what to say in reply but understanding now what he meant when he used the word " love " , it wasn't easy for me to accept and I had to tell him:

Timmy: " but you makin' me feel funny "

Tyree: " I ain't playin dawg...'fo real. I guess it's hard fo' you to take but am jus tellin' the truth .... don't tell me not to love you - please "

he petitioned, now studying my face as he reached for my hand and held it across the table.

I didn't respond but my thoughts were that this was going to be a very long day. I mean, here I was still struggling with this .... this torrid and unusual affair with him, Aji suspecting we did something, and now Pete saying he's got something to tell me, something that seemed so important, it appeared to be troubling him.

Tyree didn't press me; we just sat and finished breakfast, at least he did, ... I just finished my coffee.

Sure enough, Aji came over. I was still apprehensive about seeing him and therefore stayed in the bedroom. As soon as Tyree let him in, he enquired where I was; Tyree hollered at me and I came out into the living room and was, quite surprisingly, greeted with an unusually warm and sensitive hug from Aji. In typical fashion, he wasted no time pouncing on me.

Aji: " welcome to da club son "
Timmy: " say what? "
Aji: " son! .... I know y'all been ova here doin' da nasty "
Timmy: " what nasty you talkin' 'bout - you done lost yo' damned mind or you been burnin' some o' dat good shit real early this
                           mornin' "
Aji: " n-e-g-r-o.........ppshaw.....whateva - but ama tell you one thing tho'........treat ma boi right 'cause he good peeps, mo' than
                           you know "
Then as he turned and headed for the kitchen, added;

Aji: " he don't need another
'Mookie' drama...knowamsayin' "
Timmy: " nigga, you is talkin'
outta yo' azz....you is not makin' no kinda
sense....."
Tyree: " Yo, B....don't be
stressin' ma boi, aiight"
He just waved Tyree off and said that Ardee
said for him to let Tyree know he'd left for
Baltimore around 4:00 this morning; said he
didn't want to wake him that early. I didn't
know what that was all about and right now I
couldn't care less. On his way out, Aji looked
at me long and hard, then walked over and gave
me another hug.
Aji: " jus take things slow 'n
easy, you'll be aiight in time "
Timmy: " what? "
Aji: " ma dude, ... jus be
chill "
He answered with a sagely smile and hugged
me again, a warm and comforting hug, then
looked me straight in the eye and told me not to
worry, that I'd be alright.
For some reason, that seemed to have lifted a
ton off my shoulders .... I guess it was the
sincerity in his voice and eyes.

Well, that didn't turn out bad at all. Now I had
to wait to see what it was with Pete when he
came over that afternoon, ɔut in the meantime I

needed to ask Tyree something.

Timmy: " Tyree, who this Mookie? "

Tyree: " 'tain't nobody, dawg...don't even think 'bout dat "

Timmy: " but I wanna know "

Tyree: " ain't even worth discussin' .... complete waste o' time "

Unsatisfied with that response and from what I'd gleaned, I threw out a bold question.

Timmy: " you had a nigga befo'? "

I'd hardly said the words when Tyree asked,

Tyree: " dawg, you say ' had a nigga befo' ' like I got one now .... do I got you........ is dat whatchu sayin' - I got you? " leaving me at a loss for words. I had to struggle within myself to find an answer.

Timmy: " ahmean....Ioknow whatchu doin'....I only know we just...but....Yo, nothin' like this eva happen to me befo' B...I ain't neva done dat...you da first person I..."

Tyree: " dawg, we got lots to talk 'bout as time go by but I need fo' you to know this: I been feelin' you like dat from day one, but I ain't said nothin' .... and all da hints I ever gave you, you neva said or did nothin' dat a nigga coulda know if you down like dat.... "

Timmy: " you mus be lyin' 'cause am sure I'da picked up somethin' "

Tyree: " nope, I ain't lyin' "

174

he affirmed, shaking his head thoughtfully.

Timmy: " dang, ... so you jus gave up? "

Tyree: " hell no I ain't gave up ..... I just chill and keeps my aches and dreams to ma' self "

Timmy: " you neva gave me no hints 'bout nothin' .... I ain't dumb, I woulda known "

Tyree: " please, ... you ' ain't dumb' .... man, you know ... "

Timmy: " oh you callin' me stupid now? "

Tyree: " not like dat ... but am sayin' I did gave you lotsa hints "

Sometimes it is easier for another to spot things about yourself before you do; was I that dumb, were there really all those hints he mentioned. If that was true, and I don't doubt him .... I'd clearly missed them.

Timmy: " whatever "

Tyree: " anyway, now you bring yo' l'il sexyazz self up here 'n this happen between us 'n .... "

Timmy: " there you go again, ... Tyree, will you stop sayin' dat ..... pleease "

Tyree: " but its true, better you don't expect me to lie 'bout it. Only thing tho' .... "

Timmy: " yeah, whatz dat? "

Tyree: " Ioknow if its just a

sexual thing witchu but am lettin' you know right now - you got me like dat "

Timmy: " dang Tyree, I .... I neva tried to do nothin' to cause dat - I ain't even know you wuz feelin' all like dat .... "

Tyree: " yup, alla dat dawg .... but even stronger now "

Timmy: " on tha real .... I knew you wuz ma boi 'n I like you 'n everything but I neva thought nothin' like this .... you know, ... last night

amean but, when you did whatchu did to me .... "

Tyree: " you ma dream come through son, ma dream come through "

Timmy: " 'n this Moochie - what 'bout him? "

Tyree: " I didn't wanna talk 'bout dat shit but since Aj' put dat in yo' head, ama just say this 'bout it: Yeah, dat nigga Mookie was my shawty but he did me grimy and when I confronted him 'bout it, he threaten to blow our shit up to Liana...but dat whole shit ...... don't wanna talk 'bout no mo' - aiight dawg? "

Timmy: " aiight, ama chill wit dat .... I ain't gon press you no mo' "

Tyree: " good; but yo, talkin' 'bout Liana reminded me to ask you a favor, you 'n Pete: Ama have Yani this weekend, Liana gonna bring him ova 'bout 10:30

Saturday morning; can y'all be here by then? or even b'fo....'cause she might prolly come earlier 'n I ain't tryin' to get into nothin' with her no mo'....you got ma back wit dat? "

Timmy: " you hidin' from yo' baby momma dawg....now, datz fucked up "

Tyree: " yo, it ain't like no hidin' B....its just dat erry time she bring him ova, she always be tryin' to get some, datz why I changed my lock too,...'n since then...man she been mad as fuck. Yo, check it; couple o' months after we split up, I come home one evenin', opens ma door 'n....bang!...she in here all by herself, ma dude!....I was like, yo, I ain't havin' this shit. So, da next day, I changed my lock 'n dat wuz it. Been like a war zone eva since "

Timmy: " say word!. So whatchu tryin' to say dawg .... you can put it down like dat? ..... dat she houndin' you fo' da dick! "

Tyree: " c'mon dawg .... I handles my bi'nizz when am handlin' my bi'nizz .... what it is, is it dat nigga she got ain't handlin' his bi'nizz? Anyway, so Saturday cool then? "

Timmy: " I got yo' back son, don't worry I gotchu "

I spent the rest of the morning chatting with Tyree and watched him go about preparing dinner early. He put a whole chicken out to thaw, diced and cooked carrots & peas, and broccoli, made macaroni and cheese, fried sweet ripe plantains [just because I like it]. Afterwards he washed and set potatoes aside to be baked and made a vegetable salad, then sprawled out on the sofa.

I joined him, sitting between his legs and leaned my head back against his shoulder. It wasn't long before he shoved one hand down the front of my boxers and fondled my pubic hairs and dick which raised immediately, then shoved his hand deep under my crotch finding my butt hole and stroked. It got me excited and I lifted my leg to give him all the room he needed. He made a contented grunt as I gyrated on his finger.

Tyree: " damn son, you gonna make me wanna....shit! look at the time yo. Didn't yo' brother say he coming ova; dang, now I ain't gon get to see yo' sexy little tight azz walkin' round in them drawz no mo' ...... but don't worry, ama get you tho' .... aiight "

The buzzer interrupted him; it was Pete. I buzzed him in and hurriedly got dressed before he came up. I let him in...

Pete: " sup Tyree .... Mr. Muscles "

Tyree: " whatup l'il thug? "

178

Tyree greeted him back, still sprawled on the sofa. Pete looked nervously over his shoulder at Tyree, then turned back to face me with a worried look and whispered....

Pete: " I gotta tell you somethin'....but I can't let him hear "
then looked back over his shoulder again.
Tyree heard him and smiled thoughtfully,

Tyree: " pleeeeze, I ain't tryin' to listen in on yo' little secret boi, I got better things to do ..... pshaw...he prolly just get some pussy fo' da first time 'n wonderin' if he fuck the right hole "

Tyree could say the weirdest things; what kind of statement was that, it didn't make even the slightest sense to me. Snickering as he walked past us, he slapped Pete hard on his butt, he was sagging heavy;

Tyree: " Bwoi! ...... pull yo' shit up "
he ordered Pete and continued on to the kitchen as we occupied the sofa.

Pete: " Oow! .....dat hurt, ... I hatechu Tyree, I hate you "
he shouted, pouting and rubbing his butt as if trying to rub the hurt away while ogling Tyree with a tantalizing smile. He then whispered to me;

Pete: " You slept ova here...............in his bed? "

Timmy: " what you wanna tell

me? "

I quickly asked, avoiding his question.

Pete: " did you? .... tell me, I wanna know "

Timmy: " what tha hell dat got to do wit anythin' .... yeah, I slept on his bed "

Pete: " ooh! "

Timmy: " what is it Pete? .... somethin' wrong? "

I prodded, getting somewhat irritated at his playful excitement.

Pete: " I don't know if you gonna be mad at me, or disappointed, or both. I been wantin' to tell you fo' da longest but I just couldn't,

                     I .... I didn't know how to start or where ama start but I can't keep it no more..... am gay "

Timmy: " What! .... why you say somethin' like dat? "

Pete: " its true, I like guys...I been knowin' this almost three years now "

Timmy: " word, ...fo' real "

Pete: " fo' real fo' real .... been knowin' this fo' a while "

Timmy: " so you.....you....you know....amean.....'n you done shit? "

He nodded his head several times and wanted to know if I was mad or disappointed. I told him "NO" not at all; then he began to tell me all his little secrets.... He said he doesn't have a boyfriend but he's in love with this guy but the dude doesn't even have a clue that he feels that way about him. What made matters even worse for him, he said, is that the dude doesn't even get down like that. He then said that he has been to bed with a few guys but it was just lust. He added that the worst part of it was that he can't even tell the dude he's in love with.

Timmy: " dang Pete, this sounds like a predicament "
Pete: " I know, but it's like this is the very first and only dude I ever fantasize 'bout...you know, except fo' like magazines 'n shit; I'd be scared as hell to tell him, he too fierce yo....besides, I don't think he like me "
Timmy: " dang...son, I dunno what to say...if there was anything I could do, I'd do it, you know dat "
Pete: " I wanna be with him so bad........I wouldn't even tell you da things I do when am thinkin' 'bout him "
Timmy: " datz ok .... I don't want you fillin' ma head wit yo' mess "
Suddenly, he blurted,
Pete: " would you tell him fo' me, ... I know he ain't gorna be mad at you "
Timmy: " Tell who! ...... I don't even know who tha hell you talkin' 'bout - he live near us or somethin'? "

then he leaned over and whispered in my ear;
Pete: " It's him .... your
friend,.......Tyree "

Needless to say, I was utterly dumbstruck.
Tyree, the same man who just the night before
had given me unknown delight and erotic
pleasure; that taboo of all taboos. Now this was
just too weird. I mean, what are the chances of
something like this happening......two
brothers.......the same guy......WHAT do I tell
my little brother?

I could hardly focus on a single thought, my
head was in a tizzy....what was I to do? Well,
he had come and confided in me, as usual, so I
guess it was only right that I let him know how
it was with Tyree and me.
Timmy: " well, I might as well
tell you somethin' too "
Pete: " what? .... whatzup? "
Timmy: " well, you might like
him but he ma friend ..... me 'n him, ... we be
like dat "

Just as quickly and abruptly as that, I'd said it to
him; I could hardly believe it myself but I'd said
it. He wanted to know why I didn't tell him
before, so I asked him how come he never told
me about his situation before. I explained that
I'd just started messing around with him, then

he told me that he had been trying to tell me for a few months now but I was always busy and that he was afraid I would be mad at him and hate him.

At this point, however, I was suddenly hit with pangs of jealousy....and it was only then that I realized: The fact that somebody else was in love with Tyree opened my eyes to my own feeling of very strong affection for him. I started to imagine all sorts of things from that moment on. Then, it suddenly occurred to me to ask him.

Timmy: " so what is it you wanna do with him "

I asked out loud before realizing what I'd said.

With his shoulders pulled up and swallowing his neck, he flexed his arms, locked his fingers tightly, and placed them between his thighs, squeezing them together,.....and suddenly drifted off into a dream-like state.

Pete: " man....I want him to want me... I want him to do me...I want him to just take me...'n make me do whateva he say, 'n he just do whateva he want wit me "

Timmy: " Pete,....... trust me, you don't even know what you askin' fo' "

Pete: " I know what am askin'

for; .... I love him. He so big......all them
muscles 'n how he walk, he so sexy - he could
do anything he want wit me - I wouldn't care "
Trying to sound indifferent and brushing it off
as childish, silly, mistaken infatuation, I
replied.....
Timmy: " you crazy, you know
that "
........but he calmly nodded his head assuredly,
Pete: " no I ain't. Timmy, I jus
know datz what I like "

Pete's interest in Tyree jolted me into the
realization that I love this dude......and that I
didn't want to lose him either; besides, I
remembered one of the last things Aji said to
me..... " he good peeps " .

I needed to give Pete an answer so I convinced
him not to be scared because I knew Tyree
didn't hate him nor would he hurt or want to
hurt him. Before I could supply that answer,
Tyree called from the kitchen saying he forgot
that he's out of table salt, and he needed me to
quickly get him some.

I seized that opportunity to ask Pete to go get it,
being yet uncomfortable talking to anyone
about my feelings for Tyree. This would also
give me more time to figure out how and what
to tell Pete, who had just quickly and happily

skipped into the kitchen as I sat perplexed;
Pete: " give me the money,
ama go get it "
Tyree: " aiight... the money still
in ma pocket - shit! .... ma hands covered in
grease. L'il thug, ... in ma sweats ... you get
it...no,no, in ma other pocket son... tha left
pocket .... Ooow .... what tha fuck! "
Timmy: " wha happen? "
I hollered, quickly getting to my feet, but before
I could get to the kitchen to investigate, Pete
went flying through the front door and all the
way down the hall and into a ready elevator.

I closed the door, then poked my head through
the kitchen doorway and asked again;
Timmy: " what happened? "
Without even looking at me, Tyree quickly
replied;
Tyree: " nothin'......'tain't nothin'
"
Timmy: " then what you holla
out like dat for? "
Stuttering with his head held down as he stood
at the kitchen sink preparing the chicken,
Tyree: " I, ... I ..... ma finger ....
it got caught .... "
Timmy: " look atchu .... you,
tryin' to lie...nigga you 'n I know that is not
somethin' you is good at "
Tyree: " no, it ain't nothin' "

he lied again.

Timmy: " so whatz up, you gon tell me wha really happen? "

Tyree: " its .... it .... L'il Thug, he jus grabbed my dick 'n nuts while his hand was in ma pocket "

Timmy: " I believe you .... "

Tyree: " you do! "

Timmy: " I know dat boi mischievous ... he wanted to do dat ... he like you "

Tyree: " c'mon dawg, people don't go 'round grabbing people dickz jus 'cause they like 'em...besides, he grabbed my nuts too, ma shit hurtin'.... "

Timmy: " you mad? "

Tyree: " naaw .... but, am tellin' you dawg, you better do somethin' 'bout him. You know dat boi used to jus run up to me and jump on ma back in da park .... just like dat .... talkin' 'bout .... ' gimmi a piggy-back ride '......... with all 'em niggaz 'bout the place watchin' "

Timmy: " he don't mean no harm, he jus too damn playful "

Finally looking at me, he warned;

Tyree: " Even so, he can't do no ...... shiit, next thing you know, I wuz gon hear some scandalous shit...I had to kinda rough him up, datz why he stopped "

I was speechless; I had no idea anything like

that had ever happened - Pete never told me. I stood there watching him stuff the chicken with a mixture of bacon ends, bread and some other stuff. He sensed something, turned, and looked at me curiously;

Tyree: " what son, why you lookin' at me like dat? "

Not being able to find a delicate way, I broke it bluntly;

Timmy: " Would you fuck Pete? "

(Chapter 7)

I stood there watching Tyree stuff the chicken with a mixture of bacon ends, bread, and some other stuff. He sensed something, turned, and looked at me curiously;

Tyree: " what son, why you lookin' at me like dat? "

Not being able to find a delicate way, I broke it bluntly;

Timmy: " Would you fuck Pete? "

Tyree: " what! .... dawg what kinda question iz dat? "

Timmy: " jus answer .... would you do it? "

Tyree: " hold up now, hold up .... whatz this? "

There was no time for my response; Pete was leaning hard on the doorbell; he must have entered the building behind somebody who knew that Tyree knew him. He brought the salt, barely edged his way beyond the kitchen doorway and handed it to me; I told him to give it to Tyree. He gave Tyree a mischievous look, shoving me ahead of him to keep me between himself and Tyree, then slid the container of salt along the counter and backed away to the kitchen door again, telling Tyree.

Pete: " am sorry I hurt you
Tyree, ... I hope you not still mad at me .... "
Tyree didn't respond and almost being a nag,
Pete asked another question:
Pete: " Timmy, ask him if I
can shower here"

Timmy: " nigga, ask him yo'self
.... he ain't deaf or dumb "
I answered, somewhat irritated;
Tyree"   " you wanna stay fo'
dinner Li'l Thug? "
Pete: " uh-huh "
he quickly replied. Tyree was smiling and
shook his head from side to side in apparent
amusement as he washed his hands. He then
put the chicken in the oven.

I told Pete to go ahead and shower; he headed
to the bathroom. Tyree pulled me by the hand
all the way to the sofa, shoved me down in a
sitting position and sat next to me. Then
turning to face me with a look of heightened
curiosity, he began to quiz me.
Tyree: " aiight dawg, you
wanna tell me whatz goin' on - 'n don't try
beatin' 'round the bush .... I know somethin'
goin' on "
Timmy: " Pete say he like you
.... "
Tyree: " whatz dat s'posed to

mean? "

Timmy: " Ioknow, he say he wish you would jus take him .... do ..... you know .... whateva you want wit him "

Tyree: " say what! ..... "

He exclaimed, then quickly lowered his voice.

Tyree: " ...... he tole you dat? "

Timmy: " tole me dat shit jus now, I couldn't believe it ma'self "

Tyree: " he down like dat? "

Timmy: " datz why he came over here - to tell me "

Tyree: " but why you tellin' me alla this? "

Timmy: " Ioknow .... he jus tole me 'n I wanted to tell you, datz all "

Tyree: " if you tryin' to pass him off as a substitute or somethin' - 'tain't workin' .... I .... "

I guess he was kinda right. Deep down I knew I wanted him for myself, but handling that dick was some challenge; one that I wasn't managing well. If he was able to get into Pete and satisfy himself, it would relieve a lot of his stress and mine as well. Besides, Pete would probably be able to handle it better than me.

Tyree broke my thoughts;

Tyree: " you heard me? "

Timmy: " what? .... yes I heard

you - why you pushin' me for? "

Pete suddenly opened the bathroom door and stepped out butt naked, asking for a towel. Tyree got one from the bedroom and gave it to Pete; he pretended not to be interested in looking at Pete's naked body but I saw that he had already taken a few quick glances.

Now that he was back sitting next to me .... Tyree looked so silly, almost like a child, trying to avoid looking at Pete again - fidgeting with the TV remote. Pete was making sure he saw him by flaunting himself. Although I was willing for them to get together, I was a little disturbed at his doing that and tried to rebuke him.

Timmy: " couldn'tchu dry off in there befo' you came out? "
Pete: " what! .... I ain't shy "
Timmy: " but dat don't mean you had to come out like dat .... this ain't yo' house "
The kid made such a face; it was almost as though he was mad at me. Well, he said he wasn't shy, and, I guess if you were going to showcase your wares - what better time and way. He blurted;
Pete: " ain't nobody else here but us .... 'n it ain't like you neva seen me naked before "
Now he was trying to be slick. He knew

damned well I wasn't talking about myself.

Timmy: " I ain't talkin' 'bout dat
.... you know what I mean ...... it ain't jus you 'n
me here "

Pete: " c'mon Timmy, it ain't
like y'all gonna see somethin' y'all ain't neva
seen before .... Tyree ain't trippin' "

That cut like a sharp knife and I felt like
popping him in the mouth.

Tyree: " y'all need to leave me
outta this "

I said nothing more. Pete finished drying
himself off, got dressed, and we all sat down
and played video games. As much as Tyree
tried to hide it, I could tell he was not
completely at ease. After awhile he got up and
went to see to the dinner in the oven. When he
came back, he sat on the sofa by himself,
saying he didn't want to finish the game.

I quietly took Pete to the bathroom and went
over my relationship situation with Tyree. I
explained that we had just started seeing each
other, but since he was my brother and wanted
so badly to be with Tyree, he could go mess
with him and see if Tyree would give him what
he wanted.

I gave him a severe warning that he was still a
few months from his seventeenth birthday and

being that he was underage, Tyree might not want to do what he wanted. I also added that I didn't think he could handle what Tyree had to offer. Above all, I warned him that he would have to keep whatever happened [if anything DID happen] a secret and that I would only allow him to be with Tyree just this once.

He gleefully agreed, hugged me, and went back to the living room. Moments later, he walked over to Tyree who was now back to playing the video game and boldly asked;

Pete: " Tyree, can I sit on yo' lap? "
Tyree: " say what now! "
he asked in surprise.

I said nothing and Tyree eyed me nervously from across the room, seemingly looking for my approval - I quickly nodded my OK.

Without even waiting for a reply, Pete gingerly sat on his lap, even trying to look him in the eye but he turned his head away, strangely somewhat abashed.

After awhile, Tyree became very fidgety and didn't seem to be able to concentrate on what he was doing because Pete was being purposefully antsy, twitching about on his lap; and when Tyree kinda shifted his position, Pete put his arm around his neck. It was the first time I'd ever seen Tyree look so distressed and every so often, he would turn to look at me in nervous confusion.

Pete started to play with Tyree's beard and the next thing I knew, he was fondling Tyree's dick through his heavy sweat pants.
Pete: " oh ma gaaw .... I knew it ..... ooh, oh snap "
Tyree looked over at me for reassurance and I just shrugged. I could sense he was extremely horny but apprehensive. His testosterone won out in the long run as Pete kept rubbing his dick through his sweats. Moments later, he was struggling to pull Tyree's dick out over the waist of his sweats. When he finally got it out, he gasped:
Pete: " oh damn, ... its big .... its so big - daayum "

As soon as he regained his composure from seeing the size of Tyree's dick, he began rubbing one hand all over Tyree's abs, chest, and back down to his abs. Feverish with excitement, he traced a finger around Tyree's belly button and down to his pubes. I could see Tyree's abs involuntarily flex with each touch.

The next minute, Pete started slobbering all

over the dick. Tyree was enjoying it too, being evident from the constant twitching and shuffling of his legs, the biting of his lower lip, and the occasional nodding of his head. I sat on the other side of the room, no longer interested in watching the TV but instead taking lessons from my younger brother.

It seemed like Tyree wasn't completely sure that I wanted him to do it, but his natural intuitive power led him on. I continued to watch as he began to force Pete's head down on his dick. Next, he used both hands to hold Pete's head down, then started to gyrate, shoving his dick deep in Pete's throat which made him gag, grunt and ooze drivel down Tyree's dick and onto his pubic hairs.

Tyree: " damn boi! .... where you learn how to suck a dick like dat - gawdamn! "

Coming up for air, Pete swallowed, admired the dick's head with his tongue, licked it twice, then gloated.

Pete: " I got skillz "

Tyree: " well don't hold nothin' back, suck dat mo'fucka "

Pete: " so you like it then "

Pete boasted between slurps.

Tyree pulled Pete's tight-fitting wife beater free from his butt exposing his briefs, gave me a questioning glance, then shoved a hand down under the briefs and very low sagging jeans, massaging Pete's young, waiting butt. His eyes looked groggy as his head fell back against the wall and Pete began to try to swallow his dick down to his balls. He hastily eased himself up and used one hand to lower his pants, pulling first at the left side, then the right.

Tyree: " oh fuck boi .... uh huh, cccctt .... yo!, yo, let them nutz be son. Damn dawg, I don't think ama be .... be able to .... "
He managed with difficulty; he was very horny and was about to lose control. He was trying to tell me that he couldn't bear the tease.

Timmy: " he want it son .... let him do his thing "

Tyree: " naaw, naw, ccct ngh .... yo Timmy, you need to stop him 'cause this boi makin' me wanna do somethin' "

Timmy: " datz what he want "
He reiterated;

Tyree: " but ama do somethin' to him if he .... "

Timmy: " you still wanna do this Pete? "

Pete: " yeah, but he scared to give it to me "
Pete was actually implying that Tyree wasn't sure he could handle him; he took immediate offense.

Tyree: " don't play wit me son, I

will tear yo' l'il azz up "
Timmy: " know what, fo'get it ....
let him stop right there "
I said, reconsidering. I just knew what Tyree
could do and thought it might not be such a
good idea after all; but Pete was determined.
Pete: " but I really want him to
do it - I want it "
Tyree: " you better keep suckin'
'cause you don't know whatchu talkin' 'bout "
Tyree warned, as Pete gagged. Tyree was again
forcing his head back down, wanting him to
swallow the dick. I knew Pete had probably
never tried taking anything that big down his
throat.

Tyree lubricated his middle finger in his mouth
with saliva, then shoved his hand back down
Pete's briefs; Pete let out a squeal, winced,
twisted his body, and let go of the dick.
Tyree: " dawg, ama fuck him
..... am serious, you know I will fuck him I
can't take this shit no mo'.... gimmi a condom B
"
Pete: " let me put it on you "
As I handed over the condom and threw the
little bottle of lube onto the sofa, Tyree started
to manhandle him, lifting him off his feet. He
then threw him on the sofa. He got up in a
flash but Tyree held him down, forcing his head
into a corner of the sofa, then pulled his pants

and briefs down over his butt; they fell to his
ankles.

Tyree: " why you gon front
now, ... don't play wit me "

Pete let out a little whimper.

Pete: " ummph noo..... "

With Pete forced in that position, Tyree had all
the freedom of movement he needed; wasting
no time, he began to examine Pete's butt hole
then exclaimed ....

Tyree: " damn, tha boi open
too. Timmy am telllin' you .... this kid been
busy .... ooh .... ama see how busy you been "

There was no more protest from Pete. He
merely made muffled moans and cooed in
delight. I watched in amazement and saw
firsthand that what he'd told me was true - he
completely enjoyed what Tyree was doing.

I pondered to myself: When did he have his
first male on male sexual encounter; what was I
doing and where was I at that very moment
when he gave up his virginity to a man? .... did
I know the person he'd been with? Then I
thought, what did that matter - where was he
that night when I first got in Tyree's bed? - I'd
left him and everybody else at home to go do
what I wanted.

I continued watching as Tyree held him in that
position while he reached for the lube with the

other hand. This was turning both of them on as both of their dicks were rock hard. Tyree hurriedly rolled on the condom and squatted behind a now somewhat motionless but moaning and muttering Pete.

Pete: " ooh, take it, take it ....
Timmy tell him to do it "

I couldn't speak and only looked on as Tyree examined his butt hole again before putting some lube on him, then himself. He began to probe Pete's hole with a curious finger, apparently trying to find out just how much experience Pete had with other men. He went from one finger to two; there was a loud gasp and Pete tightened his butt cheeks and cried out but Tyree slapped his butt cheek hard as he continued to violate his hole, poking and twisting his fingers inside him.

Pete: " stop, Tyree .... stop "
Pete feigned;
Tyree: " ain't no stoppin' this now....you ...wanted it "

I suddenly remembered the dinner in the oven and rushed to the kitchen to check on it. The potatoes were done so I turned the oven off and went back to the living room, eager to continue watching the proceedings. There were still sounds of Pete's moaning, enjoying Tyree's attention, yet teasing by pretending he wanted him to stop.

Tyree: " boi, stop frontin' ....

'n keep yo' little azz still, you know you want
tha dick - 'n you best believe ama give it to
you too "

Pete: " No!...No!..... "

Tyree: " yea! You tell dat l'il
hole to be ready 'cause ama be climbin' all up in
it in a hot minit...you best believe dat "

Pete: " noo......I wuz only
playin' - stop! "

Tyree: " well, I ain't playin' ....
this fo' real, you wanted it - now you gon get it
"

Tyree crowed as he held him down, searched
for his hole and,......finding it, slowly forced his
huge hard dick between Pete's butt cheeks....

Pete: " stop, stop, you pokin',
you pokin' me, st.... Oowmph...ungh,
ah...aaaghh "

He continued to whine and fidget, dislodging
the dick. I knew how much he wanted it and
was merely teasing his aggressor, but by now
Tyree was like an enraged animal: The Alpha
Male.

Agitated, snarling, dominating, he picked up his
little five feet six inches, one hundred and forty
pounds prey and yanked him back into a
suitable position; this time propping one of his
feet onto the seat of the sofa, thus leaving Pete's
butt poking out back at him standing in the rear.

He was possessed but Pete was enjoying every moment of it and fueled his agitation by playing hard to get. He poked one finger up Pete's butt and began to jiggle and probe; then he tried two again, which made him wince, grimace and scream as Tyree warned in a low guttural growl...

Tyree: " uh uh! .... you ain't seen nothin' yet .... I got somethin' fo' you " then mounted him from behind and slowly coursed his long dick in him, then eased out almost to the tip of his dick and proceeded again. He went back in again, this time vigorously, and again,.... only this time, even more vigorously and deeper....Pete groaned...

Pete: " Uugghh..umm "
Tyree: " yeaaah...uhh uh "

Pete gripped the seat covering with both hands but Tyree dug into him again and he collapsed stomach first onto the sofa. Tyree was right there with him, on top of him and in him - deep .... his butt rhythmically rising high in the air as he moved like a well oiled machine, his dick goring and plundering Pete's hole as he anchored himself with both hands to Pete's shoulders.

Pete's body was contorted, his face buried deep in a corner of the sofa seat, his right foot hanging off over the floor flailing, and toes curling. His muffled wailing did nothing to quell the passion in a rapacious Tyree who continued relentlessly. I felt pity as Pete continued to plead...

Pete: " Pleeeeeze, please......Tyree.....Oh-oOOW, ple......aaaaagrrh Timmy, Tim...a-a-aawrrrr..... "

Tyree: " whatchu callin' Timmy fo'...man up 'n take the dick, datz what you need...is why you came ova here, ain't it "

Pete: " No-oo! "

I attempted to go over to them but Tyree quickly growled a warning;

Tyree: " you stay where you at dawg, don't come ova here, I got this,......I got this "

Timmy: " N-No!..... Tyree stop; ohmagawd .... you gonna kill him, stop now ..... stop, please ..... see, he turnin' all red "

I took one step toward them and Tyree flashed me a rebuking look and I stopped in my tracks.

Tyree: " stop worryin'...he be aiight dawg...where you goin'....keep dat l'il azz right there, don't be tryin' to wriggle outta this, you ain't goin' nowhere, ama plug this azz good ......cccttt, yeaah right there...uh uh "

Biting his lip and grimacing as Tyree dug into him again, Pete clung to his arms, sinking his fingers in deep as his toes curled and locked into that position. His eyes suddenly bulged out and he let out a shrill wailing cry;

Pete: " aayee, ay, ayiiiiii - cono "

Tyree: " oh yeah! ama make this culo talk son "

I could see he was hurting; too much, it seemed, and I wanted to do something. Lowering my voice, I frightfully and eagerly beseeched;

Timmy: " Tyreee, he ma little brotha dawg ..... oh shit! - he turnin' all red .... stop!, stop! - Tyree, you hurtin' him ..... omagawd, why did I..... "

But, to no avail. Tyree merely paused, his dick still deep inside Pete, and looked at me with annoyance written all over his face. It was as though he was sex starved and that was the last piece of butt he was ever going to have. He was behaving like a lion interrupted while devouring his prey; he snarled at me, baring his teeth, then suddenly morphed back into human form, assuring me:

Tyree: " c'mon son, da l'il nigga wuz red awready .... you worryin' fo' nothin' dawg .... jus be chill "

I could see that no amount of pleading was going to change anything as he was bent on getting what he wasn't able to get from me. I stepped back and watched in fearful silence as he continued his onslaught but somehow couldn't stay that far away and ended up standing near Pete's head.

Tyree pulled him to his feet, the dick still wedged inside him. Pete's legs were trembling and he reached for my hand and gripped it tightly, pulling me closer toward him as the much taller Tyree gripped him about his hips, his body stooped to compensate for the height difference. I looked at Pete and saw a trail of glistening precum oozing and hanging halfway down his thighs, beads of perspiration trickling down his forehead while Tyree gazed longingly at me over Pete's shoulder. He puckered his lips, I inched closer, and our lips met momentarily over Pete's shoulder.

As I felt the warmth of his breath and the magic of his fleeting kiss, I remembered we were not alone and pulled my head back.

Tyree: " you aaight dawg "
Timmy: " yeaah...am good "
I assured as he took up where he had left off, stooped behind my little brother, plowing repeatedly into him again. Pete had such a grip on my hand that it almost began to hurt. I tried to stay there for him but when I met his gaze, I couldn't. He was looking but couldn't see; his eyes were glazed over and I realized that as much as he was in some degree of pain, he was

clearly loving it.

Tyree now forced Pete down onto the rug, placing him on his back with legs wide apart before getting on top of him. Propping Pete's legs over his shoulders, he began to methodically grind and stab his way into a clearly distressed and wailing Pete. It was hard to watch; Tyree was becoming more and more aggressive;

Timmy: " no, ... I can't watch this no more "

I said, and told myself I had to leave but somehow I could not and was forced to witness every detail of it.

Tyree: " keep them legs up son....keep 'em up, don't run now.....wrap 'em 'round ma neck, c'mon....."

Pete: " yes, yes, awright,.....m-mmmph, nghf aaaggwh! "

Tyree: " see all them times you be jumpin' on ma back...this wuz what you wanted wuzn't it...? "

Pete: " yes, yes,......uuh.....ooh mm-mmph...... "

Tyree: " where you goin'...you runnin' from this dick? "

Gasping between words as he barely managed to reply, Pete panted:

Pete: " no, no,.....Ugh! - oyee, Tyreeeeee! "

Tyree: " well take the dick now
then "
Pete: " aiight, aiight.....ama
take, ama take.....aaagghhh, a-aayee..... time
out, time out....mmmph, ay, mi culo ay,
papi,....mi culo "
Tyree: " lemmi get dat bwoi "
Pete: " Tyreee....ay....I can't
take it no more - I can't take it, Tyree, I can't
take it, pleeez.....oooh
gaaawd.....Timmy!....Oooh, oh, oooh, make him
stop now! "
Tyree: " uh-uh....ain't happenin'
like dat "
Pete: " Ay....CONO! "

Seeing him like that and now hearing him resort
to his other language, I knew he was under
severe pressure. I knew I had to relinquish my
watchman's job. I think I was in far greater
distress than Pete and thought it better for me if
I didn't see any more, especially since he was
starting to make that mournful wail again...
Timmy: " I...I can't watch no
mo'...I gotta..."
But just then, Tyree began a guttural groan and
became more frantic in his movements.
Tyree: " grrr..ccccttt...don't
leave dawg...don't go
nowhere...shiiiitt..yeaaahhaaahh "

That was enough. I had to stop him, I thought, but as I stepped over to them, Tyree's movement went from rapid and furious to abatement; then he was motionless and his butt cheeks locked tightly as they clung together, both still curled up into a ball.

Pete's legs were still wrapped firmly around Tyree's waist and as Tyree grunted out the last of his cum, I could see his dick pulsate and swell with every release - making Pete moan in delight as his butt hole was made a tight receptacle for all of Tyree's pent-up emotions. Moments later, Tyree raised himself up on his knees and I watched closely as he very slowly pulled his dick out, stretching........and pulling the skin tautly around Pete's butt hole. As his dick slowly made its exit, Pete's butt hole puckered, still clinging to Tyree's dick. It must have hurt since Pete grimaced, gasped, and sunk all ten fingers in Tyree's thigh as the dick head finally came out making a popping sound. He exhaled deeply, let his arms fall limply by his sides and his head swung loosely to the right.

Tyree got to his feet and peeled off the condom laden with his cum while Pete watched him through glazed half-closed eyes. As he headed to the bathroom holding up the condom between his forefinger and thumb, Pete softly

but assertively called to him.....
Pete: " Noo, no!.......Tyree, I
wanna see it "

Tyree smiled boyishly at me as he handed it to
him as Pete lay there on the floor drained and
dazed but delighted - staring at the condom as
though it was some marvelous, prized gift.

I eased him up and he hugged me around my
waist and leaned his head against my chest but
his legs were wobbly. Tyree emerged from the
bathroom, his dick still semi-hard and walked
up to us. Throwing his arm around my shoulder
and leaning his head against mine, he brushed
his lips across my cheek in a light kiss of
gratitude while Pete slowly and adoringly
played with his abs. I suddenly remembered
Pete was naked and told him to go clean up and
put on some clothes. He ambled off to the
bathroom looking at the condom he had cradled
in his palms.

I sat next to Tyree on the sofa and reflected in
amazement at all that I had just seen.

I thought about how badly Pete had wanted
Tyree....he had even said he loved him. I
thought of how he just submitted himself under
that dick, endured it, and was happy in the end.

I wondered if I had not fallen short of really "giving it up." I had wanted him to fuck me....I still did, but I guess I was just too scared, and as Tyree told Pete...." I just punked out." I owed him that - besides, he'd been very patient and gentle with me.....and now that I'd seen Pete just "give it up" - it made me jealous. I should have been the one under it, but I'd been too scared....

My thoughts were broken by Tyree's deep, soft voice inquiring.
Tyree: " baby, you aiight "
He'd never called me that before and I guessed it to mean I'd not lost my place in his heart.   I nodded and smiled thoughtfully before replying,
Timmy: " yeah, dawg.....you happy "
Tyree: " I love you son......yeaah, thank you "
Timmy: " just this once "
I warned, as he gave me a quick kiss on the cheek before Pete came out of the bathroom looking much revived and alert. He sat next to Tyree and me and as he did so, he gave Tyree a peck on the lips and wiped a finger across it; Tyree's tongue flickered, licking his lips, then recoiled in disgust;
Tyree: " what da fuck you put on ma mouf "

he demanded, looking over at Pete who was
smiling sheepishly as Tyree wiped his lips
vigorously with the back of his hand. Tyree was
now looking very upset so I asked Pete what it
was....he lowered his head and said softly,
Pete: " cum... its jus cum"
Timmy: " who cum"
he pointed a finger at Tyree;
Timmy: " what is wrong witchu
son....what is you,...you crazy? "
Pete: " it don't taste bad....it
kinda sweet "
Tyree: " Da fuck!!....you tasted
it?....yo, yo, dawg....you need to talk to yo' l'il
broth.....Yo, L'il Thug...lissen up, don't play wit
me like dat....you is not to play wit
me.....aiight!... see, if you wuzn't ma dawg l'il
brotha...I swear...yo,Timmy,.... you need to talk
to this l'il nigga, he actin' crazy "
he fumed and stormed off to the bedroom,
leaving Pete looking like a kid who got caught
doing something wrong and was now
embarrassed and panicky, fearing his
punishment.

I gave Pete a long lecture on his hare-brained
escapade and reminded him that this was not
one of his boyz or anything like that...this was a
grown man; he bowed his head in submission
and I then asked,
Timmy: " awright Pete, you

satisfied now....you got what you wanted "
Pete: " yes,...ohmagawd "
Timmy: " what? "
Pete: " nothin'...am
jus...ohmagawd "
I guess that meant satisfaction; he was stunned
but satisfied and I could now put the whole
incident behind me.

Tyree came out and announced that dinner was
ready. We headed to the kitchen and as we sat
at the table, Pete looked at Tyree with
sorrowful eyes and apologized for his
behaviour.
Pete: " Tyree, am sorry 'bout
what I did...Ioknow why I did it... I hope you
don't hate me no more "
Tyree: " where'd you get that
from....I don't hate you son, I never did hate
you...it's jus dat... it was some dumb, stupid
shit....anyway, we just gonna fo'get 'bout
dat...but from now on jus be chill - aiight! "
Pete: " aaiight "
He swooned with a cheerful smile.

(Chapter 8)

Later that night, as Pete and I got into a cab to head home from Tyree's, my phone rang and it was Marie.

Timmy: " hey, whatz good ma...nothin' much just tryin' to get some stuff together fo' school...ohhh!...damn ma, yeah, but lemmi take care of somethin' first...yes, ama be there...later then...beso "

Pete was quiet the entire trip. As soon as we got home, he said he was going straight to bed and asked if I wasn't ready for bed yet too. I told him I was going back out. He looked disappointed or displeased, I wasn't sure which, then he grudgingly asked,

Pete: " you goin' back ova there "

I didn't want to tell him where I was going and replied casually,

Timmy: " naw .... I got somethin' else real important I gotta take care of.....I'll see you tomorrow "

and left.

Once outside, I quickly hailed a passing cab and was on my way to Marie's. With all that had happened today, I thought it was a good break that Marie had called. Besides, I hadn't had sex in about four weeks, which was most unusual for me. To be perfectly honest, although I was falling in love with her, I thought she would be more delighted to see me than I her. I was probably just glad to give myself a valid excuse not to go back over to Tyree's tonight.

It didn't take Marie long to show how much she wanted to be with me as she began a slow, sexy tease by flaunting her perfectly shaped desirable body before me. My testosterone level was at its peak and I slipped my hand under her nightie as she poured and lit another batch of delectably scented oil. I nestled my cheek against her belly and ran my hand slowly along the length of her thighs and up to her crotch. I was met by a cluster of pubic hairs and as her jasmine scented body mingled with the romantic scent of the burning oil, I toyed lightly with her clitoris. She swooned and moaned; Marie: " pa-pi.....ooh! " her body limp, she slowly tumbled over on me as I fell back on the bed face up and continued to give her pleasure with my finger. Her lips urgently sought mine and I made my mouth a ready and willing receptacle for her moist tongue. Our kisses were long and passionate at first, then fiery and ravenous with wild abandon. Our randy desires were demanding and we awkwardly fumbled to rip each other's clothes off.

I climbed atop her and she quickly furnished me with open legs. I was hard and my demand was ever pressing and as I slid slowly inside her warmth, she exhaled and muttered.

Marie: " ooh yes......Timmy, Timmy....I feel you; you're hard inside me "

I'd buried myself deep and locked onto her, my member throbbing and butt cheeks clenched tight. She felt so good I wanted to be embedded deep inside her all night. I slowly eased out, then made a couple thrusts, then slid slowly back down inside her, enjoying the warmth and inviting grip of her moist hungry cavity.

Suddenly I remembered... I'd forgotten to bring some condoms - I couldn't abort now, not now...how could I. My dick was rock hard, heart racing, my head awash with the waves and intoxicating sensuousness of her nude and tantalizing body. She was a beautiful woman, clad or unclad. We spent the night together making passionate love. It was good to be in bed with a naked woman again after such an unplanned hiatus.

At 5:00 a.m., I took a shower and quietly sneaked past her Dad pulling the garbage out onto the sidewalk. Having safely slipped by him when his back was turned, I hurried down the block, steadying the keys jingling in my pocket; they were Tyree's.

I smiled within myself as I vividly remembered when he gave them to me - it was three days after the first night I slept with him. The thought was comforting.

A whole two weeks went by and I had not been back at Tyree's but as usual, we always called each other so he knew that everything was fine. He told me that Ardee had spent almost two weeks out of town since I'd last seen him but that he'd been back since Tuesday .

I hung out with Pete, making sure he was okay after everything that had happened. I was kinda worried about him, but he had been his normal mischievous, nosy, sometimes irritating self from the very morning after. He did confide, however, that for the first few days he was so sore, he was afraid to go to the bathroom...but he was fine except for that.

I questioned him about it later that day, just to be on the safe side:

Timmy: " Pete, you sure you okay now?.....amean....is yo shit still...."

Pete: " yeah...am good now.... but dat bull! .... ohmagawd....he was tearin' ma shit up "

Timmy: " well am glad you satisfied "

Pete: " I wuz ..... "
he replied and added dreamily,
Pete: " I just always knew dat it
would be good wit him "
Timmy: " oh yeah "
Pete: " its like I been dreamin'
on it all ma life ....knowamsayin'......"
Timmy: " well, you can't say you
didn't get what you wanted "
Pete: " yeaah - but yo.....I'm
tellin' you, he wuz all up in it, a mean like
e'rrywhere - up in it "
Timmy: " well now you can
settle yo' azz down 'cause datz gon be it "
I warned, giving him a stern look. He was
completely unfazed; he just continued on in his
dream world.
Pete: " dat there nigga is a
beast...set yo shit on fire...... fo' real....I ain't
neva been fucked like dat be'fo, dat shit waz
straight up gangsta. Timmy.... it's soo good dat
I can talk to you ...you know, 'bout stuff like
this. I love you big brotha "
Timmy: " Pete,... you know am
here fo' you anytime 'n you know I love you too
"

I replied, throwing my arm around his shoulder
and giving him a tight squeeze to break his
thoughts and bring his head back down from
out of the clouds.

Another weekend was already here and I
decided to surprise Tyree by spending the night.
After all, he had not seen me for four weeks
now and I knew he probably figured I'd call
him from home later that night, seeing that it
was Friday.

In order for this surprise to work, I'd need help,
so I called Aji very early that afternoon;
Aji: " whatupwhatup "
Timmy: " boi shut da fuck up 'n
open yo' ears - anybody witchu? "
Aji: " naaw, wha happen? "
Timmy: " nothin'....nothin'....do
me a fava, ama go ova Tyree's but he must not
find out "
Aji: " he right here son "
I told him that if Tyree was not with either of
them at ten thirty tomorrow night, he should
make sure that he was not at his crib and to
keep him occupied because I planned to
surprise him by going there, and that I had to
get in before he did. He agreed, but not before,
Aji: " dang...so you ready to
give it up now dawg "
Timmy: " negro, what is you
talkin' 'bout...you always come up with some
ill shit, I ain't givin' nothin' up "
Aji: " you need to lissen to
yo' self....you think... "
Timmy: " c'mon man, it ain't

even like dat "

Aji: " yo!.........Timmy, how
long we been boyz...dawg, I got yo' back; you
ain't gotta front wit me. What you need is some
good advice, don't go ova there wit no bellyful
of food 'n... "

He explained some things to me about
cleansing - taking care of myself.   The kinda
stuff I had absolutely no idea about; as a matter
of fact, I had never even thought about that
possibility. I would have probably just gone
ahead and done it my way. We decided to meet
right away so that he could tell me in detail,
face to face, just what to do. I was truly
embarrassed about meeting him on this topic,
but then I considered what and why I wanted to
do what I wanted to do, and he was the only
friend I had in the same position, so I went and
had a valuable lesson taught to me.

I was so anxious for Saturday night to come
that I started to put a few things in my back-
pack: a change of clothes, a new toothbrush,
deodorant, a pair of slippers, stuff like that.

At 9:30 I called Aji and told him I was about to
leave. He said the coast was clear so I got out
the set of keys Tyree had given me, then
hurried out of the house before Pete returned or
anyone else in the house realized I'd left.

I arrived at Tyree's at 10:17, called Aji, and let him know that I ......

Timmy: " Aj.... am in .... he,.... he wit y'all? "

Aji: " yea boi handle yo' nizz ...... "

Timmy: " niggashutdafuckup .... is he wit y'all? "

Aji: " hold up...wuz it me who just help you set up yo' fuck...'n now a brotha gonna talk smack to me like I'm dirt....it aiight tho'

ama leave you alone, somebody else will deal wit yo' azz ..... to-night - 'n yea yo' nigga still here, we got his azz on lockdown right now so errything good "

Timmy: " well mothafucka, if nothin' else...you done two thang corrects today....'n...negro...suck-my-dick, good lookin' out tho' "

I took a nice long shower, put my phone to charge, slipped into my white boxers, and threw myself diagonally across the bed on my stomach. My mind was filled with vivid pictures of Tyree fucking Pete. Every little detail of it ran through my mind like a movie on a reel and it excited me so much my dick was rock hard.

Tonight....I was ready to give it up. I was scared like a mothafucka but I wanted him in me tonight....it was gonna be tonight even if it killed me. I thought about that lube, searched the night table drawer, found it, and put it under the bed where my hand could reach it as I lay there now.

Unable to sleep, I lay there with all sorts of erotic thoughts until I heard the front door being opened. It was a little after midnight, and Tyree was home. I tore my boxers off and dropped them on the floor next to the little bottle of lube, hurriedly wiped a large dollop of it deep in my butt cheeks, cleaned my fingers off with my boxers, and lay there.

Tyree entered the living room and turned the lights on, then off, went to the bathroom and a moment later, I heard a long, heavy stream of urine churning the water in the toilet bowl. My heart was beating faster as Tyree headed to the bedroom, realizing that the shower had not long ago been used - he turned the light on but I didn't move;
Tyree: " Ooh - damn........ dawg! "
neither did I respond; I was ready to just wait in silence until he took what I wanted him to.
Tyree: " Timmy, you asleep? "

He was the one who told me " wheneva you is ready boo " ; my mind had been made up now for days; I was ready to try it again - NOW.....

Hoping to give him some encouragement to fondle me and get something started, I shuffled slightly, moaned, and pulled one knee forward and upward, making it parallel with my waist. That move should make the crack of my butt cheeks open just that much wider and possibly show that gleaming stuff I'd just put in it.

From that point on, it didn't take him long to figure out what to do as I heard him stumbling, hastily trying to get out of his boots and clothes. He chuckled, he was excited, I could tell from his heavy breathing and raspier than usual voice as he said;
Tyree: " oh damn son...oh shit, yo, ama go take a showa, don't go nowhere dawg, stay right there...jus like dat, "
On that score he didn't have to worry, my mind was anywhere but leaving. His excitement drove mine to even greater heights and I could hardly wait for him to get out of the shower.

It seemed like ages, but I knew this shower had to be even quicker than the last quick shower I'd seen him take. He hopped into bed and started to kiss me from my neck and ears as he breathlessly threw just about every compliment

at me between kisses, his hands roaming my
eagerly waiting body;

Tyree: " damn son, you look so
good "

down to my butt, then squeezed the cheeks. I
thought my heart stopped when he slipped a
finger between my butt cheeks.

Tyree: " ooh ...... shit son, wha
did you do, you put lube on dat booty .... "

Timmy: " you gonna fuck me? "

Tyree: " yea, yea ..... am, am
ready but, ... only if you ready "

It was a suggestion and not a question. I
mumbled with bated breath, almost unable to
bear the waiting;

Timmy: " uh huh "

Surprised, he asked;

Tyree: " whatchu sayin' - you
ready? "

Timmy: " any time you ready "

taken quite by surprise at my willing readiness,
he asked;

Tyree: " you mean you don't
want me to taste it first? "

almost to the point of irritation, I shot back;

Timmy: " give it to me now, if
you really want it - take it now "

Tyree: " da-ang, ... shawty, you
is ready "

He wasted no time climbing on top of my back

and started grinding against my butt slowly and rhythmically while kissing my ears and neck and whispering sweet nothings; that big hard dick between my butt cheeks, sliding up and down for the longest, tantalizing me. It was as though my very soul was crying out, deeply desiring to feel the force of his manhood invading my most private place. I could not hold it anymore, I was imprisoned and had to be released. I needed him now, and I couldn't wait any longer.....

Timmy: " take it, take it .... mmmh Tyree .... oooh .... take it "

Tyree: " you sure you ready boo "

Timmy: " yeaah, do it mothafucka "

He began to massage my hole. His lubed finger rubbing against my butt hole made me hornier than ever and I craved his penetration, but he kept denying me. I poked my butt up several times trying to catch the finger and force myself on it, but he would always elude me - teasing, tantalizing, frustrating me.

When I was least expecting, but still had my butt poked up in the air, he suddenly drove his middle finger straight up in it and held it there. It was painful but short and although I pulled away a bit at the impact, he still had his body laying across my back so I didn't get far and as he gripped my interfering right hand by the wrist with his left, he continued reaming me with his right middle finger. It made me gasp and squirm but he would not release his hold on my hand, nor would he stop working that finger - slowly turning it, making quick stabs and pulling my hole open.

Timmy: " Tyr .... uugh, o-o-ooh ... mmmph "

Tyree: " you aiight dawg? "

I was breathless and pained but glad I had gotten this far. I took a few deep breaths and answered;

Timmy: " uh huh "

I locked my teeth onto the pillow, writhing, his finger still burning but sending continuous waves of electric sparks through my entire body.

Tyree: " oh ma niggah .... my beautiful nigga .... you gorgeous son, I wantchu "

He muttered, the inescapable sincerity of his plea difficult to go unnoticed. He was almost brutal with his finger - turning it once more; then poking and turning with each plea of his desire to put his dick where his finger was. Each plea was followed by a compliment,

Tyree: " beautiful, ... oh baby you is so tight "

Timmy: " Ty-reee, mmffhh ..... "

and that finger again which sent my legs flying involuntarily upwards.

If he wasn't as aggressive as he was, he probably wouldn't have gotten anywhere because of my timidness. But he asserted himself and did what I would not have had the courage to tell him to do.

He lay on top of me fully again, kissing and caressing and nibbling on my ear, then continuing on down my back and proceeded to shove his tongue down between my butt cheeks, flickering it against the hole.

He stopped suddenly, then whispered in my ear.
Tyree: " I ain't trying to hurt you boo .... I'm just trying to open up dat tight little thang you got there "
Timmy: " I know "
Tyree: " so you ready now? "
he crooned;
Timmy: " yeaah .... I think so "
Tyree: " you don't sound like you sure, you really wanna go thru' wit this? "
Timmy: " yes, yes ..... do me too son "
Tyree: " too? .... "
He asked in surprise; I didn't realize I'd said it until he asked;
Tyree: " whatchu mean too? ....

you ain't.... "

Drunk with ecstasy, I mumbled almost incoherently, spreading my legs wider as he continued.

Tyree: " .... makin' no sense "

Timmy: " like Pete .... like you did Pete "

Tyree: " naw, you can't take it like dat; ama get up in there but I can't do it like dat, you gon be hurt "

Timmy: " I don't care "

He put more lube on me and climbed atop me again, rubbing his dick up and down between my cheeks before sliding it down until it touched my butt hole. He gently jabbed several times, then gyrated giving me sweet memories of him and Pete and I began to imagine it buried deep inside me. I did my best to relax and soon did. I began to move with him, like dancing partners on a dance floor, together, co-ordinating, poking it up each time he was coming down.

Suddenly, with one great thrust......

Timmy: " aaarghhh .... oohgaw, glmph, mmpph .... ooh, oh fuck ..... Tyree, ohmagawd .... wait!, wait! "

I wanted to lay still but the sudden sharp searing pain sent my head and body into a tizzy.

I could find partial refuge only in the softest
thing that was closest and offered no resistance
- the pillow; ..... my mouth was filled with one
of its edges.
Tyree: " ssssssshhhh, ssshhh .....
it's aiight, it's aiight .... "
Timmy: " hellfuckin'no it ain't,
shit nigga .... Tyree .... fuck nigga let ..... "
Holding me in a rigid grip, he was like an
octopus, having me tangled by my arms and
legs.
Timmy: " let me go, ... pull it
out, pull it out "
He wouldn't let go but remarked,
Tyree: " you tha one who got
ma legs tangled up wit yo's .... relax "
Timmy: " ohmagawd dat shit
hurtin' son "
Tyree: " I know but, we aiight
now....it's in there, it's in .... we straight now,
just relax so I can get past the head; relax ....
boo, I gotchu
                               .... just release ma leg
.... daaatz right, ... there you go "
Timmy: " o-o-oh, ooou,
omagawd, owmagaaa "
Tyree: " take a deep breath boo,
relax "
Timmy: " aiight, aiight "
Tyree: " datz it, jus stay chill am
comin' in again "

227

Timmy: " Oow! .... ohmagawd,
ohmagawd .... son, son, Tyree .... "
Tyree: " I know, I know but jus
give up, I gotchu...release ma leg, breathe deep
and slow ...."
and ever so softly and calmly reassured me
everything was alright without releasing his
hold on me one bit. Slowly he gyrated, trying to
work more of his dick in; that made it hurt even
more. Oh this thing was huge! I wished he
would just get it all in but it hurt so much. I
timidly and nervously untangled my leg from
his.
Tyree: " you want more now?
.... this just da head .... want me to go deeper? "
Timmy: " nooo .... no son .... "
Tyree: " c'mon don't be so
scared "
Timmy: " please, pleeeze no .... "
Tyree: " then how it gon get
done. You ready now? "
Timmy: " Ioknow, ... o-o-ooh
.... Tyreeee ... oooh, o-woo, oow .... damn
dawg, ccctt you gon kill me? .... "
He paused and whispered hoarsly in my ear,
Tyree: " you aiight? "
Timmy: " I, ...yes .... mmm, aah,
aah... "
Tyree: " you like it tho' - right?
"
Timmy: " ye-es, it feel good but

228

you too deep .... "

Tyree: " datz where you gon
love it best, mmph .... "

Timmy: " ma gaawd!,
son...ooou,...O-Ooh "

Tyree: " damn boi you feel
good; Ooh! .... come back, don't run boo I
gotta give it to you like this .... mmm ooh baby
you is nice,

                         ooh - bwoi! "

Timmy: " fuck!....magaawd
Tyreee, it's me son.....ooiee Ay - dio, ma
nig.....yo Tyre...Ooow - Marie! "

I vaguely heard him chuckle, then he asked;

Tyree: " dang son you callin' yo'
gurl name? "

I guess that was embarrassing but I couldn't
care less now, the pain was intense and yet I
was being strangely fulfilled.

I continued to wail as he paid no attention to
my plea that he not go any deeper. It felt like
live embers shooting through my butt and
burning their way up under my fiercely
pounding heart. My entire body felt like it was
electrically charged from head to toe and
although I cried out from the searing pain, I was
ecstatic as he worked his way deeper and
deeper into the bowels of my being.

Not knowing if I would ever regain my sanity, I

229

clung to him and clawed in a fruitless fight. I
was now keenly aware of my toes, they seemed
to be on fire; and every thrust he made was a
mixture of pain and bliss. Still absolutely beside
myself with overwhelming emotion, I could
only inflict vengeance onto one corner of the
now wet pillow. I felt like his entire body was
literally inside of me, walking ... trampling with
intoxicating brute force in places deep in my
insides that had never experienced such a
feeling. I was soaked in my own sweat and
didn't care, I just listened to him talking dirty
sometimes and at other times boasting that I
was his.

Tyree: " who yo' man Timmy? "
I didn't answer, I couldn't .... not then; his dick
was too deeply embedded inside me, I thought
he was about to extract some internal organ.
My mouth was agape, I was gasping for
precious air .... maybe I should answer his
question, maybe he would let up a bit, I thought
....

Tyree: " who yo' man boo? ....
tell yo' boi "
I managed to gasp one syllable.
Timmy: " Y-You "
Tyree: " Who? "
Timmy: " you.....ohma....YOU!
- ayiii cono....malicon "
Tyree: " whatchu say? .... ha ha

.... who you callin' faggot? "

Timmy: " mmph ugh... "

I didn't know why I'd said that, I didn't mean it disrespectfully. The thought had just occurred to me that this was what they must do to each other; and here I was, doing that very thing and at my own will - enjoying it even. Tyree was totally unperturbed by it, he merely chortled and taunted me.

Tyree: " datz aiight, cuss daddy if you gots to but daddy gon treat yo' l'il sweetness right "

Timmy: " go on then, take it .... take it motha fucka; take it, gimmi whatchu gave Pete "

Tyree: " oh baby, ... I love you .... you lovin' it but you keep fightin' .... you feel yo' tight l'il hairy boi pussy stretchin', you feel me in

                 yo' belly? "

Timmy: " fuck you! "

Tyree: " yeah, but am still the one dat bust yo' cherry "

He tried to turn me over on my side to get under me and raise my legs, but when my body twisted to a different angle, his dick suddenly popped out, causing much pain. I didn't want it to come out because it hurt so much going in.

He quickly repositioned me; my legs were now

firmly anchored to his waist as my arms fought a battle of their own bracing against his hips, trying to shove the hurt away. Again he began to apply force, his large mushroom headed monster slowly snaking its way in, burning but delighting me again, going deeper, so much deeper that I found my legs slipping down from his waist, my feet trying to find some kind of anchor to stabilize myself and shift away from his rigid probing snake...

Tyree: " don't fight me son, let me get up in you .... lemmi get up in dat tight l'il booty boi, ... "

Timmy: " wait, wait ..... ohmagawd .... this shit is huge .... ugh .... go easy dawg, don't go in so deep - ughh - GHFN mmph! .....aarghh

                    Tyree "

Tyree: " I been waitin' long fo' this, gotz to get up in yo' belly tonight son ..... you want me to get up in this sweet l'il hairy booty hole,

                    don'tchu? "

Timmy: " yes, uh.... yes...yes.........mmmm"

Tyree: " aiight, move yo' hand then, you sexy l'il thing....lemmi get where I gotta go ... .just relax, give it up, ... give it up...yeaah damn you nice 'n tight boi .... yeaah boi datz ma shawty,   lemmi up in there "

Timmy: " O-MA-
GAAAAWD....you gonna tear.....uuhm, oh, oh,
aaah.....Oh gaawd....Tyree, too deep.....O-
Oohwoo SSShiit! you-gon-kill-me son! "
Tyree: " yeaah, right there ....
see, see .... it feel good now, right? "
Timmy: " Fff-uck! .... yo dat shit
is too big .... take it easy, oooh, whoo .... take it
easy dawg ... .lemmi catch ma breath .... please
....
                          phew, phew .... oh fuck
you is deep; go easy on me dawg, go easy .....
oh, ... pleeeeze"

But he was welded to me, slowly and steadily
pumping and grinding away. As gentle as he
was trying to be, he was forcefully thumping
something somewhere deep inside me with his
hard dick, stretching my butt hole, hurting,
satisfying, fulfilling the desires I had but could
not recognize; it was wonderfully intoxicating.
My legs, again around his waist at his demand,
quivered and my body shook violently as he
continued hitting that spot as he held me tighter
and rocked my curled body back and forth and
fed me his hungry dick while he made
satisfying grunts in my ear.
Tyree: " you love it dawg, you
love it? "
Timmy: " uh huh ... yes,
mmmh....mmh, yes ..... ooooh shiiiit .... oh shit

.... whatchu doin' to me dawg .... oooh ss-hit, Tyree, pleeze, ...

Fuck! ooow! "

Tyree: " oh fuck son, ... this tight booty gon make me nutt "

He croaked as he slammed himself into me hard, deeper and harder and held it there. I felt his dick pulsating and it felt so good I wanted it to stay there forever. That place where he was in me seemed to have weakened him as he began to moan in surrender.

Timmy: " gimmi .... gimmi...I want it "

I begged, as he started to propel salvos of hot cum deep inside me, lighting further the fire within me and causing my own discharge in rapid profusion, smearing both our stomachs.

I don't know how long we lay there like that - he was completely spent and so was I. But I felt a great satisfaction. I felt I'd conquered him as he lay on top of me, his body going into spasms. I listened to his breathing go from rapid to normal, and felt his heartbeat against my chest subside and heard him make continual grunts of satisfaction.

After awhile he slowly pulled his dick out and it was then that I'm sure my butt knew it was fucked. He rolled me over on top of him and kissed me passionately before we both fell off into a very sound sleep.

(Chapter 9)

I was awakened at 9:33 a.m. by the phone. Tyree picked it up on the living room extension. When I got out of bed and went to the kitchen where Tyree was preparing breakfast, I gathered the call was from Ardee who had said he and Aji would be coming over soon. Ardee wanted to holla at me, but I told him I didn't want to talk to him right now. As I was standing in the kitchen doorway leaning my head against the door jamb, still groggy, Tyree smiled at me, bowed, and with a wave of his hand said:

Tyree: " good morning Your Highness, will your Highness be having his breakfast here at this time, or will Your Highness be taking it in the Royal Sleeping Chamber? "

Timmy: " nigga you is crazy silly "

Tyree: " it is as Your Highness says. Your Highness is most perceptive .... your humble servant graciously admits "

Timmy: " well, Ioknow what this 'Your Highness ' gonna do, but ama take mine right here "

Tyree: " may I prevail upon Your Highness' wisdom and suggest the Royal

Sleeping Chamber? "

Timmy: " dat may be a very wise
decision but 'Your Highness' will take it here
with his 'humble servant' just the same "

He got up, bowed, and waved his hand inviting
me in, saying;

Tyree: " as Your Highness
desires, it is so done "

I chuckled as he joined me at the table. I
enjoyed the platter of banana, honey dew,
cantaloupe, grapes, strawberries, kiwi and small
mounds of pineapple chunks set exquisitely in
the middle of the top, followed by freshly-made
rolls with ham and cheese. The meal was
enjoyed in silence but I could sense Tyree deep
in thought and looked up to see him looking
across the table at me. From time to time, I'd
look up and we'd smile at each other. Once he
gave me a start by putting his feet up under my
crotch, then teased:

Tyree: " where that big lump
you came out here with in yo drawz earlier? ....
it disappeared "

Timmy: " oh, so you watchin'
dickz now too! "

Tyree: " I be watchin' errythin'
you got boi .... "

Timmy: " is that right "

Tyree: " yes, ... l'il tight azz

237

mofucka "

he replied, muttering the last sentence.....
snickering, as I got up and was walking to the
bathroom to take a shower;

Timmy: " I heard that "

Tyree: " yeah, yeah, but if you
need any help in there just call me dawg aiight
"

Timmy: " I don't need no help ....
what ama call you fo' mothafucka .... to do
what? "

Tyree: " who you talkin' to like
dat "

he hollered and chased me into the bathroom
before I could close the door. He grabbed me
and hugged me from behind;

Tyree: " you wuz beautiful last
night ma shawty, I can almost still feel you on
ma dick "

Timmy: " you liked it? "

Tyree: " liked it?!? .... hell yeah
"

Timmy: " good, 'cause datz tha
one time you gon get it "

Tyree: " you mus be crazy ....
except you ain't got it no mo' "

Timmy: " negro, get yo' hornyazz
away from me 'n lemmi shower "

I retorted, shoving him out and closing the
bathroom door behind me, leaving him to clean
up the breakfast clutter.

I took a quick shower and then put on my sweat pants and white tee and was relaxing on the sofa, not really wanting to face Ardee and 'em. Just as Tyree had finished cleaning up in the kitchen, the doorbell rang - it was the fellas. As soon as Tyree let them in, I ran to the bedroom; Ardee quickly came to the living room inquiring where I was, but I remained silent.

Not one to be put off, he walked over towards the bedroom and I dashed past him in the doorway and ran to the sofa. He hurriedly came over to me on the sofa and greeted me with a great ceremonious display of friendship, pulling me up off the chair, giving me a bear hug, and rocking us back and forth as though he had not seen me in ages. I figured right away that he knew what had happened last night between Tyree and me; I was mildly embarrassed but could not help laughing while looking over his shoulder at a smiling Aji.

Timmy: " nigga get da fuck off me "

Ardee: " Ha ha ha ... ma nigga got some d...ick...ma nigga got some d...ick" he cackled jubilantly, still hugging me. He then leaned forward, threw me on the sofa, held me down, and began tickling me.

Ardee: " see how you is B...you

see how you is ...uh!......how you gonna diss yo' boi like that, just 'cause you get some dick...don't even take ma call .... yo!, datz cold Black, dat is cold .... musta been some goodazz dick dat you couldn't even talk to yo' boi; y'all see this .... soon as the boi start gettin' some dick ...."

he teased, looking at the fellas, shaking his head from side to side before sitting next to me curled up on the sofa, peeping out from behind the small decorative pillow covering my face. He was tickling me again, telling me:

Ardee: " datz how a dick do to a nigga Aj? "

Aji: " what tha fuck you askin' me .... how would I know, you heard somewhere I be takin' dicks? "

Ardee: " whateva, you jus prolly mad 'cause you ain't had none in a minute "

Aji: " negro, will you get offa ma dick "

Ardee: " fo'getchu. Anyway, ma boi got .... you got some, you got you some dick boi "

he continued, turning to me.

Timmy: " we neva did shit .... y'all get this crazyazz .... da fuck! .... stop, stop yo....oh shit, ...yo, yo, get away from me yo... Ardee...

                yo...Ardee...yo, da fuck...chill son....aah...aah .... oh shhhhii......Ar-

240

dee... "

Ardee: " I know dat booty feel
good now "

He chuckled and finally gave me a break.

Timmy: " fuck you "

I barked.

Ardee: " whateva "

Knowing that this situation with Tyree was not
something I could share with everyone, and that
these, my boys, were so happy for me - I
laughed, deliriously happy that they were happy
too. Ardee slapped me playfully on my butt a
few times before Tyree intervened.

Tyree: " y'all need to leave ma
dawg da fuck alone ..... 'n yo, Ardee, you need
to watch where you put yo hands .... aiight "

Aji: " yo Black, it's yo' boi
Ardee ...., I ain't done shit to him "

Tyree: " Aj .... don't even try,
you da one who tole Ardee he ova here "

Timmy: " yeah .... get offa me,
get away from me .... big 'ole dirtyazz nigga"

I trumpeted, settling myself comfortably in the
sofa before Aji drove me off, sending me to my
regular seat.

As soon as I sat down, Tyree came over and sat
on my lap, then lovingly threw an arm around
my shoulder and tongue-kissed me in front of
everybody. They were absolutely delighted to
the extent that Ardee prodded:

Ardee: " yeaah dawg, datz yo's now .... stretch dat tongue "
before Aji chirped...
Aji: " y'all about to make me sick wit datz nasty lovey - dovey shit "
Timmy: " y'all mofuckaz need to mind y'allz binnizz .... aiight "
Ardee: " Oooh, this boi done broke out .... whadidya do to him dawg "
he teased as he sat rolling a blunt with Aji's outstretched feet in his lap, massaging his dick, causing him to be aroused. He soon abandoned the blunt and began groping Aji's butt...
Ardee: " ama just finish rollin' this blunt 'n get up in dat azz "
he declared, looking up over his hands at Aji as he sealed the blunt with his saliva...
Aji: " I ain't in no mood to do nothin' right now "
Ardee: " whatchu mean you ain't in no mood .... mmmph .... lemmi find out dat some nigga been up in dat 'n you gon find out .... "
then turning to Tyree he said:
Ardee: " them last few months I notice this nigga been acting all bitchy 'n shit .... I just hope it ain't got nothin' to do with dat nigga you was chattin' with when you came outta dat shoe store. What da fuck was y'all talkin' 'bout anyways? "

242

Aji started to freak out and pleaded with Tyree to intervene:

Aji: " Ohmagawd, Tyree, talk to him...'cause he can't hear me. I ain't done nothin' .... I swear .... Ioknow why he buggin', I ain't
did nothin' I ain't s'posed to .... why he stressin' me? "

Ardee: " You ain't done nothin' you ain't s'posed to .... what you need to do is, get yo' azz back ova here .... you know you ain't
runnin' shit so don't be actin' like you runnin' shit .... like you wanna boss a nigga around ...... 'n Tyree ain't got SHIT to do
with this ..... get yo' azz ova here nigga "

Aji meekly obeyed and tossed himself down next to him pouting.

Ardee: " you fuckin' this nigga now...you fuckin' some otha nigga? "

Aji remained calm and silent.

I was totally amazed at all of this. I'd never seen them like this before. Of course, I had no idea they were.....well, a COUPLE, and seeing them going through a lovers' spat was just absolutely spectacular. I was amused...they were lovers, two guys, in love - with each other. Oh my, suddenly my situation with Tyree didn't seem so odd to me anymore and somehow I could begin to relate to the whole situation. I certainly didn't think I would want Tyree to be with anyone else......I could not answer a lot of the things he had asked me, I didn't know how to. This whole episode had awakened me. I realized too, that Tyree had said nothing in reference to their spat and although he sat there motionless and almost expressionless, I could definitely sense that he was on Ardee's side. And.... yes....I did love him.

Jolted back to reality, I was again keenly observing the drama between my two friends.
Aji: " I...I need a smoke"
Ardee: " you don't need no smoke, what you need is to tell me what y'all was talkin' 'bout...I know this nigga, I know what he about"
Aji: " Ardee, please, don't make me try to explain somethin' that ain't neva happen"
Ardee: " boi, you gonna make me smack up yo' l'il pretty face if you won't tell me what I need to know"
he warned as he grabbed Aji by the cheeks with one hand, squeezing, so that his mouth opened and his lips puckered;
Aji: " so you gonna fight me ova nothin'...son!"
he managed before a tear trickled down his cheek and Ardee released his grip. He looked

across the room at me and Tyree, back at
Ardee, then back at us with a look of
reassurance and said:
Aji: " I tole y'all I ain't done
nothin'... 'n I ain't lying. This nigga I seen
peepin' me while I was in da store just rolled up
on me as I
                        was leavin' 'n was
like....' yo bro, I don't mean no diss or nothin'
but you look fly in them jeans wit dat
belt...where you
                        get those? ' I tole him
and was about to step when he grabbed ma arm
'n said....' could I holla atchu fo' a quick minit?'
                        ...then I just yanked ma
arm away 'n tole dat mo'fucka don't touch me
'cause I don't even know him. Dat was when
                        he start to get real
expressive 'n apologetic 'n shit.........'n I just
bounced, left him standin' right there. Datz wha
happen.
                        How many times he
gonna make me go through this kinda shit...I
ain't fuckin' dat nigga 'n I ain't fuckin' wit
nobody else, dang! "
Ardee: " Damn, B, I
thought...amean, I thought you was encouragin'
dat nigga, I know that mo'fucka...he tryin' to get
in yo' drawz...I
                        ain't mean to cause you
no stress...is just that......come here "

Then Ardee, quite rightly feeling like a dog, started to grovel, pleading with Aji while showering him with kisses all over his face and neck. Aji pretended to be uninterested and was shrugging off his touches and moving his face away from the kisses until Ardee stuck his tongue in his ear and licked his neck. Then he began to swoon with his eyes rolling back in his head; Ardee whispered in his ear:

Ardee: " you know I love you dawg, it's just that when I seen dat nigga roll up on you like dat.... I just don't like seein' dat nigga near

                    you... yo, I knows this nigga...can't nobody...yo! I know what am sayin'. So you still mad at me fo' blowin' up like dat or you

                    forgive me...uh...you gonna give daddy some of dat sweetness now?
"

He pleaded pitifully like a little child as Aji allowed him to peel his clothes off, leaving him standing there in his boxers. He eased the back of Aji's boxers down and kissed the top of his butt cheeks several times before rising to his feet and telling him:
Ardee: " come up outta 'em drawz shawty "

....even as he was sliding them down over his high-arching, honey-brown butt, letting Aji's hard dick spring up from behind the elastic waistband that had held it prisoner.

He caressed Aji's butt and thighs as the shorts crumpled around his ankles. Aji slowly stepped out of them and stood there with a fist in his palm, like a male and female coupling, rubbing them together in a kind of anxious anticipating rub. Bare, hot, ...desiring and being desired, eagerly awaiting he stood there, a picture of complete submission.

Ardee took a seat on the sofa in front of him with legs wide-spread. Then quickly changing his mind, he got down on one knee and in a flash was slobbing on Aji's dick, frantically tugging at the zipper of his own jeans. Still sucking and unable to open his fly, Ardee got down on the other knee and finally unzipped his pants, undid his belt, and released his hard, curved dick and began to stroke it.

He seemed very horny and was soon shoving his hand between Aji's legs, a hungry finger searching for his anticipating butt hole. I guess that was to be expected, considering that he had been out of town for a while - I guess he had not been sexually active.

They continued what I would have to call "the show," as though there was no one else present - even though me and Tyree were sitting right there in the living room! They didn't give a fuck.........and I was shocked. Never-the-less, I decided that I would continue to watch the show and now witnessed Ardee go about his business with fervent ardor, stripping Aji and wolfishly devouring every part of his body as Aji stood there, eyes dazed as his body and mind succumbed to his boy's bidding. Their dicks were hard, and Ardee's was jumping energetically up and down as he suddenly turned to us and addressed Tyree.

Ardee: " damn dawg, don't just sit yo' azz there like that....gimmi a condom B....
Tyree: " oh, so now in addition to usin' MA crib like some kinda Ho' House, you gonna order me around too!......yo,Timmy, go get

                          his backed up azz a condom so he can get rid of that three week old nutt "
Ardee: " now, now see..., you gon......yo, you know you ain't da one to talk to nobody 'bout backed up, look how long you ain't had

                          shit; yo' boi felt sorry

fo' yo' azz 'n only jus now gave you some.... "
Tyree: " oh, you mad now
'cause yo' boi got some?...datz cold Black"
Aji: " he prolly ain't gettin'
no mo' either "
Ardee: " knowamsayin'...ssshit, I
bet he musta had to chip dat nutt out wit a
mothafuckin' hammer 'n chisel.....you just
hatin'.......I
                    ain't got da time fo' yo'
smart azz right now....first things first "

He retorted, quickly silencing Tyree, then
turning to face me as I handed him the condom.

Ardee: " ain't dat right
dawg...mo'fucka had to chip dat nutt out right "
Timmy: " nigga you gonna take
this mothafuckin' condom or what? "

I shot back smiling, but avoiding his quip.

I handed him the condom and he quickly ripped
it open and rolled it on his dick as Aji took lube
from his own pocket and wiped some up his
butt, then rubbed what was left on his hand on
Ardee's rigid waiting dick.

Ardee made him spread his legs like cops doing
a search while Aji bent over with both palms
flat on the seat of the sofa. In a flash, Ardee

was behind him sliding his dick up a wide open butt. You could hear a pin drop as we watched in silence....then Aji wailed:

Aji: " cccccctttt, aahhh.....damn dawg...oooh...mmmph "

Ardee: " keep still boi, stop movin' dat azz all ova tha place "

Aji let out another yelp;...... he was in.

Instantly he started to pump and grind just as beastly as I'd seen Tyree do with Pete. It was turning me on, which amazed me. I was also amazed at how easily he was penetrated. Aji, who by now had his face twisted in pain and pleasure but was still trying to get out of that position, was clenching his teeth, and at times opening his mouth wide, as if he had something lodged deep behind his molars - clawing his way to the other end of the sofa, trying to get flat;

Ardee: " where you goin' dawg.....you owe me three weeks of this azz....come back on this dick "

Ardee boasted as he pulled Aji back on his big hard dick.

Aji: "
Aahhh......ccctttt...mmmm....cccccttt, easy son,
shit!!....ooh shhiittt...oooohh "

Ardee: " Mmmm huh....c'mon
work dat booty on this dick...gimmi some of yo'
moves "

Ardee grunted as he worked feverishly, making
unintelligible utterances. Tyree started to kiss
my neck and fondle my butt, looking at me with
much desire in his eyes and whispering to me:

Tyree: " wanna gimmi some
right here too dawg....right now? "
Timmy: " in front of 'em, you
crazy....besides, I can't do nothin'....I think it's
kinda sore "

I lied, but I knew he saw through me.
Nevertheless, he said nothing;

Tyree: " oh ma dawg....you ain't
mad at me tho' is you...daddy gonna take care
of that fo' you, aiight "

he replied apologetically and kissed me.

Ardee was still pounding away like a
jackhammer, this time both of them standing
erect, Aji with his head leaned back over

Ardee's shoulder. His eyes were rolled back in his head, and he cupped the back of Ardee's head in the palm of his hand.

Ardee: " who pussy this, uh!...who pussy? "

Aji: " yours "

Ardee: " say what ma shawty,.... I can't hear you shawty "

Aji: " yours, son...its yo's......aaahhh, shit son....ccctt, ahaagh, itz yours "

Ardee: " then poke dat shit out shawty....lemmi tear dat...c'mon, you know I own this shit...who own this shit uh, who own it? "

He boasted.

I knew it didn't matter that we were there watching, but I don't think Aji could have seen anything through those eyes right now. Ardee's breathing was now laboured and his movements frantic as he held Aji firmly by the waist with one hand and the other clutching Aji's hard dick.

Tyree, with his hands down the front of my sweat pants as I lay back on him with my head against his shoulder, was gently massaging my dick, pulling the foreskin back, over and over. I felt a sudden surge run through me as my dick throbbed between his expert fingers. I tried to warn him, and even grabbed his hand...

Timmy: " stop! you gon make me nutt "

Tyree: " awready dawg, Whoaa!...dang son "

Timmy: " I tole you "

I did try to get up to pull it out and avoid nuttin' in my clothes, but the excitement of watching those two and Tyree's manipulative fingers were too much and I came in my sweats.

At that moment, both Ardee and Aji were moving rhythmically and ferociously. Ardee, in particular, now roared like a threatening lion as they both fell onto the sofa, him on top of Aji, who brought his right hand behind him and clutched Ardee's thigh, sinking his fingers deep, then moments later slowly releasing his grip and letting his hand fall slowly and limply to the floor. They lay motionless for a few seconds before Ardee got up and peeled off the condom burdened with his cum, held it up high over his head and roared triumphantly.

Ardee: " Yee, Ye-es! "

Tyree: " Ha ha ha haa.......see, I tole you dat nigga was backed up....take dat shit witchu, don't be tryin' to leave dat shit in ma crib.....ole rustyazz backed up mo'fucka "

Tyree was completely in stitches and I was roaring right along with him as we watched Ardee bend over Aji, still lying on the sofa, kissing his back, butt cheeks and finally on the lips in gratification. Then he turned to face us,

Ardee: " what da fuck y'all starin' at...y'all neva seen a brotha get some azz be'fo'? "

Tyree: "damn, dawg, we ain't said nothin'...we know you jus handlin' yo' bi'nizz"

Timmy: " yeah....wit yo' backed-up azz "

Ardee: " oh! you got jokes "

Timmy: " what!.....I can't say

nothin'? "

Ardee: " yea, you got talk now
but I bet when you gettin' yo' l'il tightness
plunged you ain't got no pretty boi smile on yo'
face "

Timmy: " man-shut-tha-fuck-up "

Ardee: " it aiight, I ain't payin'
you no mind...yo' l'il shut-up azz gon get tore
up reeeal soon - remember dat "

he retorted with a smirk.

Timmy: " Whut-eva "

I quipped as he strutted off to the bathroom.

Aji got up and followed behind,.....and as we
eyed him with wry grins and snickers, gave us a
look of bewilderment.....

Aji: " what!.....we
grown,....if we can fuck then we can shower
together "

......as he sauntered by. As soon as the bathroom
door was closed, Tyree gave me a salacious
look, wrapped his arms around me, and started
to kiss me passionately, groping me, shoving

his hand under my crotch all the way to my butt hole, paying no heed to the cum splattered all over inside my sweats. I raised one leg slightly, allowing him to play with my twitching hole.

I was horny too and appreciating him being all over me like that. I hungrily returned his kisses and yearned for his hot naked body against mine but was still too timid to let him undress me like he wanted to. He nibbled on my ear and whispered, then begged,

Tyree: " you got me burnin' up shawty...I want you in the worse way...when you gonna gimmi some mo' of this "

squeezing my butt with a lustful look in his eyes as he gazed into mine.

Timmy: " Ioknow, maybe lata ....
I gotta see "

Tyree: " what you gotta see? "

He coaxed as he kissed me again and propped my leg up over the arm-rest. Now he got my butt cheeks wide open and as I was sitting on his lap I could feel that his dick was still hard. I reached between my legs to hold it and squeeze it. He moaned softly and sucked on my earlobe, whispering dirty arousing talk which turned me on even more.

He then moistened his forefinger in his mouth and then shoved his hand down the back of my sagging sweat pants. He began to massage my hole with his slippery finger. He continued with a relentless finger, subduing my body even as my mind fought.....

Timmy: " Tyree Noo! "

Tyree: " jus a l'il bit dawg - even a little taste....c'mon, jus lemmi wet ma head "

...... out of fear, not out of desire. He was increasingly making me want him more and more, but the fellas were here and although he tried to persuade me, I just couldn't bring myself to commit. But he was a very persuasive man and I was losing self control....

Just then, both Ardee and Aj came out of the bathroom and caught us. I tried to put my leg back down but Tyree held it back. Ardee looked at me and smiled broadly.....

Ardee: " see, I knew you wuz gon get dat booty plucked "

......he teased. My leg was still fighting Tyree's

strong and persistent effort to keep it up and I couldn't find anything to say with Ardee catching me in that position. Aji winked and nodded at me,

Ardee: " yeah boi, handle yo' bi'nizz...treat yo' man right "

I could only manage a sheepish smile - after all, there was no point in hiding it now. They had caught me with Tyree's hand under the foot of my pants and me holding onto his hard dick.

They both got dressed in the living room, still admiring each other with little amorous, satisfied grins. It was like Tyree and I were not present - they were in a world by themselves.

When they did finally manage to stop their visual sexual intercourse, Ardee called Tyree aside to talk with him privately in the kitchen. Aji sighed contentedly and stretched himself out on the sofa, smiling at me as he hugged one of the small cushions against his chest, then closed his eyes but said nothing.

From what little I overheard coming from the kitchen, Ardee was telling Tyree something about some guy and the money he owed them. From what they were saying, this guy was trying to "play" them and that was why Ardee

had spent so much time out of state a few
weeks ago trying to deal with the situation. I
continued my eavesdropping.

Tyree: " I told you, you shoulda
tore dat azz up long ago, instead you tryin' to
help dat little pussy - 'n see what you get.
Ioknow
                    'bout you B but ama
get ma papa back, I ain't playin' dat
shit...straight up; besides, you know how much
I wanna buy a
                    house - am just waitin'
fo' da right time, 'n I need to have dat papa
when I find what I like; I ain't tryin' to have
nobody owe
                    when am tryin' to step
forward - knowamsayin'...shhit. You know
how much interest dat coulda made me
awready? "

Ardee: " don't stress it dawg,
ama take care o' this...fo' sho'....but I might need
yo' help tho'. Yo, dawg, checkit....remember
dat
                    nigga at the gym?.......
"

Tyree: " who dat?....what nigga?
"

Ardee: " tha dude I tole you was peepin' you dat day you was toweling off at the gym.... "

Tyree: " I can't pick up .... "

Ardee: " come on bro,....dat day when we had the big downpour....the dude who came thru' to use the swimming pool..... n we gave
            him a ride to the auto shop to get his car "

Tyree: " Ooooh!, yea, yeah; you talkin' 'bout preppy boi.   What? "

Ardee: " preppy boi! .....whateva. Anyway, ma man Zach tole me he hit dat "

Tyree: " you playin' ...fo' real dawg "

Ardee: " straight up son; I tole you you shoulda get at him....see if you can tap dat azz knowin' you ain't gettin' nothin' .....he-he..... "

There was a short pause and I could just imagine him cutting his eyes unmaliciously at Ardee for the remark.

Ardee: " he-he-he; awright don't
stress it, I got this, know am
                          sayin'.....I got this! "

Tyree: " Good, but damn, you
makin' it sound like am desperate yo....
c'mon,...you know I can get just about any
mo'fuckin' azz dat
                          I want - if I want.
Still,..... Ioknow....I....I guess I......wasn't feelin'
it like dat, besides, ma l'il nigga Timmy is all I
been had on
                          ma mind all tha time.
Still, dat azz did look good tho'.....I ain't gon lie
to you son "

Ardee: " well you need to get
some...I don't like you 'round me when yo' azz
all dried up like dat "

Tyree: " negro you still scared
ama... "

That was an odd statement, I thought. I
pondered it for a moment and asked,

Timmy: " what is they talkin'
'bout? "

Aji: " exactly......you need to

261

set the man straight "

Aji quickly interjected, looking at me.
Obviously he was listening too and was now
prompting me to give to Tyree what he'd just
given to Ardee. I wouldn't concur but instead
gazed at him under narrowed brow and went
back to my eavesdropping.

Ardee: " but yo, dawg...you need
to tell me this befo' I bounce. You really finally
get yo boi....you really hit it?...I know dat azz is
                          fresh...Timmy am
talkin' 'bout...don't lie to me now, Aj done told
me dat shit "

Tyree: " mofucka, why y'all
tryin' to be all up in my bi'nizz, I ain't hit shit 'n
I ain't tole nobody I hit nothin' "

Ardee: " c'mon dawg, I know
you lyin' "

Suddenly his voice dropped but I was still able
to hear as he boasted:

Tyree: " yeaah dawg, we done
it. Yo! it wuz tha bomb too. Shawty nice 'n
tight yo, homie got tha bestest azz I eva
had.....son, if you seen dat boi butt

nekid........mmmm, m-m-mmm - Umph, ma shawty is tha sexiest thing - fa sheesy, l'il sexy got e'rrythang you coulda eva want. E'rrytime I think

'bout him ma shit go on brick....I love this boi homie, am tellin' you, I love this boi "

Ardee: " Y-E-S!.......datzwhatI'mtalkin'bout. Still, from dat first day in the park when you let him play wit us, I knew dat l'il nigga got yo' azz, its jus dat I neva thought it was gon work out...you patient like a mo'fucka tho' dawg... Ioknow if I coulda waited so

long. He know you love him like dat? "

Tyree: " I tole him, but I don't think he understand or even believe me. He prolly need time to figure shit out fo' hisself, thats all...but

it lookin' guud right now "

Ardee: " YE-ES!....you lookin' good then "

Ardee pounded the kitchen floor with his feet and shouted with glee, then came walking into

the living room pumping his fists and waking
Aji who had dozed off.
Tyree echoed from the kitchen:

Tyree: " now y'all need to get
tha fuck out now and lemmi.....see if I can get
some mo' o' this sweetness "

Ardee: " yeah, yeah, I feel you
dawg, I know how it is...yo' boi still shy. Yo,
am good now...we out...aiight, we out "

Ardee bent over and kissed Aji and told him
they had to go now. Aji got up and hugged him
from behind, then palmed his dick as he eyed
me with a provocative grin. They walked in
unison, one behind the other, toward the door.
Ardee looked at me, gave a wry smile, then
boasted at Aji's appreciation of him and what
they'd just done.

Ardee: " you love this dick, don't
you? "

Aji: " yo, Timmy...gimmi a
holla, aiight son "

Ardee: " l'il tight azz "

Ardee teased with a final big silly grin like
some mischievous schoolboy and went out the

door.

(Chapter 10)

All the compliments that Tyree had paid me when he confided in Ardee left a warm glow inside me and I couldn't help but feel special....very special. For the rest of the day those words were stuck in my head like a sweet melody and I was so happy I felt like bursting out into a song.

As soon as Ardee and Aji had stepped through the door, Tyree scooped me up in his arms and kissed me with such fervor that I started to burn all over again. I kissed him back equally as I clung to his neck with both arms, my legs encircling his waist like a scarf.

He carried me to the bedroom and gently set me down on the bed, then hastily pulled my sweats down as I struggled out of my tee. He climbed on top of me while still pulling his sweat bottoms off, finally using his feet to rid the mass entangling his legs and started to kiss all over my body. Then he got to my dick and I remembered I had not cleaned myself off since I had nutted.

Timmy: " lemmi go clean myself off "

I warned; he protested.

Tyree: " damn shawty...you ain't gotta go do nothin'...its all good wit..."

Timmy: " naaw "

he gave in reluctantly and I went to the bathroom, got under the shower and cleaned myself off. I returned to see him sprawled out on his back, hands behind his head on the pillow, and dick alert; and I found myself admitting it was a magnificent sight.

Tyree: " damn, shawty...what took you so long? "

Timmy: " long! .... know somethin', I don't think you can tell time "

Tyree: " ....come ova here - lemmi look at ma pretty l'il hairy thing "

I was still a little embarrassed by those explicit descriptions of the most private area of my body he was always gloating about.

Timmy: " Tyree! "

Tyree: " what! "

Timmy: " you nasty .... you know
dat? "

Tyree: " fo what!...... fo'
describin' a beautiful thing I seen; why you
always trip when I compliment yo' body ... you
gorgeous son, dick-raisin' gorgeous "

I declined to reply to that and merely offered;

Timmy: " I had to take a shower
"

Tyree: " I coulda done dat
boi...you wouldn't even havta ask "

Timmy: " Black, you is nasty "

Tyree: " ama show you nasty in
a minit...come, bring yo' l'il sexyazz ova here "

he commanded.

I got in bed next to him and he began
smothering me again, raising my leg and
kissing my foot, working his way up my inner
leg and thigh to my pubic area before burying
his face in my crotch, breathing heavily on my
balls. My body shook from the sheer intensity
of the warmth of his tongue and breath. It made
me writhe and my body contorted, giving way

to each and every erotic spurt that he expertly sent coursing through my body. I wished he would stop, but I wanted him to continue giving me this feeling of indescribable pleasure....I could hardly contain myself.

Timmy: " oooh ssshi-it .....
whatchu doin' to me son "

Tyree: " you ain't seen nothin'
boi "

Timmy: " damn, ooo, oooou,
ngfh ..... oh, ooh, oh shit sor.....ccctt "

Tyree: " put them legs up and
lemmi look at dat l'il tight booty hole boi
"
I eagerly raised them, propped up high by my hands under the back of my knees. He got on all fours and dove in, wetting around my hole with his hot tongue, teasing, licking everything but the hole. I kept shoving it up to where I thought I could catch his tongue but he was constantly teasing, just like before.

Timmy: " lick it, lick...oh fuck
yea.....ccctt...oooh...don't tease me no mo', lick it son, get dat shit, lick it "

Tyree: " oh you like dat shit -

269

don'tchu shawty? "

Timmy: " yes, yes, I like,.....I like
it...aaaah...fuck yea son "

I was able to manage between gasps as he
polished my hole with his sloppy tongue for
several minutes.

Tyree: " I need some of dat
right now shawty...you gonna let me get some?
"

Timmy: " right now!!.....we can't
wait till later? "

Tyree: " Liana gon be bringin'
Yani ova tomorrow son,......please don't tell me
you gonna make me wait "

Timmy: " NOO!, it ain't even like
dat, I jus got some shit I gotta do at home 'n
ama have to go ova to Maria's house after dat; I
don't

                    like....I don't like doin'
nothin' like this when ama go over there
"

Tyree: " damn, dawg.....you got
me burnin' up, ma shit is hard as fuck, ma nuttz
is hurtin', am oozin' shit...I need you son...'n

you

gonna....lissen, dawg, I
love you,..... you hearin' me dawg...I love you, I
need you to know this, am feelin' you like

dat - ever since dat
first day we played ball in da park. Timmy, I
don't use 'em words lightly or often, I don't joke
'bout

somethin' like dat... I
need you to be ma shawty....it ain't just da sex
thing. Is you gonna be ma shawty?...I need to
know

dat too...but you don't
tell me nothin'...I need... "

Timmy: " damn yo, I been havin'
a hard time wit dis...you don't know how hard
this shit is. I didn't know what to do, how to
do....but I

love you too dawg,
been like dat fo' a while, I only just realize datz
what it is...but how was I gonna let anybody,
especially

YOU, know somethin'
like dat. I didn't even know you...you...you
know, get down like dat! I always had this
strange kinda

feelin's when I be wit
you; but I think when it first kinda hit me, was
when you was grindin' up on ma azz. I felt yo'
dick

against ma azz, 'n it was hard. Then when you pulled ma shorts down 'n start touchin' ma azz...I jus felt somethin' - I liked

it,..... Ioknow why, but I....I jus did...it felt guuud...ha ha - dat shit was wack yo....... I wuzn't even mad at you fo' doin' dat

shit...its just dat Ardee 'n Aji wuz there 'n Ardee wuz....... knowamsayin'..... I ain't liked dat part ..... "

Tyree: " you tryin' to play me son? "

Timmy: " how you gonna say somethin' like dat! .... damn, we did it last night ....you gonna wear ma shit out wit yo' bigazz mo'fuckin'

dick; besides, look how much time I spend ova here, how often I be here "

Tyree: " aiight, aiight,.... ama wait till later then. What time you gonna be here? "

Timmy: " Ioknow,...... soon as I get done "

He got back on all fours, straddling me, kissing

me all over my face, neck and ears and raspily whispered in my ear;

Tyree: " ama get you shawty...jus wait 'till you get yo' sexy azz back ova here...you gon see "

He threatened with a provocative smile. His dirty talk was turning me on, but all that other stuff that was going on in my head induced me to have to go and prove myself.

We spent the next few hours around the apartment talking as I helped him make the bed, clean the bathroom, and mainly just watched as he prepared food for Yani's visit the next day. He didn't touch me even once during the rest of the morning but having come to know so much more of him now, I realized that he was trying to keep himself from getting further sexually excited and not being able to act on it. From time to time, however, he did look hungrily across the room at me, then lick or bite his lips and pucker an imaginary kiss at me and I would flirt back by opening my mouth or sticking my tongue out.

There was so much happening in our lives at this particular time. He was anxiously awaiting the call from some business place downtown; Liana was making his life difficult because he refused to get back with her; and some guy owed him twenty grand. And I guess me, for causing him a lot of uncertainty.

As for me, the only stressful situation I was dealing with was learning about Pete's sexual orientation and coming to terms with myself about what I was feeling between Tyree and me and what we did. Who was I what was I...... Pete had come to me and promptly declared he was gay. That forced me to ask myself this very pertinent question - am I gay too?

He had done the same things as I'd done with Tyree. I knew Tyree liked it, but strangely enough, I liked it too. I liked when he held me, kissed me, and did all the things that he did to me - it felt good. Why, and how was it that Pete was able to come to that conclusion....I didn't feel gay - whatever that was...Oh, I was at odds with myself!

It was for this reason I'm sure that I had to go to see Marie tonight - to prove to myself that I still wanted pussy, could still handle pussy; I needed to go over there and make wild, passionate love to her and "beat it up." All my life I had only been with women and now this...me being with a man - it felt good to me. Hell, I even loved it.

It was now mid-afternoon and time for me to leave for home - the home I spent so much time away from these past few days. I had to go now to take care of what I had to do at home and later go to Marie's. I rose from my regular single-seater chair, went over to Tyree who was lying on the sofa, one leg fully extended to the arm-rest, the other sprawled wide on the floor, one hand on his stomach and the other across forehead. It was a beautiful sight just to look at him lying there with his eyes closed and I could not resist. I walked over to him and quite spontaneously kissed him with great ardor. He pulled me down onto his stomach and returned my kiss with equal enthusiasm. When we finally separated, he sat up and looked at me quite puzzled;

Tyree: "daamn, ...shawty, what got into you! "

he enquired with a boyish grin.

Timmy: " no - thing...... what! so I can't give ma boi a kiss now? "

Tyree: " hell yeah, any time - every time ....you just took me by surprise, datz all "

he replied, scratching the back of his left ear, as

he usually did when puzzled. I told him I was leaving now and he appeared perplexed, nibbling on the tip of his thumb, his gaze cast into the distance beyond the window...

Tyree: " you comin' back ma shawty "

he quizzed, looking a bit lost, lonely, and unsure of his status. Walking over to me standing in the living room doorway, he spread his arms wide, begging for a hug. We hugged tightly for a long moment before he shoved me backwards an arm's length away and asked again:

Tyree: " you sure you comin' back? "

Timmy: " dawg, I ain't neva lied to you...ama be back "

We kissed again,.......goodbye this time, and I headed out the door as he was watching me, even until I got on the elevator.

As I rode the elevator alone on my way down, I couldn't get the picture of him and his pleading eyes out of my mind. He seemed so forlorn that I felt deep compassion for him; but he need not have worried as I was coming back.

I got home and took care of some personal things, had dinner, and hung out with Pete, just talking and joking around like old times. It seemed like so long since I'd been with him and I realized he missed me as much as I'd missed him. I checked up on his school work and found out he was still doing very well. We lay on the bed talking until I dozed off. Late into the night I awoke, dressed quickly, and hopped on the train to Marie's.

When I got there, she greeted me at the door naked except for her sheer pink nighties and pink slippers. She looked sexy and smelled very feminine.

Yes, I thought, this is da business...why would I want some man's hard dick bruising my butt and going up into my gut?!?

Before I could get any further inside, she backed me up against the corner of the wall in the foyer, raised her right leg around my waist, and kissed me with such passion I was immediately aroused and started to grope her. She had no panties on and I began to finger her clitoris, immediately sending her into wild sexual derangement; she moaned and hugged my neck tighter;

Marie: " ay papi...ay...I want you "

she pleaded, as I continued to work ardently on her clitoris while she feverishly sought to dislodge my hard dick from my boxer briefs, struggling to get it over the top of my sweat pants. I eased the waist down, giving her easier access and as she continued eagerly, my dick sprang free. I swooped her off her feet and carried her to the bedroom. I gently set her down across the bed, admiring her firm breasts, pubic hairs and pussy through her open negligee as she spread her legs wide.

I peeled my clothes off and covered her, licking her hard nipples as she writhed in delight. She encircled my waist with her legs as my dick brushed against her pubes and clit. I was about to penetrate her but remembered that I did not have a condom. My loins were burning and I just couldn't resist, so I decided to do it anyway but planned to hop off before I ejaculated.

I pulled my foreskin back and slowly penetrated her tight pussy. For a woman of twenty five years, she had a very tight pussy compared to others of a lesser age. I was grinding my dick deep inside her as she tried to move in sync with me. I started to alternate hard thrusts with grinding, increasing momentum as we lay prostrate, working and sweating - me grinding away like a boar and her willingly receiving.

We did it like that for quite awhile before I switched position to doggy style for a good twenty minutes or so, then put her back in the supine and continued to work it - evoking high-pitched, sometimes unintelligible, utterances. Frenzied and clawing at my back with her sharp nails she wailed...

Marie: " ay.....ay.....papi si.....ahi mismo, si.....rapido, mas rapido papi - ay si........Oh, ohmagaaaw baby YES! - just like that baby just like that-oooh, umm, mmm, mmm pa-pi, PA-PI! - you doing it right.....yes papi,........Timmy!....ay Timmy, Timm...omagaa, oh-ma-gawd, oh-ma-gawd PAPiiiiiii! "

She was approaching her climax and I was deep inside her. Her pussy was good and enticing, inviting and demanding me to keep myself buried deep inside her, encouraging me to dig even deeper, hoping to find just what may lay at the bottom of a pussy such as this. I found it,.....somewhere deep inside her - and pounded it hard. It was so good, too good - it was about to make me release a bust like I don't think I'd ever done before .... I knew I had to hop off, ... hop off now ..... I had to hop off before .....

She sunk her fingers deep into my bare back
and locked her legs tightly around my waist.

Timmy: " Aaah, let go - let
go..... ughf ngh ma, ma, am about to......oh shit
ma, ama....cummm ma, let go ..... Ooh Sssssh -
SSSshiii - it "

I fought to free myself but she clung to me
fiercly. I was now somewhat weakened;

Marie: " no papi, ... yes, yes,
like that ..... imitacion, imitacion papi ..... si, ay
si, darmelo, darmelo papi, ay .... Timmy, oooh,
oh Gaaa -
                         YES! ..... si,....si mi a-
morrr!...... "

I was about to cum but she maintained her grip,
squealing as she hugged me even tighter. I
barely managed to shift my body so that my
dick came out as I started to cum, but in an
instant, she grabbed hold of it and thrust it back
inside her.

Marie: " ay, yes papi ooh yes,
give it to me"

I couldn't hold it any longer and being trapped

between her warm and seductive thighs - my dick and will seemed to succumb to her hot beckoning invitation, expelling my energy deep within her.

I lay there for a moment, spent - and thought about what had just happened; the longer I lay there, the more the insanity of the situation registered deep in my brain. Why the hell did she slip the dick back in. I was so numb, too numb to do anything from that point. I finally rose to my knees between her seductive thighs, looking at her beautiful, enthralling body through dazed eyes as she cupped her breasts in her hands.

Brought back to reality, I jumped up suddenly,

Timmy: " damn ..... why you slip it back in ma ..... what if somethin' happen, what if you get pregnant? "

Marie: " I love you papi, don't worry, I want your baby "

Timmy: " con`o!..... "

Marie: " its alright Timmy, ... don't worry, if I get ..... "

Timmy: " ma, ... stop talkin'

like dat, you makin' me nervous awready "

Marie: " don't get mad Timmy, I
love you .... I don't care "

Timmy: " come on ma don't be
talkin' no mess like dat, I ain't ready fo' no
baby....I can't afford it "

I reminded her, but she was blissfully
indifferent. I lay my sweaty body next to her for
awhile thinking about it as she contentedly
played with my dick. At that point I decided I
had to go; every moment lingering with her
reminded me of what I'd just done, I asked;

Timmy: " what time is it "

Marie: " its only 12:49 "

she hummed softly and sweetly.

Timmy: " I gotta go ma "

I said as I quickly got out of bed and headed to
the bathroom where I took a long and
thoughtful shower....too long, that my phone
rang in my absence and Marie ended up looking
at it. When I got out of the shower she asked
me.

Marie: " who is Davenport "

Timmy: " what? "

Marie: " your phone rang .....
Davenport called "

Damn! I thought, why did she have to go look
at it; suppose it was any of those girls calling
me, I wouldn't want her to know about that. In
my situation I needed to be more careful; I was
seeing other girls and the way I felt about her, I
couldn't afford to let her know ..... I really liked
her a lot, a whole lot more than any of the
others. I had to play it as cautiously as possible
and therefore merely replied with nonchalance.

Timmy: " oh, dats ma
friend....aiight, thanks......Marie...... "

Marie: " eh! "

Timmy: " I gotta go - ok ma "

Marie: " I thought you were
gonna spend the night with me "

Timmy: " no, no I can't..... I gotta
go "

Marie: " couldn't you just stay

tonight?....please baby "

Timmy: " I wish I could ma but,
don't worry, ama make it up to you..... 'n ama
call you soon - K "
Marie: " alright, but I wish you
coulda stayed "

I hurriedly dressed and kissed her a long and
lingering goodbye.

(Chapter 11)

That phone-call had been from Tyree. I was so
excited, I could hardly wait to get over there.
The train seemed to take forever, but then they
were always few and far between at this hour of
the night. As I leaned against the station wall,
my thoughts turned to Tyree and how much I
wanted to see and be with him. And about how
satisfied I was with my performance with
Marie; I still could do, and did, all the things I
usually do to a woman to make her satisfied to
the point that she would reach her climax. My
manhood was in no way compromised, I'd
performed superbly. So, were there two sides to
me?

The train arrived, I boarded, and we were soon
on our way. The stops were short as the night
riders were fewer, so I made good time getting
to my stop. I thought of calling Tyree back to
let him know I was on my way, but figured it
would be more appealing to arrive
unannounced.

Hoping he would be asleep, I tried to let myself
in as quietly as I could, but no sooner had I
opened the door and peeked in the living room,
I saw him silhouetted against the pale living
room wall, sitting on the sofa. The dim lights

from the street filtering through the thin curtains descended on him, transforming him majestically into smiling hues of bronze. He rose to his feet with outstretched arms, then engulfed me as I laid my face to rest on his naked muscular chest - a subdued man. And I knew it. I grabbed the back of his head and brought it down to my face and kissed his lips hard, long and passionately. He was ready for me and I was ready for him.

Tyree: " ma shawty, I gotta ask, what dat fragrance on you? "

Timmy: " oh, I know, am comin' from ova Marie's...it's her perfume...is it bad? "

Tyree: " naw, naw...is just dat I thought it smell feminine 'n I ain't neva known you wit no smell like dat b'fore, datz all "

Timmy: " hell no, ... I don't be wearin' no shit like this son..."

Tyree: " hold up dawg, you say you comin' from Marie's, so datz where you been all night, you jus had some pussy...didn'tchu? "

I smiled as he gazed deep into my eyes as though he was trying to read my mind. He

smiled back at me. I brushed his hands away
from my chin and looked the other way.

Tyree: " ma dawg...you da
playa"

Timmy: " I gets mine "

Tyree: " I know dat dawg but I
wuz missin' you 'n wonderin' where you wuz "

Timmy: " you know I gotta do
me son "

Tyree: " yeah, datz why I called
Natasha ..... I wuz feelin' kinda lonely but guess
what!, she ain't answered .... three times I called
                          'n she ain't answered "

Timmy: " whatchu mean she ain't
answer - what, she got anotha man? "

Tyree: " naw, ... 'tain't nothin'
like dat but, am fucked if I know whats goin'
on; three times son, three times "

Timmy: " datz funny "

Tyree: " knowamsayin' .... 'n da
fucked up thing is: I can't even go by her
house; her mom don't even wanna see me ....

tellin' her

              'bout I ain't no good -
talkin' 'bout am jus tryin' to get in her pants "

I had to laugh because I knew that he was. I'm
not saying he didn't have any affection of any
sort toward her, but I knew he was trying to get
in her pants, so I replied;

Timmy: " well you is - ain'tchu?
"

Tyree: " c'mon dawg, you know
how it is. Honey fine as hell .... 'n dat coochie,
ohmagawd ..... you can't jus hit dat once "

Timmy: " fuck you, let tha girl
be, she still goin' to school "

Tyree: " Nursin' School B ....
Nursin' School, not regular school "

Timmy: " still school .... "

He gave me an evil look, but I was just joking.

Timmy: " am jus fuckin' witchu
dawg "

Realizing that he had called her first and when

he didn't get her, he'd called me, I bluntly put it to him that,

Timmy: " so since you couldn't get no pussy you think you gon take revenge .... beat me up like dat "

and he quickly tried to assure me it was not like that.

Tyree: " c'mon dawg, ... ain't even like dat "

Timmy: " yeah right, but it ain't gon happen like dat "

Tyree: " you know I ain't tryin' to hurtchu .... "

He offered and paused, then asked;

Tyree: " wanna share a small drink wit me? ..... nothin' too strong, jus some wine "

Timmy: " yeah, hit me "

I said and watched as he went for a glass and poured me a drink. After a few sips, I got up and sat on the sofa next to him; and as I turned my head to search his eyes in the dimly lit

room, I suddenly met his warm lips. His manly
scent wafted up to my nostrils, filling me
almost to intoxication as I inhaled deeply his
sudden closeness.

His wine-stained lips pressed hard against
mine, his hot tongue eagerly and impatiently
forcing its way into my mouth. My chest
heaved as I drew a sharp breath when his hand
that had been tenderly caressing my back,
suddenly moved down the back of my pants
and onto my butt. I wanted him - and he was
ready for me ..... I decided not to waste any
time.

Timmy: " what you got in here? "

I asked as I shoved my hand inside the front of
his boxers and squeezed his hard dick.

Tyree: " it's yours shawty, but
don't start nothin' if you ain't gonna gimmi
nothin'..... ma nutz is achin' already...I need
somethin' -
                         you gonna gimmi
somethin'? "

He begged with a puppy-dog gaze.

Timmy: " negro you talk too
much "

I boasted while ripping his boxers down in one swoop. I shoved him back down on the sofa and got on my knees, taking his dick in my mouth.

Tyree: " oh damn! its like dat shawty "

He exclaimed, obviously shocked at my very bold move. He soon forgot that as I sucked his dick the best that I could. Nibbling at its head, I tried to raise his leg to get at his balls but his feet were hampered by his boxers at his ankles. Even so, I still licked his sack, trying to send my tongue under his crotch.

Tyree: " oh, ooh, ooh ssshiit shawty, ... damn ...... cccctt, fuck son! "

I didn't think I was getting to him like I wanted to and so I grabbed him by the hand and pulled him towards the bedroom but again, he was hampered by his boxers at his ankles. He hastily kicked them off his feet as I dragged him along into the bedroom and shoved him over on the bed, raised one of his legs, and started to lick his balls again back to his dick.

Tyree: " oh shit son, oooh,....damn boi, you gettin' dat shit. Yeaah suck on dat mothafucka...cccctt, oh shhhit. Dat really you son....

tha fuck!...wha gotten into you dawg...I don't believe dis shit...mmph, easy dawg hold back them teeth; yeah, datz betta

playa...ccctt, aaagh shit hole up on them ballz yo...cccctt shit Timmy...oh fuck dawg, c'mon yo...ccctt aaaahh .... oh shit

Timmy - son, what you doin' boi...pphew......damn. Mmmm wash dat shit shawty ... wash dat shit yo. Oh fuck!, them ballz

again!, no dawg - ccctt aaaw fuck son, datz ma ballz yo,.....easy ma dude......ooooh......fuck nigga, fuck you,..a-ooohaaaw.....dawg! - chill dat,

shit ma shawt........ccccttttttt......I can't take this no mo' - ccbbbrrrr, let go of 'em ballz yo.....lemmi..... "

I had him completely at my mercy - I liked that, it made me feel very good. His balls were his weak spot and while he didn't mind having me lick them a bit, it appeared he couldn't handle having it done for too long. He was losing control, twisting, squirming, shaking, and panting hard.

He sat up in bed with his legs splayed, propped up by his hands outstretched behind him. He looked somewhat spent, and was still breathing heavily, his head bowed. He shook it from side to side, apparently in disbelief at how I'd rendered him powerless, if even for a brief moment and,...... hopefully was pleased and satisfied with the feeling I'd left him with. He exhaled deeply and loudly...

Tyree: " Phwee!....... damn son, datz some tongue you got there...whoo-whee...I ain't neva had nobody be lickin' ma ballz like
                    dat. Shawty, why you been hidin' dat tongue from me .... still, I don't much be havin' no nigga lick ma nuttz, not even ....
                    come ova here boi"

Timmy: " aha!... see now,... mo'fucka, I done found yo' weak spot...'tain't so much da tongue, datz yo' weak spot 'n you ticklish right
                    there - ama be on it e'rry chance I get....oooo ama getchu; 'n I ain't comin' over there either. Now shut da fuck up 'n turn
                    ova on yo' stomach nigga, I got this"

I ordered and helped flip him over on his stomach. On my knees between his legs, I tried to spread his butt cheeks open but he clenched them tightly. I tried again and he did the same thing. I smacked him hard on his butt...

Tyree: " Damn son, I neva seen you like .... ooooohh, damn shawty...what you tryin' to do, freak me?"

I slapped his butt again......

Tyree: " O-Ooow! "

.......and told him,

Timmy: " don't tighten dat shit up again, if you do ama slap the shit outta you next time "

Tyree: " Awright, awright. Damn son,...I neva seen..... "

Timmy: " shut tha fuck up! "

and smacked him even harder this time.

Tyree: " awright, ooou.....ooh, whooo....anything you say boo - you tha boss now "

He rasped between his teeth which were locked onto a mouthful of pillow.

Timmy: " yes, am tha mo'fuckin'
boss now "

I charged, looking down at his big, long, semi-
hard Black Mamba of a dick protruding
between his open thighs, still wanting to
plunder my little hole.

Timmy: " wit yo' bigazz
mo'fukkin' dick "

Tyree: " Oh you don't like Mr.
Johnson dawg - O-OOOhw! ccccttt, oh
shit......dang, you tryin'a punish me son "

Timmy: " tearin' up ma shit wit
dat big ol' mo'fucka - KEEP STILL! "

I commanded and delivered yet another slap.
He relaxed and I began to spread his butt
cheeks apart. He was still tense, raising his head
up to peek behind to see what I was about to do.
I shoved his face back in the pillow, slapped his
butt again, and listened to his muffled "O-Ooh
". With him now somewhat relaxed, I began to
slowly run a forefinger from the top of the
crack of his butt cheeks,

Tyree: " Ung, Timmy -
dawg,......don't do nothin' rough - please "

he begged with a petrified muffle as his legs began to tremble.

Timmy: " this shit mine now - ama do whateva I want "

I elected to play on his fears and started to roughly massage the base of the crack of his butt cheeks, working my way down, nearing but still not yet touching his hole.

Tyree: " Ti-Timmy.....my, ma dawg...... "

He stuttered nervously;

Timmy: " SHUDDUP!......ama dig all up in this shit now "

I threatened,

Tyree: " no Timmy dawg, don't do dat "

he whined, twisting his body trying to look at what I'd threatened to do.

Timmy: " KEEP YO' HEAD DOWN! "

I demanded sternly and watched as he fearfully

and reluctantly buried his face in the middle of the pillow. As he waited tensely in anticipation, I surprised him by merely spreading his cheeks wide to take a good look at his butt hole; a tiny brown sweat-moistened pucker that seemed an impenetrable thing. I stuck my tongue between those cheeks,

Tyree: " O-Oohw! "

flickering like a Komodo Dragon. Although relieved that I wasn't poking his hole with a finger as I'd threatened, he still began to pull his legs together and tighten up again. I licked lightly, raising my head to look for his reaction. His face was buried deeper in that soft pillow, his arms a little out and upward......and slightly above his head, clutching two handfuls of the rumpled sheet. If he'd been standing, it would appear that he was being "frisked ".

Tyree: " Aaaah! "

He exclaimed, as though being pierced by a needle.

Timmy: " you like dat?"

Tyree: " naaaw, I jus let you 'cause I thought you liked doin' it "

Timmy: " hell fuckin' no.... but
datz good tho'......'cause I don't think I liked it
either"

Tyree: " shawty, don't make me
wait no mo'....pleeze....c'mon, gimmi some of
dat.... "

I quickly rose up on my knees and cut him off
abruptly as he tried to turn himself face up,
having to maneuver his leg to get it over my
head and lay it flat. He faced me,

Timmy: " what! ...... you mean
you ain't gonna taste it 'n lick it first? "

Tyree: " Oooooh!...so you love
dat shit "

Timmy: " hell-yeah-I-love-when-
you-do-dat-shit "

Tyree: " so then, what's takin'
you so mo'fuckin' long to come up outta them
drawz shawty? "

I undressed but disappointed him by only
pulling my boxers down to my knees and
electing to suck his dick when I knew he had
tighter things on his mind. I teased him by
lightly sucking on the head of his dick and

watched as he leaned his back against the headboard, trying to watch me through glazed eyes. I'd no sooner stopped and was kneeling between his legs when he asked pitifully;

Tyree: " you gon gimmi now? "

Timmy: " yeaah "

I answered and turned my butt to him while on my hands and knees between his legs. He wasted no time. Before I had the chance to peel it off, he was all over me. Next thing I knew, he had me on my back with my feet in the air and was pulling my boxer briefs over my heels. I spread my legs wide and held them as he buried his face deep between my butt cheeks, slurping and licking and jerking my dick sometimes.

There was a pause - he was preparing a finger for me; in a moment he would be probing me with that finger

Timmy: " ccccttt, aaw, mmmh...oh shit "

Tyree: " I ain't gonna be waitin' too long wit this dawg, I need to get up in you...ama get you tonight, ama take dat shit 'n claim it...stamp ma name on yo' l'il tight fineazz ..... you hearin' me shawty "

Timmy: " yo, don't be tryin' to take it out on me "

Tyree: " I ain't doin' dat but, ama handle ma bizz "

Timmy: " uh...yeah, ccctt...oooh...yes, yes a heard...damn son you tryin' to dig it out "

Tyree: " I got somethin' different to dig this out wit boi...am only playin' wit you right now, you soon gon find out. Get on your kneez boi
                    'n lemmi taste some mo' of this....mmmph .... lemmi see dat lube...I want .... "

I reached into the drawer of the night table and handed him the lube. He daubed my butt copiously and then slowly worked a finger in, poking and turning and loosening me up.

Timmy: " yo, dawg, no matter what happen...just give it to me, just get it in there quick and take it "

Tyree: " oh! you still scared son

"

Timmy: " naw...I ain't scared
but..but I just...."

Tyree: " yeah, you keep sayin'
dat. Come ova here, bend ova the edge of da
bed...I wanna see this dick goin' up in dat tight
l'il azz
                    hole...yea, like dat,
right there...spread yo' legs,......l'il mo'...yea
right there, don't move...damn datz a pretty l'il
thang ma ....
                    shawty,....believe me,
you gorgeous all ova...mmm mmmph....aiight,
here it comes...nice 'n slow, nice 'n slow -
aiight!... "

Timmy: "
cccctt...oooh...mmmph...mmph, oh shit, ow,
oooww...aahha, aaaagh...Tyree "

Tyree: " stay right there dawg,
relax, just chill....aiight,.....come back up,.....a
l'il mo'. Ooh see, it started to go in, you made
it come
                    back out "

Timmy: " oh fuck...kiss me
Tyree...mmmph...just get it in quick
dawg...please "

He tried again and failed. Four more attempts and it still didn't work so I had to get on my back, legs up.

Timmy: " just make it go in quick...just make it go in"

Tyree: " you gotta relax tho'...try to think 'bout somethin' else 'n just try to relax ..... aiight, here we go "

Timmy: " mmm, ngh ssshii mmm, yea .... yea, keep doin' it like dat yea .... oh yeaah .... ooohh cccct fuck ..... Tyreee cccttt a-a-

                                         aha .... mmph ... ff-- uuck "

Tyree: " got it, I got it...put yo' leg back up, don't make it come out again .... stay chill boo "

Timmy: " Oooh .... aaawfuck .... fuck you, Tyree, fuck you .... mmmph .... ooohh "

He was probably halfway in and still trying to fill me up with it. As I clung to his neck and girded his waist with my legs, I wondered what my butt hole looked like, being stretched to its limit by his big dick.

He was kind, he let things settle at that point, giving me a chance to catch my breath as he kissed my neck and ears. His butt was very high in the air and that told me that I had a lot more dick to receive...more than I'd thought. Holding me by the shoulders, he continued to kiss me as he rocked me back and forth, cradled under him and clinging to him like a baby chimp clinging to its parent.

Tyree: " ama tear it tonight shawty.....you want it like dat...think you can handle dat? "

He warned lustily, his hot breath warming my ear,

Timmy: " Noo son!.....none o'.....
"

but as I tried to warn......

Timmy: " M......Mmpf!...."

...... I felt the force and hardness of his manhood.....shifting something inside of me, disrupting the rhythm of my heartbeat.....

Timmy: " Y-You said you wuzn't

gon.......Fu-uck, ccccttt aaye-yo-Uhm..... "

.....I cried out and found myself with two handfuls - an ear, and a fleshy part of his neck.

Tyree: " Urrrngh!....dang shawdy,...you gon pull daddy ear off - take it easy "

Timmy: " Oooou-woo-ooou, it hu-rrrt "

Tyree: " Ungh, I know, I know....but let go of ma ear.... "

Despite his claim of being hurt, his bestial instinct still made him relentless, keeping the pressure on and forcing his hardness into my depths, as though searching for my tenderest confines.

Timmy: " damn son - whatchu!....U-nnng - A-A-AAHHHHH!.......... "

Tyree: " you too scared .... stop punkin' - give it up "

Timmy: " Oh-magawd - Oooow! aiight! aiight!.....take it, take it any way you want....U-Oooh!....I, I....I don't care if you hurt it - jus do it how you gotta

do "

Tyree: " oooh ... .lissen to you 'n
yo' big talk... "

He teased, leaving his tingling lip touches on
my face at intervals.

Tyree: " .....pshaw...you soon
start hollerin' 'n you know it...scared to take a
l'il dick...l'il tightazz "

Timmy: " brah!.....don't act like
you don't know the size of that thing "

Tyree: " don't mind me
dawg...am just fuckin' witchu, I love you, you
know dat.....you 'n all yo' l'il sexy ways so don't
stop"

I tried very hard to condition my mind to
receive more of his hard, demanding dick and
hugged his neck even tighter. Again he rocked
us back and forth and whenever we rocked
back, he would shove deeper into me as we
rocked forward. On and on we went like that
until I could feel his dick coursing its way
through the same path it did the last time, trying
to get to that spot that made me tremble
uncontrollably with excitement and fear,

leaving me weak and limp.

I was now almost full with his manhood and he kept positioning himself to the point where he was now on his toes in a kind of stooping position and when we rocked forward and came back, he dipped hard, going deep, the head of his dick hitting...

Timmy: " OHGAA-wd...mmph...woo-wooo-wo...oh...ohgawd, ohgawd...mmmph...you deep, oh, oooh.....you love me Tyree?...Tyree, tell me you love me son...mmph, ohhh shiit,....you tearin' it nigga...you gonna bust ma shit up yo"

Tyree: " tole you I was gonna give it to you dawg...put yo' legs back 'round ma waist shawty .... you gotta learn how to take this dick

                .... you ma shawty right? "

Timmy: " yes!, yes.....do anything you want widdit....it's yo' azz now dawg, tear it, hurt it.....O-ooow!....wait!, wait, lemmi...... "

Tyree: " shawty I ain't waitin' fo' nothin' - not when I got yo' sweet l'il tight booty clampin' on ma Johnson like this "

Timmy: " damn bruh - tha fuck!
"

Tyree: " you want me to pull it
out? .... "

Timmy: " No! no!....don't
ta....don't take it out, mmph Unng....don't make
it come out "

Tyree: " so you love this dick
then .... you wanna sit on it? "

Timmy: " Hell no bruh! "

Tyree: " how come you say you
love this dick 'n you scared of it "

I was hurting like crazy.....

Timmy: " mm-mmph, fuck you
Tyree; UUMPH, oh-ma-gawd - if it come out
then you gon be forcin' it back in again "

Tyree: " oooh,.....ma l'il shawty
"

.......he crooned in my ear....

Tyree: "Awright, hole tight 'n

stay on tha dick, ama turn ova on ma back so you can be sittin' on it - dat way you can take whatchu

want - you ready? "

Timmy: " yea. Pheeew!....am ready "

I did as he said, but now that he was on his back, I had to put my full body weight down and absorb all that dick. That was a clever move on his part, getting me to sit on his big dick. It was more than I could bear and I found myself squatting over him rather than sitting plumb on the dick. He reached out and took my hands, holding them straight down against my sides as he gyrated and jabbed wickedly at my hole....

Timmy: " A-Aaayeeee!.....ssshit "

I did my best to be as quiet as I could and bore the hurt..... revelling in the intoxicating bliss of his sexual prowess and captivating personality.

Tyree: " this yo' dick, ride it, ride dat nutt out of it....rock it shawty...rock dat shit, - it ain't far, rock it .... don't punk this now ..... rock

dat shit 'n take this

nutt...c'mon...I know you like it, see how hard yo' shit is .... ROCK DAT MOTHAFUCKA!.....yeaah "

He goaded as he released my wrists then grabbed me firmly at the waist, pulling me up and down while he jabbed and gyrated, with a pool of my precum, emanating from the still hanging trail oozing from my dick, just below his navel.

The pounding was becoming more intense, and I could feel the swelling up of his dick, throbbing against the resisting muscles of my butt hole as he continued to force me to grind on the dick.

Tyree: " take it shawty....yea, take dat dick, itz yours...c'mon, l'il tightazz ...ooh yeah...stay on it shawty...stay on it, yeaaah go ahead and

break dat mo'fucka off up in dat tight hole, don't be shy boo, treat yo' nigga right...uh huh, yea, work ccctt ....

damnyougotsome guud azz boi...c'mon shawty work wit me lemmi tear dat azz...don't run shawty...dont run, how da fuck

ama get this azz if you keep runnin'...mmph; fuck!....boi, you got some bombazz booty you gonna make a....oh

309

fuck son,

fuck! you tryin' to
make...hell no, not yet...fuck shawty, chill,
chill....ooh fuck nigg....you gonna...damn
shawty, its comin',

rock dat shit 'n take this
nu .... "

In a flash he flipped me on my side, raised one
of my legs, fastened himself behind me, and
was fucking me with a vengeance. I was trying
to pull that leg back down as he had me so wide
open I had no balance and could only claw
away with my hands. Ending up with my upper
half hanging over the edge of the bed was not
the best position to be in and he nailed me even
moreso, I think, because of my efforts to
escape. This made him agitated and even more
aggressive.

Timmy: " Oohhh fuck son I
can't take it any more .... "

He stopped, then said we had to go back to my
sitting on it. He again tried to have me force
ride his dick but this time it was that much
more unbearable and I did all I could to get off
it. He eased me off, pulled me to the floor at
the edge of the bed, and raised one of my legs
up, throwing it wide on the bed and
immediately forced his way back deep in me

for several minutes before he had me climb back on top of him giving me more of that prostate pounding.

To my utter surprise, I began to feel a degree of high emotional excitement as my own cum was beginning to surge through my loins with each ebb and flow of the rocking motion and his hard and pulsating dick being thrust against what I thought had to be - my prostate. There was no more hurt now, only the pure and warm ecstatic splendor from before which made me suddenly send a gush of ....sperm flying across his chest and stomach just as he...

Tyree: " ooh fuck son.....B-brrrrr....aaaaw, aaaagh! "

We both lay limp as I'd fallen back on his chest and he hugged me across mine while we regained our strength.

Tyree: " ooh.....dat nutt been yo' nutt fo' a long m'fuckin' time dawg"

Timmy: " damn, negro, wuz you tryin' murder me? "

Tyree: " naaw ma shawdy .... dat was jus some good fuck, datz all " he assured, and kissed me as we lay still in the dark.

A few moments went by before I felt for and held onto his now flaccid weapon of pain and pleasure, thinking of how he had made me feel. He sighed and snuggled up behind me, assuming his usual sleeping position - him cuddled up behind me in the fetal position - and we fell off into a very sound sleep.

(Chapter 12)

I was awakened from vivid dreams of Tyree and me having sex, so vivid that my dick was rock hard and my heart racing. I slowly gathered my senses and looked at the clock. It was 8:33 a.m. and Tyree was sleeping like a baby.

I'm not a good cook but I decided to make omelettes for breakfast - Tyree's favorite. As I was cooking, my thoughts drifted to Tyree and I wondered what his dad looked like. Was he as strikingly handsome, masculine, and with the same distinctive and pervasive quality?

Oh!...I suddenly remembered.....Yani, Yani would be coming over today to spend the weekend with his dad. I immediately turned the flame off under the eggs and awakened Tyree to remind him.

Timmy: " Tyree, remember Yani comin' ova today!...what time?..."

Tyree: " oh shit, what time is it? "

Timmy: " 9:07...I gotta go, I don't want her to see me ova here this early in da mornin' B "

Tyree: " chill out son, chill
out...lemmi think......mmmm, call Aji, tell him
to get his azz ova here......immediately, if not
b'fore. I don't
            need to be alone up in
here when Liana get here 'cause she can't seem
to get it through her head dat I ain't tryin' to get
            wit her no mo'...I'm
over widdit..... can't take the mess, it wuz either
me or her parents "

I could see that there was hurt in his eyes; he
may still be in love with her but from what I'd
gathered so far, her parents were the problem.

Having spoken to Aji, I closed the phone and
turned to him;

Timmy: " said he be here in ten
to twenty minutes...he at da pharmacy gettin'
some things for his moms "

Tyree: " tell him to get here
now, twenty minutes too long, he need to get
here before Liana and Yani "

I immediately fulfilled his request, watching
him moving about in a frenzy before turning the
flame back under breakfast. Aji said he was

dropping everything and would be here in a few minutes as he'd just hailed a cab. At 9:16 Aji was buzzing the intercom. I quickly let him in and a few minutes later he was at the door. He came in, gave us the usual hug and pound, then Tyree explained the situation to him as we tried to relax, chit-chat and be as casual as we could be.

The intercom buzzed at 9:43 but when Tyree answered there was no response.

Tyree: " that would be Liana, somebody musta let her in...watch out fo' it now...'n watch y'allz moufs, ma son gonna be in here "

He warned.....

Aji: " Black, don't even start accusin' me 'bout nothin' 'cause she ain't even here yet 'n I ain't said nothin' "

......looking back......

Tyree: " Aj,....I know how you be - but jus chill,.......aiight! "

Aji: " will you jus let the lady come in be'fo you start accusin' e'rrybody "

315

.....as he unlocked the front door, then went and seated himself at the kitchen table.....waiting as he started to eat his omelette.

I promptly headed for the living room and stood there watching some news on CNN, leaving Aji leaning against one of the kitchen door jambs. Moments later the door knob jiggled and the bell rang. Aji stepped backwards and reaching behind him, opened the door. As soon as Yani saw me, he ran excitedly to the living room with his little arms outstretched....

Yani: " Uncle Timmy, Uncle Timmy! "

..... and I scooped him up and hugged him. Liana had slowly walked in, stopped in the foyer and was eyeing both Aji and Tyree, although with Aji, her look was one of disdain. She then took a few steps past him, shifted the drapery, and peered into the living room. She looked at me but said nothing - her look said it all: She did not like seeing us here. Pulling her head back out, she inquired;

Liana: " Dang!.......y'all don't live nowhere! - why is y'all always over..... "

an icy and sarcastic response from Aji.....

Aji: " I sleeps in da park.... "

......and he gave me a glance...mischief written
all over his face. He then turned his head and
looked at Liana, adding,

Aji: " datz ma boi, we hang
out... "

Tyree: " where ma son at?"

Tyree interjected. Yani shuffled his feet upon
hearing his dad's voice, becoming fidgety, an
indication that he wanted to be set free. I let
him down and he ran towards the kitchen. I
followed, watching him leap into Tyree's arms
and lap. Liana, wearing an evil scowl, turned
her head to either side looking at me..... and
Aji, loudly and scornfully demanding,

Liana: " y'all don't work
nowhere!.......up in here so early in the mornin'
...... y'all need to get a job - fuckin' scrubs "

Aji: " whatchu say!......hole
up now......who you call...... "

then Tyree interjected calmly,

Tyree: " Liana,.......is this
necessary! "

Liana: " why they always gotta
be.... "

and I engaged her with a rational reply,
intoning softly,

Timmy: " its Sa-tur-day ma ......
it's tha weekend "

and she fumed, cutting her eye at me.

Liana: " whateva "

Aji: " you too bitter, ... I
ain't even gon bother "

Aji retorted sarcastically, dismissing her quietly
with an edge of disdain as he looked at and
through her under thickly raised brows.

Tyree: " Liana, why you gotta
come up in ma house disrespectin' me and ma
friends? "

Liana: " what friends? "

She exclaimed, sounding a bit calmer but hissed
through her teeth; then turning to face him with
her hands akimbo, she demanded;

Liana: " so you fuckin' dat fat bitch Ayishia now! "

Aji looked at me in shock, and I merely shrugged my shoulders. I had no knowledge of it. I knew they were kinda close but couldn't say whether her accusation was true or false.

Tyree: " what! ..... whatchu talkin' 'bout ..... "

Liana: " don't even try to deny it ...... that fat bitch, wait till I see her ..... I still can't believe you fucked that nasty bitch "

Tyree: " Liana, why you always be tryin' to embarrass me.... in front of ma friends too?...dat was totally uncalled for - 'n it's rude.

                 This ma house, 'n I invited them over here...you need to watch yo' mouth "

Liana: " you talkin' 'bout them, am done with them ..... am talkin' 'bout that ho' ..... "

Tyree: " Look, Liana, you better stop now. Am very sorry fellas, am really sorry...you ain't gotta leave. Ma-an.....this is soo damn embarrassing "

She gave Aji and me another nasty look and turned back around to face Tyree who was standing there with little Yani in his arms. He was the perfect picture of agitation, but - notwithstanding, remained very calm and dignified. I think, in addition to finding us there, his mannerisms only helped to fuel her indignation; talk about "a woman scorned."

She was about to hold onto Tyree's upper arm and, seemingly, kiss both him and Yani but Tyree immediately held Yani up - chest high between himself and her - with outstretched arms; rolled his eyes, sighed very audibly and turned his face aside.

I guess she kissed Yani, I couldn't say, as I had turned my head away. I returned my gaze only to see her turn about sharply, walking away but not before pausing momentarily to look back at Tyree, then blurting angrily as she stormed toward Aji and the doorway, her head bowed and fists tightly clenched by her sides.

Liana: " Ooou....I hatechu Tyree Davenport - I hatechu - Ooooou! "

She declared in a fit of rage;

Tyree: " Bye Liana,.....wave bye to mommy Yani "

She purposefully bumped into Aji as she exited the kitchen in her fury and on her way out the front door;

Aji: " Hey! .....remember, I didn't do nothin' to you ma! "

and, quite unnecessarily hollering back at Tyree from the hallway on her way to the elevator.

Liana: " YOU JUS TAKE CARE O' MA SON!..... "

Aji could hardly believe it......

Aji: " Daayum! "

Liana: " ......'N YOU BETTER CALL ME! "

......nor could I, but we'd heard and seen it - me for the first time. I joined the trio of Tyree, with Yani in his arms,.....and Aji, outside the front door of the apartment watching her.

Tyree: " see that, am sorry dawg.....CALL YOU WHEN? "

She was too irate and didn't even bother to respond to Tyree's question, instead she unnecessarily warned from the elevator door:

Liana: " you make damn sure you here when I come back fo' my baby "

Now that was a lesson to be remembered. We returned to the kitchen. Aji asked if he could help himself to a sandwich and without waiting for a response made himself one; I was already making one for myself. While wolfing it down he remarked,

Aji: " I feel fo' you dawg...I see what you talkin' 'bout now - she never stop "

Tyree just nodded as he busied himself with his son. I imposed upon them, trying to change the atmosphere by asking Yani;

Timmy: " Yani, how old are you? "

he cheerfully held up five fingers as he nibbled on the fruits Tyree had prepared for him earlier. I smiled as Tyree instructed;

Tyree: " no, no,...Yani is

322

three....see, three, like these...ok "

he corrected, holding up three of his fingers.
He tried hard and finally managed putting up
his three middle fingers, then chirped,

Yani: " like theeese! "

...delighted he'd managed the three finger
indication. That earned him a hug from his
dad.

At this point I needed to make my exit, but as I
was about to leave, Aji leaned against the
kitchen door jamb, grinned, and muttered under
his breath;

Aji: " so it true, ... you hit
dat? "

I looked on in anticipation; I wanted to know
too.

Tyree: " Aji, why you so nosy "

Timmy: " I wanna know too "

Tyree: " it ain't none o' y'all
bi'nizz .... see that Yani? "

Without even looking at him, and far removed

from the situation, Yani was licking the fruit juice off his fingers and nodded in the affirmative.

Tyree: " see, they all tryin' to be up in daddy's business "

Aji recoiled in raucous laughter, holding his stomach with both hands, his back pasted to the door jamb as he slowly slid to the floor.

Aji: " so it is true, ... "

When he'd finally composed himself, he warned;

Aji: " wait till I tell Ardee this "

Tyree: " you best shut your mouth if you know what's good for you "

Aji: " it don't matter what you say, ama tell him. As a matter of fact - well....I ain't sure whatz goin' down but he 'sposed to

                     be hollarin' atchu soon
"

Tyree: " he wanna talk to me and you - don't know what it's about - sound kinda strange "

In spite of all the talking they were doing, my mind was on the latest bit of gossip from Liana's mouth. I tried to imagine Tyree on top of Ayishia - both of them going at it - and teased;

Timmy: " ss-oo - tell me dawg:
Was it good? "

Tyree: " Timmy, will you leave
me alone "

Timmy: " man, I'm just asking
you a simple question - 'yes' or 'no' ..... it's that
simple "

Tyree: " you know what, my
little man is here and I'm not prepared to
entertain any ..... "

Timmy: " alright, alright but,
we'll find out "

Aji: " yeah, we will but, right
now I gotta go "

Tyree: " ok I'll give you a call
later "

Aji: " good, if you need
anything just gimmi a holla 'cause I see your
hands gon be full this weekend "

Timmy: " yea, and ama step
too...but lemmi get a hi-five from ma little man
right here "

Little Yani quickly and eagerly accepted my
high slap as I bent down and met his little hand.

Timmy: " well,....that's it, Timmy
is outta here "

As Aji and I were followed to the door by
Tyree, Yani said sadly...

Yani: " Daddy, Uncle Timmy
gone? "

Tyree: " yes son, he and Uncle
Aji have to go home now "

Yani: " Uncle Aji gone too? "

Tyree: " yes Yani,....he have to
go too "

...and with a pound and a hug apiece from
Tyree, we both headed to the elevator - me
feeling kinda empty, having to face an entire

weekend with absolutely no thought as to just what I was going to do to occupy my time. It was becoming apparent that my life now without Tyree was lacking something and I was sad.

Aji seemed to sense something was wrong - was it the silent ride from the elevator to the corner of the block? I didn't even want to think about what he might have thought, I just knew that this was going to be a very long and lonely weekend.

My thoughts were disrupted by a quick, playful thump to the chest and an even quicker reassuring squeeze of my shoulder from Aji. It was just like my boy Aji to offer comfort and reassurance to me; that felt good. He had been a great support and source of advice these last few months, guiding me along this new path of life that had come my way. We went our separate ways further down the block and promised to call each other later.

I arrived home, took a shower, and threw myself across the bed. Pete, who seemed overjoyed to see me, offered to treat me to a movie if I felt like it when I woke up. I accepted his offer and when I awoke some nine hours later, he was dressed and ready to go.

I thought the movie was a good idea as it would take all the other things off my mind. In addition, it also gave me the opportunity to enjoy my brother's company again after what seemed like ages. It did offer some help, but every so often my mind would drift off to Tyree. It was hard to think that something like this could be happening to me: Here I was at the movies with Pete, which I usually enjoyed with complete satisfaction, but this time it was different - I wasn't completely in the present.

After the movie we decided to get something to eat. We couldn't decide where to go and since Pete had treated me to the movie, I decided to go along with his choice which was narrowed down to the nearest Wendy's or Popeye's..... and the latter came out the winner so we headed to the nearest franchise.

Even at this point, Tyree still flooded my thoughts. He loved chicken and seafood. Damn, I thought, is everything going to remind me of Tyree? Pete's elbow to my ribs jolted me back to my surroundings. I smiled at him, but it wasn't a nudge to bring me back to talk our normal brother to brother talk.

Pete: " I know him...I know him! "

he exuded, referring to a guy, I'd say around my age range, that was just walking into the restaurant.

Timmy: " calm down son...don't get loud now "

I warned in big brother fashion. He tried to calm himself, holding onto my arm and digging into my flesh,

Pete: " I know him,......he datin' one of ma friendz at school "

Timmy: " aiight, aiight...so......you know him 'n he datin' yo' friend...'tain't like he a celebrity or nothin'...chill "

Pete: " yea.......he so cute tho' "

he whispered excitedly.

The guy really was good looking. He was now returning from the restroom with his jacket front unzipped; his blue jeans crumpled at his ankles as a result of being halfway down his butt. A long faux silver chain was clinking against a possible false, silver-studded belt. He was very noticeably dressed in all black, except for his white turtle neck undershirt and was waddling in our direction where we stood in line.

As I took a good look at his reflection in the large mirror on one of the Eatery's side walls, he toyed with his phone. He was about 5'9" with a dark complexion, slender build, and boyish face. His black du-rag was now more visible as he'd raised his knitted red skull cap with its peak turned backwards to sit askew to the right on his head. Another accessory was a "diamond" bracelet adorning his wrist which he kept adjusting from time to time while still toying with the phone; the bracelet was probably new, or the phone, or both - I thought.

I feared him looking up and finding me taking such keen note of him, especially since he was so near. But I saw through the "street tough" image he was trying to portray.....to me, he was definitely more of a "girls' plaything" than anything, with his handsome, near baby-face, sparkling eyes, and captivating smile.

He was standing in line behind me, with Pete ahead of me as we waited to place our order. When we'd received our order we occupied one of the four-seaters as nothing else was available. As we began to eat, I noticed Pete was eyeing the fellow every now and then,

looking up from his chicken and fries. I
remarked:

Timmy: " please don't tell me
you gon sit here wit dinner 'n be..... goo-goo ga-
ga ova this boi "

Pete: " am jus lookin' yo' "

Timmy: " man, I can see right
through you...why you lyin' "

Pete: " he cute tho'...right? "

Timmy: " man, pl-eeze...Ioknow
what you lookin' at..."

I lied.

Pete: " datz 'cause you don't
know cute "

Timmy: " be cute - ER if he
pulled some o' his shit up, he practically walkin'
on them jeans "

I replied, having just seen the guy reach for his
order only to give me a good view of half his
backside and his long johns.

Pete: " he look good "

331

Pete countered,

Timmy: " whateva...now, can I have ma dinner.... please "

I had no sooner taken a mouthful when the guy came walking over to our table with his meal. Pete swallowed hard and was kinda wide eyed for a moment.......and I thought: He was about to choke; he was completely beside himself.....

Pete: " he comin' this way, he comin' this way.......ooou he comin' ova here "

.......getting more and more excited as though Royalty was approaching;

Timmy: " EAT! "

I scolded calmly with my head down in my meal.

Pete: " but he comin' ova here!
"

Timmy: " will you shut tha hell up 'n eat bwoi!..... "

I hissed, now outraged at his trivial outburst.

Timmy: " ......'n keep yo' l'il drawz on "

Sure enough, this little negro walked right up to our table and calmly asked,

The guy: " is it aiight wit y'all if I sit here? "

Pete seemed to have lost his tongue so I told him,

Timmy: " feel free, it's jus two of us "

He displayed rows of pretty white teeth, sat directly opposite Pete, and without looking up, ravenously began to devour a chicken leg. When he finally surfaced for a sip of his soda upon completely devouring that leg in less than ten seconds (I would swear this dude must not have eaten all day), he looked up at Pete and said;

Shareef: " I know you...I seen you somewhere before, I don't remember where, but I know I seen you...Ooh, ma badd, ma name Shareef "

Pete finally found his voice and introduced us.

Pete: " am Pete, this ma brotha
Timmy "

Shareef: " oh, aiight...so y'all live
'bout here? "

He questioned, smiling at Pete, never losing eye
contact. Pete nodded,.....and he offered:

Shareef: " I live in da Bx "

Pete: " where,...how far from
here? "

Well this was turning out to be an interesting
evening. I do believe this guy was trying to
pick up Pete and Pete was willingly taking the
bait. I would never have figured this out if Pete
had not told me of his sexual status. The guy
was about my age - a year younger maybe - but
he was definitely trying to get at Pete. He had
wolfed down his food long before us and spent
the rest of the time talking, eventually giving
Pete his number before we left.

Once outside, he pulled Pete back as he walked
next to me.

Shareef: " can I holla atchu fo' a
minit ma nigga "

Well, he was certainly presumptuous; " ma nigga "?....Didn't this guy, like...just meet Pete? Anyway, I walked ahead a few feet and waited, standing there in the cold while they talked about what seemed to have no end. I kept looking back, wondering if Pete had forgotten that he had me waiting. Realizing my displeasure, the next time he managed to catch my eye, Pete brought the conversation to an end and came running up to me, grinning like a fool......and without so much as an apology.

Timmy: " ok...so we goin' home now, right? "

Pete: " he said am sexy "

Did he not even hear a word I'd just said?

Timmy: " da fuck! ....y'all got dat far in one night...wha he knew 'bout you dat he coulda say somethin' like dat to you? "

I asked, glaring at him.

Pete: " I tole him I know he datin' ma friend, 'n he say they ain't seein' each otha no more "

Timmy: " so what!...you gon fuck wit this nigga? "

Pete: " Ioknow, I ain't say all dat "

Timmy: " you don't...know what, I ain't gettin' into yo' bi'nizz "

Pete: " you gettin' mad 'n I ain't even did nothin' "

Timmy: " I ain't mad atchu Pete..... am jus sayin' you don't even know this dude "

Pete: " I know him, he........ "

Timmy: " dat ain't knowin' - you seen him - 'n he used to date one o' your friends....but he can't be all over..... "

I had to change my words and be as blunt as possible for the sake of understanding.

Timmy: " ...... am sayin' he can't be all up in you jus because o' dat - datz what am sayin' "

Pete: " I kno-ow dat!.....I jus like him Timmy - datz all "

He belabored, and I warned.....

Timmy: " might turn out to be
more than - 'datz all' before y'all get through
so make sure you know whatchu doin' "

.....turning my head left and gazing into his eyes
as we now tried to navigate this busier bit of
sidewalk near some clothing store.

Pete: " I ain't givin' up nothin'
jus like dat so you ain't gotta worry "

I was pleased to hear him say that.

Timmy: " I love you - you know
dat, right brother? "

Pete: " I know,......I know you
jus lookin' out fo' me "

He smiled, looking up at me.

I awoke the next day a little after noon, called
Aji, chatted for a while, took a call from Marie,
chatted for over an hour and just when I was
about to go have my late breakfast, my phone
rang.

Timmy: " hello?.... "

Tyree: " good afternoon sir,
may I please speak to Mr. Gooden "

Timmy: " ha-ha-ha, nigga you is
stupid and crazy, I was gon call you in a l'il bit
- I jus got up "

Tyree: " I been missin' yo' l'il
sexyazz like carzy boi - whatchu been doin' -
where you at? "

Timmy: " ain't doin' nothin'
much,.....I tole you I jus woke up; wuz chillin'
with Pete 'n shit...we went to a movie last
night....'n... "

Tyree: " Oh word!.....you seen
anybody in there dat look like me? "

Timmy: " naaaw, naw,....nobody
dat..... "

I chortled, taking a quick look over my
shoulder - I was alone.

Timmy: " .....nobody dat look dat
good....I waz thinkin' 'bout you tho'....yo, I gotta
tell you 'bout this shit dat happen last night at
tha

                    restaurant...aah...um,
can I come through in a little bit...amean, if you

ain't doin' nothin'...amsayin'...I know you got
Yani 'n..... "

Tyree: " ma shawdy,...you can
come ova - a-n-y-t-i-m-e! "

Timmy: " aiight, am coming right
now "

Tyree: " aiight but I ain't there
right now, me and Yani on the road.....I jus got
him a big ol' fire engine. We headin' home now
tho' but you might get there
                              before us. Ma
mom's comin' thru' too - when she leave
church,... "

Timmy: " Oh! "

I heard myself saying. I realized I was hoping
to have him alone. What was I thinking,.....he
had Yani - and I couldn't even remember that.
That might have been easier to accept but now
his mom was going to be there - my thoughts
were broken....

Tyree: " .....you still there
dawg?...... I said ma mom comin' thru too -
anyway, ama see you then - aiight? "

.....Tyree's voice now suddenly was audible, I

replied.....

Timmy: " yeah, yeah.....no doubt,
no doubt "

......then hung up.

I was most eager to be over there again, just to
see and touch him. Quickly making a sandwich
for my breakfast, I wolfed it down as I watched
mom preparing dinner. Dad was in the living
room with Pete reading the newspaper.
Without even saying anything to mom, as soon
as I was done I grabbed my phone, snuck out of
the house, hastened down the street and hopped
on the first available bus going to the West
Side.

As soon as I got off the bus and was hurrying to
his apartment building, I saw him and Yani
going along the walkway to their lobby
entrance. I followed quietly, unbeknownst to
them until Yani looked back, saw me and
pointed in my direction and shouted,

Yani: " Daddy!.....I see uncle
Timmy....daddy, uncle Timmy is coming "

Somehow, he managed to pull away from
Tyree's grip while Tyree was talking with the
building Superintendent and came charging

down the pathway at me. Tyree spun around to chase him but when he saw me, he stopped and little Yani ran up to me and grabbed my legs. I bent over and scooped him up, much to his delight. He started to tell me about his new Fire Engine, and I listened to his gleeful chatter until I caught up to Tyree who by then had finished talking with the Super.

I set Yani down and he held onto Tyree's hand and we headed to the Lobby. We took the elevator up and I sat and watched as Tyree removed Yani's jacket and boots, then went to the bedroom to get his house slippers and a more comfortable change of clothes.

Yani began to help himself by removing his clothes but was having a hard time keeping his mind and hands off his new toy; he stopped in the process and began playing with the bright red truck. Tyree returned with his clothes and finished the job for him, then asked him...

Tyree: " would you like something to eat, an apple, a banana, some grapes maybe....or would you prefer some soup, I made

                            some nice soup "

Yani: " yes "

Tyree: " Yani...what did I tell you "

Yani: " yes daddy "

he replied, bashfully lowering his head as Tyree knelt in front of him sitting on the sofa next to me.

Tyree: " which would you prefer "

Yani: " grapes!....I want grapes "

Tyree: " aren't you forgetting something...where's that little magic word "

Yani: " may I please have some grapes daddy "

Tyree: " there you go...that's my man ....then grapes it shall be young Master Davenport "

Yani: " daddy you're funny "

Yani giggled and continued to engage himself again with his new toy, running it on the sofa before turning around, holding it high with one hand as he imitated the sound of a wailing

342

siren, following behind Tyree who was in the kitchen preparing the grapes. I followed and as soon as Tyree had him sit at the table and begin to eat, Tyree headed back out to the living room.

We were alone, so I groped his dick and he squeezed my butt. My heart was racing and my desire for his touch and to touch him had to be quelled. Not wanting to get physical with Yani being there, we just looked longingly at each other and tried to be satisfied with that.

He then told me that his mom should be there soon and that he would make us a drink so they could see us drinking when she arrived. He quickly whipped up a Gin and Lime concoction, poured it into a martini glass and garnished it with a red cherry. Of course, this was merely to make things appear casual in the presence of his mom and her friend, but I wondered if they wouldn't conclude that I was too young to be drinking what seemed to be alcohol; never-the-less, that was how it was going to be - me having paid him a visit and him having offered me a drink.

Moments later, the phone rang, and it was his mom; they were coming up the walkway, he said. We heard nothing further from her until the doorbell rang and Tyree let them in.

Ma Gladys: " where my precious
gran' baby at? "

She asked excitedly as she hurried to the living
room, followed by her friend. I got up to make
room for her and Yani by taking the single
chair.

Ma Gladys: " oh ba-by!, you've
grown so big...give 'ma Gladys some sugar
honey "

she cooed, hugging, kissing, and smothering
little Yani with love as he hugged her neck
tightly. He was showing off his new truck
when Ma Gladys realized she had not even
introduced her friend or said hello to anyone
else.

Ma Gladys   " oh my goodness me!,
y'all need to forgive me...this little man made
me completely forget my manners: Tyree, how
you
                          doing baby...remember
Miss Walker.... hi Timothy ....did I get that
right? "

Timmy: " yes Ma
Gladys...everybody call me Timmy though,
.....Miss Walker, pleased to meet you ma'am "

Tyree: " how you doin' Miss
Walker. Mom, would you like something to
drink, some tea perhaps - or coffee - Miss
Walker may

                    I please offer you
something "

Miss Walker: " I'll have whatever
Gladys is having..... with a little of what he
having in mine "

Ma Gladys: " coffee for me baby, no
cream - remember.... and two sugar...thank
you "

Tyree: " coming right up,
Timmy could you give me a hand my brotha "

he winked and walked off to the kitchen. I told
him in a minute as I went to the bathroom first,
washed my hands, and while drying them,
overheard;

Miss Walker: " Gladys, that boy get
finer than ever as each year go by.... I told you
that boy was going to turn into a fine,
handsome young

                    man and see.....girl, if I
was ten years younger I swear.... "

345

Ma Gladys: " Clarese!....the man got enough woman problems already. That's why I can't even see my precious little grand baby   sometimes when I want,....besides, you know you old enough to be the boy's mother...or better yet his.... "

Miss Walker: " now Gladys, don't you make no statement that you can't substantiate dear "

Upon hearing that, I was about to burst out laughing, but managed to compose myself and think of a way to let them remember my presence. I coughed loudly, opened the bathroom door, delayed a moment to give the ladies a chance to regain their composure, then came out and hurried off to the kitchen. As I got to the doorway, Tyree was coming out and I perched myself against the kitchen door jamb;

Yani: " ma Gladys, daddy gave me a baff......'n we went to the movie - ma Gladys, daddy have a big Mr. Johnson "

Miss Walker: " how big baby? "

Ma Gladys: " why Clarese! .... you ought to be ..... take control of yourself "

Yani struggled off the sofa, got to his feet,

stood in front of them, and held his two hands straight up over his head, indicating what he'd seen.

Tyree: " Yani!....come here....what did I tell you....you go apologize right now "

Yani ran to Miss Gladys' lap, crying.

Yani: " ma Gladys...daddy mad at Yani "

While she soothed him and Tyree came back to the kitchen, I told him about the little episode between Miss Walker and his mom. He chuckled, straightened himself up, then announced that the coffee was ready. Still smiling, he put it on a tray, went out, and served it to the ladies who continued their chit-chat while playing with Yani until Miss Walker discovered that the little bit of "what he having" [the gin] was not in her coffee and promptly asked about it.

Tyree: " Miss walker, I thought you were just joking...I'm sorry, I'll pour you some "

Ma Gladys: " Clarese!.....I swear, woman, we just got out of church,.....oh for goodness sakes! "

Miss Walker: " now, Gladys, don't tell
me you don't know that a little spirit is good for
the body "

We all had to laugh at her candor, in that she
wasn't hiding the fact that she wanted the
alcohol in her drink.....and as Tyree was about
to pour a jigger into her cup, she hastily sipped
a mouthful of the coffee to lessen the amount in
her cup.

It wasn't long before her cup was noted to be
half empty. When Tyree poured himself a
drink, she promptly told him........ "pour me
another one baby"; and so he did, much to her
delight. I was about to burst wide open with
laughter and had to dash off into the kitchen so
as not to cause any embarrassment.

When Tyree returned to the kitchen with the
bottle, he was also chuckling. We tried our best
to put on a straight face to rejoin his guests in
the living room. More chit-chat as I sat in my
usual chair, sipping my drink and listening to
Ma Gladys brag about her "gran' baby" and
how much he was the spittin' image of his dad
and so on. Miss Walker nodded her
acknowledgement before taking another sip of
her gin-spiked coffee. By then Yani had

urgently worked his way off the sofa and was heading toward the bathroom, pulling at his pants.

Miss Walker: " yes, he is one beautiful little boy.... just like his daddy "

When she finally noticed him, she exclaimed;

Ma Gladys: " where are you going baby "

With his arms outstretched, palms turned upward to emphasize his statement, he declared with wide-eyed urgency:

Yani: " ma Gladys, ... I have to pee "

Ma Gladys quickly scooted him off to the bathroom and took care of him. Not long after, Yani came running out without his pants, followed by his grandma who quickly snatched him up and asked Tyree for a change of pants for him. Tyree went to the bedroom, and Yani leapt from his grandmother's lap and took off to the bedroom, just as Tyree was returning with fresh underwear.

Tyree: " go let ma Gladys put your pants on "

The kid took it and made a hat of it by pulling the waist over his head and with his arms spread wide, tried to walk blindly over to her; this kid was spirited and full of pranks.

Ma Gladys: " bring that here!....you little scallywag "

She reprimanded, grabbing him by the hand as he neared her, and pulling him between her legs. As she sat there dressing him, she asked Tyree (who was in the bedroom searching for a change of pants for Yani):

Ma Gladys: " Mr. Davenport .... "

Tyree: " yes Mrs. Davenport, what is it now? "

Ma Gladys: " you're not going to make my little grandson grow up without a brother or sister, are you? "

Bearing a pair of brown and tan pants, Tyree entered the living room, teasing with a straight face;

Tyree: " mom, I don't have a brother or sister "

She rolled her eyes, turned her head in Miss Walker's direction, and gave her a knowing look; she merely raised her eyebrows and, not surprisingly, pried;

Miss Walker: " Mr. Timothy, do you have any children, ... or when you settle down do you plan on having a large family? "

Timmy: " I, ... I, ... well, I've never really thought about it Miss Walker "

I was caught completely off guard; however, Ma Gladys wisely stepped in.

Ma Gladys: " oh Clarese, the boy is still young "

She offered,...... and having dressed her grandson, she pulled him toward her, cupping his little cheeks between her well manicured hands and kissed him. By the time she'd let go, he'd spread his arms and puckered his lips, seeking another kiss.

Miss Walker: " that boy gon be randy just like his daddy 'n grandaddy "

Ma Gladys: " Clarese! "

I was looking at Tyree in wide-eyed disbelief

when the delightfully inquisitive Yani suddenly and repeatedly kept tugging at his dad's shorts; he didn't address him immediately and he tugged harder, asking;

Yani: " daddy! daddy, pay 'tention "

Miss Walker was pleased and amused at his precociousness. She turned to Miss Gladys....

Miss Walker: " isn't that just cute "

Ma Gladys: " you know that little thing think he grown "

.....she replied with a satisfied smile. Meanwhile, Yani was getting his question answered, albeit flippantly.

Tyree: " I'm sorry Yani, what is it? "

Yani: " what's a scallywag "

Tyree: " you! "

Ma Gladys: " oh my goodness, I can't be too careful what I say around you "

Ma Gladys beamed, as Tyree went on to to

explain the meaning to him.

Ma Gladys: " baby when you going to settle down .... I don't like how Yani's back and forth between you and Liana "

Tyree: " moms, please....let's not go through this again. I told you I'm not seeing her like that anymore, we just have to keep a civil
                relationship; that way Yani don't have to suffer...I have him two weekends each month, she have him the rest - nothing
                between us, strictly platonic - not interested anymore mom, it's done "

Ma Gladys: " well baby if you would come to church you would probably find yourself a nice wife.... "

Miss Walker: " oh let the man live a little Gladys .... he's still young "

Miss Walker intoned, setting her cup down.

Ma Gladys: " baby you're young, but you shouldn't be alone like.... "

Tyree: " mom, mom...you're
doing it again "

Miss Walker reiterated her opinion,

Miss Walker: " Gladys, let the man
have some fun with his life before he go tie
himself down "

then turned her attention to Tyree and advised;

Miss Walker: " you take your time son,
don't be in no rush to find no mate....she will
fall into your hands... just like a blossom fall
from a tree and the wind blow it to you...don't
force it, let it come to you "

Ma Gladys: " Ooh well.....I guess I
can't do anything about it. Anyway...we have
to leave now baby, but you take care of yourself
and
                         don't let anything harm
my precious little grand baby now,......y'hear "

Tyree: " under the present
circumstances there is not too much I can do
but I'm doing the best I can "

Ma Gladys hugged and kissed him, then
smothered Yani with hugs and kisses once
more, then picked up her pocketbook.

Ma Gladys: " come on Clarese, remember you promised to help me find those curtains today "

Miss Walker: " don't rush me Gladys, let me say goodbye to the young people "

She hugged and kissed Yani, then hugged Tyree, then said goodbye to me and with a final wave, they disappeared out the door and down the hallway.

It was now late afternoon and Yani was beginning to show what I think was the strain of his day's activities and started to doze off. Tyree made him comfortable on the sofa, putting his pants and slippers back on and covering him with a blanket. He then stood looking down at him in silence. It was a touching moment,.....a moment in which I don't think he even remembered that I was there. That very personal and special few seconds I made sure not to disturb - I just sat and watched in admiration. Yani was secured, and after another few moments Tyree looked up from his travels, smiled a thoughtful, kinda nervous smile....

Tyree: " sorry dawg, I jus got carried away fo' a moment "

...... and apologized for what he, no doubt, deemed his indiscretion.

Timmy: " no thing bro, you doin' tha right thing "

He smiled approvingly, jerked his head toward the living room door indicating that I should follow him and walked off; I got up and followed. Once in the kitchen, we sat down with our drinks and got to talking about us.

Timmy: " yo son, datz a healthy little boy you got there - fo' real "

Tyree: " datz ma pride 'n joy son, am jus sorry we not together 24/7 "

Timmy: " yeaah ...... but, at least you have him over every two weekends a month "

Tyree: " mm-mmm, yeaah .... "

He muttered thoughtfully, then suddenly spoke up.

Tyree: " .... we need to do some serious talkin' dawg "

Timmy: " 'bout what? "

Tyree: " 'bout us...datz the what.
On da real tho', I need to let you know how I
do...amean, you say you awright wit being ma
shawty
                    but I got rules.... naw, I
think I put dat wrong 'cause I don't want you to
feel like I think you less than me or nothin'
but...but I...
                    ....I love you...'n if you
ma peeps...you ma peeps - only. I ain't gon put
up wit you fuckin' wit anotha nigga 'n think... "

Timmy: " but I ain't tryin' to fuck
wit - why you comin' up wit this shit I
don't even know nobody else who.... "

Tyree: " Timmy, please, please
understand this: I ain't tryin' to fuss or fight
witchu...am just sayin'...what if you meet
somebody 'n
                    you feelin' him.... "

Timmy: " you need to stop, I ain't
gon meet no fuckin' body, shit..... "

Tyree: " dawg..... shit happen;
'n am jus sayin' dat if dat eva happen, it's best
you jus lemmi know...don't be feelin' sorry fo'
me -

thinkin' you can't tell me... jus lemmi know 'cause I ain't gon be sharin' you wit some nigga - you feel me "

Timmy: " this some fucked up shit ...I...I don't even know why you sayin' somethin' like this to me "

Tyree: " I gotta tell you this dawg, I prolly shoulda tole you awready but, I can't jus have us go on 'n you not know how I feel 'bout it "

Timmy: " negro.... you makin' me mad.... I ain't tryin' to be wit nobody else. You ain't lissenin' when I tell you somethin'?.... "

Tyree: " but I do listen "

Timmy: " do you know how mo'fuckin' long I struggled wit this shit befo' I could tell you dat I love you...I didn't even know what it was

                dat I was feelin'.... but when I found out, I tole you - 'n I wasn't lyin' then 'n I ain't lyin' now. If anythin', you da one who gon do

                some shit - not me "

Tyree: " how you gon say

somethin' like dat "

Timmy: " man please - I see how you get as soon as you see some butt somewhere.... you a prisoner to dat shit "

Tyree: " dang, how you gon do me like dat...you ain't neva seen.... "

Timmy: " Tyree, don't even bother, I know what am sayin'...you don't see it 'cause it's you "

That silenced him and I sat there with him explaining my feelings. We spent a great deal of time talking about us until the house phone rang; I picked it up, and it was Ardee. He said he needed to talk to Tyree and I handed him the phone. As it turns out, Ardee said that he saw Liana walking up the block as he was driving by and gave her a ride. She said her destination was his apartment. Tyree had to put him on hold as he was getting an incoming call - it turned out to be Liana, she was coming up the walkway. Tyree's quick advice was for me to stay in the bedroom while he hurriedly put Yani's stuff in his bag, hoping to just hand it to her and send her on her way. However, Yani was still asleep so we knew things would be moving a little slower.

She didn't even buzz the intercom, she'd come straight up and rang the doorbell. Somebody who knew her must have let her in because nobody gets in this building if they are a stranger; even I have had problems entering when I tried to get in behind a tenant. He was blunt in denying me and I eventually had to buzz Tyree.

I tried my best to be calm but I was scared that she would find out that I was here and suspect something. As soon as she was inside the apartment, she asked to use the bathroom. When she came out, all was quiet for a little while until she confronted Tyree with a question,

Liana: " Tyree, why you always ignorin' me like I got somethin'..... I need some dick too "

Tyree: " Liana!...what is wrong witchu? "

Liana: " ain't nothin' wrong wit me - whats wrong witchu! "

she shouted back at him. He replied calmly,

Tyree: " am ok Liana "

Liana: " 'ok'.....you keep avoidin' me - WHY?...... "

Then there was a space of absolute silence before she cooed,

Liana: " you don't remember this coochie, don't you want some?....remember all the good times we used to have... "

Tyree: " Liana stop,.....that's not gonna work no more - the last time was a mistake, it's over - am done "

Liana: " whatchu mean done ...... you turn gay now or somethin'...why don't you want my pussy...it jus as good as before...why? "

Tyree: " Liana, I ain't even gon get into that, the answer is NO - 'n fo' da last time, leggo ma dick "

Liana: " I know you still want it,.....gimmi some o' this good dick "

Tyree: " MMMMRR Liana Stop!....oh-ma.....what is wrong witchu - stop, stop....you squeezin' me Liana....Liana!...stop! "

Liana: " see, you hard as hell -
let's do somethin' "

Tyree: " .... oh-ma.... Liana you
got a man "

Liana: " he can't do me like you
do.... come on baby.... "

Tyree: " I don't wanna know
nothin' 'bout yo man "

Tyree: " well come on then "

Tyree: " Liana stop, you rippin'
ma fuckin' shirt, let da fuck go.... am warnin'
you "

Liana: " I need some of this
good dick today "

Tyree: " let go o' ma shit Liana,
you got a man .... I ain't .... "

Liana: " what! ma pussy ain't
good fo' you no more?. Every time I come ova
here 'n try to get witchu, you keep avoidin' me...
you
                      playin' hard to get?
.....look how hard yo' dick is, 'n see this pussy,
see how wet it is.... it want this dick "

This kind of man and woman affair was a sad thing to have to hear and I so wished I wasn't there - my head was a boiling pot of spaghetti but I couldn't help but overhear.

Tyree: " Liana, I wish you wouldn't do this... "

Liana: " come daddy, come take care of me like you always do "

Tyree: " Liana, please, close yo' legs,don't show me nothin'. Why you always be makin' ma life difficult, I try to get along witchu
but you always do some shit to hurt and embarrass me - even in front of other people. Lissen, am tellin' you...for da last
time: It's not working, it's not gonna work - am done, it's over....stop Liana, stop or ama - ohmagaa, Liana don't make
me have to hurt you - tha fuu!......look whatchu done, you ripped ma shirt. You know what - I said stop, don't make me have to hurtchu "

Liana: " you ain't gon hurt me "

She said boastfully. Suddenly Yani started crying. I don't know why but he was real loud.

Tyree: " see what you done now...you satisfied now! "

There was the sound of another little scuffle....

Tyree: " let go of me,....you done woke my son up "

Liana: " that's no big problem, we is mother and father "

Tyree: " oh my gaaa....I can't do this anymore....don't make me have to hurt you Liana - MM-MMmphf! "

Liana: "
Oooww,......mothafucka, you hit me.....oh my god,......YOU NEVER HIT ME BEFORE! "

Tyree: " I warned you Liana, I warned you...you better leave - now! "

Liana: " OK, Tyree Davenport, treat me like dat......it's da last time you gon see your son "

Oh I knew he was mad now; there was a moment of silence,....then he spoke, calmly, distinctively, and with conviction;

Tyree: " Lemmi tell you
somethin' Liana...don't ever - EVER ....try to
use ma son as a weapon against me... you do
dat 'n you
                    gon get to know who I
really is......LEARN 'N KNOW THAT
NOW......know what, ...I ain't tryin' to upset
Yani any more than he already is...take his
bags, ama bring him down 'n call you a cab "

All during the time Yani was awake, he didn't
stop crying; now suddenly, this babe was
consoling,

Yani: " mommy don't
cry.......daddy, mommy crying "

Tyree: " Ooh man,...no, no
Yani, mommy's ok, she's just crying because
she's happy...c'mon let daddy get you a cab "

There were movements but no words for about
a minute, then I heard the front door slam hard,
then there was quiet. I waited a few minutes,
then slowly and nervously opened the bedroom
door. The phone rang, startling me, but I
regained my composure and looked at the
Caller ID and saw that the call was from
Tyree's cell phone. Still, I was nervous when I

picked it up..... I spoke softly;

Timmy: " yeah "

Tyree: " lissen "

the voice said, it was Tyree's and he repeated himself.

Tyree: " jus lissen, ama keep the line open "

I hardly wanted to speak and managed a soft....

Timmy: " k "

.....while figuring he was just trying to keep me up to date on what was going on between them outside, as I could hear the noise from other people in the background and concluded that they were out on the curbside awaiting the cab.

Like people with some daytime radio "Soap Opera," I kept the phone to my ears and listened until I heard Yani crying and him saying goodbye. Another moment of silence, then:

Tyree: " you aiight dawg? "

Timmy: " yeah am aiight "

Tyree: " everything
cool.....sorry I put you thru this - am on ma
way up "

(Chapter 13)

A few minutes later, Tyree came up looking distraught. I thought he needed some consoling and although I had not fully recovered from my own encounter with this live drama, I immediately gave him a hug and a kiss on the cheek. He expelled a very heavy sigh and shook his head.

Tyree: " Timmy...dawg, Ioknow how much more of this I can take...this shit is killin' me. Amean, 'tain't like am tryin' to diss her or

                    nothin'...knowamsayin', she the first girl I ever love... but I been tellin' her it's done between us - ova 'n ova - 'n she still

                    keepin' up this shit .... "

Based on his demeanor and how he was pacing non-stop, I knew the best thing I could do to console him right now was to just be quiet and listen; so I tuned in and focused.

Tyree: " .... you see how she pop up sudden like dat...don't even gimmi a call to say she on her way. She came here wit no

                    panties on - no panties, son!.....then she gon sit 'n open up her legs showin' me alla dat - talkin' 'bout how wet she is.

Datz so fuckin'
embarrassin' .... amean, she ma son's mother 'n
.... I don't wanna see her like dat, like she
desperate ..... then on top of

dat, she threatenin' me
too, tellin' me I ain't gon see ma son again...she
know me betta than dat tho'...she know better
than to fuck wit me
like dat...she know I will murder her azz "

Oh he was livid....

Tyree: " I know a lot a the shit
she be doin' is on account of her mother,.....she
the one responsible for alla this turmoil "

......and had to vent - I completely understood
that. It was heartfelt; his emotions were
overflowing, and I had to allow him to let it all
out. I suspected that the only reason why things
did not get any worse than they did between
them just now was because Yani was present. I
continued to be his shoulder.

Tyree: " Dawg, I try so hard to
be nice to her...if she need help with somethin' I
help her, I do anythin' just to make sure ma son
don't suffer because of
me not being with her but when it come to the
fuckin' part - am done, done, done

knowamsayin'....done;

if I try to get wit her like dat again, Max might find out,.....datz the main reason I ain't doin' it; it could make dat man resent

me and ma son would suffer for it - he'd mistreat ma kid, see what amsayin'? "

He poured out, searching my eyes for my understanding, and I nodded agreement;

Tyree: " normally she don't give me no problem in seein' ma son but this shit she startin' up wit now 'bout not lettin' me see him -

I know it comin' from her moms "

Timmy: " dat is not no kinda wise advice - if datz what she really doin' "

Tyree: " it's full time she get it through her head dat it ain't happenin' like dat again 'n stop da bullshit games she playin'. "

what da fuck mo' can I do...how many times do I gotta say it....c'mon now....am tellin' you, this woman is gettin' to me....

yo,....I need a drink ....
"

Timmy: " am a get it .... whatchu
havin'? "

Tyree: " anythin'...any
mo'fuckin' thang, jus gimmi somethin' "

I thought the best thing for him at the moment
was a double shot of that Remy Martin
V.S.O.P, so I went to the kitchen for a glass,
came back and poured it, took it to him
and,....now that Yani was gone, I sat on his lap.
Just then his cellphone rang; dang! I thought. It
was Ardee, and he would be coming over in a
little bit, Tyree said.

Timmy: " it's gon be aiight dawg;
what you need is distraction.... knowamsayin' -
take yo' mind off this shit "

I told him as I got up off his lap, stood in front
of him and turned my back. I pulled my pants
down and bent over. As I peered between my
legs, he was smiling broadly; he reached out,
held me by my waist with both hands, pulled
me toward him and began to trail his tongue
between the crack of my butt before finally
burying his face deep, licking that spot that I
love him to lick. It wasn't long before I was hot

371

and ready, my blood coursing through my veins
at high speed and,.....between gasps I managed;

Timmy: " see...I know whatz
good fo' you...I know you can't resist no azz "

Tyree: " damn shawdy, why you
gotta make me look so cheap "

he answered as he pulled me back onto his lap
and onto his ready dick.

Timmy: " but you is cheap "

Tyree: " c'mon now dawg.... "

Timmy: " you think I don't know
yo' azz by now.....funny how Liana couldn't get
you to hop up in dat pussy but as soon as you
see ma azz -
                         yo' flag run right up the
flag pole 'n you dive right up in it - whatzup
wit dat "

I teased, revelling in the comfort of his arms.
He brushed his lips against my ear and kissed it.

Tyree: " datz cold dawg, don't
do me so grimy "

Timmy: " if you don't fuck Liana

no mo' you ain't gettin' this again "

Tyree: " oh you think you funny
.... don'tchu? "

He quipped, pulling me roughly back against
his chest and began tickling me, sending me
twisting and turning as he held me firmly by
my waist. After it went on for too long I started
to protest, begging for him to stop but he
wouldn't.

Timmy: " ooooh sshit.....stop
bro! "

Tyree: " this a joke bwoi -
what! you don't like jokes no mo'...huh? .... "

He chided playfully, before he manhandled me
and shoved my head down into his crotch,
yanked my pants all the way down to my
ankles, and started to smack me on my butt. He
wasn't too keen on having my butt so far from
his face and quickly pulled my face out of his
crotch and spun me around to begin nibbling on
my butt again.

As usual, his hot expert teasing sent delightful
shivers up my spine. Hot with passion, I began
to take my boxers off but only managed to get
one leg out before he started poking a finger

between my butt cheeks, trying to pry them apart. I gave him access so he could get his tongue in from every possible angle.

Timmy: " oh fuck son ..... ngh, damn .... oh, cccctt, yea, yeah ..... a-aaah - cccctt, Sssh-it! ..... "

Tyree: " sssshh, remember the neighbours "

Timmy: " yeah ..... Tyree mmmph, oh yeah, get dat mo'fucka, wash dat shit son - eat it up, eat-it-up "

I was red hot, burning for his dick. I could see why Liana had difficulty leaving him alone. It was very ironic: Now Timmy Gooden and her were competing for the same dick!

Tyree: " go get tha lube ..... hurry! "

He didn't have to tell me twice. I quickly slipped my leg back in my trousers and dashed for the bedroom, returning in a flash, butt lubed and all, wiped some on his dick, then eased the back of my shorts down and squatted over him as he commanded.

I was more than willing to sit on that monster.

After several attempts, he finally got his dick head in but had to force me to stay on it. Slowly he kept pulling me down on it until it was to the point where I could take it and where I was able to enjoy it.

Then the buzzer suddenly went off. He got up to go see who it was - it was Ardee, he let him in, and came back to the living room where he insisted that I get back on his dick. I wanted the dick but Ardee would be up any minute and I didn't want him to see me like that.

Seeing my apprehension, Tyree got behind me, held me by the waist with his left hand, and shoved me in the back to bend over. I was petrified because of the expected company and tussled with him, making verbal protest as well. Needless to say, he won the battle by shoving my head down into a corner of the sofa and began to try and work his dick back in me.

Timmy: " Tyree no! ..... Ardee comin', don't make him come see us "

Tyree: " But I want him to see "

Freaky is what that really was; as much as I knew Ardee, I didn't have that kind of courage and continued to make verbal pleas since my physical protests weren't getting me anywhere.

Timmy: " No Tyree, no ..... don't
do ..... lemmi go B ..... pleease ..... no! ....
Tyree! ..... aaargghh "

He was suddenly partially in me again and
quickly turned around and sat on the sofa,
bringing me down with him so that I was now
straddling him. It felt so good, those painful
little jerks he forced me into. I tried to stand up
but was powerfully held, with him slowly
grinding and me trying to keep him off some by
placing both hands on his thighs to limit those
wicked little movements he was throwing.

We were taking a great chance with Ardee on
his way up. There was the hurt, but his dick was
sending such delightful sensations of sheer
eroticism through me, especially when he had
me turn around to face him with the dick still
embedded in me.

That single movement of turning around on his
dick was so exhilarating that I went limp and
dizzy with delight.

Timmy: " Ooo, Tyree ... Tyree,
oooohh Tyree ..... mmm, mmph, ccctt oh, oh ....
Ty-reee omagaaw, stop now ..... stop son .... "

Tyree: " l'il tight azz, you lucky

I can't tear it like .... oh shit son, why don'tchu want me to get up in there, stop runnin' .... "

The doorbell rang once ..... twice .... three times, but he wouldn't go get it. He just kept breathing heavily in my ear, making those little jabs as he tried to peer into my eyes as he talked dirty.

Timmy: " Lemmi get the door! "

For a fourth time the bell rang and suddenly the door swung open. Ardee strutted straight into the living room;

Ardee: " Ooh!..Ooooh ..... daayum, ... damn dawg! .... I, I neva knew y'all wuz ..... daaaamn ..... "

In my moment of hysteria, I didn't know where to turn or what to do; I'd been completely paralyzed and couldn't decide whether to get up and run, thus exposing what I was really sitting on, or just keep sitting and try to appear unperturbed - but the way I was wearing my pants wasn't normal, ...there was no way I could rationalize that.

Ardee stood frozen in the middle of the living room doorway, jaws agape, speechless for a moment. Then he exclaimed as he groped his dick:

Ardee: " damn Timmy, datz
freaky as hell! "

Me! ..... of all the ..... why would he think that I
had anything to do with him finding us like
this?!? I tried to get up but Tyree had me well
held.

Tyree: " it's awwight dawg, jus
be chill ..... don't be shy, it's only Ardee "

I was about to die - and I knew it, but I was
going to murder Tyree first.

Timmy: " whatchu...mmphf ..... "

I tried mumbling a feigned protest and Tyree
tried to reassure me as Ardee stepped forward
placing his hands on my shoulders and pushing
me back down on Tyree's dick.

Ardee: " handle yo' bi'nizz boi
..... I can come thru' later .... 'tain't no thang "

Tyree: " go sit yo' azz down
nigga, we can talk later "

I just wished Tyree wasn't so insistent that he
stayed.

I sat still, nervous and embarrassed, but Tyree kept jabbing every now and then.

Ardee started to slowly step back, still groping his now hard dick; saying he'd leave and come back but Tyree wisely advised;

Tyree: " it's aiight dawg, ma boi still too shy anyway "

I was reaching for my shorts on the floor without getting off the dick. I didn't want to stand there fully naked.

Ardee: " I likes to see dat - ma dawg fixin' up yo' back "

Timmy: " fuck you! ..... suck ma dick "

I said, hopping off and running toward the bathroom.

Ardee: " oooh, he gettin' nastier 'n nastier ..... I likes dat "

I knew they were talking about me behind my back but it didn't seem to matter so much. They stopped their conversation when I came out and Ardee pulled Tyree aside quickly and whispered in his ear as I turned my back to them and quickly slid into my shorts. When I'd turned back around they were uniformly taking a seat; and as Ardee eyed me with a roguish grin, he said;

Ardee: " dawg, maybe I got some good news "

Tyree: " good... spit it out "

he prodded, but Ardee was still gawking - and I didn't really care anymore.

Ardee: " damn-yo'-boi-got-a-pretty-azz!...... "

It felt good hearing Ardee also say that.

Tyree: " dawg,....pay attention, where yo' mind at! "

With his hands in his pockets and his mouth half open, he threw out another compliment.

Ardee: " .....he a sexy l'il mo'fucka ..... mm, mm, mmm - damn! "

Tyree: " datz my good news B; what's your good news?.... yo, yo, ... look at me dawg, don't be peepin' ma shawdy like dat?

"

Ardee: " ma badd, ma
badd......damn Tyree I neva knew homeboi wuz
so fine with nothin' on.....gaaawddamn!..... "

Tyree: " Ardee.......whatz yo'
good news? ...... son, wake up ..... hel-lo-o! "

Ardee: " Oh! yeah - ma boi
Darnel, he bought his'self a house B...a whole
mo'fuckin' house in Va. - thru this Realtor he
know in
                    Brooklyn; said if I eva
need a Realtor - dat be ma man...he'll hook you
up good, jus tell him I sent you ..... oh, lemmi
                    give you his bi'nizz
card..... here "

Tyree: " you know I been
thinkin' 'bout dat...but I know ma money ain't
right ..... "

He offered, eyeing me strangely; Ardee's
expression seemed a little odd too.

Tyree: " mmmph ...... Rasheed
Duncan. Yo, dawg, you need to get ma money
from dat l'il bitchazz...datz interest am losin'
right there...been well over a year now "

Ardee: " I know dawg, I know, but Virginia is a ways off 'n ama have to make the time "

Tyree: " I know dat but sshiit, ... it's almost two ..... "

Ardee: " I know dawg - 'n I ain't gon make you lose yo's after all you done, ama settle dat - trust me "

Tyree: " almost two years - at that interest rate I'd be gettin' wit what I got in there now,....dat woulda been some respectable papa, yo' nigga costin' me good money dawg "

Ardee: " I know, I know - 'n he ain't my nigga! I wuz jus doin' dat mo'fuck a favor by lettin' him do dat - I coulda used somebody else
but I felt sorry fo' his azz. Ama make sure you get yo' papa back dawg - soon...real... "

Purchasing a home of his own sounded like a good idea and I wondered where he would decide to live, so I asked;

Timmy: " where you wanna buy tho', in the city? "

Ardee: " oh, so you can talk now, huh!...you too shy dawg...you ain't gotta be shy 'round me...ain't no shame in ma game B... I will
                    handlez ma bi'nizz right here in front of y'all...y'all know what time it is...I don't give.... "

Timmy: " yea, yea, we know..... dirtyazz nigga, we seen you, grindin' up 'n diggin' up in ma boi...big ole dick durtyazz nigga - you nasty
                    too ..... lickin' at his booty 'n shit "

Ardee: " negro, fuck y-o-u .....you jus hatin' 'cause you ain't had yo' shit licked yet .....but wait, you gon find out "

Timmy: " ppshaw, whateva "

I said, waving him off.   Never had mine licked!.....well, what he didn't know couldn't hurt him, I thought, smiling to myself.

Ardee: " ama ignore you boi...leave dat l'il tight azz to ma man here - you gon get yo's "

Tyree: " yo...fo'get Timmy right

383

now...you need to run me ova there "

Ardee: " what is wrong witchu
son...dat azz gone to yo' head.........it's Sunday
B, Sun-day...ha-ha haw..... you got ma boi
whipped
                              wit dat booty "

Timmy: " Ioknow whatchu talkin'
'bout but I know yo' azz whipped
tho'.....whipped good too....buggin' out 'cause
some nigga talkin' to
                              Aj .... ha ha - now
datz funny "

Ardee: " shut tha fuck up.
Dawg, you gon jus stand there 'n let this negro
sass me like dat "

Tyree: " dat negro ma boo son,
'n you tha one who fucked wit him to start. But
back to da Realtor bi'nizz, ama need you to
gimmi
                              a ride ova there
tomorrow then - so I can see what da deal is "

Ardee: " no doubt son, no
doubt.... you know I gotchu, jus holla when you
ready.... I ain't got no special work fo'
tomorrow, what's
                              there Aj can have them

fellaz handle it. I can jus take some time out 'n
leave Aj in charge o' the Shop - Oh! did I tell
you dawg.... Aj comin'
thru' lata "

Tyree: " nigga, don't be tryin' to
run no game on me...you know you ain't tole
me nothin'. So, what! e'rrytime y'all wanna
fuck y'all
gon come use ma crib?
"

Ardee: " you ma dawg son, you
s'posed to have ma back "

Tyree: " naaw, you wouldn't
like dat, I'd tear yo' shit up "

Ardee: " see dat now Timmy -
he ma boi, 'n look what he wanna do to me "

Tyree: " not only dat - ama
have to start chargin' y'all a fee to be comin' up
in here tearin' ma crib up "

Timmy: " yeah, ... the money
you woulda made offa his hornyazz.... whoo,
dat woulda ..... "

Ardee: " negro, stay outta
this...you jus got yo's 'n now you hatin' 'cause a

brotha tryin'a get his "

I wasn't going to respond to that so I continued with my ribbing.

Timmy: " amsayin'.... but you don't live here tho'.... you need to take yo' hornyazz home ha-ha-ha; be off wit dat shit "

Ardee: " yeah, you funny nigga...you real funny "

Timmy: " ooh, now he all hurt 'n shit ...... ma badd, ma badd ...... you know am jus fuckin' witchu dawg - it ain't no thang "

Suddenly, the intercom started to buzz without ceasing as Ardee's phone rang. He quickly answered it and said it was Aji downstairs so Tyree released the door letting him in. In a few minutes he was at the door greeting Tyree with the usual pound and a hug. Moments later he was led into the living room by Ardee holding his hands,.....and being surprised to see me, he pulled away from Ardee and came over and gave me a tight hug. As we separated, he held me at arm's length, grinning;

Timmy: " what? "

Aji: " he-ey - 'sup Timmy

dawg? "

Timmy: " same ol'....you know
how we do, we chillin' - jus chillin'....'sup
witchu? "

Tyree: " sssshh,.....Aj, Yani in
the bedroom sleepin' "

Tyree lied, winking at me. I didn't know the
reason for it but thought it might have been that
he'd made an agreement with Ardee, giving him
permission to again use the apartment for a
sexual rendezvous with Aji. At any rate, I
decided to go along with the prank and had to
try and keep a straight face as their dismay
began to show.

Aji: " fo' real! - I thought
this wuz yo' free weekend "

Aji exclaimed. I could see the disappointment
on his face.....

Tyree: " naaw, you got dat
mixed up "

Aji: " Ioknow how I slip up
wit dat,....I mus be losin' ma damn mind.... "

387

.....as he seemed to accept the situation in a subdued manner, obviously still trying trying to work out in his head where he went wrong.

Ardee, on the other hand, was completely peeved, and didn't even try to conceal his displeasure as he immediately put on a scowl and glared at Tyree, who pretended not to notice. Meanwhile, Aji took a seat on the sofa with a thoughtful look, apparently still considering the dilemma....

We were talking for no more than three minutes when Ardee, sitting back with his arms fully extended across the back of the sofa, began repeatedly swinging his legs open, then closed. The next moment, he quickly shoved one hand down the front of his pants, rearranged the position of his apparently hard dick, and quickly pulled his hand back out. Moments later, with raised brows, he impatiently asked Aji, who was on bended knee by the side of my chair:

Ardee: " damn...'sup dawg, you gon spend all yo' time over there? "

Aji: " am talkin' to ma boi son....dang! "

he fumed with a frown.....I immediately knew why Tyree winked at me and Aji got to his feet. Walking over to Ardee, Aji reached into his pocket and pulled out a few "Dutchmasters."

Aji: " where da weed at? "

Ardee: " ain't nobody tryin' to burn no weed now son .... "

Tyree: " good, 'cause Yani's here "

Ardee: " ...... who interested in any damn weed now; come, sit next to me.....look here! .... see whatchu cause, whatchu gon do
                         'bout it? "

He exclaimed, pulling the front of his pants and boxers forward off his waist so Aji could peek in and see his hard dick.

Aji: " so we ain't gon smoke? "

Ardee: " hell no, you heard tha man. Anyway ....not right now.......lata son, lata...right now.... "

He pulled Aji over to him and began to kiss his

neck and ear. Three phillies fell to the floor -
one rolling under the sofa as Ardee threw a leg
across Aji. Tyree emerged from the kitchen and
on his way to the bedroom:

Tyree: " I hope y'all remember
there ain't gon be fuckin' goin' on here
today.....that or whateva else y'all thinkin' "

Timmy: " right "

I chortled.

Ardee: " yo dawg, I wish you
wouldn't say nothin' right now "

Timmy: " dang,....you mad as
hell - ain'tchu - but it ain't ma fault "

Whenever this dude wanted some booty, he
could be like an ill-tempered bull who couldn't
get in the bitch because another bull was
already locked onto her.

Timmy: " ain't nothin' dippin' in
nothin' today "

I taunted with a snicker. He turned to Tyree
with a complaint;

Ardee: " Tyree, tell yo' boi to

chill out - aiight "

Tyree: " I can't stop the man
from talkin' B....you stupid "

he replied with a frown and shrug of his
shoulders; that was highly jarring, his last nerve
had just been plucked. Tyree saw it and burst
out in laughter.

Ardee: " this shit ain't funny
bruh "

Tyree: " awright, awright "

With an arm about Tyree's shoulder, his
demeanor changed quickly and he began to
speak in a soft low voice;

Ardee: " dawg,...can'tchu set
somethin' up; if you 'n Timmy stand watch here
in the livin' room me 'n Aj can jus go in the
kitchen so I can get ma shit wet "

Tyree: " in ma kitchen - is you
crazy! "

Then he made another desperate plea;

Ardee: " aiight, aiight....we can
do it right there in the foyer "

Now Tyree didn't have any more excuses and threw the old one back at him.

Tyree: " But Yani might wake up "

Ardee: " come on dawg, jus do this fo' me - you know we don't wanna go to no hotel - you know how dat shit be "

I began to wonder when Tyree was finally going to bring an end to this prank;

Tyree: " man,.....whatchu expect me to do?.... "

Ardee: " damn dawg, can't you show a brotha a l'il love; Holmes ain't gon wake up now "

Tyree: " Love!.....you want me to give you love! the only love..... "

he squeaked, looking him up and down as he held onto his dick through his pants.

Ardee stared at him, awed.....and forlorn. Then breaking out in a snicker, Tyree set his mind at ease.

Tyree: " awright,....y'all can use
the bedroom but hurry tha hell up.....he-he-he...
"

Ardee: " but you..... but you said
Holmes.... aaah c'mon dawg,....you mean you
played me like dat!....I shoulda opened the
damn bedroom door "

Tyree: " how you gon open up
ma private room door - s'pose I got somebody
in there! "

With a gleam in his eyes, Ardee looked back at
Aji who had heard everything;

Aji: " 'n all this time you got
us...... man you somethin' else "

Tyree: " datz fo' fuckin' wit ma
shawdy "

Aji just looked at him, shook his head, and
began to head for the bedroom.....

Aji: " Ardee you comin' wit
me or what! "

Ardee's face immediately brightened.....and he
stepped off behind Aji, and looking over his
shoulder, he charged,

Ardee: " y'all had dat shit
planned long before I said nothin' 'bout Timmy
"

And I was finally able to release my pent up
laughter. Ardee smiled and gave Tyree a hug
before eagerly and gladly heading back to the
living room, taking Aji by the hand, and leading
him to the bedroom. Poking his head around
the drapery of the living room, Tyree teased.....

Tyree: " 'n it's gon have to be a
quickie too......yo' thirstyazz ain't gon get no
chance to break ma bed down "

......and he retorted,

Ardee: " shut tha fuck up
Tyree.... "

while Tyree had a good chuckle....

Ardee: " ......tryin'a spoil ma
shit.....go ahead boo "

.....as we watched the pair enter the room.
Before Ardee slowly closed the bedroom door
behind them, like a little kid, he made a jeering
face at me but I just laughed it off. I turned to
Tyree, asking;

Timmy: " why you play a cruel
trick like dat on the bro - man,.......you really
somethin' else "

Tyree: " I know it looked
fucked up but I had to get him - you know
how he always fuckin' wit me 'bout 'backed
up'....well his azz wuz backed up - they ain't
done shit in a minit, I had to get him "

Remembering that made the prank sweeter to
me and I found myself laughing again.

Tyree: " You see how he looked
like he wuz gon die when it looked like he
wuzn't gon get nothin' "

Timmy: " I shoulda whipped out
ma phone,..... I woulda have dat shit to show
him e'rrytime he mess wit me "

I added as we sat down in the kitchen. I should
have guessed it wouldn't be a normal sit down
for no sooner had we sat down, I felt his feet
poking at my crotch from under the table. At
first it felt kind of ticklish but as he wormed his
toes further and brushed against the head of my
dick hanging down my left thigh, I began to get
excited. I spread my legs wider and slid down
a bit in my chair so he could get at me better.

All during this, he kept searching my eyes with a lustful gaze as he asked,

Tyree: " you gon gi me somethin'? "

Timmy: " am broke "

I chortled,.......and he sneered,

Tyree: " Ha - Ha,....you funny.... "

adding,

Tyree: " .... if I wanted anything outta yo' pocket it would be the back pocket "

I tried to make it funnier by replying,.....

Timmy: " well, I ain't got nothin' in there either "

...... and his legs suddenly left my crotch. Just as suddenly, he slid off his chair and was under the table and before I knew what was happening, he was pulling my dick out. By the time he got it out, it was rock hard and as I sat anticipating a nice handjob, I felt a wonderful warmth peeling the foreskin of my dick over, invigorating it even more......

Timmy: " A-aaah - ccccccccttt "

......and continued doing so, developing into a
steady pace,........a sweet, drowsy, jaw-dropping,
eye-closing pace.

Timmy: " ooooh, ssssh - oh shit
Black! "

Only able to hear his slurping at intervals, at
one point I wondered if I was having a dream
but I could tell my head was going down as his
oral skills weakened my neck and brain, falling
and resting on my arms as they lay tight-fisted
on the edge of the table in front of me.

When I felt his hands at my hips pulling my
pants down, I was more than eager to ease my
butt off the chair to give him access and as they
folded at my ankles, he was feverishly pulling a
sneaker off one foot. As quickly as he got it
off, he slid that pant leg over my heel and
started to shove my leg high off the floor. His
hot breath under my balls told me where he was
going and I slid down further; he took my legs,
pants and all, and put them on his shoulders.....

Timmy: " O-oooh cccctt - wh-
oooooooh! "

.....and almost sending his hot tongue between the already opened crack of my butt cheeks. It got very frenzied,.....he was eagerly and sloppily devouring my hole and I was ladling it out, so much so that my lower back was now on the seat of the chair. I was uncomfortable and didn't know it, having to grab onto the edge of the table with one hand while the other was on the floor supporting my weight.

He ate without any kind of good manners, slurping and slopping like a pig - but at the moment,....at this table,....his manners were highly accepted. Quite without warning, he suddenly stopped and crawled out from under the table. As I pulled myself back up onto the chair, he glanced toward the kitchen window, no doubt to see if anyone was at the kitchen window of the apartment almost directly across from ours.

Two quick steps and he was by my side of the table, yanking me off my chair and pulling me behind him. Shackled by my pants on one leg and haphazardly trying to follow, I kept reaching down to pull my pants up but to no avail.

Where was he pulling me to, I pondered, still trying to reach my pants - and he suddenly

398

stopped at the bedroom door. Still holding onto my hand, he pressed his ear against the door, listening to the erotic sounds coming from within; he need not have, as I could hear all the gruntings, moanings, and hissings clearly. A little less than a minute later he was pulling me up against him.

Timmy: " Tyree!...come away 'n leave them.... "

Tyree: " hell no,....I wantchu to lissen "

Timmy: " Noo! "

Suddenly, a careless voice thundered from the other side,

Ardee: " I know y'all out there!..... "

Tyree only snickered; and even as I tried pulling him away from the door, he pulled me back. Quite to my surprise, he opened the door.....

Aji: " NNNgh!....daa-ddeeeee "

.....for me to witness the soles of Aji's feet

dangling just over the side of the mattress and
Ardee over him, pumping,....his fuzzy butt
cheeks wide open and his booty hole twitching
as he gruffly barked orders at Aji who was ever
so slowly sliding off the bed. His dick was
wedged in Aji, stretching his hole from the little
I could see until all became partially hidden by
his big balls. His left hand was resting on the
night table and his right foot, along with the
upper half of Aji's body, lost over the far side of
the bed. Peering behind even as he sunk
himself deep in Aji again.....

Aji: "
Oooh,........Ardeeeeeeee! "

......he spoke to both of us, Aji first - then us;

Ardee: " STOP RUNNIN!.....
you think I give a fuck? "

then grabbed Aji's right hip and yanked him
back.

Aji: " Ohma.... -
Uuuhmmmm! "

Too rapt in thought to speak, Tyree was busy
pulling his dick out of his pants as he continued
to watch keenly, the muffled, bitter-sweet
wailing from Aji echoing from above and under

the bed with its rumpled sheets. Some of the pillows and shams were on the floor at the foot of the ottoman,..... and on the ottoman, seemingly hastily tossed aside. Pulling me even closer to him and looking deep into my eyes, Tyree pitifully renewed his pleas;

Tyree: " dang dawg,.......they fuckin' 'n you ain't go let me get nothin'! "

Timmy: " Tyree noo "

Tyree: " pleeease dawg,.......look how you got me - I can't even fit back in ma clothes "

Timmy: " sshit,.....it ain't the first time you eva looked like dat "

I retaliated, trying to sound completely uninterested; I was still against doing it publicly.....

Tyree: " don't be like dat dawg, gi yo' boi some "

......and accused,

Timmy: " .....besides, you gon try to kill me 'n everybody gon hear; I ain't doin' nothin' " shoving him off my neck as he continued his grind on my butt.

Tyree: " noo son, ama jus take a little.....jus nice 'n slow like how you always want it "

He tried to assure, whispering in my ear while slowly pulling the bedroom door shut.

Timmy: " yea right! "

I shot back, as we stumbled back against the bathroom door. He was opening the door and pulling me in; I followed, half wanting and half not and as he sat on the toilet and pulled me down onto his lap, I found myself sitting on his hard dick.

Tyree: " lemmi get a little dawg - even if it's jus the head "

I got up and moved toward the bathroom door but he held me back and slammed the door shut. Pulling me back, he slowly shuffled backwards until he found the toilet again and sat. He spun me around and began kissing my butt while he played with my dick....

Tyree: " lemmi put a l'il bit in

you dawg "

He begged as his moist finger searched for and
found my hole.

Timmy: " ccctt-haaaw! "

He withdrew the finger and began to lick,
feasting until I was on tip-toes. Between my
cheeks was a messy mass of saliva and when he
stopped I heard a "thwat",..... he'd spat in his
hand. Moments later he was tugging at my
hips, wanting me to sit down; I descended
slowly, begging....

Timmy: " Be easy, Tyree, be
easy "

Tyree: " I ain't doin' nothin' -
ama letchu take it in - however much you can
handle "

.....I could scarcely handle any - him giving or
me taking; I sat anyway, feeling that blunt
demanding thing ready to un-blunt itself when
it found my hole.

Timmy: " ccccctt ff-FUCK!..... "

As I was going down he was coming up......

Tyree: " OH YEAH - don't-move-dawg-don't-move! "

.........he entreated with ardor, great urgency in his tone. Then suddenly, he shuffled his feet, seeking and finding a position,..... then stabbed at me,.....and to my great surprise, the head of his dick just popped my hole and set it afire. It was burning like he had an entire basketball he was trying to get up inside me;

Timmy: " OOH! - omagawd, omagawd no - wait!....... "

Tyree: " don't move, don't...... "

His arms were so tight around my waist, he was squeezing hurtfully, so I begged....

Timmy: " .... Uh!..... whatz wrong witchu bruh, dat hurt "

Tyree: " my badd my badd......awright, you try 'n take some more "

Timmy: " Hell no!.....I can't even take it like...... "

.....but he made me, sinking his chin in my back and quickly using his legs to reach out and pull mine in, planting them between his, like a lion

who had just brought down its prey; man he
could be cruel sometimes.

Tyree: " don't move ma
dawg......please don't move "

I couldn't. I was held firm and any kind of
wiggle I made, I was sure his dick was making
a tear in my hole. He slowly moved his chin
and replaced it with his cheek, still holding onto
me and I panted. I remembered I was supposed
to stay calm and relax. I tried and waited until
the burning subsided a bit but by now, he was
rubbing my chest, stomach and thighs.

Tyree: " oh yea dawg,....we
cool, don't fret, I ain't tryin'a take no mo' - jus
gimmi whatchu can "

Timmy: " I can't gi you nothin'
more! "

I flared, his big dick pulsating in my hole,
stretching it and making me mad....

Tyree: " yes you can, jus move
a l'il.....like this "

Timmy: " O-Ooowooou! "

Tyree: " ooh baby........ "

I don't know how long we were in there, his dick slipping out and him fighting me to put it back in.

When he finally gave up, pulling his pants up and going out the door, I was only moments behind him, still pulling my pants up. I looked up as Tyree was about to sit in his swivel chair and from the corner of my eye, I made out the pair of Ardee and Aji all cuddled up on the sofa. It made no sense to turn back to the bathroom to fix my clothes so I hurriedly secured my belt and plopped myself down on my chair at the other end of the room from Ardee and Aji. I'd barely sat down when I felt eyes on me. I cast my gaze up.....Ardee had pulled his lips off Aji and was grinning like a fool.

Ardee: " Mmmm, y'all wuz doin' sumptin' while we wuz doin' sumptin' in there! "

I said nothing, neither did Tyree; Ardee snickered and went back to smooching.

Suddenly Tyree spoke,

Tyree: " you mean to tell me after alla dat tearin' up y'all still carryin' on! -

dang! "

Tyree questioned as he walked over to join me.

Aji: " what - you jealous
'cause am gettin' some? "

Tyree: " Aj......you need to shut
tha fuck up or ama havta start chargin' yo' azz
by the hour next time y'all come
thru'.....squealin' 'n
                                        tearin' up ma
bed "

With the smuggest grin, Aji muttered under his
breath.....

Aji: " wouldn't be gettin'
much 'cause we wuzn't even in there fo' no hour
"

.....but Tyree heard....

Tyree: " 'n you wuz carryin' on
like dat "

......and replied in like fashion,.....but Aji
silenced him,

Aji: " wuzn't no mo' carryin'
on than y'all wuz - we huurd you......beggin'

like a dog "

and Ardee added in,

Ardee: " been a minit B,.....we
need to get some luvin' jus like you "

In one quick fluid move, Ardee got out from
under Aji and stood before him with his dick
and balls sticking out over the waist of his pants
and boxers. Aji began to suck his dick as he
ripped the pants down below Ardee's butt at the
same time. Cradling Ardee's butt in his palms,
his head began to bob slowly at first, then
gathered momentum. Soon there was a loud
pop as Aji pulled his mouth off the dick - then
he did it again.

Ardee: " oh shiit ..... son ......
cccccctt, yeaaah, daamn ..... lemmi see dat booty
again son, c'mon "

Aji stood, and as he pulled his pants down
about his ankles, Ardee spun him around,
shoved him back on the sofa, raised his legs and
got on his knees. He licked Aji's butt hungrily,
making him moan with delight while his
tangled feet dangled above Ardee's shoulders,
at times violently causing his boots to bite into
Ardee's back - his wallet and money fell to the
floor.

Ardee: " damn son, take them
Timb's off...you gon make a hole in ma back "

Aji: " ssh_it, look how long
you been tryin' to make one in mine "

Now we just couldn't take that one without
falling apart with muffled laughter.

They were making me hot just watching, and
Tyree wasn't helping any by fondling me. I
wanted his dick all the more because of his
lubricated finger playing with my hole. It
seemed he was taking his cue from Ardee as
whenever he did something, Tyree would
follow.

Now he was forcing me to spread my legs
across each arm-rest of my chair, after easing
my pants down, so he could also lick my butt
hole. My protests fell on deaf ears as he
continued to weaken my resolve and clear away
all my doubts and fears by blowing, nibbling
and sticking his tongue in my ear...kissing my
neck, gently tracing his forefinger along the
edges of my lips, then whisperingin my ear,

Tyree: " don't be so scared
dawg, they don't give a fuck.....c'mon, let me
lick dat azz "

Timmy: " Tyreee.....noo....please,
don'tchu see them right the......oooh cccctt,
mmmph, oh ma.....Tyree nooo - I
can't.......cccctt FUCK, DAMN Tyree - Aaaah!
"

With his hot, persuasive tongue licking my hole
like that I was no match, I was powerless and
he knew it too; and so he continued, further
licking, slurping, melting my futile resistance -
my very being into nothingness.

His trip from the kitchen to the bedroom earlier
had been a tricky one. As it turned out, he had
condoms and lube in his pocket and didn't have
his boxers on. He had made preparation fully
knowing what he was going to do when he
came out. Not that it mattered; I was yearning
for his dick so badly, now I was ready to drop
right there whenever he gave the word.

As he lubed me up, I watched Ardee, who was
oblivious to anyone or anything but Aji and his
quest, move the coffee table aside, making
room for Aji to spread himself out on the rug in
eager anticipation of his dick.

Both bulls were ready. Condom-covered dicks
just waiting to plunder lubed butt holes.

Aji raised his legs high, his butt hole exposed to me for the first time (I'd never before thought of seeing him like that), ready to receive Ardee's hard and eager onslaught.

I couldn't see myself opening up out there like that, under the present circumstances, and Tyree must have thought I would have difficulty readily accepting that - which was why I think he sat back on the chair and told me to sit on his dick. Several times he tried to penetrate me but without success, and he became agitated and overly aggressive, mainly from seeing Ardee digging into Aji and him getting nowhere.

Tyree: " you too tense boo, loosen up .... relax ...... you gon make me fill this condom up 'n don't even get up in you - don'tchu want yo'
                    dick too? ..... "

He cooed softly;

Timmy: " am try-in' "

Tyree: " I got a nutt waitin' in here fo' you son ..... c'mon, don'tchu want it? "

He rasped in a low voice. I nodded several approvals, and when we tried again, after he

411

spent a little time licking my hole, the head popped in. He held me so tightly I could not get off it and he suddenly rose to his feet with me clinging to his neck.

He slowly got down on one knee,.....then the other, putting me on my back right next to Ardee and Aji.

Aji's face was turned in my direction. I couldn't look him in the eye - I turned my head the other way. For a moment, I was caught up in hearing Ardee and Aji's moans and groans as they locked chests and shoulders. Aji kept his legs firmly wrapped around Ardee's waist.

Ardee was hard at work dipping into and grinding gracefully, evoking the erotic soft moans and squeals out of Aji. Our closeness seemed to have spurred him on. Once, when he made a deep penetration, he clenched his butt cheeks tightly and clung to Aji motionless for a moment.

Aji: " O-ooowmph .... Ar-deeee, ooh, shiit "

Ardee: " datzwhatamtalkin'bout "

Tyree seized the opportunity of having me on

my back on the floor to gain leverage by anchoring his toes into the book cabinet, and with one sudden powerful plunge, submerged half of his ten inches of dick inside me like he had never done before.

I could not contain myself - the power and sudden force of his massiveness made me let out a long, loud wail.

Timmy: " Ooou-oooow! .... "

Tyree: " ssshh, ssshh, ssshh ......
you ok? "

Timmy: " oh-my-gaawd! mmphf
"

Tyree: " it's ok, it's ok "

He assured breathlessly, and engulfed my lower lip, squeezing his hungry, thoughtless, big-headed monster deeper into my reluctant hole. I wiggled and squirmed, denying him from reaching where he was so desperately trying to get.

From out of nowhere Aji found my flailing hand and held it. I gripped firmly and held onto it as I winced and wiggled in my quest for escape but to no avail, as Tyree would not release his hold on me nor give me time to catch my breath. He was feeding me more dick even as I cried.

He quickly covered my mouth with a hand; there was no escaping, I could only express muffled wails as me and Aji gripped each other's hand, to the point of hurting sometimes, and held on tightly - two friends under pressure, sharing the same agony, the same pain (although I guess mine was less tolerable).... trying to run from it, wishing it would stop - but still somehow wanting to take it.

It wasn't getting any easier as Ardee was goading himself and Tyree on with dirty talk. Aji was really feeling it too, I could tell from his grunts, moans, the vein that popped up in the center of his sweat-covered forehead, and the squeezing of my hand.

It was as though we were communicating through our hands, looking each other in the eye now from time to time. I don't know what my appearance to Aji was, but to my surprise, the intimacy and camaraderie of the moment stripped me of my shame and liberated my closely guarded inhibitions.

Aji: " oooow ssshhhit .....
Ardee, oh, oh, ooh yeah son, wear dat shit

414

out.....O-oowooo - Ard .... "

Ardee: " yea son, it's me ..... datz
ma name "

Aji: " mothafucka!..... "

Ardee: " take this dick boi, am
here to tear this azz up, show you who own this
..... you know who this, uh! .....

Aji: " yes, yes, take it, it's
yo's "

Ardee: " whatchu holdin' his
hand fo' .... leggo his hand, you can't do nothin'
fo' him, his man got him "

Tyree and Ardee were drunk with the pleasure
of domination and from the squeals and moans.
They kept working feverishly, digging,
grinding, plundering - Ardee more laboriously,
searching to find the satisfaction for their
unified desire as I fought desperately to repress
any outburst.

Ardee: " you gettin' dat azz
dawg? "

Tyree: " uh-huh "

Ardee: " then tear it dawg .....
give him dat shit gangsta son .... tear it "

Tyree: " oh damn Timmy, cccctt
damn son, this shit ..... Oh fuck ma shawty .....
uumph ..... grrr.... aaahh ..... oh yes! - yes! "

Timmy: " oh gaawd Blaze .....
no-ooo .... "

Ardee: " yea boi, you gettin dat
azz waxed now "

Timmy: " oohmagaw..... ay!
cono..... you gon kill me son? .... ssssshiit ay
Papi! ...... Aji! .... "

Aji: " bear it son,....uh,....it
be over soon "

There went the hand over my mouth again and I
struggled to remain silent as he lay still atop
me. Ardee though, was making good his earlier
promise to show ownership. To that end, he
was successful but was now, none-the-less,
brought down to a stuttering, panting, snorting
semblance of the trash-talking man who had,
not so long ago, so boastfully taken on this task
of satisfying himself and Aji ....

Ardee: " oh ssshit shawty, ga-

gaawddamn, you pullin' errything outt....
Unghf, ngh, oh, oh, oooh ssssshhhhiiiiit "

Yes!.....he'd succeeded.

My hand was still in Aji's, although now only
limply, as all four of us lay on the floor spent.
They had both succeeded - we were conquered.
Well, at least I'm sure I was. Tyree had never
fucked me like that before; he was so very
aggressive and - well, really, really brutal.

I think he had completely lost his senses, for the
Tyree that was now gently kissing me and
earnestly inquiring if I was okay, was a totally
different one from the one that had me under
him a couple minutes ago. He had made me
feel like his personal possession, owning my
body and soul. All that I did not want him to
do - he did, hurting me, but at the same time
setting my body and soul alight with delightful
fires that were still burning within me.

And as I lay there under him, his now semi-
hard, condom-covered dick laden with his cum
still inside me, still sent electrifying urges
through me. My thoughts returned to times
past - little intimate moments when I'd just
watch his bearded face and lips, especially
when he ate - but most of all, our first sexual
experience.

As his dick pulsated one last time, rekindling the raw, yet unsubsided fire in me, causing me to twist and squirm, I felt a great and overwhelming surge from my loins and my sphincter contracted several times, squeezing his dick tighter and sending raw eroticism through me. I was about to ejaculate and the sheer magnitude of the sensation lifted my back off the floor pressing my body hard against his.

Timmy: " Tyree....oooh, oh sshit ...mmmph.... damn! "

Tyree: " wha! ..... oh damn ..... baby boi ..... you .... oh damn "

Timmy: " am sorry "

Tyree: " no boo, am glad you did ..... you aiight? "

Yes, I most certainly was - completely.

He slowly pulled out of me but I clung to his neck as he got his feet and walked us to the bathroom. I peeled the condom off him, placed it in tissue and discarded it, then sat on the toilet looking at my cum smeared on his stomach. He wiped a forefinger in it and tasted it, wiped the finger again, held my head and extended the finger to my lips.

Timmy:　　　　　　" No! .... no, Tyree .....
Noooo ...... phwat ..... you nasty "

Scurrying up to the bathroom with Ardee right
behind, Aji joked;

Aji:　　　　　　　" y'all ain't had enough!
..... we need to get in there! "

The rest of the evening, we joked around,
smoked, and drank beer. There was something
about Aji that had always endeared him to me,
and from that evening onward, we got along
better than ever before.

I had planned on going home to spend the
night, but after the fellas said they would be
spending the night at Tyree's, he said he wanted
me to spend the night there too and I agreed. In
the morning, he and Ardee would go see the
Realtor and I was going to go with him.

We talked for awhile longer before we all went
off to bed, me and Tyree in the bedroom [of
course], and Ardee and Aji opened up the day
bed in the living room and slept there.

(Chapter 14)

Daybreak Monday morning, I was the first to get out of bed to find Ardee and Aji all cuddled up in bed. Ardee was on his back, legs spread wide, his right hand around Aji's neck and half his dick hanging out the fly of his boxers, jumping every now and then like a hopping toad. Aji was on his stomach and had his left cheek and right arm on Ardee's chest while his right leg, bent at the knee, was on and between Ardee's thighs.

I quickly tiptoed back to the bedroom and woke Tyree to come look at them.

Timmy: " you gotta come see this shit "

Tyree: " see what? "

Timmy: " c'mon, you'll see "

I whispered as we moved cautiously and stealthily out into the living room and stood over them, trying not to laugh out loud. Tyree snickered,

Tyree: " yo .... ssshhh, watch this, ama scare the dog shit outta them. Go get the baseball bat under the bed "

He always kept an aluminum baseball bat under his bed. I quickly fetched it and found him standing at the foot of the daybed holding the large cast iron skillet.

Tyree: " gimmi the bat "

He whispered and signalled for me to stand back. I stood behind him, peeking out from his right side as he held the bat and skillet over their heads and banged loudly on the bottom of the skillet.

Tyree: " INMATES!.....R-i-s-e 'n shine mo'fuckaz....it's a new day!! "

Ardee leaped from the bed like he'd just received an electric shock. On his feet but in a somewhat crouching stance, his eyes darted left and right before he quickly straightened up and tried to stand at attention; then appearing as though he was about to faint, his body swayed back and forth a little bit before he suddenly put his dukes up and bellowed;

Ardee: " Yeah,.......bring it mothafucka......Oh!.....ooooh sshii-t! "

and promptly fell back on his butt on the bed. He was pissed and yet amused that Tyree had caught him with that trick and lay with an arm across his eyes. Aji had jumped up but sat in bed with both arms outstretched behind him, supporting his weight as though he could not sit up all by himself. His head was hung down and, if you asked me, still asleep. Ardee had now come to his senses and realized that his now soft dick was hanging out of his boxers.

Ardee: " what tha fuck!! "

Tyree and I were laughing so hard we couldn't stand. I tumbled over on the bed with them and Tyree, dropping the skillet and the bat, flung himself on the settee in raucous, uncontrollable laughter.

Ardee: " What tha
fuck.......dawg, dat wuz fucked up - fo'
real,....dat shit wuz fucked UP - Damn! "

Tyree rolled, twisted and eventually folded himself up in the fetal position, holding his stomach as his eyes watered. He still couldn't speak and neither could I. It was Aji who seemed to have just walked into the land of the living and asked in earnest surprise;

Aji: " Wha happen? "

Ardee: " damn! ..... you mean a

nigga can't even get no sleep in this mo'fucka "

Aji, now fully alert, reiterated,

Aji: " wha happen? "

and Tyree finally found his tongue;

Tyree: " it's yo' boi - you
shoulda seen him, his shit pokin' out o' his
drawz ..... haahaha....then, then .... finally went
..... FLOP .....
                                ....oh ma-gawd..... dat
shit wuz funny yo "

Ardee: " oh you think so "

He frowned, getting to his feet and shoving his
dick back through his fly. Then finally offering
a deceitful grin, he mumbled jokingly,

Ardee: " it's aiight dawg we gon
see how funny you think it is when it's yo' turn
"

He walked to the bathroom, pulling out his dick
as he went. He took a leak and returned;

Ardee: " what kinda mo'fuckin'
host you be ..... you couldn't even make a
brotha get some sleep son, this how you treat

yo'

mo'fuckin guests? "

Tyree: " nigga - you ain't no guest, I jus took pity on yo' azz 'n let you stay over "

Sitting on the edge of the bed next to Aji, who was scratching his head as if he still wasn't sure if he was asleep or awake, Ardee asked;

Ardee: " you got breakfast ready? "

Tyree: " first y'all press out ma sofa, 'n now you want free breakfast? "

Ardee: " cost you less than the doctor bill fo' tha fuckin' trauma you caused "

Well, at least his sense of humor was still intact.

Tyree: " I couldn't pass dat one up dawg...fo' real fo' real; you shoulda seen yo' azz - dick all hangin' out 'n shit - when Timmy showed me y'all...I was like - yo.... "

Ardee: " slick, real slick.... Timmy... but ama get you back "

424

Timmy: " Me! ....but I ain't did nothin'.... why you gotta single me out, you scared to cuss yo' boi out son? "

Ardee: " ama get both o' y'all "

With that, Ardee headed to the bathroom again, this time to brush his teeth and freshen up. Aji joined him and took a quick shower. Tyree and I followed after which we all had orange juice, toasted bagels, coffee, and some fruit.

After breakfast, we boarded Ardee's truck and he dropped Aji off to open the shop then headed off to Brooklyn. It was about 9:30 a.m, and the heavy traffic caused us to get there later than we had planned. Finding a parking space was so difficult that Ardee decided to drive around until he could find one but suggested that Tyree and I go on ahead.

The office was operated out of the bottom level of an apartment building. There was an older woman sitting at one of the three desks and she greeted us, saying her name was "Mrs. Grimes" and I detected an apparent haughtiness in her voice as she asked;

Mrs. Grimes: " how can I help you? "

Tyree: " we're here to see Mr.
Duncan "

Mrs. Grimes: " what is the nature of
your visit? "

Tyree: " to speak to a Mr.
Duncan, is he here? "

She didn't answer the question and was still
pressing to find out why we wanted to see this
Mr. Duncan. That was so rude and silly; it was,
after all, a Real Estate Office and it should be
more than evident that we desired to conduct
business of that nature. She still insisted on
knowing the nature of our visit and Tyree
merely stated what he'd said before. This
seemed to have infuriated her and she promptly
informed us that she could assist us in his
absence. Tyree insisted that he needed to see
Mr. Duncan in person, but she continued on to
the point where it was bordering on
belligerence. She had pushed too many of his
buttons and he stated with a calm authority I'd
not seen in him before,

Tyree: " if Mr. Duncan is not in
his office, and it's not a problem, we would like
to wait or ......would that be ok? "

Her nostrils flared.

Mrs. Grimes: " well, it would be best if I knew what you were here for "

Just then, the door to the small cubicle at the back of the office opened and a fairly tall, slender-built, good-looking, dark-skinned man in his mid to late twenties came out. His haircut was low, highly sheened and wavy on top; a pair of naturally neat eyebrows sat as awnings over his radiating dark brown eyes and a well tailored moustache spanned the length of his lips, tapering off to pencil point thinness.

Dressed in a dark blue suit, sky blue shirt, and an ice blue and white polka dot tie, he would have looked more like an executive with a regular tie.......but that was his choice. He looked at us curiously, flashed a pleasant and welcoming smile, and said to the woman.

Mr. Duncan: " is there a problem Mrs. Grimes? "

Softly,......and it may well have been for my benefit, Tyree exclaimed,

Tyree: " preppy boy "

I remember the occasion I first heard him use

that moniker.

Tyree: " preppy boy "

Tyree muttered again, as he raised a fist to his
mouth, feigning a burp and searched his pocket
with the other for the business card.

Mrs. Grimes: " well, sir, these two men
say they are here to see you; they refused to
disclose the nature of their visit and I was just
trying

                    to..... "

Mr. Duncan: " it's ok Mrs. Grimes, I'll
handle it from here.... thank you "

Dejectedly, she walked back to her desk, sat
down, and immediately began to fumble with
some papers. Mr. Duncan then turned to us;

Mr. Duncan: " well,..... gentlemen,
how may I help you? "

Tyree: " I'm Tyree Davenport,...
this is my partner Mr. Gooden. We are here on
the recommendation of a very good friend "

Mr. Duncan: " oh good! "

Tyree: " that's how we happen

to be visiting you "

Mr. Duncan: " well gentlemen, I apologize if you were inconvenienced in any way "

Tyree: " oh, we'll be alright "

Tyree said sarcastically,..... and this man immediately looked sheepish. He shook Tyree's hand but lingered a little too long, I thought...then he shook mine and quickly invited us into his office where he offered us a seat.

Mr. Duncan: " ......please, you must forgive Mrs. Grimes, she's a little, er...... eccentric and somewhat overprotective "

.......apologizing again. Tyree kept his lips sealed but I knew what he was thinking.

Mr. Duncan: " what can I do for you gentlemen today? "

Tyree dipped into his sport coat pocket and took out the business card Ardee had given him; he handed it to Mr. Duncan. He looked at it, turned it over, and appeared to be reading something from the reverse side.

It had been Tyree's dream to own a house and he was very excited to have been recommended someone who was most polite and accommodating. I would have to say he went out of his way to satisfy us - showing us every catalogue and attending to Tyree's every little whims and fancies. He even showed us houses, some nearby while others were way upstate with exorbitant price tags - leagues out of Tyree's capabilities.

Strangely enough though, Tyree spent some time looking at them in detail and asking questions. When he had exhausted the index of catalogues, Tyree questioned him about private sales. He leaned forward in his swivel chair, scratched his chin, then leaned way back, cradling the back of his head in both hands.

Mr. Duncan: " well Mr. Davenport, I don't have anything suitable for you - at this moment. However, I do know of something that might

                          interest you. It's not available just yet, nor has it even been put on the market, but the owner has expressed a definite desire to sell "

Tyree: " how big are we talking? "

Mr. Duncan: " actually it's five bedrooms...two on the lower level... three and a half bathrooms "

Tyree: " mmm.... sounds interesting, what you think Timmy? "

He asked, pulling me into the discussions and taking me by surprise; I had to ad lib.

Timmy: " might be worth a look-see "

I offered casually.

Tyree: " maybe we should do that "

Mr. Duncan: " what exactly are you looking for "

Tyree: " space, quiet, sturdy .... I think I might have to wait until you have something else "

Mr. Duncan: " mmm, you never know, you might wanna take a look at this one though "

Tyree: " you think it fits the bill? "

Mr. Duncan: " it's nice, might be what you're looking for but, like I said, there is a willingness to sell - and it's not on the open market "

Timmy: " what about the neighborhood?.... that's very important "

Mr. Duncan: " very decent and respectable, Mr. Gooden, but, mind you, this is in the upper price range "

Tyree: " mmm .... Timmy, I think this calls for conferencing "

Mr. Duncan: " tell you what, if you care, you could leave me a number where I could reach you and I'd be only too happy to accommodate you gentlemen as soon as I have positive news "

Tyree: " sure, sure, if I'm not available at that moment, I'd really appreciate your leaving me a message and I'll be sure
to return your call as soon as possible "

Mr. Duncan: " well, it's settled then and you can rest assured you'll be hearing from me as soon as I have some good news "

Timmy: " we appreciate that "

Mr. Duncan: " I'm always happy to help the friend of a friend "

Tyree: " we look forward to that "

Mr. Duncan: " anything else gentlemen? "

Tyree looked at me for a response and I shook my head in tacit response.

Tyree: " no Mr. Duncan, that seems like it for now "

Mr. Duncan: " ok, ... Mr. Davenport.... Mr. Gooden, it was a pleasure. Good day to you both and thanks for coming "

Timmy: " our pleasure, I'm sure "

I replied politely as we shook hands again.

As we were leaving the office and nodding goodbye to Mrs. Grimes, I could strongly sense Mr. Duncan's eyes on us and just as we were about to go out the door, I turned my head quickly and saw that he was staring at us from his office door.

As soon as we were outside, Tyree asked;

Tyree: " did you see how dat
woman wuz dawg?....damn "

Timmy: " for a Receptionist .... "

Tyree: " good god "

Timmy: " ..... I jus did e'rrything
to try 'n act decent "

Tyree: " some people seem to
think dat 'cause you a thug, or dress like one,
you gotz to be some ignorant-azz negro "

Timmy: " she need to be working
in some back room - if at all "

Tyree: " them type o' people
seem to think you neva been to no school, can't
even write yo' name, don't know or have good
                    manners 'n can't tell a
mo'fuckin trollop when they see one .... c'mon
dawg, let's go find where Ardee parked at "

I was amused by Tyree's deep indignation at
this woman's behaviour; she deserved it
though,......and I knew he was not a misogynist

434

- not the way he treats Yani's mother and other women that I'd seen him associated with.

All through the meeting I had noticed how this Mr. Duncan looked at Tyree with a kind of shy but lustful look; never-the-less, I tried to put it out of my mind and think about other things - things like just what awaited Tyree in his quest, as an unemployed single black man, trying to buy a house, and now in particular, a house through this Realtor whom I couldn't help feeling was not behaving in a straightforward manner. And what could it be that was written on the back of that business card? I guess that would remain a mystery as I thought it wouldn't be proper to ask.

Tyree: " you see Ardee truck anywhere? "

Timmy: " no, he prolly parked blocks away or maybe he still circlin' - can't find nothin' "

Tyree: " after all this time...naw...I don't think so.... ama call him "

He called Ardee who said he was a few blocks away and that we should wait where we were.

A few minutes later, I saw his truck coming

slowly up the street. He pulled up, we hopped in, and were on our way back to Harlem. Tyree and Ardee talked about what happened back at the Realtor's office but my thoughts were somewhere else.... I just didn't like Mr. Duncan. He seemed like one of those sly, underhanded people. Peering between the seats, Tyree looked back at me sprawled out in the back seat of the Navigator.

Tyree: " damn boo, you awful quiet back there, whatchu thinkin'.... why you ain't wearin' yo' seatbelt? "

Timmy: " nothin' "

I replied thoughtfully, then sat up, buckled myself in, and stared out the window at the now somewhat lessened late morning traffic.

Tyree: " put it on son "

Ardee: " ha ha ha, it's dat dick from last night ....homie still wore out "

I didn't feel like responding to Ardee and so a few minutes later, Tyree turned around again.

Tyree: " 'sup B, you aiight? "

Timmy: " yeah, am good "

I lied. It was immediately detected by Tyree, who now turned himself almost completely around and looked at me very curiously.

Tyree: 		" naw, naw...somethin' ain't right...don't make me have to come back there and squeeze it outta.... "

Timmy: 		" dang son, I did say I wuz aiight...didn't I? "

Ardee: 		" oh shit!........ I know somethin' comin' now "

Timmy: 		" Ardee, who this Mr. Duncan? "

Ardee: 		" who...who Mr. Duncan? "

Timmy: 		" dang, is dat so hard to understand? "

Tyree: 		" what up Timmy? "

I didn't address him; I continued to press Ardee with a comical chuckle.

Timmy: 		" I know dat crazy mix o' liquor done wore off ..... why you stutterin' son? "

Ardee:　　　　　　　" naw, naw, I ain't
stutterin' ..... you jus ask a odd question 'n I
wuz wonderin' whatz up wit dat .....datz all "

Timmy:　　　　　　　" yeah - whateva "

Something was afoot.

Ardee couldn't answer my question without
stuttering and Tyree had not offered a word of
explanation, as he normally would. During our
goodbye handshake, I could have sworn Mr.
Duncan had given Tyree's hand an odd squeeze,
like some trifling tryst on the sly. I just hoped
that I was wrong. Even so, I firmly voiced my
opinion.

Timmy:　　　　　　" I know y'all know I
ain't no damn fool "

Tyree:　　　　　　　" c'mon now, ain't
nobody callin' you no fool "

Ardee:　　　　　　" whatchu mean dawg? "

Timmy:　　　　　　" exactly what I said .....
I ain't blind ..... Tyree know what am talkin'
'bout "

Tyree: " Timmy, I got no clue
what you tryin'..... "

He was genuine, he didn't know; I put it bluntly
on the table.

Timmy: " what's wit dat
handshake between you 'n Duncan? "

Tyree: " ain't nothin' funny; he
put his hand out, I put mine, - 'n we shook!.....
he shook yo's too! "

He quickly replied, his voice raising to a higher
pitch.

Timmy: " oh yeah .... but, decent
and respectfully tho' "

Ardee: " ooh shit ..... y'all got
somethin' you wanna tell me? "

Well, apparently, it was nothing Ardee should
have known or suspected.

Timmy: " I ain't got nothin' to tell
but am jus wonderin' what tha fuck wuz up wit
dat handshake "

Tyree: " oh, you mean like dat.
Well, I did think he held ma hand a l'il too long

fo' somebody you jus meetin' but I jus wrote dat
off

                             as 'eager to please,' but
I ain't thought nothin' of it "

Timmy: " good, then we gon
keeps it jus like dat "

Ardee: " Daaayum, assertion!
Dawg, is dat Timmy back there? "

He looked back at me - beaming, and proudly
declared;

Tyree: " sho' nuff - datz ma
shawty "

I was satisfied.

Later that evening after returning to Harlem,
just as soon as we had finished our meal, Tyree
sat silently rolling a blunt when he suddenly
declared;

Tyree: " I think ama drop this
shit ..... an occasional smoke but - datz it "

His reasoning was that it was not good for Yani
to see him doing that or get too familiar with
the smell of it in his home; he didn't want to do

anything that might encourage him to start smoking weed as he got older. Tyree was so careful with him that whenever he was around, we couldn't even speak our normal ebonics. Still feeling for a smoke, though, he decided me and him would share one blunt.

As I sat waiting for the blunt to come back around to me, I looked at Tyree as he took a long pull and exhaled. I watched the twirling wisps of smoke wafting upwards, thick and slow at first, then darting left or right, thinning as they snaked their way overhead, then quickly darting about and dissipating. Peering deeper into the swirl of smoke, I thought I saw the moment of my first sexual encounter, when Aralia opened her legs to take a dick for the first time in her life - it was my first time too. I knew I smiled.

I couldn't tell when or where that vision ended and when the one where I saw Tyree squatting in front of me sitting on the sofa with his dick hanging out one leg of his boxers; I vaguely heard myself chuckle, then heard Tyree saying my name.

Tyree: " you lit tha fuck up, I don't think you even heard me "

For some reason, that sounded extremely funny

- I laughed.

Tyree: " good shit - right? "

I laughed again and responded with a sharp:

Timmy: " yeah "

Tyree: " you sexy as fuck -
you know dat? "

I chortled,

Timmy: " you got a bigazz dick "

That was sudden and completely unexpected.
I'm not even sure I knew why I answered like
that and wondered if the words came from my
mouth.

Tyree: " stand up "

Timmy: " fo' what? "

Tyree: " stand up, I wanna see
somethin' "

I did.

Tyree: " take yo' clothes off "

I did that too - slowly, giggling.

Tyree: " turn around, turn yo'
back .....
                         daaamn ..... put yo'
arms up, above yo' head - yeaaah ...... "

I was easily compliant, and he was perfectly
pleased.

Without warning, he trailed his hand down my
chest while the other held my arm up from
under the pits; he slowly ruffled the hairs there,
causing me to shiver, then slowly trailed down,
now using both hands, to my legs. Moving
from squatting to kneeling, he turned me
around and gently shoved me a few feet
forward, about arm's length;

Tyree: " bend over "

I was again a willing participant.

Tyree: " oooh damn Timmy,
ccccttt aaah! ...... "

He hissed, and palmed my butt cheeks,
spreading them apart. Using a finger, he gently
stroked the hairs around my hole before
suddenly getting to his feet.

Tyree: " stay right there, jus like
dat "

.... he ordered as he reclaimed his seat. I was
looking at him upside down - he was holding
onto his dick, his lips slightly ajar. Finally he
bit his lower lip, then puckered, muttering:

Tyree: " oooh maaan ..... you is
beautiful - I could bust a nutt jus lookin' atchu
"

I straightened myself up and he was off his seat
in a flash, enveloping me in his arms,
suffocating me in his embrace. Showering my
neck and face with kisses and intermittent
words, he panted:

Tyree: " If I never tole you
before .... mmmuah, mmuah, I ...... I ..... muuah
..... love you Timmy Gooden, mmuah, I love
you "

I knew he wanted to fuck, but while I too was
burning with passion, I also knew I couldn't
handle it .... not now, not so soon after the last
time; I was sore.

Timmy: " Tyree, please don't try
to fuck me "

Tyree: " dang son, Why? "

I explained. He showed a little disappointment but then cheerfully said,

Tyree: " come to bed wit me, we gon lie down nikid - if we sleep, we sleep, but I need to feel you up against me "

And with that, we went to the bedroom. It was almost 3:00 a.m., and after cuddling, licking, kissing, and fondling, we finally dozed off.

(Chapter 15)

There was this honey named Charm whom
Ardee used to be with. He had set her up out
there in Virgina just like he'd set up this brother
Marlon after he got out of the Penitentiary and
was wandering around aimlessly - broke,
homeless, hungry, and destitute - he couldn't
even get a job. Only difference was, the
business was really Ardee's and Marlon
received a fixed percentage - the rest was
supposed to be turned over to Charm, who kept
it until Ardee collected it from her.

Marlon had been coming up short for quite
some time and always had some lame excuse,
but reassured Charm that he would pay up by
the end of the next week. After this had gone
on for too long, she'd put Ardee on the alert
because she said she wasn't prepared to
continue supplementing Ardee's take with her
own cash anymore. Ardee told her to continue,
however, and he would always pay her back.
All this happened without Marlon being the
wiser but now, Ardee was ready for his money.

After weeks of prodding from Tyree (since
most of the money was a loan from him), Ardee
finally came up with a plan to get the money
they were owed.

From what he explained, he'd told Charm what he was going to do to get his money back and that he would call her the very moment before he was on his way back there again. In the meantime, she was to ply Marlon with liquor and the promise of her pussy, which he'd been trying forever to get. She was mainly into women but would only, on very rare occasions, go after a man if she really liked him and thought he could put in some good sexual work. When Ardee called, she was supposed to pinch Marlon's cell phone and distract him with herself as the lure.

Ardee chose to make the trip on a dark and dreary Friday, and asked Tyree and me to join him on the trip. We estimated our arrival there very late that same night, at which time he'd call Charm and ask to speak to Marlon.

With three pairs of fresh eyes sharing the driving, we got there about 2:30 a.m. and parked far away from any street lights or lit buildings. Ardee immediately called Charm to let her know; she hinted that at the moment, Marlon was high from smoking weed and drinking cognac. She said he was to the point of falling asleep, but he told her to wake him up so he could speak to him. Ardee put the phone on speaker so that we could hear him as they spoke.

Marlon: " yo, what up ma homie
.... whatz guu ..."

Ardee: " yea, yea, neva mind all
dat shit, this biznizz right here - meet me down
da block next to the restaurant - 'n ... yo, hurry
yo'
                              mo'fuck azz up - aiight
"

Marlon: " aiight B, ama be there
"

Twenty minutes went by and there was no sign
of him. Ardee was getting very antsy. He lit a
cigarette and began filling the truck up with
smoke; Tyree took two from him, lit them and
handed me one. As the truck began to become
overcome with smoke, every now and then I'd
roll my window down to let in some fresh air.
When we finished our cigarettes, Marlon still
hadn't shown up and we were now all edgy.

Ardee: " where tha fuck dat
nigga at? "

Ardee mumbled impatiently.

Just then, Tyree, who was peering into the

dimly lit streets, declared with scorn;

Tyree: " here come his bitchazz
crossin' da street ova there "

Timmy: " about mothafuckin'
time "

Ardee: " knowamsayin' .... look
at his bitchazz, all dressed up 'n blingin' like a
mo'fuckin' starlight - I got news fo' his azz "

Ardee cursed in disgust as he recognized him
struttin' down the sidewalk. Ardee turned his
tail lights on and off quickly, Marlon spotted
us, and then scurried along the sidewalk. Ardee
released the lock as he approached the truck
and rolled his window down. As he
approached and held onto the open window,

Marlon: " whatzup homie? "

Ardee: " what da fuck took you
so long? "

Marlon: " I .... I was .... "

Ardee: " get in, get in "

Ardee ordered impatiently.

As soon as he hopped in, Ardee pulled off, letting in a rush of the cold, fresh night air and dispelling the rest of the smoke from his second cigarette before tossing it out and putting the windows back up.

Having boarded the truck so quickly, I was only able to see this Marlon under direct light for a few seconds before the door closed. As Ardee quickly navigated the strange and traffic-less streets, I caught a better glimpse of him from time to time as we zipped under the street-lights and by some brightly lit store windows, creating a flash camera effect as we zigged-zagged our way out of town.

It was enough to show that he was a grown man in his mid-twenties who I thought was fairly handsome. He had a fresh low-cut and groomed sideburns incorporated into his beard; the facial hairs were separated only by his thick, well-formed lips between them and his moustache. He was about Ardee's height, with a dark chocolate complexion, a gold ring, two long chains around his neck, "ice" on his slim wrist, and two gold-capped upper front teeth. He had a slender body but it was obvious from his open jacket that he'd seen the inside of a gym at least a few times.

So this was the man Ardee and his long-time

acquaintance Dwayne had saved from being raped in prison; this was the man he'd entrusted his money with. Ardee had finished his short and almost juvenile stint, leaving them both in the "Pen"; then when Marlon was released, he'd sought help from Ardee - and got it, only now he wasn't paying him his money and on top of that, had the nerve to be late.

Ardee: " nigga, you know I don't be waitin' fo' nobody "

Marlon: " I know homie but .... "

Ardee: " don't be tryin' to bull shit me nigga, you heard I wuz waitin' "

Marlon: " had to take care of some serious binizz bro, you know how I do "

Ardee: " lissen to this nigga sittin' here lyin' to me ... what! you think am stupid, ... you think I don't know what's goin' on "

Marlon: " I...... I had to put ma clothes on boss .... I wuzn't dressed "

Ardee: " nigga! what did I tell you 'bout dat .... 'BOSS' shit? "

He roared, taking Marlon by surprise. Marlon made a dissatisfied face, then began looking out the window and remained silent from then on. It was just as well, none of us wanted to chit-chat with him.

Ardee was putting distance between us and the city at near mach speed when Tyree said in a calm, low, and raspy voice:

Tyree: " yo, go easy on dat right foot son "

Hardly paying heed to Tyree's warning, as he only reduced speed by about ten miles per hour, we continued on. Except for those few words of caution from Tyree, nobody had spoken since Marlon entered the truck and we had been driving for about twenty minutes now. Suddenly, Marlon spoke up with curious concern:

Marlon: " where we goin'? "

Ardee: " what tha fuck you care .... anyway, we almost there "

He answered in frustration, then opined with cynical satisfaction:

Ardee: " you look like you eatin'

good tho' nigga "

Marlon: " well, you know ..... a
nigga gots to feed hisself ..... keeps workin' it
.... it goin' aiight, knowamsayin' "

Ardee: " I hear dat....good, good,
datz good .... good to know somethin' goin'
right "

Marlon: " but boss, this way
outta ..... "

Ardee: " there you go again
nigga! .... whatz wit all tha talkin' .... you
swallow a radio or somethin' .... you here to
lissen, not run
                              yo' mo'fuckin' mouth
off ...... 'n dat 'BOSS' shit - I tole you, you
need to drop dat shit ..... call me dat one mo'
time 'n .... "

Marlon: "awright, awright, ... am
jus sayin' we way ..... "

Ardee: " nigga, you need to shut
da fuck up - aiight! "

About ten minutes later, Ardee swung hard to
the right, putting us on a dark, lonely dirt road
densely populated with trees on either side. He

453

continued for about another five minutes or so before coming to a stop deep in the thickets overlooking a ravine. He shut the engine off, lit another cigarette, then turned around and looked at Marlon.

Turning his head from side to side and peering out into the darkness as though he was expecting to see someone, Marlon quizzed;

Marlon: " where da biznizz at Black? .... I can't see nobody "

Ardee looked across at Tyree sitting next to him in the front seat and said,

Ardee: " yo, ... homie .... talk to this nigga, tell him how it is "

Tyree: " nigga we ain't here fo' no mo'fuckin' debate "

Tyree snapped, eyeing Marlon with utter disdain.

Ardee: "
WHEREMAMONEYATNIGGA? "

Marlon: " oh, ... that, ... man ... I ..... I been havin' a l'il pro'lem wit some peoples bro, but .... "

Ardee: " nigga, I ain't got time fo' yo' personal affairs; I ain't got no mo' ears fo none o' yo' stories .... man, step outta tha ride"

As Marlon reluctantly stepped out, we all followed - Ardee first; he walked around the front of the truck, to where Marlon was standing a foot away from the truck and went by him. As soon as we began to follow Ardee, Marlon began to look over his shoulder, eyeing us curiously; I know he was anticipating me and Tyree doing him some harm.

At that very moment, Ardee, quite unexpectedly, turned around and threw a powerful right to the side of his head sending him reeling backwards on me. Alert and following all movements carefully, I quickly stepped aside and let him fall. He never saw that move coming either. So much for his anticipation.

Ardee: " get up nigga.... "

Ardee ordered calmly and continued to gloat.

Ardee: " ....whatchu doin' down there? .... come, show me how slick you is "

He staggered to his feet, holding his head, but

couldn't find his balance and ended up tumbling into the side of the truck, holding onto it to steady himself.

Ardee: " ma brand new ride nigga, you bangin' into ma brand new ride "

It was beyond me what Marlon was thinking. Instead of apologizing for having done that, he started complaining - he must have thought he and Ardee were too good of friends and that was the end of it.

Marlon: " that's a sucka punch ..... you neva had to do that bro "

He said, wincing in pain as he staggered to his feet and tried to regain his composure.

Ardee: " well if dat wuz a sucka punch it's 'cause you a sucka motha fucka. C'mon .... put 'em up then, 'n don't be takin' no 'su-cka'
                                        punch like dat, you ain't no pussy - is you? "

Marlon: " we ain't gotta get physical man "

Ardee: " you got ma money witchu nigga? ... a hope so, 'cause if not, you gon pay yo' debt in full tonight - in full "

Marlon: " I ain't got it on me
dawg but ama get .... "

Again without warning, Ardee stepped forward
and gave him a hard uppercut to the solar
plexus. Marlon crumpled at my feet and I
shoved him off with my foot to send him
sprawling on his stomach.

Timmy: " pretty boy messin' up
his clothes? "

A snicker escaped Tyree's lips as he put a hand
to his mouth.

Ardee: " tell me somethin' nigga
.... you fuckin' ma girl Charm? Huh? "

Marlon: " Ardee, I .... we .... "

Ardee: " we mothafucka .... ain't
no 'we' - whatchu doin' ova there this time of
da mornin' dat you gotta go put yo' clothes on,
                         huh? ..... "

Marlon: " we was jus....... "

Ardee: " ..... don't even open yo'
mouth, it only gon be worse fo' yo' azz. Think

457

you a slickazz, don'tchu....after all da shit I done fo'

yo' azz: Findin' you a place to stay, feedin' you, settin' you on yo' mothafuckin' feet so you could eat - 'n puttin' papa in yo' pocket! "

Marlon: " Ardee, I can explain everything to you brotha "

Ardee: " 'brotha' .... "

He hissed;

Ardee: " .... wasn't fo' me, I know yo' azz woulda been back upstate awready bein' some nigga'z bitch - 'n you tryna play me, then turn around callin' me 'brotha' ... I know you know me betta than dat - 'brotha.' Oh, you

musta thought I wuz gone so soft you coulda .... "

Marlon: " no bro, it ain't nothin' like that "

Ardee: " hell yeah it is. So, you be thinkin' you real slick...eh, mothafucka - mmmphhh, yeaah....have dat.. bitch "

Marlon: " owww, no, no....

please .... boss - Ardee, don't hit me no mo'
bro! "

Ardee: " you know what ....
come back ova here "

Marlon staggered forward apprehensively,
covering his lips with his hand. Before he
could get any closer, Ardee ordered;

Ardee: " get ova there - pull ma
nigga dick out 'n slob on dat shit "

Marlon: " c'mon Ardee, you
know I don't be suckin' no .... you know I don't
getz down like ..... "

Ardee appeared calmer now but was beginning
to show a cynical disregard for anything to do
with Marlon's well-being. He suddenly
whipped out his 9 mm from his coat pocket and
waved it menacingly under Marlon's nose as he
spoke.

Ardee: " ama tell it to you like
this here .... nigga, you lucky 'cause ama give
you some choices: One: You polish ma boy'z
knob 'n take
                        some dick. Two:
Take me to ma money - all ma mo'fuckin'
money or - Three: You can collect some a

these here shellz

          as a souvenir............

whatz it gon be? "

Marlon: " why you gon come up
wit somethin' like dat man, ... you know I
don't ..... "

Ardee: " now, now see....datz
how mo'fuckaz like you get shit done to 'em....
stand yo' bitchazz up 'n drop yo' drawz....nigga
you

          missed this back in da
pen but tonight is yo' party, c'mon .... you know
what time it is ..... "

Marlon: " you know I don't gets
down like dat, come on dawg "

Ardee: " what! ..... don't nobody
give a fuck how you do, turn yo' pussyazz up "

Marlon: " come on bro .... that
kinda thing only gon fuck a brotha up "

Ardee: " you done tha same
thing to me ..... after I saved you from bein'
e'rrybody b-i-t-c-h .... "

Marlon: " I know you looked out
fo' me man but, ... no bro, don't do this "

Realizing that Ardee wasn't joking, Marlon fell on his knees and pleaded - but Ardee was deaf to his pleas. Instead, he grabbed Marlon by the chin, squeezed his jaws together, and stuffed the cold 9 mm between his puckered lips.

Ardee: " this whatchu beggin' fo' nigga? .... I can give it to you, ... you know I don't GIVE a fuck "

Marlon tried to speak but the gun was still in his mouth. He decided quickly - tearing away at Ardee's fly and pulling Ardee's dick out while muttering;

Marlon: " datz a low down dirty trick "

Ardee: " nawww bitch, you wrong again: This down low .... a 'Down-Low' dirty trick, but bitches love dat shit "

Me and Tyree had to fight hard not to laugh; that was one funny pun. Even so, Ardee was in no joking mood and he barked another order at Marlon.

Ardee: " Get it! "

Marlon: " Ardee, you know I

can't do this man! "

Ardee: " 'nuff talk, ... SUCK,
m-o-t-h-a fucka! "

Putting the dick in his mouth with disgust,
Marlon's efforts didn't measure up to what
Ardee wanted so he pulled his dick out and
poked the gun in Marlon's nostril.

Marlon: " don't do this to me bro
... don't kill me, pleeze "

Ardee: " you a real pussy....
ain'tchu - rob me o' ma money but can't stand
up. Look at yo' sorry snivellin' no good azz,
you ain't

                         breakin' nobody heart
... this gon be like back up in da big house
nigga;..... but you outta luck, 'cause this time....
you

                         really get fucked ..... yo
dawg, hold ma piece "

He put the safety catch on and tossed the nine
to Tyree, who was groping his hard dick. He
let go, stepped aside, and caught the gun,
bringing his hands down low with it as he
caught it so as to ease the impact of its landing.

Ardee reached in his pocket for a condom and

462

lube, strapped up, and stuffed the bottle of lube in Marlon's trembling hand.

Ardee: " handle yo' bi'nizz nigga, ama be right behind you "

That was cold and outrageously wicked, I thought - making Marlon lube himself up! But then, coming from an irate Ardee, it was no surprise. I knew that side of him - he could be brutish.

I watched as a dejected Marlon loosened his belt - the heavy metal buckle was enough to pull his already sagging, baggy jeans down and they fell compactly to his ankles, revealing his black boxer-briefs with bold "glow in the dark" images.

At first, we couldn't tell what was on it, but since it was glowing in the dark, we were curious. Tyree went for a flashlight, putting the light on at close range so as not to create any great amount of light in the otherwise pitch black night.

A quick look revealed lettering printed along the waistband that read: "PLAYA" ... "WHO'S YO' DADDY" ... and "BAD TO DA BONE" - with the image of a hard dick over the fly. We were amused at his fancy underwear and quietly made fun of them before Ardee gave his last words of warning.

Ardee: " y'all see this Victoria Secret shit this nigga be wearin'.... bitch, pull yo' l'il panties down....bitchazz.... you wuz jus waitin' to
                          get fucked, wuzn'tchu ....'n you better stop frontin' like you don't want this dick up yo azz too .... "

Marlon: " Ardee, am beggin' you man! "

Tyree: " shut tha fuck up nigga - fuck him Black! "

Ardee: " .... so be ready - 'cause we is "

Marlon: " please bro, I know I can't take that "

Ardee: " you ain't gotz to worry 'bout takin' nothin' ...... ama give it to you! "

Ardee was getting cynical and funny at the same time, and he was bent on teaching Marlon a lesson - and I was willing and glad to watch.

Timmy: " burn dat azz B "

Tyree: " about time "

Strapped up and ready to ride, Ardee coldly
demanded:

Ardee: " grab yo' ankles nigga....
"

he taunted as he stepped forward, muttering....

Ardee: " ......I know you gon
love this...... "

.....even as Marlon began to accept his fate with
a soft-spoken prayer as he rubbed his palms
together.....

Marlon: " oh-please-don't-make-
me-die-tonight "

His skinny, long, limp dick was now shriveled
beyond half its normal flaccid size and now
barely able to dangle. Ardee continued his
taunt:

Ardee: " .... yup, yo' drawz got
all kinda fancy shit printed on it but dat azz got
this dick printed all ova it - shit is mine tonight
boi "

Marlon: " come on Black, you
know I ain't down wid that "

Pointless pleas; he was talking to a stone wall,
if not the darkened expanse of the skies.

Ardee: " mmmph,
mmmph...keep still nigga, you think am playin'
- I ain't gon take no mo' shit from you, I jus as
soon put two caps in

                                yo' azz 'n send you ova
dat ravine "

Ardee threatened coldly. Stark fear now
accompanied Marlon's uncomfortable look as
he realized the seriousness of Ardee's threat and
that the moment was finally at hand.

Ardee: " stand yo' bitchazz
up.....fallin' all ova da mo'fuckin' place like tha
drunkazz ho' you is...... "

...... and Marlon begged:

Marlon: " come on Ardee, you
know dat shit gonna hurt "

He whined as he made a face and kept rubbing
his buttocks as if feeling the pain already.

Ardee: " I ain't feelin'

shit......face down - azz up..... you 'bout to get some o' dat upstate Pen fuck up yo' azzhole "

Calmly and deliberately he toyed with him, stroking his dick while looking down, treating the whole thing as a trivial matter. It would have been reasonable for Marlon to conclude that as long as the dick was out, it was an indication that Ardee might just do as he'd threatened; however, he seemed to be entertaining other ideas and begged:

Marlon: " Ardee, ... remember we boyz bro, we can work somethin' out like back in the day bro "

He was referring to when they were both back in the penitentiary. Back then, Dwayne (the guy who had caused Ardee to end up doing some time) had quickly taken Ardee under his wing. Marlon was very young and fresh when he went to prison, the perfect candidate for a jailhouse gang rape. Dwayne and his posse, including Ardee, had spared Marlon that experience by being his protector. If they hadn't, it was a sure thing that Marlon would have been gang-raped and/or made somebody's "Bitch." Knowing Ardee, I think the reason Ardee protected Marlon in prison, and later put him back on his feet when he was released, was probably because he was hoping to fuck him sometime in the future!

Tonight, however, Ardee wanted his money and wasn't in the mood for showing any "love" this time!

Ardee: " there he go again on dat jailhouse penitentiary shit - you mus love dat shit "

Pleading as he held onto Ardee's legs as though taking him in confidence, explaining something to him, he continued:

Marlon: " come on dawg, back in the day ..... "

Ardee: " see now, you still got this shit all twisted ..... this ain't no day, this tha night - 'n I ain't 'back in' in nothin' yet motha fucka "

Ardee calmly ordered:

Ardee: " bend ova mothafucka "

Marlon: " oh dear god - Ardee please man .... "

Ardee: " ohhh, so you a preacher now motha fucka? "

468

Ardee taunted as he placed an open hand on his back and positioned his dick at Marlon's hole.

Tyree: " dat aiight, jus pull dat rod out 'n preach in his azz "

Now it was my turn to snicker. Ardee made a few gentle stabs;

Marlon: " ccct, mmmph, easy Ardee - please! "

Ardee: " if you say ma name one mo' time ama shut you up fo' good "

Marlon: " awright, awright .... ohgod, ohgod "

Ardee: " shut tha fuck up nigga "

Ardee seethed and delivered a sharp jab to his ribs. From then on until the time he finally got his dick in him, the only sounds that came from Marlon were sobs and whimpers.

Looking on, I thought about Aji, and how he'd be livid if he ever knew Ardee was doing something like this. But I couldn't tell him. Surely it would be difficult for me to look Aji in the eye after this. But I had to shake that thought out of my head and concentrate on what was happening here.

After prolonged efforts Ardee dipped low .....

Ardee: " uh-huh ...... yea, yeaah .... "

.... and came up hard, slamming his groin against Marlon's butt.

Marlon: " Fuck!.... aaagh, aaw sssh-i-it man, you gon tear me up! "

He pled as his legs trembled and the branch he was holding onto swayed, causing him to pitch forward and away from the dick. He turned his eyes up to the dark beyond;

Marlon: " please, please, don't do this! "

Ardee was unmoved. In fact, he was all the more furious. He now had his foot on his neck, in a manner of speaking, holding firmly onto Marlon's hips; and as a patch of grey clouds slowly drifted by, a pale but silent moon took a fleeting, unconcerned glance at the proceedings below as Marlon's eyes bulged and he gasped for air. He was on his own, not even the master of the night skies paid heed to him.

Marlon: " aawk, a-aaahh - fuck yo! "

Ardee: " straight from preacher to cussin' like a mo'fuckin' sailor ..... you a piece o' work ain'tchu "

Tyree: " yea, church on Sunday 'n cuss all day Monday "

Marlon: " come on bro, why you gotta say stuff ...... "

Timmy: " you payin' attention to dat? .... thought the dick wuz yo' problem "

Suddenly, Marlon folded like a maiden broodmare.

Marlon: " Haaaaaw! Black ..... "

Ardee: " what? "

Marlon: " why you gotta..... Nghf .... go so deep bro ..... I, ... I do anything for you man, jus pull it out ..... please! "

Ardee: " yeah, - anything? "

It was high drama to me, watching this play

out; I found it amusing and I listened intently.

Marlon: " yeah bro, jus spare me this pain man! "

Ardee: " good, then you take some dick 'n gimmi ma money or you take that last option - dat suicide capsule from ma nine "

Except for low moanings and groanings as Ardee worked his way up into him, grunting like a boar, he was quiet after the reminder of that last option.

Ardee: " yeaah.... you feel dat dick up in yo azzhole?......yeah!...datz whatz up nigga ....don't run - you ain't gon get nowhere.
          Uh-huh, datzwhatamtalkin'bout...oh yeah. I bet you been wantin' some guud dick fo' a long mo'fuckin' time huh... "

Marlon: " a...mmphf .... don't be doin'..... "

Ardee: " shut da fuck up.....stop runnin' bitch ....come get back on the dick - you think this some kinda game am playin' witchu? grab ahold a that dead tree 'cause yo' azz ain't goin' nowhere this time "

472

Marlon: " show some mercy on me Black ....I can't take it no more...... "

Ardee: " what da fuck you know 'bout mercy...shut da fuck up 'n bend ova...pussyazz...pussy good too boi..... "

Marlon: " take it easy bro, am beggin'..... take it easy, you killin' me bro "

Ardee: " nigga you oughta know you ain't gotta beg me fo' shit ..... look what I done gave yo' azz 'n you ain't begged for it "

Much to Ardee's disgust, Marlon continued his weepy begging.

Ardee: " somebody come put a dick in this nigga mouth to make him keep quiet "

Quite unexpectedly, Tyree gave me such a sudden push, I ended up about two steps forward from where I was standing. There I was, standing between him and the action. I looked back at him, realizing what he was indicating. I was apprehensive about it but he further encouraged with a wave of one hand while holding his dick with the other.

Tyree: " go ahead son, get yo'

shit cleaned ..... 'n if you feel any teeth - bust his fuckin' lip "

I thought, ... why not? So I went over there, dick in hand, and stuffed it in his face. I was excited beyond words, my dick was rock hard, and I waved it in his face, wiping the head against his lips. He clenched his teeth and it made me mad that he was rejecting me, so I slapped his face real hard.

Timmy: " bitch suck that dick .... da fuck you think this is "

He reluctantly locked his thick lips around the head of my dick and I shoved forward, peeling the foreskin over between his lips; his mouth was very warm and tantalizing, his tongue so accommodating. He was gagging and Ardee was filling up his back end. The sound of this grown man gasping and groaning, making muffled pleas with his mouth filled with dick had turned me on beyond my wildest imagination.

After letting him suck my dick for some time, I stepped back and stood next to Tyree, leaving Ardee to continue his onslaught on the defenseless Marlon. Minutes later, and quite to my surprise, Ardee called me, motioning with his arms for me to come over, saying:

Ardee: " throw dat shit back
nigga ..... hell no, don't be tryin' to run from this
dick, get back on it, back dat mothafucka up .....
uh-huh, there you go bitch, put dat jailhouse
bi'nizz on dat dick ...... oh yeaah
                        ..... damn! ......
payback's a bitch ain't it .... bet you neva
thought yo' AZZ wuz gon pay fo' all dat slick
shit .... where da fuck you goin'? when I put this
dick on you - stay widdit, mothafucka .... now
come back on da dick nigga "

Ardee gloated and slammed hard into him.

Marlon: " N-Ngha!.......ma azz
bro! "

Ardee: " yo' azz?.....this shit
mine tonight! "

Marlon used a hand to tend to his burning hole.
Examining his fingers as he brought his hand
up, he whined like a fearful pup:

Marlon: " I think you tore...... "

He didn't get to finish his statement....Suddenly
Ardee taunted:

Ardee: " yea - what 'bout yo'

azz? "

Marlon: " don-don't slam me
so..... "

Ardee plunged his curved dick deep into
Marlon with a single, powerful thrust.

Marlon: " ......Aarrggh!....
hard....bro "

Ardee: " what! you teachin' me
how to fuck or somethin'? "

Marlon: " no man but jus show
....Ungh .... ooh-ma-gaawd "

Ardee: "..... mmph ccctt ....
mmmph, damn boi, this azz really need to get
sum dicks. come 'round here pretty thug, ...
you need to come get yo'self some of this tight
azz too. Stay tuned mo'fucka, mo' hits comin'
soon! "

Marlon: " Nngh!,...nghf, u-uh-
oooh ..... please bro, you gon kill me! "

Ardee: " not wit no dick I ain't
..... datz too sweet a death fo' yo' azz "

Marlon: " wo-ooou, woo, ooou -

can't take no mo' - can't take it "

Ardee: " ain't no beggin' gon help you nigga...this what it is...man up 'n back yo' azz up .... ungrateful pussyazz bitch "

I wasn't sure I wanted to do this. But the one thing that I was absolutely sure of, was that I did not want to convey the wrong message to Marlon. There was no way that I wanted him to even begin to think there was any kind of schism between us three - or even that this would be my very first time. I didn't really want to, but I knew they wanted me to, and needed me to help enforce the message. I hoped and prayed that Ardee wasn't going to kill him, but I wasn't going to show weakness by begging Ardee not to, at least not here in Marlon's presence.

Tyree's gentle coaxing in my ear and little nudges did little to help make up my mind about fucking this guy. However, as he shoved me forward and kept up behind me, I took a very deep breath and began to step forward, still apprehensive.

Marlon: " gimmi a break, dawg ..... don't make him do this to me man .... look at him, he jus a kid, please bro"

That sealed my decision and Ardee's encouragement was added incentive.

Ardee: " Ummmm 'kid' huh? - well dat mean you be aiight then - c'mon dawg, don't pay this nigga no mind - get up in dat shit "

I took the condom from Tyree and rolled it on as Ardee continued battering Marlon's hole. So this was it, my first piece of ass - my chance to find out what it feels like!

Ardee beckoned me to get behind him as he started driving his dick harder and deeper into Marlon. A few minutes later, as he worked even harder and faster, his knees began to buckle and he emitted low guttural growls, signifying that he was ejaculating.

As he pulled out, Tyree nudged me again, then shoved me forward, rubbing my back and (away from Marlon's eyes) squeezing my butt cheeks. I summoned up all my courage and I pounced, forcing my four and a half inches thick dick in him with one single thrust! He lunged forward, hollering:

Marlon: " am a man jus like you son ..... show a brotha some mercy man .... please "

Timmy: " it can't be all dat bad nigga, ama do to you whatchu did to ma boyz "

Marlon: " you a nice young man bro, jus a l'il kid 'n am a grown man, please ..... don't do this to me man "

He begged, holding onto and gently squeezing my upper arm. Little did he know that his pleas were falling on deaf ears. I didn't know him, but I knew what he'd done to my friends, after they'd helped him out in such a difficult situation. Besides all that, he had the nerve to call me a "little kid" and thought he could sway my mind. I'd always hated patronizing, and now he was trying to use psychology on me. That really made me decide to give him more of what he'd just got and I told him:

Timmy: " ama give you l'il kid..... this 'kid' dick up in yo' azz is all da mercy you be gettin' from me nigga .... put yo' mo'fuckin' leg up on dat log and lemmi put this dick in yo' lyin' bitchazz .... Mr. Casanova man - you creepin' wit ma boi honey ....

you done fucked her,....right! .... now YOU get fucked bitch! "

479

Ardee:			" yeaaah son bust dat azz open wit dat thickazz dick .... don't pay his azz no mind, I know he lovin' dat shit, he a hoe ....a nasty bitchazz ho'.... 'n you bust yo' nutt on his face too "

Timmy:			" oh ama pay him mind, I know he love attention - you seen 'em l'il panties he be wearin' - Victoria Secret wearin' bitch.
			Can't tell nobody you ain't had no dick after tonight "

Ardee and Tyree chuckled and bumped each other's fists in approval at my sadistic remark. Without trying to be gentle in any way, I got behind him and immediately ripped into him.

Marlon:			" o-uuaahaa, oh-oh, oh gawd...too hard, too hard son ...aaagghh, oh ma gaa...a can't take it, a can't take it "

Timmy:			" you is takin' it bitch "

Ardee:			" oh shit son!, ... yea.... datz it son .... pin dat mo'fucka down 'n bust dat azz open, don't let him run .... yea, dick him			good, ... fuck da dog shit outta him .... ooweee, oh! ohshit, you got him now son "

Oh, this was something else! If I had thought his mouth was warm and tantalizing, then having my dick deep in his butt hole was hot and beguiling! It felt damn good; his butt hole was tight and warm and intoxicatingly sperm-pulling. It reminded me somewhat of my first heterosexual encounter, although there was no tenderness or fragrantly scented bosom involved here! This had a different feel to it that I could not determine completely .... but one thing was for sure, and that was that it was strangely and unusually exciting! I knew that I would not be long in loading this condom.

Tyree was standing a few feet behind me, watching my every move. After a few minutes, he approached me very slowly, then gently, slowly ran his hand down my back, tracing my spine from the back of my neck to my butt, squeezing it briefly before directing a finger at my hole. That sent further waves of eroticism shooting through me, terminating at my dick and butt hole. It left me feeling almost breathless to the point that I thought I was gasping for breath.

He whispered softly but hoarsely:

Tyree: " yeaah son, work dat azz ..... yeaah, datz ma boi, work-dat-azz "

I knew he was referring to my butt and so I worked it all the more while he kept playing with my hole. I tried to capture his finger in my butt hole but he would always elude me, irritating me somewhat. He was freaking me; I had goose pimples all over my body and was wishing he would fuck me right then and there while I was still deep inside Marlon. He wouldn't, and I finally realized that I didn't really want that either; it was just the heat of the moment. However, he did allow me to snare his finger once and when he did, he left me to use my movements to work it in. As he licked the back of my neck, he whispered:

Tyree: " get yo' nutt boy, get dat nutt "

My unavoidable faint whimpers caused him to stop. He was so very perceptive - he was not going to unmask me in the presence of this unsavory character and complete stranger. It wasn't too long, however, before I could feel my cum surging through me as Tyree faced a subdued and wailing Marlon who, by now, must have come to the conclusion that Tyree was about to be getting his too....

But I was about to cum - now - and how .... oh!, how I wished Tyree was buried deep inside me that very instant!

Timmy: " fuck!....cccctt....grrr,
fuck, you 'bout to get a nutt bitch! "

I grunted and emptied my load in him and
slowly pulled away.

By then Tyree was pulling his dick out over the
top of his sweatpants. Marlon took one look at
it and began to sob. He got down on his knees
with his hands clasped, looking up at Tyree
towering over him; he was sobbing like a
whimpering puppy to a totally unmoved and
uncaring Tyree.

Marlon: " Oh my god - brotha,
am beggin' you .... ple-ase, don't put that on me
man .... you seen .... I done took enough
awready
                         .... look how they
done me ..... I know I ain't gon ..... "

Ardee: " yea .... 'n took what
wuzn't yo's; you a taker so take somethin' mo'
now "

Marlon: " spare me just this one
time bro "

Tyree: " you talk a lot, don'tchu!
.... aiight, you can keep talkin' but ama rip this

azz apart, you best believe dat, ama get paid -
'n

get the interest too "

Marlon: " please bro, I ain't gon
manage dat there dick "

Tyree: " ama manage it mo'
fucka, you ain't gots to worry 'bout dat "

He replied coldly as Marlon groveled at his
feet, holding onto both his ankles and
snivelling. Tyree pulled out a condom and held
it between his teeth, putting his hands akimbo
and muttering:

Tyree: " c'mon nigga, wet this
dick up "

Marlon hurriedly began to suck, I suppose in
the hope that might satisfy Tyree. But after a
few minutes, he heard the condom being ripped
open and looked up.

Marlon: " Ohhhh -
Gaaaaaawddamn bro! "

Tyree: " yessir, this what it is "

Tyree proceeded to roll on the condom as
Marlon dropped both palms to the ground and

placed his forehead on them as though he was praying. His sobs were that of a distraught and broken man; he'd finally come to the conclusion that there was no escaping this.....

(Chapter 16)

Finally looking up and seeing the condom-ready hard dick over his head, Marlon now wept uncontrollably. Tyree pulled him up by the collar and growled in a low guttural voice:

Tyree: " remember how it is: face down - azz up, motha fucka ...... you gon show these boys how good you is "

Marlon: " my brotha,.....please, I know I don't even know you but am beggin' you again .... am beggin' you .... look at what you got,

                  you gon hurt me brotha .... dat thing gon hurt me man - lemmi suck your dick, I can suck your dick real good yo .... "

Tyree: " y'all heard dat? ..... he say he a good cocksucka, he jus wanna suck this dick "

Ardee: " fuck dat! "

Timmy: " what da fuck up wit dis nigga!...first he don't suck no dick, now he wantin' to suck dick...da fuck...put da dick in his mouth

dawg, he talk too
mo'fuckin' much.... 'n when you get done - you
tear his azz up too "

Ardee: " see nigga, you ain't got
no friendz out here - rip dat shit dawg "

Marlon: " don't lissen to him bro
.... look at me dawg - yo' two boyz done
fucked me up awready - jus be easy on a
brotha man, ama suck
                    yo' dick for you "

Tyree: " you got this shit
twisted nigga, I ain't here to lissen to nobody -
'n I ain't yo' fuckin' bro-tha. Now you gon suck
                    this dick like a good
boy 'n then ama tear dat azz open "

He readily jumped on the dick, sucking and
slobbing like he knew his life depended on it;
Tyree was pleased with his performance.

Tyree: " .... yeaah, suck dat
shit...uh huh...swallow it...swallow dat
mo'fucka...da fuck! - whatchu coughin'
for...put dat shit back in
                    yo' mouf ..... and take it
all da way to da back of yo' throat...yea, go
down...deepa...all da way down mo'fucka.
Whoo - this

nigga ain't no joke....
boy can suck some mothafuckin' dick! "

Tyree only had him on his dick for a short
while before he roughly shoved him off, wiping
the dick all over his face and telling him to stick
out his tongue. Then he used his dick to beat
Marlon's tongue.

He then rolled on the condom and told me to
toss Marlon the lube. I tossed it on the ground
and watched in silent amazement as this grown
man wept like a child - but still had to bend
over and pick it up, snivelling and sobbing,
muttering about his dread of what he saw Tyree
would be using to pound him. As if that wasn't
demeaning enough, he had to apply the lube to
his own already well beat up butt....

Tyree: " TURN YO' AZZ UP
BITCH - 'n shut da fuck up,.....my turn now "

Marlon: " am begging bro, ...
don't do me like dat, am a man jus like yo'self "

Tyree: " I know you ain't like
me motha fucka, ... datz why you gon have
this dick up yo' azzhole "

Surely now, in spite of all his pleas, Marlon
must have resigned himself to his unpleasant

488

fate.

As soon as Tyree had put the condom on, he shoved Marlon over and forward, positioning himself behind him with his dick in hand. I closely watched his movements as his butt tightened - once, twice, thrice, a fourth time, and then he slammed his body up against Marlon.

Marlon let out a sharp, long, frightening yelp and ended up on one leg, on his toes, trying to balance himself. Were it not for the fingers of both hands touching the log, with the other leg fully extended behind him and past Tyree, who still had him held firmly by the hips, he looked like a clumsy ballerina. It was a laughable sight but I managed to control myself.

Tyree: " do it hurt?.... huh, do it hurt - bitch? "

Marlon couldn't speak, he was gasping and trying to raise himself back up. As he settled his hands on the fallen log, his arms now began to shake violently.

Tyree: " nigga, you better not go back down again "

Tyree had rammed him so hard with that one

thrust, his dick was about halfway in. Marlon rose slowly; he was midway up but unable to support himself on his arms; nor could he stand his ground - his legs were extremely wobbly, too wobbly to stand on. But Tyree pounded a fist on his back, indicating that he should lower himself a bit. He was slow in getting there and Tyree leaned over on him, transferring his weight onto Marlon's back. Crossing his arms with a change of hold, he slammed into him again;

Marlon: " A-Aarrrgh! - Ohgod......oh gaaawd, go easy on me bro, am hurtin' "

Timmy: " shut tha fuck up "

Ardee: " yea, yakkin' like a l'il bitch - fuck the shit outta him! "

Tyree: " hear dat nigga ...... you can moan 'n groan as much as you like but - one mo' word outta you 'n ..... "

Those words served as great impetus, and to say he was mercilessly pounded by Tyree would be putting it mildly; Tyree dug into him, plowing him like virgin earth and as he disobeyed and uttered his first word, Tyree punched him in the rib.

Tyree: " a-a-aah, you talkin'
again nigga "

As he was assaulted again, he remained
wordless, but not silent;

Marlon: " mmmm-oow!, ... OO-
Ooo - phew, phew......pheeew "

Tyree had struck again;

Marlon: " uhm-mheee ......oow "

and again;

Tyree: " datz it pussy, - meow
"

Marlon: " Ga-aaaw-engh, ohmnn
.... ghn, ghn .... "

and yet again;

Marlon: " Mu-Mmm-oooo "

Timmy: " oh shit, he raisin' up
tha whole fuckin' farm "

He was actually trying to stifle his sounds;
that's what made him sound like a domesticated

animal. He made just about every conceivable sound, trying not to utter a word. Well, even if he wasn't an animal, between the three of us, we were going to tame him tonight!

Tyree held him firmly by his waist, supporting him, but Marlon was still wobbly and appeared to be dead weight. This was a different side of Tyree, one I'd never known. He was so cold, calloused, and completely unmoved by Marlon's beseeching.

Marlon: " you gon kill me brotha ..... I told you I couldn't take that thing man... "

Tyree wasn't responding to anything he said. He was suffering but to be truthful, he wasn't getting all that Tyree could give. Tyree loved to throw you on your back and get on top of you but this wasn't lovemaking, it was revenge - a vengeance fuck. And he was getting it on his feet. But still he couldn't handle it and would, every now and then, beg like a sniveling bitch.

Marlon: " ...... uh, mmmphf .... I got a son and a baby girl man, don't do me like this ..... you gon kill me "

Tyree: " y'all come hold this motha fucka down 'cause he actin' like a fuckin' tired camel "

Ardee: " I oknow why dat
mo'fucka keep squattin' like a bitch - somethin'
wrong wit yo' legs nigga? "

Tyree: " turn it up nigga,
....head down, grab yo' ankles 'cause am about
to get ma moneys worth.... you can holla as
much as you

         want but you gon get
this dick...uh huh,...erry which way up in dat
azz.... datz what you need - a man to climb up
in yo'

         back "

Marlon: " mm-mm-mmf .... go
easy bro, take yo' time .... easy,
please......aaahgrrr .... mmph, oh, oh, ooooh .....
haw, haw, oh, ha, ha .....

         ooohhaaa ..... ooh shit
..... Fu-u-uck! .... oh .... "

Tyree: " some good dick -
right? "

Marlon: " oooh.... ha, ha, haaw....
ngh, ayi, ayi .... mmmmm O-ooooh! Oh god!
ma azzzzzzz "

Tyree: " bwoi if yo' daddy could

see you now ..... big ole dick up in yo' azz hole.... "

Ardee: " 'n he lovin' it too "

Tyree: " mmm...uh huh, yea, stay right there nigga...ama make this azz talk to-night...ohh yeaaah, keep it right there mo'fucka...yea

                    bitch, this what I want...right there... "

Marlon: " Ayiiieeeee, whoooo, ...Nghffuhm "

Ardee: " yea, stifle dat fuckin' hollarin' "

Tyree: " yea motha fucka mmphhhh...yeaaa datz what am talkin' 'bout....don't run, turn dat pussy out "

Marlon: " wha-aiiiiee, mmm, mmm, mmph, ... lemmi rest a minit bro "

Tyree: " motha fucka, this ain't no game "

We watched as Tyree dominated his victim, drilling a larger hole behind him than he already had. When Marlon fell to his knees,

Tyree stayed with him, riding him as a jockey would a horse. He was clawing at dirt, and his forehead was where his hands were, in the dirt. He was weeping and writhing in agony but Tyree was nailing him every which way he went. It was, as they say, "poetry in motion" watching as the artfully adept and agile Tyree maneuvered and outcrafted Marlon's every little means of not getting the full impact of the dick; it was like a cat toying with a mouse. I could almost feel pity for him; he was, after all, under great duress. Still, he had only himself to blame.

Tyree: " get on yo' feet, stand up wit me .... don't lose dat dick or ama have to fuck you up .... damn, this mo'fucka azz pullin' da
                    rubber offa ma dick "

They came up together slowly, Tyree's arms around his waist, pulling him up. When Tyree told him to put one leg on the nearby dead log, he could barely manage to lift a leg up. With one side of his face pasted to Marlon's back and his arms locked around his stomach, Tyree dipped low and came up grinding, moving smoothly like a belly dancer. tossing his hips from side to side as he grinded into Marlon's hole, twisting it with each sideways movement. Each time Tyree did a slow grind, coming up hard and slamming into him, Marlon would wail.

At one point he raised up off Marlon's back and stood straight behind him, delivering five or six violent stabs as Marlon hacked and spluttered....

Marlon: " A-Ahk-k-k! twhoo, wh-o-ooooo "

......and Tyree jeered.

Tyree: " yea motha fucka, take dat dick! "

Marlon's body slumped in near lifeless fashion.

Marlon: " O-o-ooh - ohgaawd "

Tyree: " I know you like dat bitch "

Marlon: " Nooo bruh! "

Marlon was on his tip-toes; his mouth was wide open and a thick trail of silvery saliva was streaming from one corner of his mouth. His quivering fingertips were barely touching the log he was supposed to be using for support; Tyree had gripped and held him so firmly, pulling him back against his groin. He tightened his butt cheeks and remained buried deep beyond Marlon's tight resisting hole.

Marlon: " spare me!,......spare me bro..... "

He begged, but Tyree only made fun of him all the more, throwing caustic, sarcastic, yet amusing phrases at him.....

Tyree: " datz what am doin' motha fucka! "

.....moving from a vexingly slow but punishing rhythm to rapid grinding and stabbing as he penetrated the depths of Marlon's now well-worked and tired butt hole. The man knew how to fuck; even his beautiful and envious moves could devastate or delight and as his feet began to shuffle from one position to another I knew he was about to release his load. Further assurance came when Marlon began to wail in pain, talking drivel:

Marlon: " aah, aah, ooooh...aawk...ahk...... don't put it back in there bro or you gon kill ......Ohoɔ-ooW..... ama de-ead man now .....
                                        ooowwee, ayii, who gon take care a ma kidz...... Kiki ..... aarrrrgghh - dear god he gon kill me "

Tyree: " yeaaah, this wha you need mo'fucka...don't think I ain't gon bruise this azz....ccctt fuck yeah "

Marlon: " ma, maa, aagh.....Kiki, Kiki.....aaarrghh, ooh, ooh, ooh, o-o-h....o-oooh, mmm mmphf - A-ay...haaaw - ka, ka aagh.....one a ya'll help me....help me!....y'all - he gon kill me! "

Tyree: " you 'fraid o' dyin' bitch - don't fret, this tha best way you gon die then "

Marlon: " aaag-ga-gaaaah!....m-mmpf mmm....ohgawd, ohgawd, ohgawd.....ogaw........ma, maaaw.......I can't take....no mo' - bro..... "

Tyree: " YO MOMS! - whatchu callin' yo mama 'n yo bitch fo'...you want them come see you wit a bigazz dick wedged up in yo' l'il

         azz hole?.... yeaah, they woulda been proud of yo' azz tho' 'cause they already know you a fuckin' faggot... "

Marlon: " ooohh...gaaaww...brotha man...phew, phew...aaaaawww....don't put it back there bro...plu--eeze .....lemmi .... lemmi ....

aaaarrghh .... gimme a chance to breathe bro...ama... "

Tyree: " courteous bitch .....jus lissen to yo'self....a real l'il pussy....hold still....lemmi bust yo' l'il azzhole up; yo mama nor yo' bitch
                    can't help you now 'PLAYA' .... play this,..... who's bad to tha bone now, uh - mothafucka? "

Marlon: " Mercy.....mercy, mercy bro.....ooh GAAA....oh, oh - aaaagghk, oh my Gaawd "

Tyree: " get da fuck up 'n come pull this condom off bitch! You lucky as fuck tonight, ma boi ova there ready fo' anotha round - but
                    he got otha shit on his mind, he 'bout dat papa now...hurry up...now slob ma shit...wash it off.... "

Marlon: " but, but...you got cum all ova..."

Tyree: " 'n datz why I tole you to wash dat shit off Bitch......put it in yo' mouf - yea, you wash dat shit off real good....uh huh...
                    now swallow dat shit,

cum-bag.... "

He made a face and closed his eyes, but he was
obedient; he swallowed, at least, I thought so.
Tyree demanded;

Tyree: " open yo' mouf.......what
dat you got in there - swallow
mothafucka!...drink alla dat shit up........ "

Marlon quickly gulped it down as Tyree stood
over him with both fists at the ready.

Tyree: " yea, ...nasty-azz trick
"

Suddenly, Marlon made a gurgling sound, and
Tyree spun around .....

Tyree: " nigga, ... do dat 'n it be
yo' last vomit "

Ardee: " bust a cap in his mouf,
dat'll make dat nigga swallow "

Marlon: " NO!...no......see,
see,........it's gone! "

he quickly assured, opening his mouth wide.

Tyree: " yo gimmi a bottle of

water, this mo'fucka got dirt all ova me "

I handed him a bottle of water and he washed his dick and hands. As I handed him the hand sanitizer, Ardee told Marlon:

Ardee: " clean up bitch, get dressed, we goin' into town - 'n hurry da fuck up "

Timmy: " yea, we got a date "

Ardee: " 'n he ain't gettin in ma ride wit no dirt "

I tossed him a bottle of water and put a roll of paper towels on the dead log next to him, got in the truck and watched as he feebly tried cleaning his butt but stopped short and plopped himself down on the log, exhausted with his head hung limply to the side.

Ardee: " don't try testin' me no mo' nigga...I promise you won't love dat shit...what you need to do is get yo' mo'fuckin self
                      together 'n clean yo'self up 'cause you ain't getin' in ma ride smellin' like da pussy dat you is "

Slowly, and with great care, he got to his feet

and finished cleaning himself with the tissue and water, then ambled over to the truck where Ardee growled:

Ardee: " where yo' bank at...we goin' there "

Marlon: " on Third... Third....mmm...... "

Ardee: " is you stallin' motha fucka? "

Marlon: " No! ... no, Third 'n da corner.....mmmhh...corner 27th and Third.... "

It was obvious to me that Marlon was in great distress, and he could hardly sit comfortably. And although I think I had the slightest feeling of pity for him, I knew nobody else gave a damn. No one spoke during the ride into town as Marlon lay crumpled on the middle row seat, holding his stomach with both hands as though he was about to vomit. Ardee drove to the middle of the block on 27th and parked on the opposite side of the road.

We waited a couple hours and as soon as the bank was opened, Ardee took an empty back-pack from under his seat.....

502

Ardee: " what da fuck you waitin' fo' nigga...this why we spend da whole night here, no mo' waitin'...now, hurry yo' azz ova there 'n bring me ma money........you think am playin' - get movin' bitch! "

Marlon swallowed hard, got out, and walked off, crossing the street with a clumsy, shambling gait and entered the bank. Tyree followed a little distance behind and went into the bank, stopping at the front desk and pretending, I think, to be filling out one of the bank's withdrawal forms.

As we sat alone in the truck, Ardee looked back at me through the rear view mirror and when I caught his gaze, he confided:

Ardee: " Timmy,......me 'n you...we cool, right? "

Timmy: " no doubt son, no doubt...you ain't got to ask dat "

Ardee: " aiight, aiight....then don't say nothin' to Aji 'bout wha happen tonight...aiight "

Timmy: " pshaw...don't even trip son...it ain't no thang "

That being said we remained silent.

We weren't able to see Marlon too clearly through the glass, but with Tyree present, we didn't worry. There weren't many customers and we wondered why it was taking so long; then we saw Tyree get up and walk deeper into the building. Twenty two minutes later, Marlon was walking out the door with Tyree close behind - the back-pack on his back.

Tyree barked an order at him and he immediately quickened his gait to get across the street and enter the truck. Tyree followed quite leisurely and joined us in the truck, showing no sign of excitement.

Tyree: " we got da goods son, I count dat shit ma self.... twenty gran. Yo this nigga got ova forty G's in dat bitch - I made him take

                    out half - he prolly got mo' accounts all ova da mo'fuckin' place too "

Timmy: " shiiit... 'n this nigga tole us he ain't got dat much up in there "

Ardee: " lyin' mo'fucka, you really think you slick, don'tchu nigga.....all dat shit you ran by me.... Dwayne got yo' money 'n won't pay

you - but you gon get
it. You is one ungrateful mo'fucka......after all I
done fo' yo' azz, am da first nigga you should
think

'bout payin' - think I
wasn't comin' back fo' ma money! "

He continued:

Ardee: " lyin'azz mo'fucka.
You lissen up real good, ama be back up here at
the end of tha month...'n that time - you come
up short

on me again...'n ama
show you somethin'. Ma money gon be
accordin' to da books...dat mean yo' funeral
plans postponed - but you eva come up short
on me any mo'fuckin time
again...jus...once........well, I ain't gotz to tell
you nothin' mo' -

you read da rest. Now
get da fuck outta ma truck "

Ardee warned, pointing a finger at him even as
he started the engine and shifted into drive.
Having accomplished the mission, we
immediately hit the road for New York City,
leaving Marlon standing alone on the
pavement.

(Chapter 17)

Back home, at last! I felt like I'd been gone for a whole week. The sound and smell of a noisy, bustling New York City was like music to my ears. I guess it's just the fact that it was - home. Ardee and myself decided to crash at Tyree's but before we could get off to sleep, Pete called:

Pete: " 'sup, son...dang, it's like you don't live here no more......I don't even see you no mo'...you aiight.... where you at? "

Timmy: " Tyree's...but yo, Pete, am dead beat, I need to get some sleep, I'll holla lata...aiight "

Pete: " I knew datz where you wuz... can I come ova there later this evenin when I get done here? "

Timmy: " yea .... aiight, lata son "

I jumped in the shower right after the call and was joined a couple minutes later by Tyree. We were in the shower for several minutes when Tyree started to scrub my back. Then I did his and as I started to rinse myself off, he hugged me from behind, pressing his hard body against my soapy butt and to grind on it for a moment.

Kissing the back of my neck gently, he spoke for the first time - a very soft baritone serenely penetrating the realm of my daydream as the shower's rain cascaded, falling first on his head and shoulders, then down to me, pooling in a steady, soapy stream in the center of my back and down to my legs.

Tyree: " tired gorgeous? "

Timmy: " yeaah, l'il bit "

I muttered, as I raised my hand above my head, happily and contentedly palming the back of his neck as he leaned over my shoulder, sinking his chin in my clavicle.

Ardee: " y'all betta not be startin' no shit in there...remember yo' boi out here need to take a shower too "

Ardee shouted jovially, awakening me - I smiled, even from deep within. I was done anyway, so I stepped out of the shower and took a towel, leaving Tyree to finish. As I headed through the bathroom door, I saw Ardee naked, smiling with his hard dick in his hand, about to enter the bathroom. He looked at me in astonishment:

Ardee: " oh shit!...so you can walk 'round naked now...you ain't shy no mo' nigga?..... "

Timmy: " ppshaw! "

Ardee: " Daayum! .... boi you got a phat hairy booty .... "

Timmy: " dat all you can see? "

Ardee: " don't be givin' me no sass boi, jus take the compliment - uh huh ..... now I see why Blaze wouldn't stop till he gotchu "

Timmy: " whateva "

I replied proudly but nonchalantly as I continued to dry myself off.

Ardee: " damn, a nigga ain't scurred no mo' "

Timmy: " am a grown azz man mo'fucka ... I ain't scared of yo' eyes...now get outta ma way wit yo' big ole rustyazz dick "

508

I replied, laughing, and as Ardee entered the bathroom he asked Tyree:

Ardee: " tha fuck you done to dat l'il nigga dawg?...you done turned him da fuck out, boi walkin' 'round buttazz nekid 'n am in da
                    house.....a can't believe dat shit. Damn son, dat boi even finer than a mo'fucka when he nekid "

Tyree: " datz ma shawty "

He boasted;

Ardee: " you seen them abs on him since you got him doin' them crunches 'n push-ups...damn! "

Tyree: " you peepin' ma shawty dawg? "

Ardee: " shawty look gooder than a mo'fucka "

Tyree: " finer than wine dawg, all ova - 'n mine too "

Ardee: " you can't blame a brotha fo' lookin' - not at somethin' like dat "

Tyree: " no, ... but remember, you got phoineazz Aji "

Ardee: " c'mon now dawg...am jus sayin'....dat boi a heartbreakin' dick-raiser... if he wuzn't yo' peeps, I swear I woulda gone after him "

Tyree: " you been seein' him comin' up in tha park alla time "

Ardee: " yea, but he wuz so little 'n .... "

Tyree: " you wuz blind, besides ...... it wuzn't fo' you "

Ardee: " whateva .... but damn, you don't see how dat flat stomach accentuate his hairy bubble butt .... boi got his daddy booty "

Tyree: " damn dawg, ama have to start coverin' him up whenever you come 'round here"

It was pleasing to my ears but even so, I pretended otherwise.

Timmy: " I can hear everything .... y'all need to get offa my dick "

Ardee: " aaaw fuck you bwoi ....
but you know what am sayin' Black "

They showered and came out together birthday
naked, Ardee in front with Tyree close behind,
dicks hard and towels over their heads. Ardee
stopped in the center of the living room, bent
over, and started to dry his legs when Tyree
came up behind him, grabbed him by the waist,
and began to gyrate against his butt.

Ardee: " tha fuck! .... dang
dawg, whatchu tryin'a do! You mean I can't
trust you 'round ma azz no mo'? "

Tyree: " not if you keep bendin'
ova in front o' me like dat, I could see all them
l'il hairs 'round dat booty hole "

Timmy: " son, you shoulda tore
into dat azz right there ....it was still wet "

I chuckled, looking at Ardee.

Ardee: " datz fucked up, you
tryin' to have yo' boi fuck me "

Timmy: " hell yeah, you got a
booty too "

Just as he was about to raise up, Tyree looked at me, grinned, and gave me a wink. I caught on immediately and nodded; he grabbed Ardee from behind and started to search for his butt hole with a finger.

Ardee: " Yo! Black! "

Tyree: " don't fight me son, lemmi feel dat cherry "

I laughed uncontrollably as they fought and ended up on the area rug. As big, muscular, and powerful as Ardee was, he was no match for Tyree, who succeeded in poking a forefinger up his butt hole.

Ardee: " A-Aaaaarrrrgghhhh! ..... "

Tyree slapped his butt cheek hard, then teased;

Tyree: " booty hole tight boi "

and released him.

Ardee: " what da fuck dawg, ... dat wuzn't funny "

Remembering my incident, I asked rather calmly;

Timmy: " how come? "

I laughed and went to the bedroom.

Pouting in embarrassment, Ardee blared:

Ardee: " I better not hear this
outta Aji mouf "

I laughed again and I threw myself on the bed
to sleep. Tyree came in soon after and the last
thing I recall was Tyree snuggled up behind me
with his hard dick like he wanted to poke me
but I just fell asleep.

I have no idea how long I was asleep, but I was
awakened by strange sounds of people in the
living room. Tyree wasn't in bed and I
wondered where he might be so I got out of bed
and quietly made my way to the bedroom door
where I heard Tyree, Ardee and Pete talking in
whispers. At first, I thought they were trying
not to wake me, but as I listened, I got the
feeling something funny was going on.

Pete: " Tyree, you got anything
like - juice? "

Tyree: " I can't even remember
what in dat fridge .... go see whatchu can find "

Ardee: " yo, son .... l'il nigga
look all grown up now ..... you seen all dat
booty he got saggin' outta 'em tightazz jeans -
damn! some nigga
                             bound to try 'n hit dat
azz "

Tyree was non-commital. I thought that was
most noble and very respectful of him but
knowing him, I didn't expect anything less.
Ardee kept up the subject and I thought that
must have made Tyree very uncomfortable but
he was saved by the bell when Pete asked from
the kitchen:

Pete: " Tyree...come
here...whatz this... in the jug...ama have... "

Tyree got up and went toward the kitchen
saying,

Tyree: " naw, naw .... datz ma
power drink...you can have one of these
cranberry/apple juice tho' "

Pete: " ugh...dat thing taste
nasty, can I have one of these frozen fruit bars
instead? those good "

Tyree: " they Yani's but, ...

yea, go ahead "

I decided it was time to make my presence known. I opened the door and was greeted by a big hug from Pete who leaped from his seat as soon as he saw me.

Pete: " dang...wuz you hibernatin'....I thought you was gon stay in there foreva; you remember I tole you I was comin' over, right! "

Timmy: " I ain't forgot...I was madd tired son, I jus fell out...fo' real. So whatz good "

Pete: " nothin'...I jus wanna chill witchu fo' a while, I don't be seein' you like...you know "

Timmy: " we here now so it's all good "

Tyree: " dang, son...you fell da fuck out...you wuz tired "

I was, more than I'd realized.

Sitting next to Ardee in the sofa, Tyree was mainly silent. I sat at his computer desk while Pete sat across the room in the chair I usually sit on, unnecessarily slurping and licking the fruit bar as he eyed Tyree. That "come on" did not escape an astute Ardee who was flashing glances at Tyree, who pretended not to have noticed Pete. I was peeved but maintained my composure so as not to cause any kind of unpleasantness.

This continued for several minutes before Ardee made an excuse, saying he wanted to talk to Tyree about something very private. They got up and went into the kitchen where Ardee began to talk eagerly in a subdued tone. I was only able to hear a few words here and there at the beginning, but I picked up enough to know that Tyree was being pressed about Pete's sexual status. As they continued, their voice levels raised a bit and sitting that close to the kitchen, I was able to get the full scope of it.

Ardee: " c'mon dawg, I know you seen how L'il Thug wuz lickin' on dat pop - lookin' atchu "

Tyree: " what is you talkin' 'bout Black?..... "

Ardee: " ha-ha-haaw c'mon son, it's me - Ardee - yo' boi, talk to me "

Tyree: " I been tole you

awready "

Ardee: " stop playin' B "

Tyree: " we ain't DID nothin' -
'n I ain't seen nothin' "

Ardee: " aiight, then look me in
ma eye, ... c'mon, look "

Tyree: " this some bull shit, ...
nigga, will you let go o' ma head; know what, I
ain't even gonna .... "

Ardee: " ha-ha-ha-haaw, yes you
do motha fucka, 'cause you know I ain't gon
stop till you tell me - you hittin' it - right? "

Tyree: " Ardee, I tole you - I
ain't did nothin' wit him "

Ardee: " don't even lie like dat
dawg, I know you better than dat .... "

Tyree: " you don't know shit! "

Ardee: " oh yea! ..... y'all did
shit, if you ain't fucked - then he slobbed yo'
shit ..... dat l'il nigga know what time it is ....
c'mon, talk to me
                       son - what went

down? "

Tyree: " jus fo'get dat shit 'n leave it alone. Dawg .... you know sometimes dat boi be actin' like he on somethin' "

Ardee: " not like this B, ... this plain as day. 'N now you tryin'a make a nigga feel like he delusional "

Tyree: " you mus be, lissen to yo' self "

He had Tyree in a spot and I didn't know if he could work his way out of it. Ardee was going to be persistent to the limit; when it came to something like this, that's how they both were and he knew that Tyree was lying.

Ardee: " uh-aaw, dat line ain't gon work, I know what I seen "

Tyree: " you need glasses or somethin', ain't shit happen' nowhere "

Ardee: " it's aiight dawg, I see you hidin' somethin' ..... you can't tell me nothin', I know what I seen - 'n you seen it too but, what is you

           hidin' from yo' boi ..... c'mon son - cough "

Tyree: " ain't nothin' to cough up, ... yo' imagination is as wild as Yani's "

Ardee: " now datz cold, you tryin' to make yo' boi look like a novice ..... know what ama do? ..... ama step to him ma'self, ama ask him "

Tyree: " nigga, you can ask him whateva you want, dat don't change nothin' "

Ardee: " B, it woulda been good fo' you if you wuz a good liar - dat way, I woulda brush tha whole thing off but - no, somethin's up "

Now Tyree was trying a different tactic; moving from the "ask him if you want because there's nothing to find out" to "look at how stupid you'll look when you find out you're wrong "

Tyree: " I ain't gon be tha one lookin' like no fool "

Ardee: " damn, I wish Timmy didn't wake up so soon "

Tyree: " you gon drop dat shit now? "

Ardee: " o-ho! - see, you gettin'
worried now. Somehow I'm not swallowin' this
- you really want me to ask him dat dawg? ....
you know
                    I don't know him like
dat .... "

Tyree: " I ain't tole you to ask
him shit! "

Ardee: " dang, if only it wuzn't
fo' Timmy, I'd ask him right now - real talk,
'cause I'd bruise dat l'il azz 'n hope Aji don't
find out nothin' "

Tyree: " well, fo'get dat shit
then "

Ardee: " I swear you lyin' - 'n I
ain't droppin' shit "

Tyree: " can we go now? "

Ardee: " dang son, why you
findin' it so hard to talk to yo' boi ..... what tha
fuck happen? "

Tyree wouldn't tell him anything but that only
prompted Ardee to push him harder and try to
get to the bottom of it.... no pun intended. I

swear, sometimes I felt like I could strangle that Pete! With his mind now fully made up that he was correct, he began to attack Tyree from yet a different angle:

Ardee:　　　　　　　　" Whoa! ..... you fuckin' both of 'em - tha two brothaz! Yo, I done did some shit in ma time but yo, ... you ...... is one slick motha
　　　　　　　　fucka, ama give you dat "

The silence indicated that Ardee was waiting for a definite "yes" or "no" but when Tyree still stood his ground, he threatened:

Ardee:　　　　　　　　" well you gon have to fight ma azz but ama sure as hell gon tell him dat you tole me he down "

Tyree:　　　　　　　　" oh c'mon dawg .... don't do no shit like dat .... 'taint even nothin' like whatchu thinkin' "

Ardee:　　　　　　　　" then you ain't got nothin' to lose "

Tyree:　　　　　　　　" you cause any shit between me 'n ma shawty - me 'n you gon have it out "

Now he was satisfied.

Ardee: " you hittin' it - 'n yo'
boi know! ..... dang! "

Tyree: " can we drop this
subject now bro. What we need to do is deal
wit dat papa, we ain't been into it since we been
back "

They returned from the kitchen with Ardee
eying Pete more than ever as Pete continued his
shenanigans. He was my brother whom I loved
dearly, but if he was trying to have Tyree again,
it was not going to happen .... not by any
means. I decided to put a stop to it right away.
I snatched him by the arm and took him to the
privacy of the bedroom.

Timmy: " Pete.....what is wrong
witchu, why is you actin' like a little ...... "

Pete: " what!...... whaddid I do
now? "

Timmy: " you know damn well
what you done, you need to stop dat shit. Datz
what you came ova here fo'?.... "

Pete: " why you buggin'....I
ain't did nothin' "

Timmy: " 'n you ain't gon do
nothin'. Lissen up, if this how you gon be, then
you can't come ova here no more...ya heard "

Pete: " see........you don't even
want me to have no fun no more "

Timmy: " don't even try dat shit,
you ain't gon run dat little brotha shit on me wit
this....look!, don't make me mad Pete, do not
make
                         me mad "

Pete: " but what if he like
me...what if.... "

Timmy: " what if who like you? "

I was about to completely lose it;

Pete: " Ardee, he, ... you
know, he down? "

I was damned sure he was not having Tyree and
neither was I about to condone him fucking
with Aji's man, at least not in my presence. I
would do all I could to prevent it. But then
again, this wasn't my house, and if Tyree wasn't
going to stop them I'd leave it at that, but I'd
definitely tell Pete to leave. I knew what would

happen because I saw the look in Ardee's eyes
and, while Tyree would refuse him I was
damned sure Ardee, with that rape look in his
eyes, wouldn't.

I think I did lose it, I poked him in his chest
hard with a forefinger;

Timmy: " you done lost yo' damn
mind. Come, get tha fuck home "

Pete: " but am not ready yet "

Timmy: " whatchu mean you
ain't ready yet - bounce "

He suddenly pulled his already almost halfway
off trousers down to his thighs and sat on the
edge of the bed; then folded his arms across his
chest and sat back, pouting and adamantly
declaring:

Pete: " you can't make me
leave, it ain't yo' house "

Timmy: " tha fuck! "

I roared, raising my hand to slap his face,

Pete: " you can't hit me, if you
hit me ama hit you back "

I couldn't believe my ears; he was never, ever defiant with me like that before.

Timmy: " Bounce - Now! "

Pete: " No! .... you can't make me leave "

Timmy: " Like hell I can't "

I grabbed him by the arm and was pulling him out into the living room, trousers at his ankles and all, when Tyree and Ardee came rushing toward the door;

Tyree: " what happenin'...why y'all fightin' dawg,.... keep it down "

Timmy: " y'all need to talk to this boi right here.....he done lost his fuckin' mind buggin' out on me... datz what happenin' "

Ardee was quick to jump in and hold Pete as he fought desperately to rid himself from my grip. Both Tyree and Ardee spoke at the same time,

Tyree: " wha happen? "

Ardee: " why you fightin' big brotha son? "

But before trying to answer, I was pulling Pete back toward me. Ardee grabbed and held him from behind in a sort of "Bear Hug" and Pete started to wiggle ...... but he wasn't really trying to free himself, he just wanted to rub his brief-clad butt against Ardee's groin.

When I saw that, I reached across and slapped his face; he began to swing wildly at me and I evaded his hands and grabbed his collar; Tyree held me immediately.

Tyree: " calm down Timmy, ...
calm down "

Pete was struggling in Ardee's grip, trying to get back at me. When he couldn't, he yelled;

Pete: " You can't make me
leave "

Tyree: " what? "

Pete: " he say I can't stay here,
..... I can stay if I want - right? "

Tyree: " I don't get it, whatz all
this 'bout? "

Pete: " jus 'cause ..... "

Timmy: " if you eva say a word - I swear ama kill you. Pull yo' fuckin' pants up "

He wouldn't, and stayed glued to Ardee.

Tyree: " pull yo' clothes up L'il Thug "

As he bent over to pull up his trousers, I saw Ardee's hard dick fighting to get out of his shorts and, behaving like a little "Trick," Pete only pulled his pants up as far as the bottom of his butt. Ardee quickly put both hands in front of him in a sly way, trying to conceal his lustful desire. I shook my head in disbelief;

Ardee: " wh-at! "

Tyree interjected with a wave of his hand.

Tyree: " fo'get it Timmy "

Timmy: " am sendin' him home "

Pete: " you always treatin' me like a l'il kid "

Tyree: " c'mhere dawg, lemmi say somethin' to you right quick "

While Tyree was pulling me aside, I kept my eye on Pete. Ardee was putting his arm around Pete's shoulder, gently squeezing while pulling him close to his side. He bent over, whispering softly in Pete's ear, pulling him down on the settee with him, enquiring:

Ardee: " whatz wrong witchu son, you need to calm down "

Pete: " but he tha one who started it "

I wouldn't even dignify that with any kind of reply. Instead, I tried to hear what Tyree had to say.

Tyree: " Timmy, lissen: First of all, I don't think it's the best thing to send him home in this state o' mind - under the present circumstances.

                    Now, Ioknow what he done but you 'n me know he hot headed, don't send him out there like this now "

I supposed he was right; Pete couldn't leave home as he pleased, and the fact that mom had given him permission to come visit me meant I was solely responsible for his well being until he got back home. The kid was horny and I did believe he came here to see Tyree and not me, hoping to possibly rekindle something again.

Timmy: " I suppose "

Tyree: " me 'n you know what the boi want .... don't send him out there now 'n make him go pick up some or fall victim to some, some .... "

Timmy: " I know, but it's so hurtful 'n fuckin' embarrassin' seein' him throwin' his'self at y'all like dat - I know Ardee will fuck him, ... I heard
                    y'all in the kitchen "

Tyree: " you heard? "

Timmy: " yep "

Tyree: " aaight, well, hear me out. I ain't tryin' to be cruel or nothin' but, ... I think it's better Ardee wax dat ...... er - ..... "

I couldn't resist a little smile at the candid and explicit way he delivered his sermon.

Timmy: " y'all is somethin' else - you, Ardee - 'n him too "

Tyree: " No, ... amean, am jus

sayin' .... "

Timmy: " you ain't gots to
explain nothin' more, I know exactly whatchu
mean "

Tyree: " c'mon Timmy, don't
take it like dat, ... you gotta see what I mean
by dat "

Timmy: " I ain't takin' it like
nothin' - I ain't no fool, you woulda do him
again 'n since you can't, you want yo' boi to do
it.   See whatchu
                         doin' now, now you
gon have me aidin' 'n abettin' 'n I don't even like
dat shit - fo' real dawg "

Tyree: " .... am jus sayin' - it's
better you let Ardee give him what he need "

When I thought of Aji, it hurt me to let it go
down like this and I swore that if the day ever
came when Aji found himself in a similar
situation and was about to get or did get some
other dick, I wouldn't say a word to anyone.

As Tyree and I stood in the middle of the living
room, we watched as Pete sat comfortably in
Ardee's lap while he folded his arms across my
brother's belly.

Moments later, they were slowly but eagerly exploring each other's bodies. Ardee was fervently passionate, kissing and mesmerizing Pete, quenching his long desired satisfaction; Pete was beside himself with pleasure as Ardee devoured him.

As we stood in the middle of the living room face to face, me looking at Tyree and wondering if I was doing the right thing, Tyree gave me a gentle pat on the shoulder and a reassuring nod.

Ardee nuzzled his lips against Pete's neck and puckered. Pete stiffened himself, shoving his shoulders hard against Ardee and let his head fall against his cheek. Slowly, he shoved a hand behind him and Ardee began to reposition himself in the seat - Pete still sitting on his lap. The next moment Ardee was nibbling at his ear;

Pete: " aaaaahhhhh "

he expelled a soft mutter. I was tense, my nerves taut; I clenched my fists and gritted my teeth. Tyree pulled me slowly, gently shoving me down onto the arm-chair and perched himself on the right arm.

Tyree: " be chill son, jus be chill

"

I was mad - not at Ardee, just the entire incident and how it had occurred.

Unable to bear the fondling without actually seeing the dick, Pete slowly slid off Ardee's lap and proceeded to plunge an impatient hand down the front of his shorts to massage Ardee's dick. Ardee spread his legs wide and allowed him to pull his dick out.

Pete: " whooa ..... wikkid "

He exclaimed when he came face to face with its actual size and saw the curve. In a flash he was on it, toying with its head, trailing his tongue around and then flickering his tongue at the hole on the tip. Without warning, he took half of it in his mouth.

Ardee: " mm-mm-mmmph cccccctttt - damn! "

Pete: " you like dat? "

Ardee: " yeaa suck it "

He croaked, finally opening his eyes. Pete looked up at his face and went back to sucking. A leg suddenly and involuntarily kicked forward; Ardee now looked at us, at me for the first time since the fondling had started, and asked;

Ardee: " you mad at me dawg? "

Timmy: " nope "

Pete got off his knees and threw himself atop Ardee and hugged him. Ardee hugged his butt and began to suck his nipple under his Polo shirt; Pete quickly ripped them off, standing in front of Ardee and groping his hard dick protruding out the left side of his tight boxer briefs. He stood there with his eyes closed as Ardee clawed at his chest and nipples in a state of heightened delirium. And when Ardee, starting from the back, trailed a lone finger under his crotch, he half squatted; and when that finger settled at what must have been his hole, his legs wobbled ....

Pete: " wait .... ama take it off "

and just like that, he was out of his underwear like a snake out of his old skin; there was absolutely no apprehension. As Ardee spun him around and pried his butt cheeks apart, Pete readily bent over, touching the floor with his hands. Ardee slapped his butt playfully,

Ardee: " daayum .... L'il
Thug, you ain't got no hole. Yo Black, you
gotta see this shit - psshaw - .... boi you pretty
as fuck,

                    damn! nice l'il booty
son ..... ni-ice "

Pete: " datz 'cause I don't be
gettin' none "

Ardee: " you want me to take it?
"

Pete :   " yeaa but lick it first "

Ardee: " aiight, but come put
some mo' dome on this dick first "

He asked, and Pete went back to sucking with
his butt in the air. It only took a few seconds
for Ardee to start fingering his hole. His back
arched instantly and he began to spasm with
each powerful twist and slurp.

Administering expert moves as he sucked, Pete
continued driving Ardee into a frenzy with his
tongue. It was too much, and Ardee began to
tap his hole with a finger as he pulled his balls
over the top of his shorts too. Seemingly
uncomfortable with that, he hastily tore his
shorts and boxers off and tossed them to the

floor.

While Pete was completely shameless, Ardee was like a ravenous wolf, absolutely and completely unperturbed by our presence. That I could understand. But I was seeing Pete in a new light - he was more than horny for some dick, and quite unabashed. Wasn't he doing anything with any of his school friends, I wondered, as he ate up Ardee's dick with uncommon fervor.

Ardee: " son, you know how to work some dick "

Pete: " I know "

he retorted rather proudly, and threw an inviting look at us. Tyree was just trying to fondle my nipples and I'd brushed his hand aside - just in time; I wouldn't have wanted Pete to witness anything like that between us.

Ardee: " lemmi see dat booty now "

He hastily and gladly got up on the settee seat, kneeling with his hands placed flat on the wall behind it, gyrating and poking his butt out, backing it up in Ardee's face, taunting him to come and get it .... I was totally shocked by his matter of fact demeanor, and I simply had to opine;

Timmy: " Pete, we sittin' right here; you mean to tell me .... you ain't in the least feelin' funny? "

Pete: " No! "

Timmy: " you is somethin' else "

Before he could respond, Tyree quickly whispered in my ear;

Tyree: " leave tha boi alone - don't get in it "

Pete: " but it's jus us! ..... "

Timmy: " boi you is shameless.... "

I added and Tyree quickly put a hand over my mouth. He had just leaned over against my ear to say something else when Pete added, simply,

Pete: " ..... it's jus like when Tyree 'n me ..... "

Tyree: " oooh shit, damn! "

I'd said too much - rather, I shouldn't have said anything at all. Ardee was just about to plant his tongue between Pete's butt cheeks but now that he'd gotten confirmation for what he was pressing Tyree, he instantly pulled his head back and gave Tyree a questioning stare, followed by an enormously wide grin.

I didn't try to see Tyree's response. However, Ardee had far more important and pleasurable business to attend to than bothering to address that issue now. He was salivating and desperately wanting to taste Pete. Prying him apart again and taking a good look, he exclaimed:

Ardee: " bwoi! ..... you got some pretty bush guardin' dat l'il gate - 'n lookit dat l'il hole! "

Pete: " Ooow! "

Ardee had poked a section of his finger in.

Ardee: " you ain't been gettin' no dick boi? "

Pete: " I tole you "

Ardee: " well ama give you some today - you want dat? "

He crooned, and kissed his hole.

Pete: " O-ooh! ..... yes, yes "

As he positioned his dick, he advised;

Ardee: " push dat booty out ....
no, no, the hole, push it out 'n make it wink at
me "

We were completely out of lube and condoms
and I thought that might have dissuaded either
of them, but Pete was adamant that he wanted
to be fucked and told Ardee to fuck him raw
using some of the baby oil in the bathroom.
Ardee was only too willing, explaining that he
was certified "clean." As for Pete, he'd never
had a test but then again, he'd explained to me
that after the time he'd had sex with Tyree, he'd
never done it again.

I didn't care to witness too much explicit detail
of the actual thing. It was Tyree who insisted
that their backs be to our end (probably so he
could see up under everybody). Typical Tyree.

I could hear the squelching of his dick with the
baby oil as he tried to force its head in.

Pete: " O-oowoooou ..... "

and entered.

Ardee: " I gotchu, I gotchu ..... "

but Pete was still falling sideways, clawing at his thighs. Ardee caught him and pulled him back, keeping the dick in place;

Ardee: " you aiight? "

Pete: " uh-huh "

Ardee: " aiight - you ride it "

Ardee placed himself on the settee with Pete on his lap. As Pete sat on Ardee's dick, grimacing and too timid to go all the way down, Ardee grabbed both of his wrists, pulling him down as he made gentle jabs from his seated position with his legs splayed wide and Pete between them. The look on Pete's face was one of intense pressure. I just knew he'd just caught that wicked curve on Ardee's dick.

Pete: " wooo, ooo, ooh -
Ardee! "

Ardee: " you want it? "

Pete: " yes! ...... I want it "

Ardee: " lemmi give it to you
then? "

He coaxed, and transferred their position to the
floor; an even better vantage point for us, to
which I'm sure Tyree would attest. He tossed
Pete a cushion, which he put under his head and
without any prompting, Pete got on his back,
raised his legs, and held onto his toes.

Ardee: " oh damn, look at dat
shit "

Further priming his dick with the baby oil,
Ardee continued to "ooh and aah" at the site of
Pete's hole and how he was making it wink at
him. He got down on his knees to lick Pete
again; Pete draped his legs over his shoulders
and began to gyrate.

Desperately wanting more than to lick, Ardee
soon turned his attention back to fucking.
Tossing Pete's legs over his shoulders, he
forced his dick in just beyond the head and
began a slow grind, performing his operation on
his knees as Pete clung to his neck with one
hand while the other tenderly caressed the back
of his head.

Ardee's butt cheeks were wide open, his almost

sealed butt hole twitching as his dick made love to Pete's hole. Gradually, he went deeper and deeper; and the deeper he went, the more his butt hole twitched. Tyree grabbed his own dick, muttering:

Tyree: " daamn, look at ma dawg booty hole! "

I said nothing but I had to wonder at his being so ravenous - would he fuck Ardee?

Tyree: " dang son, he makin' me wanna do somethin' "

Timmy: " trust me, you ain't goin' over there - 'n I ain't doin' nothin' so get dat outta yo' head "

I knew that made him mad, which is why he turned on Ardee.

Tyree: " Dang! ...... stop playin' widdit, take dat azz like you want it nigga "

Ardee: " boi nice 'n tight as fuck - he gon make a nigga bust ..... boi, you got some sweetazz booty - Damn! "

Pete: " mmphf, you like it? "

Ardee: " hell yea "

Pete: " it's yo's papi - O-o-
oohh, yes, yes, ye-es ..... Ohgawd - YES! "

Ardee: " ama go up in it son,
ama go up in it "

Pete: " yea, do it ...... do it .....
A- aaahhaayiiiii ! - Pa-pi "

He squealed, clinging to Ardee's neck with one
hand and shoving at his hip with the other.

Tyree: " oh Shit! ..... he 'bout to
...... "

Ardee's dick was deep past the curve; he'd
stopped his movements now but I could see his
dick pulsating and his hole twitching.

Ardee: "
Gaawddamnsonyougonmakeme - bus!
.... ssshit ccccttt - where you want it! ....
o-oooh ssshhh..... "

Pete: " give it to me! give it to
me, I wanna feel it "

Timmy: " No! .... "

542

Putting a tight grip around Ardee's back and his legs firmly plaited around his waist, Pete heaved his body upward, taking and holding the dick while Ardee went into spasms and his butt hole twitched like a flashing strobe light.

Tyree: " Gaawddamn! "

I was numb with disbelief and just sat there. When Ardee regained his strength, he just rolled over on his back with his arms and legs spread wide. Pete quickly jumped up and began to suck his dick like there was no tomorrow, sending Ardee's body back into spasms; he had to beg him to stop.

At that point, Pete snuggled up against him, still groping his dick; a moment later, he released his hold, threw his thigh across Ardee's groin and lay his head on his chest. Ardee threw a loving arm about his neck and closed his eyes. Tyree got up, brought out a blanket, and covered them.

Timmy: " ch ma.... I, I don't think ama be able to sit here 'n watch no more o' ..... "

Tyree: " take it easy son...jus chill. Why don'tchu go lie down in the bedroom "

For the next two hours I sat on the chair in the corner of the bedroom and listened to Tyree as he lay across the bed telling me how much he thought it was time I "cut Pete some slack." We talked on it at length until they started fucking again. I had to fight off Tyree as he was hell bent on fucking me; I was horny and hot and bothered too with all the sounds filtering through the slightly ajar door, but I was afraid to risk it.

Eventually, he convinced me to let him sit on the chair while I sat on his lap. However, he'd cleverly pumped some body lotion from the bottle that was sitting on the chest of drawers and as soon as I was in a crouched position to sit, he shoved a hand under the foot of my shorts, plastering my butt with the lotion.

Timmy: " whatchu doin'! .... Pete out there "

Tyree: " why you so scared, he can't see nothin' now "

Timmy: " I do not want him to see me "

I shot back.

544

Tyree: " aiight, aiight - don't get mad "

And thus the tussle began. I couldn't overpower him - I couldn't win; I settled for timidly sitting on it and just taking the head. So it went, with me slowly rocking and grinding, taking what I wanted and having some quick, hot fun.

Unsatisfied with not being all the way deep in me, he propped one of my legs over the arm-rest and tried to shove more dick in me.

Timmy: " Haw! - Blaze! "

Tyree: " datz jus the head! "

Timmy: " well, I ain't takin' no more "

It was burning like hell - but it felt kinda good at the same time.

Tyree: " dang shawty, can'tchu jus do this? "

Timmy: " I ain't takin' no more 'n datz it "

Tyree: " aiight boo let it stay right there, ... you wanna work it? "

Timmy: " No! "

Tyree: " all you gotta do is rock on it "

Eventually, I did, and it felt oh so good. I continued to rock on it. It was barely the head - I knew because I'd feel with my hand from time to time. He held it trying to keep the head in there - and, I knew, to sneak in more also.

Pete was wailing in delight and Ardee was grunting and calling him every sweet name in the book, asking if he loved the dick; Pete responded by saying " yes, breed me papi ".

That inflamed every ember in me, and I had to jerk my dick.

Tyree: " hear dat son, l'il shawty gettin' his, c'mon, get yo's too .... fuck the dick boo - l'il tightazz mo'fucka "

Now I was driven even more by his dirty talk; frantically, I pumped my dick as I rode his dick and I could hear his laboured breathing.

Not long after, I could feel my own strength ..... fighting, desperate to burst through my loins; it was coming.

Tyree: " oh shit, chill shawty, chi ...... "

Timmy: " m-mmm, ... ye-es, gimmi dat shit too "

Tyree: " ...... oh damn son, don't make me ..... Nghfm, nghf, nghh, nghnnn "

It was done; my ejaculation had greedily and jealously evoked his own eruption and I felt his hot love juice plaster me. We quickly cleaned up with a paper towel, as best we could, tossing the used ones under the chair till the coast was clear. He threw himself back on his stomach on the bed, looking at me provocatively, pointing an accusing finger and warning,

Tyree: " dang son, I wuzn't even in it "

That I already knew; I had felt it all over my crotch and butt hole - still, I was more than satisfied; but he was not.

Tyree: " negro, you owe me - remember dat, you owe me "

I could live with that.

When that sexcapade in the living room was over, Ardee took Pete to the bathroom and they showered together. While they were doing that, we came back out into the living room. As they got out of the bathroom, Pete asked,

Pete: " you still mad at me big bra? "

Timmy: " no son, I ain't mad atchu ..... but you gettin' yo' azz back home now "

Pete: " awready! "

Timmy: " either dat or l call yo' mother 'n tell her to come get yo' azz "

Ardee: " I know you mad at me tho' dawg "

Timmy: " No, but I jus don't wanna talk to you right now "

Tyree was repeatedly making a throat-cutting sign with his hands under his throat, but Ardee didn't see.

Timmy: " I suppose you awright now "

Pete: " uh-huh "

Timmy: " boi get offa me "

I joked, as he had me in a tight hug.

Pete: " am jus sayin'..... you mean you don't even wanna give yo' brother a hug? "

Timmy: " am jus jokin' - you know dat "

Now that he'd gathered his sanity, Ardee seemed to want to talk....I guess to apologize or something ....

Ardee: " Timmy dawg .... "

But it was unnecessary. I wasn't mad but I didn't want to talk about him and Pete right then.

Tyree: " let it go dawg.......damn...........let - it - go "
Pete: " so ain'tchu comin' home too? "
Timmy: " No Pete! "
Pete: " awright, I see you whenever you come home "

Ardee: " come L'il Thug, ama
take you home "
Timmy: " ama come home when
am ready "
Pete: " whateva............ lata
gator "

"Later Gator" was a phrase dad always said to
him when he was very small and he'd never
given it up since. He grinned happily; I smiled
as I walked him to the door and Ardee hurried
ahead to the elevator.

Timmy: " lata "

Chapter 18

When Ardee returned from taking Pete home, he took me by surprise, immediately planting a big kiss on my lips.

Tyree: " hey, hey...."

Ardee: " keep yo' drawz on bro, dat wuz jus a friendly kiss "

He admitted and headed straight for the settee.

Plopping himself down with a satisfied smile, his legs sprawled wide in front of him with his eyes closed, he locked his fingers together and joined both hands at the back of his head. He didn't move or even open his eyes.

As for Tyree, he had a half worried look as he searched my eyes, waiting for it....he figured he knew something was coming.

Tyree: " oh shit!...Timmy, lissen, jus........ "

Timmy: " jus what, I ain't sayin' nothin' .... "

Ardee still didn't stir or even open his eyes.

Tyree: " you .... you mean you ain't gon blow up now? "

Timmy: " you might wanna check yo' boi Ardee tho' ..... see if he still alive "

Upon hearing that, Ardee sat up.

Ardee: " you mean you ain't really mad dawg? ..... but I ..... "

Timmy: " well you wrong then, ain'tchu? "

Ardee: " I came back figurin' you gon cuss ma azz out "

Timmy: " 'n then cuss Pete out too. Ardee, I know if it didn't happen here today, YOU wuz gon find a way to do it - and dat boi

                would jus be waitin' "

Tyree: " Phwhoo! ...... datz a relief ..... "

Timmy: " well you needn't sweat it "

Ardee: " he wanted it Timmy 'n I jus couldn't resist his l'il cuteazz "

Timmy: " it's cool Ardee, I ain't even thinkin' 'bout it like dat no more - jus drop it "

I guess he wasn't really at fault for what happened - I was mad at Pete more than anything else; it had to be Ardee's conscience that was at work because it seemed he couldn't get it out of his mind.

Tyree later fetched the bag of cash and set it on the floor between himself and Ardee, then sat at his desk and swiveled his chair around to face Ardee as Ardee opened up the bag and began to take out several stacks of one hundred, fifty, and twenty dollar bills. He counted out ten thousand dollars and handed it to Tyree, then he counted out another five thousand, looked up at Tyree, and said:

Ardee: " this fo' all yo' troubles B....thanks......this otha five is fo' me, fo' ma troubles.....all dat time and gas dat mo'fucka made me

waste goin' down there all them times - 'n this.....this fo' you Timmy dawg, you a real nigga, you had ma back "

He said, walking over to me with a very broad grin and handed me a wad of notes. I counted them quickly.

Timmy: " fi'teen hundred! ..... jus fo' ridin down wit y'all ...... dang bro, this da best days' pay I eva had ..... this tha kinda job I need; thanks

                Ardee .... a-ha-haa, if you wuzn't a man I'd kiss you.... you tha ma-an "

Tyree: " datz aiight dawg, he can get a kiss from Aj ..... ssshit, I'll even kiss him fo' you if you want "

Ardee: " hell no, you about somethin' else ..... I can't trust you nigga! "

Tyree: " damn skippy "

Timmy: " yep, I think he will fuck you "

Ardee: " he ain't gon get no chance like dat "

Tyree: " what! .... well, lemmi catch yo' azz asleep ova here again ..... I will tie his azz up, gag him - 'n fuck tha shit outta him "

Timmy: " see what am talkin
'bout "

Ardee: " datz some fucked up
shit right there, ... sometimes I wonder
'boutchu - dat woulda been war between me 'n
you "

Tyree: " c'mon, you know you
woulda love dat shit "

Ardee: " yo, let's drop dat shit ....
you gettin' way too .... "

I broke out in such laughter, Ardee looked at
me like he thought I'd lost my mind.

Timmy: " what! you mean I can't
laugh? ..... "

Ardee: " I don't see nothin' funny
"

Timmy: " it's damn funny. Fo' a
minit, I thought you wuz gon strap dat bag to
yo' azz 'n run outta here "

Tyree: " c'mon dawg, stop
trippin'.....you know am jus fuckin' witchu -
'xcept if you really wanna gimmi....ha-ha,

ha.....hahahaaaaw "

He was really rattling Ardee but then, he
calmed down.

Tyree: " ma bad, ma bad ..... but
I had to go there "

Looking at the money in my hand, my thoughts
quickly went back to serious matters, financial
matters, like how I was going to use this
money, and once again I offered my gratitude:

Timmy: " Ardee, thanks man .....
I know exactly what ama do wit this "

Ardee: " 'tain't no thang son.
But anyway, besides helpin' us tear dat nigga
up, 'n beat him down...you wuz a driver
too...'member,

                    you wuz da one who
took da wheel on da last leg home when we
wuz tired "

Tyree: " fo' real dawg, ma boi
handle his bi'nizz like a man...a true G... fo'
sho'. I stay up wit him fo' a while then I jus fell
out... I don't

                    even know when "

Ardee: " we wuz knocked tha

fuck out .... I wuz surprised when you woke us
'n said, ... we home "

Timmy: " ama have to step now
son, gots to take care o' biz ..... Tyree keep this
safe fo' me till I get back "

I asked, stuffing the wad in his hand.

Tyree: " I gotchu son, go handle
yo' bi'nizz "

Splashing on a dab of cologne, I looked in the
mirror to make sure I was street ready. I left
them there talking business, my single thought
now - the girl I was going to meet and later
take to a movie.

When I got back later that night, Ardee was still
there and Aji had joined them.

Just as I sat down, the phone rang. It was
Tyree's mom.

Tyree: " hey mom, I was going
to call you later; I had some things me and Mr.
.... er, the fellas wanted to put to you and I
wanted to
                    know what you would

like for Mothers' Day, I don't wanna get you something you don't............aw mom, not that, you know

I don't like ..... aiight mom, anything for you .... I'll be there .... yeah mom, ...no, not yet but I think I'll hear from them soon ....

...ok...yes, bye...love you too mom "

He told me that his mom would like him and Yani to attend church with her next Sunday for Mothers' Day, saying that would be his Mothers' Day gift to her. He asked me if I would come along too and I quickly told him yes.

Ardee: " Y'all need to gimmi some room 'cause me 'n ma boi need to take care o' biz "

Timmy: " Oh, I ain't gon be standin' in yo' way, am goin' in the bedroom "

I bolted for the bedroom, pulling Tyree along behind me. I felt a streak of mischief and decided that tonight I was going to mess with his head and find something out in the process. I knew what he was going to be wanting now that we were alone in the bedroom, especially considering what was going on out in the living room.

I was biding my time; we kissed, groped, cuddled, and I waited until he had finally stripped me naked and was hot and ready - then I delivered the bomb.

Timmy: " Let me fuck you "

Tyree: " Wha! "

Timmy: " I wanna fuck you "

I said, trailing my hand down his back, finally filling my deceitful hands with his butt cheeks. Oh, the look on his face! I wanted to laugh but had to keep a straight face, especially when I saw his dick slowly limp away in defeat. He struggled to find words:

Tyree: " I, Tim.... er .....
Timmy, I .... I don't get fucked - I neva know you woulda want to do dat .... a .... amean - jus always
                        thought ..... "

Timmy: " c'mon son, ... then ama letchu do me; c'mon turn ova on yo' stomach "

He sighed heavily and reluctantly, but obeyed.

But no sooner had he done that, I requested:

Timmy: " no, no, turn over on yo'
back "

I helped flip him over as he grunted, groaned,
and defiantly locked his jaws. He looked
absolutely wretched. I quickly raised his legs
in the air, wet my forefinger in my mouth and
rubbed his ass hole as he began to stiffen his
entire body. I licked it, although I really didn't
like to ..... then tried to poke my finger in but
he shoved me off.

Timmy: " c'mon son, stop playin'
"

Tyree: " Timmy, I ..... "

He started to protest;

Timmy: " shut tha fuck up 'n
lemmi look atchu "

I demanded and he raised his legs high,

Timmy: " hold them up there like
dat ..... yea, jus like dat "

Tyree: " yo, ... dawg .... "

560

Without any warning, after stroking his hole with my saliva laced finger, I poked him;

Tyree: " A-Aaaaaahh! .... "

he roared and quickly sprang to his feet.

Tyree: " .... Fuck! Nghf ......
yo Timmy, I can't do dat ...... "

Dismissing his protest, I tried to pull him back onto the bed. With his gaze to the floor, he stood shaking his head adamantly and quickly declared;

Tyree: " naw, naw .... it ain't gon be like dat shawty, I don't even like.... I can't do this "

Timmy: " whatchu mean you can't do it?, I did dat shit ..... C'mon, turn .... "

Tyree: " Timmy, let's talk 'bout this "

Timmy: " Talk! ..... now! .....
c'mon son "

His troubled face said it all; he looked absolutely petrified and I thought he was about to break out into a cold sweat. Bu I was willing to push it further. He opened his mouth but could find no words and in that quick moment, I offered:

Timmy: " don't trip dawg, lemmi get at dat booty "

He licked his lower lip nervously and fretfully,

Tyree: " Timmy, ... I, ... if we ..... look boo ..... "

but I pretended to be frustrated with his indecision and .....

Timmy: " ..... c'mon son, I wanna get some o' you - I know dat mus' be better than Marlon's "

Now I was sure he thought he was going to die for denying me what he'd always said was so good when he got mine; now why wouldn't I want to get the goodness that he'd gotten but never given to anyone else? Stuttering, like an apprehended fool, he tried to explain:

Tyree: " I, ... er ..... see ..... Timmy, ... lissen boo, I love you but, ... I know I can't do this, I don't get fu..... "

Timmy: " c'mon, lemmi get yo's

son ..... you got mine "

Tyree: " datz different "

Timmy: " Different! ...... how'z
dat? "

Tyree: " oh damn son ..... you a
shawty - ma shawty "

Timmy: " so datz why you won't
let me do it ..... if I wuzn't yo' shawty then you
woulda gimmi "

Tyree: " Hell no! "

He found those words quickly. I lowered my
head dejectedly and mumbled;

Timmy: " oh! ..... I see "

.... still pretending.

He was quite crestfallen;

Tyree: " Daamn! ...... don't take
it like dat boo, ... amean, ... amjussayin' ......
ooh ssshit "

And I couldn't help it, I began to chuckle and
hugged him around the waist. He hesitantly

hugged me back and I squeezed him a little harder and pressed closer into him, resting my cheek on his chest for amoment, content in the fact that he was what he was. I think he felt that as his chest heaved and I heard him sigh. Relieved, he chuckled; I looked up at him, he smiled and shook his head, then pulled me back close to him.

Timmy: " I wuz jus playin'.... I wuz testin' you "

Tyree: " Testin' me!..... shawty...don't eva play wit me like dat again...you had me worried there fo' a minit - fo' real. You had

                                        me thinkin'...like...what da fuck is this! ..... you mean ama lose ma shawty...man, yo...I wuz about to bug da fuck out -

                                        straight up "

Timmy: " Tyree "

Tyree: " sup shawty? "

Timmy: " you love me? "

Tyree: " c'mon......without question... you know dat boo "

Timmy: " soo, you don't love
Pete? "

Tyree: " noo son, it ain't like dat
.... why you ask a dumb question like dat for? "

Timmy: " Ioknow...Ioknow...I
jus......Ioknow "

Tyree: " whatchu mean you
don't know ....we need to talk dawg, we need
to talk - NOW "

Timmy: " talk 'bout what? "

Tyree: " me 'n you "

He retorted, looking at me incredulously.

Timmy: " what now! "

Tyree: " whatchu lookin' at me
like dat fo'? "

I didn't respond but wondered: What could it
be that he had to say now? I hoped he wasn't
going to complain about me telling him some
time ago that while I thoroughly enjoyed
getting into bed with him, I couldn't handle
getting fucked on an everyday basis, nor did I
want to; that there were times when I really

wanted it and there were times when I really didn't. He continued by pressing the issue.

Tyree: " you not gonna answer? "

Timmy: " if I don't look how you expect ama see? "

I finally answered with a laugh.

Tyree: " c'mon boo, am serious "

Timmy: " ok, ok ..... why you actin' so uptight? "

His only response was straight to the point.

Tyree: " wuz you serious when you tole Pete you wuzn't comin' home tonight? "

Timmy: " yeah "

Tyree: " good, so we can talk, 'cause we gotz to talk. Lissen, da weekend almost done, Yani gon be comin' ova next weekend 'n
                    you gon be busy all week wit school...I mean, you doin' yo' finals 'n

566

errything, then graduation 'n all dat. I don't want you to
have yo' mind clogged up wit unnecessary stuff 'n not ace yo' finals, knowamsayin.....so we gotta get somethin' straight
right here right now...aiight, I know I tole you before... I love you ... I think you prolly ain't gave much thought to it because
you new to alla this 'n still grapplin' wit stuff .... I understand dat, but am fo' real ..... fo' real son ... fo' real. I wanna spend
each 'n erry day witchu but I ain't rushin' you 'cause you got yo' own life 'n family, 'n school - 'n I do want you to make a
success of everything you tryin' to do......so I pull back 'n try to give you yo' space to think 'n work things out but, ...I need
you .... you gotta
believe dat "

Timmy: " you mean you ain't jus sayin' dat? ... I wanna believe you but sometimes I wonder .... you know, do he prefer Pete over me
or... "

Tyree: " naw, naw, naw ... 'tain't
nothin' like dat son. Look here, there wuz a
whole lot a peeps I coulda been wit since I met
you -

                    dudes 'n honeys ......
damn Timmy, I got peeps still sweatin' me 'n I
ain't even made a move .... dawg, I been months
                    without doin' nothin'
be'fo I met you .... 'n after I met you .... I ain't
done nothin' till me 'n you dat night - fo' real
.... you know I

                    don't even play wit ma
shit like a lot a men do so I ain't even had a nutt
"

Timmy: " you mean you wuz jus
waitin' fo' me? "

Tyree: " from da first day in da
park son. What! you think it wuz your bball
skills why I wanted you to play wit us so much
.....

                    ..... pshaw, nigga a seen
yo' skills 'n am glad you on our team but, it wuz
da rest of you dat got me .... I wuz like, WOW!
....

                    this l'il nigga is a TEN
"

Timmy: " dang, ... you wuz
lookin' at me like dat back then? "

Tyree: " yep. Timmy, I don't know if I can find tha words to really let you know jus how I feel 'bout you .... how much I love you .... I want

               you son .... I need you - 'n I ain't tryin' to lose you "

Timmy: " I ain't goin' nowhere "

Tyree: " best song I heard all day "

Timmy: " song! "

Tyree: " datz music to ma ears shawty "

Timmy: " ha ha ...... ok "

Tyree: " but look, I got lots of stuff on ma mind these days .... da house, Yani havin' to go back 'n forth every otha weekend; this

             thing am expectin' them to call me 'bout soon .... but wit alla dat I got you on top of ma mind too "

Timmy: " I feel you son. Me, am jus

             tryin' to ace this MRI

course 'cause my moms gon get me hooked up at her hospital.... "

We spoke at length about what he wanted to do with his and Yani's life - not that Liana was completely out of the picture, but from how he explained it, he was a single father doing his best to maintain a civil, platonic relationship just for the kid's sake. He said he did not see a future with himself and another woman settling down together again, although he would continue to pursue and see whichever other women he chose. But he avidly pointed out that he wanted me to consider myself the permanent partner in his life.

He said his main focus right now was his financial situation, whatever that meant. I mean, his home was never really out of food, nor had I ever heard any complaint about his rent not being paid on time. The only job I'd known him to do was on a few nights, mainly on weekends, when he would say he had a gig at some posh place as a waiter or bartender and be gone.

Now, when he talked about buying a house, I concluded that he was doing something on the side like Ardee, and I left it at that. He was quite determined that he was going to own a house and see that Yani was raised the proper way. He also said he had taken out an Endowment Insurance Policy on Yani that would mature when he turned eighteen. He even confided that Ardee owned a house somewhere in Virginia, and that the Auto Repair shop where Ardee and Aji worked, actually belonged to Ardee and that one day he would show me the shop.

There was still so much that I didn't know about these guys that had befriended me and whom I'd accepted as my best friends; and the fact that he was telling me all this must have meant that I was being fully inducted into his circle of friendship.

He went on to say that the money he had was the result of a settlement on the accidental death of his dad on his job; that began to throw a whole new light on the situation. Then he finally said that in order for his life to feel complete, it would be up to me to decide whether I wanted him, and wanted to be in his life permanently.

It was a lot for me to digest, but I was sure that I wanted him and did not want anyone else to have him. I realized that clearly when Pete came around, trying to seduce him. I did love him - everything about him.

As we lay there on the bed with my head resting comfortably on his chest, just clinging to each other, I thought of how good it felt, how very good - I felt at home, at complete ease - a part of him. He kissed me gently on my lips and I felt warm and secure ....

On the other hand, did I really want to be with him permanently? Could I handle that? Would I still want to be with women if we got into a permanent relationship? These were pressing questions that weighed heavily on my mind and that I needed the answers to.

I guess only time would tell.

NOTE:

TO BE CONTINUED...

JUST A SLIGHT PAUSE...

BE SURE TO BUY:

"ThugPassion – ThugLove"

(Volumes 2 and 3)"

on SALE NOW

visit:

www.DNAeBooks.com

www.DLowe.us

www.ThugPassion.us
and

www.ThugLove.us

**THANK YOU FOR READING
ALL MY BOOKS…
and
THANK YOU for YOUR
CONTINUOUS SUPPORT…**

One Love - D.Lowe

**Thank you, for your purchase.
"Thug Passion – Thug Passion" (Volume 1)
By D.Lowe**

**For More Info about this Author and
our other Authors and Writers please visit
our websites.**

visit:
www.DLowe.us
and
www.DNAeBooks.com

DNA eBooks Publishing Company

DNA eBooks Publishing Group

Book Description:

THUG PASSION - THUG LOVE, is the story of Timmy, *a somewhat sexually confused and very curious young man, who by chance meet three good friends on a hot summer's day. That meeting would result in a considerable change in his life forever.*

One of those friends, Tyree, *the most dynamic of the trio, falls head over heels in love with him; this leads to eventual sexual advances which at first were spurned by* Timmy, *but later reciprocated.*

Timmy later found himself battling those deep lustful thoughts, which plagued his mind for years, about his real true feelings for Tyree.

Timmy, had to admit to himself, but couldn't fully explain why things were the way they were; but finally came to grips with the realization of his relationship with Tyree, and spent years living a secret life of love and passion, with him; even though he had a beautiful wife and several lovely children.

He prodded and quickly shifted his position, evading my hand as I try to grab his balls "

Timmy: " motha fucka! ..... mm-mm-mmmphf .... Oh Fuck! - AAIGHT! .... aiight .... mmmph, mmph, I surrender "

Tyree: "see...I tole you" He gloated and dug into my sides once more.

Timmy: "fuck you Tyree...ccccctt, ooh, ... SHIT"

Tyree: " you can't be surrenderin' 'n cussin' like dat in front o' grown folk, you surrender or what? "

Timmy: " yes, yes,...yes, I surrender .... lemmi go"

Tyree: " you sure? "

Timmy: "yes, you, tha boss, you tha master, jus move yo' hand, please"

Tyree: "well you best behave yo'self now" Without warning, he straddled me; kneeling on the sofa and pinning me between the back of the seat and his stomach.

Tyree: "I want you boi...."

Timmy: "you got me"

Tyree: "I ain't talkin' like dat .... am talkin' 'bout some o' dat"

Timmy: "some o' what .... I ain't GOTS nothin' to give you"

Tyree: "am serious, 'specially from I seen how you tore dat nigga Marlon up, .movin' dat booty like dat" Pretending to be uninterested in his quest, I suddenly changed the subject, asking as I toyed with his belly button;

Timmy: "Tyree, you say you love me...why?"
Tyree: "dang son, you gon ask dat now!"
Timmy: "tell me...a need to hear" He hastily got off me, tilted my chin up, knelt before me and looked deep in my eyes before he bowed his head, shook it slowly from side to side, sighed heavily then looked back at me.

Tyree: "Timmy, I ain't got no more words to explain it to you, I ain't got no more ways I, I, don't know what to tell you except that I love you, am torn apart e'rry day jus thinkin' 'bout you...datz what I do all day every day -jus think about you".ain't nothin' mo' dat I know dat I could say, you jus gotta let time prove me right or wrong...but I do love you...more than you eva know"

Timmy: "what is it about me dat you love?"

Tyree: "dang son, datz 'errythang...shiit; from yo' temper, how yo' chest move up 'n down when you mad, da way you walk, them very hairy, slightly bow legs, yo tight little muscular butt, all dat pretty black hair on yo' butt, stomach, yo' pubes, under yo' arms, them hairy ballz, dat nice l'il 'stache, thick eyebrows 'n lips, yo' bright dark brown eyes, rich coco 'n

577

cream complexion, da way you talk. dang son, Ioknow. jus da way you squeeze me back when I hold you. I know son, e'rrythang.jus e'rrythang, fo' real - I jus saw you 'n wuz like wow! .this kid is bangin'.'n on top o' dat you fresh - 'n intelligent too...its too good. Son you what I been lookin' fo' all this time"